REIGN OF DARKNESS

PRINCE ASSASSIN #2

ARIANA NASH

Reign of Darkness, Prince's Assassin #2

Ariana Nash - ***Dark Fantasy Author***

Subscribe to Ariana's mailing list & get the exclusive story 'Sealed with a Kiss' free.

Join the Ariana Nash Facebook group for all the news, as it happens.

Edited in US English.

Version 1 - November 2020

www.ariananashbooks.com

CHAPTER 1

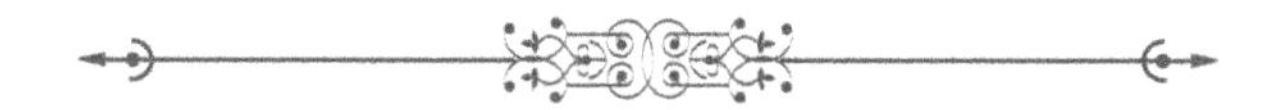

Flames licked at the palace's exterior walls, climbed from blazing doorways, and spiralled from smashed windows. Staff ran through the grounds, coughing into their clothing, eyes streaming and wide, their faces soot-blackened.

Niko should have been among them, but he'd abandoned his horse to push through the terrified crowd on foot. Screams barreled from left and right. His heart thumped too hard, his head full of memories from front-line battles, the moans and screams peppered by the ringing clash of swords. This was no battle, but it felt like one.

Bucket lines manned by guards stretched from the wells in the grounds. Buckets sloshed from hand to hand, but their impact was no more effective than pissing in the wind.

Any fool could see the palace was lost.

A Caville must forever hold the flame.

If the Caville bloodline abruptly ended, the horror

harbored within their blood would be set free upon the land. There were few certainties in this world, but keeping the dark flame from escaping was one of them.

He drove forward, forearm raised against the hissing flames, shielding his eyes.

Heat lashed in waves, beating him back. Flames roared and howled, spiraling into the skies, drowning out the sounds of the bells. The fire was alive now, a huge, breathing, feeding thing, devouring everything in its path.

"Get away from there!" a guard bellowed.

Niko staggered back, only half hearing.

He had to get inside. The Caville palace was a nest of snakes. In the flames and confusion, whatever violence had been brewing during the year he'd stayed away would surely boil over. Vasili—the only damned Caville who gave a shit about the dark flame—couldn't fight *this*. Rumors had proclaimed him sick. Rumors said a lot of things during the past twelve months. But Niko knew, in his soldier's gut, that if he didn't get to him now, all would be lost.

Vasili had to live.

A hand grabbed his arm, pulling him back. "Get back!" the guard barked.

Niko yanked free. "Where's Vasili?"

"Who?" The guard grunted, making a grab for Niko again, as though he were some fool who needed to be dragged away for his own safety. Niko smacked his hand aside.

A sudden superheated roar blew out a window above, raining glass and burning wood onto the ground.

"The prince!" Niko yelled. *"Where's the damn prince?!"*

"Pull back!" The order rose from among the retreating others. "Withdraw!"

The guard shook his head and backed up. "Go in there and you're a dead man!" He turned on his heel and bolted.

Another blast of heat plunged from above, and Niko ducked, covering his head with his hands. Glass rained. Screams mingled with howling flames.

He staggered back from the cracking walls and squinted up into the spiraling embers. "A Caville hasn't killed me yet."

The tunnels.

Vasili had shown him another way inside. One that took him to the very heart of the royal wing. He bolted through the gardens and stables, avoiding the stablehands desperately trying to soothe the spooked horses, and tore through the undergrowth, searching for the concealed tunnel entrance.

Ripping back a wall of ivy, he plunged inside the cold, dark tunnel, feeling and stumbling along to the sounds of his own ragged breathing.

This was taking too long. Everything was taking too damn long. Soon, there would be nothing left of the palace. If Vasili died, all the flame would jump to Amir—and the gods only knew what that wretched fool would do with it. But if they both died... Chaos. Darkness. Worse than the war. Monsters, man and beast, would be free upon the land.

It couldn't happen. He wouldn't allow it.

Light eventually lit the tunnel ahead, pouring in from a tight spiral staircase. Niko climbed higher, emerging in one of the rough, little-used service corridors. A heavy oak door barred his way. It had been a year. The door hadn't been there before. Or if it had, he didn't recall it. He tried the handle. It rattled, but the door didn't budge.

A swift kick blew out the lock.

He charged on. Wind tore through the corridors. Flame torches spluttered in their sconces. But the fire wasn't here. Not yet.

The deeper he ran, the more smoke boiled above and heat tightened his skin.

One staff member ran at him, her skirts pressed to her face to keep from inhaling too much smoke.

"Vasili?" he asked.

She ran by, eyes wide.

The hiss and snap of fire grew louder. He turned a bend in the corridor. Heat and flame surged in a great wave. Niko recoiled and darted back the way he'd come, veering down another corridor. If he got lost inside the burning walls, he might never make it out.

The maze-like palace corridors finally took on the more familiar colors of the royal quarters. "Vasili, you slithering bastard, where are you?" He wouldn't be dead. Not yet. He'd survived eight years as a prisoner to the elves. He'd survive this until Niko could get to him. He had to.

Niko's heart pounded, hot and heavy behind his ribs.

Smoke laced his nose and throat. He coughed into the crook of his arm, trying to filter the smoky air through his sleeve. His eyes burned, making the bright royal colors swim.

Gods, this was insanity. Returning, for the prince, just like the prick had said Niko would. *I will not ask or order you, Nikolas Yazdan, but you will return.* Niko almost laughed at the memory. How was it Vasili always got what he fucking wanted?

"Niko!"

He whirled at the sound of his name, and, squinting through the broiling smoke, saw the figure looming ahead, hand reaching. Niko lunged, laced the slim fingers with his, and threw his shoulder against a nearby door, pulling the woman inside. He slammed the door on the smoke and stepped back, watching it seep beneath the door and creep toward them.

"Niko?" Lady Maria coughed hard and slumped against the wall. "Walla, save us. This infernal fire has taken everything!" Her voice was wrecked, her layered silk gown stained by soot, but she didn't appear hurt.

"Maria," he caught her shoulder, helping to hold her up and offering some support, "where's Vasili?"

"Darling Niko," she smiled fondly, red eyes streaming tears. "You came." She reached for his face.

He caught her hand. "Where is he?"

"The library." New tears glistened in her eyes.

He released her and glanced at the door. This room was typically royal in its flamboyant decoration. He vaguely recalled the palace layout. The library was in the same wing, but deeper within the palace, closer to the firestorm's eye.

"He went for the books," she said.

"No book can be worth his life." Niko started for the door.

"Wait!" Maria took up her shawl and tore a great strip from the fabric, then dumped it in the nearby washbasin. She brought it to him, wrung out the excess water, and handed it over. "Cover your mouth and nose. You'll need it." Her warm hand was suddenly on his cheek, her gaze intense. "Take him away from this cursed place. Take him and go. *Never* come back."

He nodded, easing her fears. "There are tunnels. Take the northern corridor—"

She smiled a strange, defeated smile, cutting him off. "I cannot leave Amir."

"This place *is* cursed, and that prick isn't worth saving. Leave while you can."

She smiled sadly. "The poison has him. Nobody else can slow its course. Go free our bird, Niko. He needs you."

There was too much to say, too many questions, but the fire raged with every second, and Vasili might already have succumbed.

Maria captured his hand and squeezed fiercely. "Take him or Amir will. You must save him." She shoved Niko back a step. "Go!"

He left her inside the room, wondering if he'd just abandoned her to the flames, but he couldn't save them both. With the cloth smothered against his nose and mouth, he plowed deeper into the choking smoke, recognizing the twists and turns of the wretched palace layout.

Sweat ran down his back and dripped into his eyes, blurring his vision. The walls he brushed against simmered hot beneath his hands. No ordinary fire could consume a stone palace in such a way. The timber windows and doors and trusses, yes, but this fire had a life of its own. Did Amir start it? Was it part of the flame?

He'd think on it later, if they survived.

The library door lay open ahead. Fire danced up the doorframe and boiled from inside.

"Vasili?" Smoke poured down Niko's throat. He smothered his mouth and nose with the cloth again, but a fit of wracking coughs doubled him over.

It was too late to turn back. He had to go in there, had to find him. Nobody else would save the "tainted" prince. Damn that bastard for being right, but Niko prayed to Walla that Vasili still breathed.

He calmed his head and heart and plunged through the flaming doorway.

CHAPTER 2

The world burned.

Heat made his skin crawl. Burned his eyes. Singed his face.

How anything could survive among an ocean of furious flame was a miracle, but someone did. The tall, cloaked figure stumbled from amid the inferno. Impossibly, the flames appeared to bend around him, letting him pass, but then hastily licked at his rippling cloak, blackening its edges. He clutched a smoldering book to his chest.

A flash of blond hair, the defiant tilt of a straight chin. Even beneath his hood, there was no mistaking him.

Niko flung out his hand and Vasili's cool fingers locked with his.

He pulled the prince back through the blazing doorway, leading him anywhere. *Away*. That was all that mattered. He had to get away from this inferno.

The prince's fingers slipped free of his grip.

Niko staggered to a halt. Thick smoke almost obscured Vasili slumped against the wall, head down, shoulders heaving. Niko pressed Maria's damp cloth to Vasili's mouth and nose. The prince's hand came up to hold it in place. His brilliant blue eye flashed a scathing warning not to touch. His lips probably found an ungrateful sneer behind the cloth too.

He could sneer all he liked, just so long as he survived.

Orange flame poured down the corridor behind them. If Lady Maria hadn't escaped, there was no going back for her now. Fire bubbled across the ceiling, devouring plaster, making flame drip to the floor, where it hastily simmered against the carpet.

Niko lifted his own damp, soot-caked shirt to cover his mouth and nose, grabbed Vasili by the arm, and hauled him stumbling along. The corridors—so thick with smoke—all looked the same. They could be walking in circles or heading deeper into the fire. Shit, what way would see them safely clear?

Niko took a left, but Vasili pulled back, urging him another way.

Smoke poisoned Niko's lungs, burned his tongue and clogged his throat, making every breath shorter and tighter. His heart thumped too loudly in his ears. A few more rattling, thorny breaths and he'd be on his knees.

Vasili kicked open a door into a plain bedchamber. A servant's perhaps. Niko let the prince go and slammed the door behind them. Smoke still hung in the air, but the room was clear enough to see and pause and breathe.

A moment's rest. A breath. Coughs tore through Niko, doubling him over, making his eyes stream.

Vasili tossed Maria's scarf aside and threw open a pair of windows. Wind tore into the room, pulled the prince's hood down, and whipped his hair about him. Air hissed under the closed door, sucking out the smoke like some bizarre beast was inhaling somewhere deep inside the palace.

What came after a dragon inhaled...

Thunder rumbled the palace walls.

Fear flashed across Vasili's face.

Niko bolted for the window.

Whatever was outside better not be a long drop.

A hideous, bone-rattling boom splintered the door. Heat and splinters flew and then flame boiled the air. Niko grabbed for Vasili, latched on to his arm, and jumped from the window, yanking the prince with him.

A pitched roof rushed up. He hit hard, knee first, then rolled, lost his grip on Vasili, and slipped downward, sliding from slick tiles. Heat and light, glass and wood, exploded inches above his head. The edge of the roof vanished. He fell with nothing to grasp but air.

His back slammed into the ground, knocking air from his lungs. The world was still and numb and quiet. Flames waved at the black sky like a thousand Caville flags. It might have been beautiful if it weren't so deadly.

The roaring in his ears returned, along with a whole lot of hurt.

He turned his head to see Vasili crawling on his front, reaching for the book in the grass.

A trio of guards loomed from the smoke, their demeanor not that of saviors. Blades drawn, they bore down on Vasili. Vasili hadn't seen. His only care was the book he'd almost died for.

Niko took a breath to shout a warning. Coughs made his lungs writhe in his chest. He spluttered and heaved.

The guards all bore the grim mouths of men ordered to use force.

Dammit, he hadn't saved Vasili from the flames only for him to be murdered by his own guards.

Niko groped for his sword, remarkably still attached to his hip. His arm felt too heavy, his thick fingers uncoordinated, but he managed to grip the handle enough to yank the blade free and swing it into the dirt to lever himself onto his feet.

Vasili was on his knees now, the book under his hand, his face full of relief.

The foremost guard swung for Niko. Niko's reflexes kicked in quicker. He blocked the blade with his own. Metal sang.

A second guard plunged his sword down toward Vasili.

"No!" Niko yelled.

Vasili rolled at the last moment. The blade snagged his cloak, pinning the fabric to the ground and trapping the prince.

A gauntleted fist struck Niko's jaw. He flailed backward, his face a riot of pain. He tried to catch a breath to steady himself, but his body was submerged in molasses, his thoughts too slow. A second fist landed in his gut. He buckled around it, stumbling to a knee, and spat bile.

"Stop!" Vasili's shrill bark pierced the chaos.

The tears in Niko's eyes burned. He wildly swung the sword and hit something that felt like it should have been another man. Cold steel pressed against his neck, freezing him.

"Stop, damn you! Obey your fucking prince!"

"No half elf is a prince of Loreen," a guard growled.

Niko, on his knees, lifted his head and met the guard's

glare. They could be the same age and wore the same ragged lines around the eyes. A flicker of liquid dark swam across the man's irises. There and gone again. Or perhaps Niko's battered mind had hallucinated it. The guard grinned.

"Release him," Vasili barked.

The guard's grin grew, but whatever thought went through his head in that moment was his last. The small, shining blade flew from Niko's right—from Vasili—and plunged into the guard's throat. Niko watched, numbed, as the guard stumbled back, dropped his sword, and clutched at the dagger sticking out from his neck in the hope he could yank it free. If he did that, he'd bleed out in seconds.

The guard dropped, but then the other two sprang into motion. Both lunged for Vasili.

With a desperate burst of speed, Niko launched off his back foot, swung the sword, and managed to block the first deadly swing. That one had intended on taking Vasili's head.

Momentum drove him into the second guard, and they both tumbled to the ground. Niko scrambled on top, wrapped the fingers of his left hand around his neck, and drove his thumb up under his chin. The old, familiar, blood-chilling need to kill tore out all reasonable thought until there was just one driving desire left. His enemy would die.

Vasili's cry shattered Niko's blind rage. He tore his fingers free of the gasping guard's throat and scanned the grass for Vasili.

He lay on his back, the guard looming over him. Vasili could have brought a leg up, could have kneed the guard or kicked his weight-bearing leg out, or scrabbled backward, but he did none of those things. He lay still, frozen. Rapid, shallow breaths sawed out of him. The guard leered, savoring his moment.

Niko rose unnoticed. He pressed the tip of his sword up under the man's palace armor, against his lower back, over the right kidney.

The guard tensed.

"Toss your sword."

He tossed the sword aside.

One guard was dead. Another lay gasping in the grass. And now the third was disarmed. Their chances of escape weren't going to get any better.

Niko slowly circled around to face the guard. He kept his blade aimed at the man's middle and offered his left hand to Vasili.

The prince didn't move. Didn't look. Didn't *see*. Wherever he was in his head, it wasn't here.

"Vasili," Niko snapped.

He blinked, startled out of his fear, saw Niko's hand, and grabbed it. Niko hauled him to his feet and backed through the grass, away from the guard, keeping his sword up. "Run."

Vasili ran, the guard lunged for his sword, and Niko whirled, sprinting after Vasili's rippling cloak.

Nowhere in the palace was safe. Once again, they had to flee, and fast.

"The stables," Vasili called back.

Niko chased after him. The stables were a terrible idea. "The first place... they'll look," he panted, but Vasili was too damned fast and already strides ahead. Niko dashed into the cobbled stable yard behind Vasili to find the stalls empty. The horses had been set free, saving them from the flames.

Vasili turned on his heel and stalked by Niko, boots striking the cobbles. He flicked his hood back up. "He'll be in the fields." He coughed and staggered but righted himself and marched on as though nothing had happened, as though his home wasn't burning and the ash of his life wasn't slipping through his fingers.

It took a moment for Niko to realize who "he" was. "Wait." He grabbed the prince's arm without thinking and received a scathing glare that scorched as hot as the fire. Niko let go, but the prince's glare only darkened.

"This is madness," Niko wheezed, throat as dry as sand. "We could spend hours looking for Adamo. Find another damn horse."

Vasili's glare turned murderous.

"The guards want you dead. You have to get off the palace grounds. Take to the road. In the chaos, you'll go unnoticed."

"Amir has poisoned *everyone* against me." Vasili threw the words at him, as though this were his fault. "Adamo is all I have left." His voice cracked.

That sudden, lonely confession had Niko choking on words he dared not speak. Words of comfort that did not belong with Vasili. Words of safety and protection that Niko had no right thinking. Whatever the prince was or had been or might have been, that had all ended before anything had begun. Niko owed him nothing. His service to Vasili Caville was over. But the prince clearly needed help, and as much as Niko's head told him to abandon the bastard, some other part of him couldn't do it.

He could help him escape Loreen. He could do that. But no more. Vasili's troubles were not Niko's fight.

"I have a horse," Niko said. "I rode him here. He'll return to the forge. You can take him and leave Loreen." There wasn't anywhere in Loreen where Vasili wouldn't be recognized. His only choice was to flee the city. If it cost Niko a horse to get Vasili out of his life, so be it. "The guards won't look for you at my forge, not for a few days."

Bitterness twisted Vasili's thin smile. "Very well, Nikolas. Take me to your home."

CHAPTER 3

Vasili's hooded cloak hid him among the stream of people fleeing the palace. A passing farmer took pity on them, probably due to Niko's hacking cough, and offered a ride on his hay cart. The rattling cart made Niko cough harder, earning him another furious scowl from Vasili.

Thankfully, the ride was short. Niko's cottage and forge took up a corner position along Trenlake's dirt street, among other recently rebuilt houses. The farmer dropped them outside and headed toward his fields to collect his cows for milking. Red skies behind the forge cottage spoke of dawn approaching. Unlike the red skies behind them, which signaled what would surely be the end of Vasili's home.

Embers still throbbed in Niko's cottage fireplace grate. Inside was warm and dark and safe, and he'd never been more grateful to be home than he was in that moment. Assuming Vasili loomed behind him, he grabbed a few pieces of kindling and stoked the fire back to life.

Once the fire was roaring again, Niko glanced to confirm Vasili was still present. He'd been so damned quiet, he might have disappeared. If only he were that simple to be rid of.

Vasili had removed his scorched cloak, draped it over the back of the chair at the table, and reclined in Niko's favorite armchair. He almost looked to be sleeping. His eye was closed, his chest rising, hands resting on the chair's arms. The whitening fingertips gave him away. He held onto that chair like it was his lifeline. Vasili didn't sleep.

In the soft, shifting firelight, all Vasili's sharp angles had lost their edges. Soot blackened his cheek and chin. He looked like that chair was his last sanctuary. Vasili Caville looked disarmingly vulnerable.

A tickle in Niko's throat erupted his coughing all over again. He hacked and wheezed and dropped to his ass in front of the fire, leveling each breath until his lungs settled.

Vasili opened his eye and watched him from the armchair. Deep lines set into the corners of his mouth. He stared at the fire like he despised it.

Vasili Caville was furious.

Niko might have cared if his jaw and gut didn't throb from the guard's beating and his heart didn't ache from the fact he'd escaped the bastard seated opposite him for a year, but it hadn't been long enough. He'd need a whole lifetime to get over Vasili and what that palace had done to him. Now, Vasili was sitting in his favorite chair, in his cottage, in his life all over again, and he'd hardly changed at all.

He'd tell him to leave.

Tomorrow.

Until then, he wasn't sure he could stand to make it up the stairs to his bed. He shuffled backward and rested against a second armchair—this one far less comfortable than the one Vasili had taken—and rested his head back against the seat cushion. He was warm, alive, and safe. And sometimes that was all a man needed to get through the night.

~

SUNLIGHT POURED in through the small cottage windows when he opened his eyes again, and the fire had burned down to ashes.

Niko tried to shift from the floor, but everything ached, making him rise like an old man. He stretched out the aches and spotted Vasili. The prince had folded his tall, lean self into the armchair, one leg drawn up to his chest, the other stretched out. His head rested on his drawn-up knee, eye closed, his face so relaxed he could only be asleep.

Gods, it might have been the first time Niko had seen the man truly at ease.

A few waves of silvery blond hair had fallen over the prince's shoulder and lay across his cheek. Slightly parted pink lips looked softer when they weren't sneering. All of him looked smaller, tucked into that chair, like he could be someone's loving son, someone's brother, someone's lover.

Niko winced at that last thought and settled back down in his seated position to stare at the cold fire instead of the vulnerable prince. His gaze wandered back anyway.

To think that a man, the same age as Niko, had the

weight of the dark flame on his shoulders. All this time, he'd been fighting to save Loreen from elves. And now the palace was gone. His home turned to ash. His father dead, and his brothers... Well, one was dead, and the other was trying to ruin him by turning the people he'd sacrificed everything for against him.

It wasn't as though there was any real love in that palace. Perhaps Vasili would be relieved to have it gone?

Niko now knew one thing: Vasili did sleep after all.

He carefully got to his feet and crept from the room, then drew a few buckets of chilling water from the well in the back courtyard. Stripping off outside, he washed the smoke and soot from himself, then threw on fresh trousers and a shirt. Vicious bruises mottled his skin, but their ache would pass.

Carrying the second bucket into the house, he set it by the kitchen stove and was about to start making some hot tea when movement outside caught his eye.

From the kitchen window, he often looked out to the forge's hitching post to see who had left their animal for shoeing. Today was the seventh day of the week and a day meant for rest. There were no horses due until later. But one waited at the post, biting at an empty feed bag. "I'll be damned."

Niko quietly unlatched the back door and ventured around the front of the forge. The morning air nipped at his clean skin.

Adamo snorted a greeting, vapor clouding his nose, and stamped a hoof. The big white charger rocked its head, highly dissatisfied with an empty feedbag. Someone had managed to get a lead rope on him but no saddle. Adamo had probably bolted the second he'd been moved from his stall.

"There's a good boy." Niko brushed his fingers down the horse's nose and let him snuffle his palm. "No carrots today." Adamo's nostrils fluttered. Niko took the lead rope and guided the horse around the forge to the back of the cottage and tied him out of sight from the road. Vasili would be pleased. Typical the prince's horse showed up but Niko's old nag hadn't found its way home.

Niko briefly ran his hand over Adamo's flanks, checking for any sore spots or scuffs. He seemed remarkably well, although his brilliant white coat had greyed with ash in places.

"You found him." Vasili leaned against the back-door frame. He'd washed the dirt from his face. A few damp tendrils of hair had escaped his quick, messy ponytail. Burns had crimped his clothes in places. The trousers were ripped at the knee. His collar gaped where a few fasteners had been torn free. For all the scuffs and tears telling the story of last night, his expression was soft. Probably because of the horse.

"I suspect he found you." Niko patted Adamo's neck and hung a straw bag for the horse to chew on. If only princes were as easily pleased.

Vasili made an agreeable noise and sauntered over to dote on his hoofed companion. He lifted a hand to let Adamo snuffle the backs of his fingers. The horse flicked its tail and went back to prying the hay from the bag with his teeth.

A smile broke out across Vasili's lips. It was a bright and brilliant thing to witness and completely unfamiliar on his face. Like this vicious, callous man had a real heart somewhere. From everything Niko had seen, that heart was reserved for Adamo only.

Niko cleared his throat, upset his cough some more, and headed inside, away from Vasili. Adamo was here. That was good. Niko would make breakfast, because Mah had always told him it was the polite thing to do for guests, even if one despised their guest, and then Vasili would take Adamo and leave. And Niko would never have to see him again.

He cut the stale end off the bread, found the middle part fresh, and toasted a few slices on the stove, then set the kettle onto the stovetop to boil. All very normal. Even if having Vasili inside his cottage was far from normal.

He'd rebuilt every wall and window and nook and crevice with his own hands, and there was much still to do, but it was finally a place he could call home. Vasili was the first soul he'd let step foot inside.

"I lost the book."

Niko glanced up. "The one you went into a burning library for?"

Vasili stepped from the courtyard into the kitchen, and all at once, the room shrank around his presence. "I went in there to save *all* the pertinent books." He scanned the shelves, reading the hand-scrawled labels on the jars for herbs and flour. "That was the last." Vasili regarded the stove, with its burbling kettle and toast rack. The last time they'd shared anything nearly as domestic as this, Julian had been between them. Now, there was no Julian to distract. Just a whole lot of judgmental Vasili. "I dropped it in the grass. It's probably still there."

If he went back to that palace, the guards would kill

him. They'd made that clear. But it wasn't Niko's place to advise a prince.

He waited, but when Vasili didn't offer up any further information, his mind turned to that moment after falling from the roof when Vasili had tried to reach the book and the palace guards had turned on him. "Amir controls the guards?"

Vasili blinked, leaned back against the small countertop, and folded his arms. Considering they'd both fallen from a palace window and almost been killed, he didn't seem hurt or even bruised.

Vasili raised an eyebrow, and Niko averted his gaze. "I was just checking you weren't hurt."

"His influence began slowly," he said, ignoring Niko's comment.

Niko steered his attention from wandering up the length of Vasili and gathered the toast instead. He tossed the pieces onto two plates, then hastily strained some tea in cups. When he handed Vasili's out and received a soft thank-you, he wondered if he'd fallen from the palace roof and struck his head a lot harder than he'd first thought. This softer, bedraggled Vasili was too much like the Vasili from the farmhouse—the Vasili Niko had savagely kissed in a starlit field.

"After what he saw in Talos," Vasili said, "Amir must have realized the truth in our mother's tales and began rethinking them. Before, when he was younger—and not on spice—his mind was sharper."

Niko wrapped his fingers around the hot cup. He'd tried not to think of Amir since leaving the palace. Vasili didn't know the details of what had happened between Niko, Julian, and Amir, but the prince could guess from the state of Julian's body, the fiend's remains, and from whatever Amir had probably boasted of. It was enough. Niko had no wish to mention the fragments he remembered—like that terrible moment he'd ended the life of the lost soldier nobody had saved. He had enough horrors in his head without inviting those back in.

"He found ancient texts in a sealed-off section of the library," Vasili continued, his crisp, royal voice loud in the small kitchen. "Books even I didn't know existed. Books regarding the Caville sorcerers, those tied to the crown. And he began experimenting with the flame."

Niko met Vasili's gaze. The prince stared back, the ramifications too big a thing to convey with words alone. The small hairs on the back of Niko's neck rose. As much as Amir was a dangerous, spice-addled prick, if he managed to wield real power, he'd be as terrifying as his father. Lady Maria had mentioned the same. And gods, he'd left her there with a prince high on a power he barely understood.

"He used whores at first," the prince nonchalantly continued. "Placed his own blood in their wine."

"He spiked his doulos' wine with blood?" Was there no limit to how low Amir would stoop?

"You're surprised?" Vasili's brows rose.

"I wish I was." Amir had been fond of spice. Consuming it, snorting it, forcing it on others. Now he'd found a new substance to torture his pets with.

"It changed them like it did Julian."

A few sips of tea helped clear the knot in Niko's throat. It had been a year since he'd killed Julian, but some days the hurt still crept up on him. Did Vasili feel it, too, or was the viper still as cold and emotionless as he'd been when he'd used Niko as a distraction?

"But doulos aren't the most reliable of subjects. A few lost their minds. So Amir moved on to the palace guards."

Niko recalled the flicker of darkness he'd thought he'd seen in the guard's eyes, a tiny fragment of the dark he'd once seen in Vasili's eye. Then it was real. "He's poisoned the guards against you."

"It was subtle at first."

"Amir doesn't do subtle."

"That's the same mistake I made, assuming he can't change. A few months ago, a squad ambushed me in the corridors. I only survived because the other palace staff intervened. I had no choice but to recuperate in my chambers. In my absence, Amir began spreading his rumors. I'm sure you've heard them..." His cheek flickered, belying the nonchalance in his voice.

Those rumors had spread through Loreen. Vasili was half elf, Vasili fucked elves, which was why he didn't engage with any doulos, Vasili was mad, Vasili was poisonous. All rumors Vasili could have ended had he been visible. But he'd been wounded and absent, and so the rumors gained weight.

"Did Amir set the fire?" Niko asked.

"I suspect not. Amir would not willingly destroy our home. With the guards distracted or under Amir's thrall, anyone could walk right in and set a blaze."

"Elves?" Niko asked.

"Possibly. They've been quiet. But we've had no reports of elves in our land since Talos's death."

"They'd benefit from the palace's fall. Loreen is vulnerable without the royal seat."

Vasili sipped his tea instead of replying, his thoughts wandering. He hadn't touched his toast. Niko looked at his, now cold, and didn't feel much like eating either.

The palace could be rebuilt, but Vasili had lost his influence, which left Amir to oversee the reconstruction, and the middle prince clearly had other priorities.

There was one way out of all this, one solution Vasili hadn't yet mentioned but was surely on his bitter lips. "If you were to *deal with* Amir, permanently," Niko said quietly, "all the dark flame would funnel to you."

Vasili set his mug on the countertop beside him and lifted his head, his face carefully guarded. "You say that as though such a thing is trivial."

"It's not as though you haven't hired assassins before."

Vasili's thin smile cut across his lips. Probably remembering the moment he tried to buy Niko in the Stag and Horn pleasure-house. "Yes, but that is not the only challenge to overcome."

When the flame poured into Vasili, he'd have to control it, and the recent Cavilles had proven how hard a thing the dark flame was to wrangle.

Fucking Cavilles. And all because someone, seven hundred years ago, decided to charge them with the dark flame's protection, or curse them with it. Niko still wasn't sure on that. "All of this could have been avoided had a less insane family been charged with protecting the flame," Niko mumbled.

"The flame corrupts what it touches."

Niko arched a brow. "I'd noticed."

"The Cavilles are victims."

"Uh-huh," Niko replied, ironically. "You can also argue

the sky is down and the ground up. Doesn't make it right, though."

Vasili's lips twitched somewhere between a snarl and a grin. "I've missed your bluntness."

"I haven't missed you. So, if you're done recounting your familial drama, you can take your horse and go, Your Highness."

The small smile fell from Vasili's lips. "You'd turn me out during the day in the middle of a village in which I'll surely be recognized? How far do you think I'd get? A few miles? Maybe you'd prefer to watch the guards take me back to the palace grounds and whip me for all to see? Petty vengeance does not become you."

Mention of the whipping was deliberate. Niko still bore a few scars from the lashing Vasili had ordered, apparently to prevent him from being executed. He still wasn't sure whether that was true or if Vasili just got off on whips. "Nightfall then. But unlike princes, I have to work to eat, so stay away from the windows and keep your hands to yourself while I see to my customers."

Vasili glanced about the kitchen, with its messy shelves, range of mismatched pans, and tatty chair. Whatever he saw in the chaos, he kept it from his face.

"Humble," he said, and for some reason, that irked Niko more than had he stayed silent.

"And remove your damn clothes. You're stinking up my house."

Vasili's lips parted. He looked down at himself, and Niko almost barked the laugh crawling up his throat. Vasili tugged at the shirt, as though only now realizing how he looked.

"I'll fix them up for you." He regretted it before the words had left his mouth.

The prince raised a silvery eyebrow. "Needlework seems a little delicate for your"—a theatrical pause —"rough hands."

He snorted. Asshole. "Mah was a seamstress."

"Ah, yes, to Lord Bucland." Who was apparently Niko's real father. Vasili didn't say it, but the implication glinted in his eye.

"I can wield a needle just as well as a hammer. Leave the clothes at the foot of the stairs. You'll find some spare shirts in my room—don't touch anything else."

Vasili's face scrunched into an expression caught somewhere between horror and surprise. Niko chuckled and left the kitchen.

Vasili believed he knew Niko. He had no fucking idea who he was. A toy soldier, a pet assassin—those things Vasili had made Niko into. It was almost a shame Vasili wouldn't be around long enough to witness the real Nikolas Yazdan, the blacksmith who had built a new life with his own two hands.

CHAPTER 4

With the day's horses shod and the forge quenched, Nikolas would normally have begun work on the cottage, but today he washed and dried Vasili's clothes and stitched the tears together as good as mostly new. Admittedly, he was not as proficient with a needle as he'd made out to Vasili, but the repairs were passable.

Vasili had spent much of the day in the courtyard, brushing down Adamo, preferring the horse's company to Niko's. The sight of him in Niko's oversized shirt had all manner of complicated thoughts springing into Niko's head. None of which he lingered on.

Niko left the folded clothes on the kitchen table and tended to a passing customer wanting to purchase a pair of door hinges. By the time he was done, he had returned to find the clothes gone and the kitchen tidied. Pans that he'd left on the side had been neatly stacked on shelves, their handles facing the same way. The herbs had been organized in alphabetical order. Even the stove had been freshly stoked and logs stacked beside it. Vasili had been in the cottage for less than a day and already he was changing everything.

The sound of boots rapped down the cottage stairs.

"I liked the pans the way they were." Niko folded his arms.

Vasili—all neatly reclothed in his stitched-up finery—cast a gaze about the kitchen as though he had no idea what Niko referred to. "However did you find anything?"

"I knew where everything was. I didn't need to *find* it."

Vasili waved a hand. "It's done."

"Your horse is fed, watered, and reshod."

The prince's gaze skipped to the back window overlooking the courtyard where Adamo dozed at his post. His cheek fluttered, thoughts drifting toward his next move. He took his cloak and threw it over his shoulders, clasping it closed at his neck. His fingers were quick, smooth. No wonder he was deadly with daggers.

"Where will you go?" Niko asked, then wished he hadn't when Vasili's intense gaze swung back to him.

"You do not need to know."

Fair enough. He didn't need to know. And didn't want to. Niko leaned back against the sink, leaving Vasili's path to the back door clear. He could leave anytime he pleased. There was nothing here to hold him back. It was time.

Vasili's fingers still fiddled with the cloak clasp, unnecessarily adjusting it.

Where he went next was not Niko's business.

As soon as the prince left, that would be the end of it.

"I should thank you, I suppose." Vasili looked up.

By the three, Vasili really must have been shaken from his fall. "What for?"

"The library—"

"I didn't return there for you."

"The flame, of course. *Loreen* should thank you. But as they don't know of your service, my word will have to do." Vasili lowered his hand from the clasp and straightened. "A griffin must forever hold the flame. You have been instrumental in its protection. Thank you, Nikolas Yazdan, for your service to the griffin."

His first instinct was to tell the griffin where it could shove its thanks. Vasili's thanks didn't erase the abuse and lies and betrayal. But he'd never expected the prince to even acknowledge his help in any of it, and now he had, he wasn't entirely sure what to do with that. Maybe he had changed in a year.

Vasili's gaze skipped away, and then the prince ducked out the door, in motion and *leaving*, exactly as Niko had wanted. So why in the ever-loving fuck was his heart racing like he was about to make a terrible mistake in letting Vasili go? Why did his body give a damn that the prince was adjusting the saddle Niko had supplied and would soon be galloping away, probably into obscurity?

Niko stepped into the doorway. He'd gone into the burning palace to prevent something terrible happening. He'd risked his life to protect Loreen from the nightmare of the Caville curse. And now he was about to let half the source of that curse leave with no guards, no advisors, no protectors? Vasili only had that damned devil horse that would probably one day throw him just for the hell of it, and Niko was just going to let him go?

Vasili had been alone since the moment the elves stole him from the palace gardens. Even if he wanted help, he probably didn't know how to ask for it. Cruel and vicious as he was, he also bore the weight of a terrible burden. One few knew of. The cuckoo in the nest. *Free our bird.*

Niko cleared his throat. "I suppose, if you wanted—"

Vasili slotted his boot into the stirrup, grabbed Adamo's reins, and hauled himself into the saddle. Adamo stamped his hooves, sensing his rider's tension. Vasili turned the horse away from Niko and settled the reins loosely in both hands.

He smiled. "I'd like to say it's been a pleasure knowing you, Nikolas, but it really hasn't."

Niko arched a brow. "Fuck you too, prince."

Vasili's smile flourished into a grin. He nudged Adamo with his heels, clicked his tongue, and urged the horse to trot out of the yard.

Niko loitered at the yard wall. The prince pulled his hood up, and Adamo trotted down the road toward the forest on the outside of the village. Dusk painted the sky red ahead of him, turning the trees into silhouettes of jagged teeth. Lamplight flickered in the windows of the cottages he passed. Darkness would soon settle across the land.

And the three gods be damned because Niko's heart raced harder, anxiety gnawing on his nerves.

He hated the man, but he'd also seen the truth inside him, and whatever the future held, Vasili was unlikely to survive the flame alone. He'd told Niko as much. He knew his future was dire. And still he walked toward it with his head held high.

The horse and rider were distant now, about to disappear over the brow of a hill.

Vasili had saved Niko from the elves. He'd said it was because Niko was his tool, but there were other tools, other men Vasili could manipulate. Yet he'd stalked the elves and trampled one to death to save Niko when he should have returned to the palace to stop Julian, the real traitor to the griffin. Instead, Vasili had taken Niko to safety and sat by him as he'd recovered, wasting time and risking the palace's security.

Was the man as much a viper as he appeared, or was he something—someone—else? Someone so damaged he didn't expect help and wouldn't ask for it. He was a brat of a prince, there was no doubt in that, but he was also a thousand other complicated pieces of a puzzle that Niko barely understood. He'd seen moments in him, softer moments from the man beneath the ice. He did exist, but he was damned difficult to get to beneath Vasili's tendency to push everyone away.

However, for all their disagreements, they did believe in one thing: protecting Loreen.

The rider was out of sight now, and night was fast approaching.

Vasili was gone. He didn't need Niko anyway. Snakes like him always survived.

Niko returned to the cottage and stopped at the sight of the pans on the kitchen shelves. Small to large, each neatly placed. He had half a mind to shift them around again.

He would tomorrow. But it was late and there was little left to do but retire for the night.

Sleep wouldn't come. His mind played over the image of Vasili riding into the dark. He'd go south. East was out of the question. Elves waited there. The rigid mountains lay due north. West was eventually the ocean, but with little between Loreen and the sea. South... to the hot, exotic city of Seran, where the houses were built on top of one another around dusty, sand-strewn streets, against a backdrop of glittering ocean.

Or so his mah had told him.

The perfect place to disappear.

A clattering of approaching hooves grew louder outside. Unusual for the hour. Niko threw on trousers and a shirt and leaned against the wall, catching a glimpse of the mounted group out the window.

Six riders gathered outside, blazing torches in hand. Two were dismounting. No armor or insignia, but only palace guards rode horses like theirs.

A thumping sounded on the cottage door, threatening to break it off its hinges. "Open up!"

If Niko ran out the back, they'd spot him. Running implied guilt. If he stood his ground, denied knowing anything, they might get rough, but they wouldn't want to risk waking the village and would eventually leave. There was no reason to suspect Niko had harbored the prince. He was just a lowly blacksmith.

Niko grabbed his sword and headed downstairs. He rested the blade against the wall and unlatched the front door.

"Nikolas Yazdan?" The man standing on the step looked to be no older than Niko. He'd probably fought elves in the war, maybe seen the same things Niko had. A small scar marked his chin, either put there by a razor or an escape from their enemies' bigger blades.

"Yes?"

Scar's expression remained flat, most uninterested. "We've been sent from the palace. We have some questions. Can we come in?" There was nothing friendly in the way he asked. The words were hollow.

"Can't this wait 'til morning?"

"No."

"I think it can. Come back at dawn." Niko closed the door, but Scar's hand shot out, blocking it.

"Don't make this difficult, Yazdan," he leered, leaning in. "Just let us in and nobody gets hurt."

The remaining riders dismounted. Six on one. Niko's sword would even the odds. He stepped back and reached for the blade.

The door flew in. Niko snatched for his sword, used his own momentum to fall against the wall out of reach, and swung the blade toward Scar's lunging figure. Clashing metal sang, the impact shuddering up Niko's arm. The man sneered, coming in hot and fast. He swung his short-sword high. Niko ducked, and the blade slammed into the back of the armchair Vasili had been resting in just the night before.

More men spilled into the cottage. Guards, they had to be, but dressed lightly, quick and easier to attack.

Panic tried to trip Niko's thoughts. He buried it beneath a rising anger.

They'd brought their flaming torches with them.

Firelight danced, painting the walls with moving shadows.

One of them plunged his torch against the tired old chair by the fireplace.

"Don't!"

Too late. Fire quickly licked up the weathered upholstery.

A sword pommel struck Niko's jaw. In a blink, he was on his knees. Fingers locked in his hair and yanked him back to his feet. Fire rippled up the cottage walls. It could still be saved. All his work, all the time invested... It wasn't too late.

Niko roared and whirled blindly, lashing out with the sword. Its edge caught one of them, making him wail. Niko slammed his head back, hitting the man who held him. He grunted, grip loosening, and Niko thrust his elbow back, meeting something soft. The man oomphed over. Niko slammed the blade handle into the side of his face, smashing bones.

Heat and light surged overhead.

No, no, no... He couldn't stop it now.

A fist landed on Niko's lower back. Black, searing heat scorched up his spine. He barked a cry and dropped to his knees again.

"Courtesy of King Amir!" Scar hissed in his ear. Fingers wrapped around his throat. "Where's Vasili?"

Gods, there were too many of them, and the fire, it was out of control like it had been at the palace.

"Where's Vasili, huh?" The grip tightened—squeezed.

Niko dropped his sword and dug his fingers into those choking him. His chest burned like the fire surrounding them. His heart pounded hot and loud in his ears—he couldn't answer anyway.

Scar suddenly let go.

Niko fell forward, gulping and spluttering air.

"Where is he?!"

His sword. On the floor to his right. Fire reflected

along its blade. He reached forward, stretching his fingers toward the handle.

A kick dug into his side, ripping air from his lungs. Niko rolled, clutching to consciousness even as his head throbbed.

Fire boiled across the ceiling and dripped down the walls. He coughed hard, choking on smoke.

"Not much of a butcher now, are you?" Scar grinned. Smoke—darker than that filling the cottage—swam across his wide, bloodshot eyes. There and gone again. Possessed.

He straddled Niko and grabbed his throat again. "You're going to tell me where Vasili is, and then I'm going to take you back to King Amir. How does that sound, butcher?"

Couldn't he see the fire? Wasn't it burning his skin? His eyes streamed, his face flushed with heat and sweat, but he leered at Niko as though there was no fire. Perhaps in his madness, all he cared about was following Amir's orders.

Niko's scrabbling fingers wrapped around his sword's handle, and he thrust the sword into Scar's waist, plunging it through, beneath his ribs, and out his other side. Scar's hold still clamped hard and his smile stayed. Didn't the bastard know he had a sword in his middle?! Then his manic grin stuttered, his body reacting to the blade through his guts. Blood bubbled from his lips. Finally, his grip on Niko's throat eased.

Niko yanked the blade free and kicked the man backward, straight into a wall of flame. Fire rushed up his clothes, devouring him and his screams in seconds.

Blistering heat scorched Niko's arms and face. He rolled onto his front, staying low, beneath the smoke, and crawled forward—sword in hand—toward the doorway.

Guards waited outside. One lunged, grabbed him by the arm, and hauled him away from the cottage. They'd burned his cottage, his home, the only damn thing he'd had left in this wretched world. Rage and dismay flipped into a state far more deadly.

Niko dropped his sword, lurched off his back foot, tackled the guard to the ground, clamped his head in both hands, and slammed his skull down, feeling it crack like an egg. The guard's bladder let go, wetting Niko's thigh.

Instinct pulled him back, made him turn at just the right time to duck a blade's swing. Niko punched the bastard in his weight-bearing knee. Bone popped, snapping into an odd angle, and the man screamed as he went down. It required no thought to take the guard's shortsword and slash open his throat. He knew, like he'd known at the front, that he had to kill or be killed. And killing came *so damn easily*.

Too soon, the guards stopped coming. Niko stood in the street, watching his life burn, while Amir's palace guards lay bloody and motionless at his feet.

Fire roared from his cottage, spewing from windows and spiraling from the roof, spitting hot embers into the night sky.

His home burned like the palace.

Amir would pay for this.

They'd all fucking pay for this.

He switched the stolen shortsword to his right hand, grabbed a second fallen blade and walked away from the flames toward a horse brought by the guards. Mounting up, he dug his heels in, kicked the animal into a screaming gallop, and doubled down, racing along the same road Vasili had taken hours before.

CHAPTER 5

He rode hard through the night and into the day, exhausting the horse until it plodded into the industrial town of Tinken. Dusk had pulled the smoke from the mining stacks down into Tinken's streets, cloaking Niko's arrival.

He hadn't been sure, at first, whether to come at all. Oh, Amir had burned his cottage, but the destruction at the hands of the Cavilles had begun long before that. It had all begun in the Stag and Horn with a prince offering him a bag of coin. From that moment on, Vasili had toyed with him like he wasn't a man, like he was a dog. A beaten dog, just as Amir had called him.

The burning of the cottage had been the last damned lash of the whip.

Niko was going to remind Vasili how he was very much alone now, in a world that would kill him for the poison in his blood.

Vasili would be in Tinken, because the fucking prince knew Niko would come. Just like he knew Niko would return to the palace eventually. He just didn't know Niko was coming with a rage in his heart as hot as the fire that had taken his home.

He dismounted outside the inn they'd visited all those months ago and shoved through the door inside, finding it as packed as usual. Nobody noticed the blades he'd tied to his back or the blood and smoke about his clothes. Adrian spotted Niko's approach, narrowed his eyes, and leaned over the bar. "No trouble now, eh? What do you want?"

"The man I came here with before—"

"Upstairs, first door on the right. If you kill him, you clean it up."

Niko's smile couldn't have been the sanest of smiles, given how Adrian recoiled.

The door to Vasili's room opened, unlocked. But the prince wasn't inside. His grey cloak was tossed over the chair, so he was nearby.

Niko grabbed the armchair by the bed and dragged it to the window, then shrugged off the swords, rested them against the chair, and settled into its embrace. From that position, he watched the door.

He didn't have long to wait.

The door opened with an aged creak. Vasili strode in and came to an abrupt halt. He lifted his chin like he did every time he was about to launch into some lashing remark.

He'd lost the fancy clothes somewhere and wore plain trousers, knee-high boots, and a billowing white shirt, the kind with ruffles at the open V-neck. A make-do patch of grey fabric covered his scarred eye. The plain clothes did little to diffuse his royal air of superiority.

"You knew I'd come," Niko said. His voice scratched,

made rough by smoke and exhaustion. "You knew I'd come to this tavern. That's why you're here in this one, instead of the half a dozen others nearby." Of course he fucking knew. If the guard hadn't mentioned Amir, Niko might even have thought Vasili sent them, just to make damned sure he had nothing left either, and of course he'd trudge after Vasili, like the faithful dog he was.

Vasili stepped to the side, heading toward a sideboard. Did he have a blade stashed inside? "What happened?"

Niko gripped the chair's arms beneath his fingers. "Guess, Your Highness. Look at the blood and smell the smoke, and fucking guess what happened."

Vasili turned his back on Niko—a dangerous thing to do considering he must have sensed how Niko itched to spring from the chair and deliver the kind of justice he should have given Vasili long ago.

Glass chinked, and when Vasili turned around again, he held two drinks.

The prince approached, boots striking the floor. Stopping in front of Niko, he offered a glass.

Niko swallowed. His throat was parched. He'd stopped to drink from a stream only once. But taking the drink seemed an acceptance, like admitting nothing had changed. Vasili still stood over him, wielding all the control, and Niko still looked up to him.

Vasili stiffened again, tilted his head, and then set the glass on the bedside table, within Niko's reach. He sipped his own drink, eyeing Niko over the glass. His gaze dropped to the bloody blades leaning against the chair and then back to Niko's face.

"I didn't know you'd come. I chose this tavern because it's the only place I know outside of Loreen."

"Fucking liar."

"What is it you think I've done, Nikolas? I did not burn your cottage. I did not force you to ride south. What terrible crime have I committed to earn your ire?"

"Would you like a fucking list?" He wasn't going to voice all the ways in which Vasili had screwed him. The prince knew them all, he just wanted to hear them be acknowledged.

"Had you stayed in the palace, this would never have happened," Vasili said, sounding like a brat who hadn't gotten his own way.

"Stayed?" Niko frowned. "Nothing could have made me stay. Fire was too good an end for that place. I'm glad it's ashes." Niko pushed from the chair, scooped up the drink, and downed it in one. It burned, but in a way that warmed his empty soul. Knowing the palace was probably a ruin relieved some of the weight from his shoulders. He'd been living in its shadow all year. But at least he hadn't been living *in it*. Vasili had. "Did *you* burn the palace?"

"Why would I?"

"Because the damn place is cursed."

"The people are cursed."

Niko held the prince's glare. Vasili gave nothing away, just stared back, as emotionless as a rock. He hadn't denied it, though.

Striding around the prince, Niko grabbed the wine bottle and poured himself a fresh glass. He downed it in a single gulp. Vasili could have set the fire, but so could any one of the remaining Cavilles, and did it really matter? The palace was gone, and so was his cottage.

Vasili watched him warily. He'd eased to the side, keeping the door within sprinting distance.

Niko wasn't going to hurt him. He'd liked the idea of it, but now he was here, hurting Vasili changed nothing from the past, and there's where all the pain truly came from. Now the anger had waned, he was just bone tired.

He approached the prince and raised his glass. "To destroying your prick of a brother." The third glass went down as smoothly as the first. Vasili silently observed and judged and despised, like he always had.

Niko dropped onto the edge of the bed and lay back, not caring he lay on Vasili's bed for the night. The prince could sleep on the floor. He just needed to rest a while, just think... just... close his eyes and go somewhere the Cavilles couldn't reach him.

If only they didn't chase him in his dreams too.

CHAPTER 6

Niko woke in the morning still sprawled across the bed, fully clothed and stinking of horse and blood. A clattering sounded in the room. He winced into the daylight.

A serving girl curtsied beside a tin bath. "Paid for by your companion, sir. Leave your clothes by the door, and we'll see they're cleaned and dried."

She left, and Niko stared at the steam swirling off the bath. He staggered to his feet and crossed the room, half expecting to see snakes slithering beneath the water. It seemed the sort of thing Vasili would tease him with. Although, Vasili had, in the past, proven he could think of others as well as himself. After whipping Julian, he'd made sure the soldier had enjoyed a bountiful breakfast and day off. Payment for pleasures rendered. If Vasili couldn't pay by coin, he'd buy loyalty another way. Was that what this bath was? Payment for joining him?

Niko had half a mind to ignore the bath, but the stench of blood, smoke, and sweat wafting off his clothes overrode his pride. He stripped to his undergarments, left the clothes outside the door—nobody was going to steal that ragged mess—and once naked, stepped into the steaming water. Filth flaked off his skin.

By the three, he needed this more than he'd realized. Blood had dried inside the cracks in his hands and ash fell from his hair. He dunked his head and ran his fingers through the wet locks.

The cottage hadn't been much, but it had been his. Bastard Cavilles. He'd make that weaselly prick Amir pay, but not like he was, with no resources, just a horse and a blade, and a prince he hated.

He could get Vasili away. Go south, to Seran, where they'd both regroup. He'd figure out the rest on the way there.

After climbing from the tub, he wrapped himself in a towel and used the shaving implements to take off the rough beard. The road ahead would be hard. Not least because he had to share the month-long journey with Vasili. It'd be a miracle if he didn't kill him himself. There were coaches, but those large, fast wagons were routinely looted. Better to travel alone and take to the old tracks where their passing would go unnoticed.

A knock came around lunchtime. His clothes were delivered, cleaned and dried. The efficient service must have cost Vasili one of his many rings. Niko hastily dressed and headed down to the bar. They'd lingered long enough. It was time to move on.

He found Vasili seated at the bar, casually tucking into a lunch of bread and sausage alongside a man draped in a heavy but colorful, multilayered riding cloak. Vasili said something through a smirk, the man laughed, deep and smooth, and the gem in the rider's ear twinkled.

Having lunch with strangers on the road was the last thing Vasili should have been doing. The mistake was unlike Vasili, as was the grin on the prince's lips. What was this then? Some game to get a rise out of Niko?

The stranger leaned in, muttered something under his breath, and carelessly touched Vasili's hand. Vasili's pale lashes fluttered at the touch. His throat moved, but his smile stayed, albeit more wooden than before.

"Ah, Lycus." Vasili pulled his hand free and grinned at Niko like he'd had a pleasant personality transplanted into him while Niko bathed. "Come, meet Yasir Lajani. He's traveling south and offered us a place on his wagon as we're heading the same way."

It took a moment for Niko to understand Vasili was talking to him. *Lycus?*

Yasir lifted dark eyes, his grin inexplicably widening as Niko drew closer. He offered his hand. Niko shook, noting several sparkling rings. He had small golden loops dangling from his ears too, as was the custom in the south. If Vasili was a viper, this man was surely a fox. What a wonderful pair they made.

"Well met, Lycus," Yasir said, his voice heavily accented, making some words roll. "I had a disagreement with my traveling partner," he grinned like the disagreement was entirely deliberate, "and find myself without companions. You'll be doing me a favor, just so long as you can ride alongside and keep an eye out for thieves."

"Lycus is a competent swordsman," Vasili added, finishing his lunch and washing it down with ale. Yasir didn't see his quick, sideways glance aimed at Niko.

"More than competent, eh?" Yasir's eyebrows lifted appreciatively. "I know a soldier when I see one. With your looks, you've got some southern blood in you too?"

Niko grunted noncommittally. "My mah was southern."

Recognizing a fellow southerner, Yasir's grin broadened. "How long did you serve on the front?"

"Eight years."

"The whole war," Yasir said, impressed. "Must have Walla's luck on your side." Gods, he was loud and animated, like a southern clown seated beside Vasili's restraint.

"I killed elves before they killed me."

Yasir conceded with a nod. "I dare say that's it." He glanced at Vasili, who returned the man's light smile with one of his own. It wasn't real. Niko knew his real smiles, and they were fleeting, twitching things he rarely released into the wild. What game was this now? What did Vasili want from this man?

"And where were you, Yasir, during the war?" Niko asked. He didn't look like a soldier. He had the wiry physique of someone better-suited for stealth than swinging a blade. He reminded Niko a little of the poet he'd known, and beautiful men like him hadn't lasted long in the ugly face of war. "Which front did you fight on?"

The man's grin slipped sideways. "There'll be plenty of time for talk on the road. Are you both ready? Time and tide wait for no mortal soul." He donned a wide-rimmed hat designed to keep the rain from his neck and tossed a few coins on the bar. "I've had more than my share of Loreen's damp air and your huddled little houses. The south, she does-a beckon me into her ample bosom." He strode from the bar with a swirl of colored cloak, taking his dramatic flair with him.

Niko frowned after him, then arched an eyebrow at the prince. "Lycus?"

"Old Loreen for wolf."

Niko snorted. "Better than dog, I suppose. And what am I to call you?"

"Varian," Vasili slid from the stool. "I trust you won't get confused." Vasili's gaze snagged on Niko's and lingered.

Did he want Niko to ask about the traveler? Niko didn't even know where to start. "Why? We don't need him."

Vasili glanced at the door. "He has a wagon," he said.

"Oh. Well. I'm sure that will be some comfort when he stabs us both in the back, steals our horses, and hands you over to Amir. I shall say to myself, *At least he has a wagon*."

A glimmer of Vasili's real smile thawed some of the ice in his eye. "Come along, *Lycus*." He straightened the bar stool and realigned his cloak and hood. "Didn't you hear? Time and tide wait for no soul."

Niko gestured with a flick of his wrist for Vasili to walk ahead and muttered, "Assuming you have one, Your Highness."

Yasir said a whole lot. In less than a day, he'd spilled how he came from a coastal family of six brothers and one sister, all of whom were apparently older than Yasir, who, as a self-proclaimed free-sprit and the youngest, had broken from his familial fisher business to set up trade in silk. He talked about trade and about his beloved city of

Seran, and Vasili rode alongside him on the wagon on the uncovered bench-seat, silently soaking up the information.

Niko rode ahead to watch for damaged sections of road or thieves. Adamo was hitched to the rear of the goods wagon, content enough to plod along behind its clattering wheels.

Earlier in the day, when they'd stopped to water the horses, Niko had taken a look under the wagon's covers and found colored silk, just as Yasir had said. But something about Yasir and his tales made Niko's instincts itch, and it had nothing to do with the way he occasionally watched Vasili when the prince was looking away, a hungry look in his eyes like those men and women from the Stag and Horn who'd just been shown a fat bag of coin.

Admittedly, Vasili outside the palace—with his hair loose and his porcelain skin warmed by the sun—had a magnetic elegance Niko had too often caught himself admiring. Like the easy, graceful way Vasili mounted Adamo, or the brush of the reins through his long, elegant fingers. Or when he thought nobody was watching and he tipped his face skyward. Niko could hardly fault Yasir for noticing Vasili when the prince was so difficult to ignore. But Yasir had no idea all Vasili's allure held a rotten core. Niko would make sure to tell him later.

Yasir had a loud mouth, a velveteen accent, and a quick tongue that had probably gotten him in trouble time and time again. Even Niko caught himself chuckling at some new scandalous tale Yasir filled the quiet with. He was an easy man to like.

Julian had been an easy man to like too. And that hadn't turned out so well.

They made camp under a broad yew tree, ate roasted

rabbit and dried rice cakes, and Yasir was out like a lamp the second he laid his head on his bedroll. Vasili lay on his side by the fire, propped on an elbow, one leg stretched out, the other bent. He stared into the flames as though their little campfire held all the answers.

Niko watched the road from the edge of their camp. The fire would keep wild animals and the chill at bay, but it would draw any nearby thieves and elves toward them.

Vasili moved from the fire after nightfall and approached Niko. "What are you thinking?" he whispered, leaning against a tree.

The fire crackled and hissed behind them, throwing its light over Yasir's sleeping figure.

"If he's a spy, you're making his job a whole lot easier."

Vasili gazed into the darkness beyond the firelight, where moonlight painted the snaking roadway white. "He's not my brother's spy."

An owl hooted far away, then its partner answered somewhere overhead.

Niko huffed, folded his arms, and glared at the road, keeping Vasili in his peripheral vision. The prince couldn't know Yasir was harmless for certain, but he had spoken as though he'd been absolutely sure. And Niko *believed* him. Even knowing he shouldn't. Vasili had known Julian was a liar. He used everyone by understanding what motivated them. If Yasir was a spy, Vasili would know it, and he'd probably use it.

So, if he wasn't a spy, what was he to Vasili?

"You did not ask me what I'm thinking," Vasili said softly, his face tipped gently toward the stars.

Niko arched a brow. "Because your head is a dangerous place. What are you thinking, Varian?" He didn't believe for a single moment that he'd get a straight answer.

"How I might enjoy the south." He returned to the fireside to settle on his bedroll, leaving Niko frowning after him. What did he mean by that? Niko rolled his eyes and faced the road again. If only it were as easy to turn his thoughts from the prince too. He had no hope of understanding Vasili. The best hope he had was to survive him. Considering how everything the prince had touched of late had been reduced to ash, even that hope was a dying one.

If only Niko hadn't seen the dark flame with his own eyes, he could walk away right now. Though, even that thought felt like a lie, like Vasili was in his head somehow, turning his own thoughts against him. Because for all his dreaming of leaving the prince, he couldn't bring himself to abandon him.

CHAPTER 7

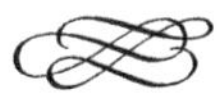

The ragged old carthorse had thrown a shoe. The creature had probably walked the roads its entire life and looked as enthused about their journey as Niko was. Yasir suggested Adamo would make a fine trap animal and received a look from Vasili that was the closest the prince had come to revealing his Caville bloodline during the three days they'd been on the road, making Niko snort a laugh.

"Only if you want to lose your wagon and your life." Niko patted Yasir on the shoulder and unhitched the horse. Walking the animal to a flat verge, he spotted a brook through the trees. "A good place to make camp for the night?"

Yasir agreed, and when Vasili had no objections, Yasir built a fire while Niko saw to the horse's cracked hooves. Black clouds rolled in at dusk, followed by a persistent rain that drove Yasir and Niko inside the wagon. At least the silks were soft.

Vasili volunteered to take the first watch. Draped in his

cloak, he swung into the driver's seat. Yasir, predictably, fell asleep in minutes. The man clearly had no nightmares haunting him.

Sleep proved elusive for Niko. After hours of listening to the rain tap on the wagon, he threw on Yasir's riding cloak and left the dry comfort of the wagon. Vasili gave him a small nod, and he climbed onto the bench beside him. The prince had been alone in the rain and the dark for hours.

"Yasir is fast asleep," Niko said, leaning a little closer so the patter of the rain on the wagon roof didn't drown him out. "You can head inside, if you like."

"It's fine."

A flash of silver caught Niko's eye. He glanced down at the unsheathed dagger in Vasili's lap.

"I still see them in the shadows even though they aren't there," Vasili explained. His hood hid most of his face, revealing only the tilt of his mouth as he spoke. "I hear them... all the time."

Niko pressed his teeth together and stared ahead. The light was so poor, he could barely make out the road, just tree trunks in the dark like prison bars. The only elves here were those inside Vasili's memories.

Julian had told him how elves had kept Vasili caged and bled him for the power in his veins. A power he hadn't fully possessed at the time. There were details Niko wished he didn't know, and while Julian's tales could have been lies, given the evidence, they were all likely true. Julian had lulled the young, tortured man in the cage into his confidence, befriending him, freeing him, all the while the elves had fed Julian Vasili's blood, making him their efficient tool, seeding him inside the Caville palace.

Vasili had trusted him.

Julian's betrayal was absolute.

Niko rubbed his chest, over his heart, where it ached whenever he thought of the war and the terrible things he'd seen, and of Julian.

Vasili's hooded head bowed, hiding all his face in shadow. "I led them to me." Rain patted on the wagon roof behind, puncturing the thick silence. "When I was twelve, I used the tunnels to leave the palace. I'd visit a smallholding outside the city walls—met a farmer's son." Vasili paused, weighing the memories. "Alek. And while I was with him, I wasn't a prince, the dark flame didn't haunt my blood. I was... nobody." He paused again, perhaps to capture the memory, or to guard himself against it. "I collected eggs, milked cows. It was mundane and earthy, and I... Joy was rare in the palace, and I... enjoyed my time outside its walls."

Niko closed his eyes. Gods, to think of Vasili in such simple surroundings did things to Niko's resolve. He saw Vasili chopping wood again in a memory that had never seemed real, even when he'd watched it happen. That memory and his words twisted Niko's idea of the cruel prince, made him think things, realigned how he saw the man.

"My father discovered my excursions," he continued, voice thinner now he'd wrung all the emotion from it, "barred me from the tunnels and from Alek. So I found another way, and I kept going for years, even after Alek's father realized who I was. People saw me dressed in drab clothes, my hands filthy. Nobody cared." He still stared at the trees, as though talking to them and not Niko. "The palace staff got so used to my wandering, they made sure to leave the doors and gates unlocked. Until, well... " He waved like he could wave the war and his torture away.

The elves had discovered a valuable Caville prince's wanderings. Gods-damn those bastard creatures. Had Vasili been left to mature as the true king, the war, the curse, it might all have been so very different. But they'd stolen him away and countless lives had changed in that moment, not just Vasili's. Loreen went to war for the missing prince. Families torn apart. Generations wiped out.

Because Vasili left a gate open.

Vasili's heavy sigh carried with it the weight of all his sins. "I didn't know there was a war. I didn't know if anyone searched for me, and as time went on, I stopped hoping for rescue. The memories of Alek and those days on the farm stayed with me. But on my return with Julian, I learned how Talos—looking for someone to blame—had Alek and his father executed not long after I was taken. All those nights I'd thought of that life, and it was already dead and rotting in the earth."

Niko swore under his breath. Had the man speaking been anyone else, he'd have offered a comforting hand, but the prince was locked behind his unemotional armor, and if Niko touched him, he'd earn himself another scathing glare.

Vasili blamed himself for his capture and for the death of the family who had shown him a kinder way. All this time, he bore the weight of their deaths and the subsequent war.

His hood still hid his face. A good thing, because Niko wasn't sure what he'd do if he witnessed the pain he'd surely see on it.

"There was no reason to suspect there were elves anywhere near Loreen," Niko said, hoping to offer some comfort. "You couldn't have known they were watching you."

Vasili turned his head, and it wasn't pain Niko saw on his face, but pure, cutting rage. "Had I known, I still would have gone," he snapped. "The palace—the curse—I watched it take my brothers, my mother. There was a babe, my sister, born before me. Her eyes were black. Talos drowned her before she took her first breath, probably as a sacrifice to the flame, making it stronger. The flame has been devouring our family for generations. It makes us its slaves. It *will* take me. It's inevitable."

The odds did seem likely, given all Niko knew. Yet, Vasili wasn't like the others. Aching for that simple life, sacrificing everything for his people. That wasn't the actions of a Caville, not the Cavilles Niko knew. "You'll fight."

Vasili's hollow laugh briefly echoed before the sound of the rain swallowed it. "Amir used to paint. He'd have painted the whole palace if he could have, and he loved it. Color and light. When he was five, I had the staff bring us the finest paintbrushes, and together we painted all the walls. He loved sunflowers. He'd paint them to the ceilings."

Niko had seen those colors. He'd thought them ugly, but he hadn't known their origin. Now he did, and his heart ached all over again.

Vasili pulled in a deep breath. "Now those walls are black." He exhaled hard. "Fight, you say. What choice do I have? I'm all that's left, and if I don't stop Amir, if I can't control it, Loreen will fall, and that will be the beginning of the end of everything. *Fight,* like I am free to choose another way."

The rain had eased some and didn't drum so hard on the wagon roof. It still swirled like a mist and muffled the night. Niko listened to the quiet and to Vasili's rapid breathing. He did not know the right words to help him, didn't even know if words were enough. But he was here. Perhaps he just needed to hear that? "I've told you before, Vasili, you have my blade. But you must fight. Surrender, and we're done."

Vasili looked over and sneered, "And what good is a blacksmith's blade against the force of the dark flame?"

"A single blade is better than none."

Vasili's lips turned down at their corners. He turned his head away, making his hood hide his face again. "Go inside, Niko."

Niko tightened Yasir's riding cloak at his neck, tucked his chin in, folded his arms, and hunkered down. "No, I don't think I will." Vasili could bark at him all he liked; Niko had no intention of leaving his side. He'd been alone for so long, nobody had fought for him, but that had changed now. Because Niko wasn't abandoning him, even if the prick did keep pushing him away. For the good of Loreen.

CHAPTER 8

Vasili and Yasir were talking atop the wagon's driving seat. Niko rode too far ahead to hear their words, but the occasional laugh traveled across the thinning trees and low brush. Vasili never laughed, not genuinely. He tossed out a few bitter barks every now and then, but nothing real. But the laughs he gave Yasir sounded real, and something all too similar to jealously poked at Niko's resolve to stay detached.

Earlier, he'd overheard Vasili telling Yasir how he'd met Niko in a pleasure-house. Yasir had assumed that meant Vasili was paying Niko for *privileges*, and Vasili had laughed so damn hard. It had sounded damn real, that laugh. So real, Niko wondered if Vasili did offer him coin for pleasures, whether he'd accept. It wasn't as though he hadn't dreamed such things, using the fantasy as fuel for when he'd woken, his cock stiff as a board.

Maybe Vasili should offer Yasir coin for those privileges. They seemed to be getting along.

Perhaps Yasir could protect the prince. Perhaps Niko

would just ride on ahead and not look back, see if Vasili laughed then.

He probably would laugh if he knew the direction Niko's thoughts had taken.

Of course, how Vasili was around Yasir was all an act. Niko just hadn't figured out what Vasili wanted from the merchant. It certainly wasn't his silks.

Niko let his horse plod along. The landscape had changed. Hills had flattened into a long horizon line and the greens of Loreen had turned to rusty browns. The land seemed so unlike what Niko had known that it left him unbalanced. Mah had said the south was hot, and the sun beating down on him now was certainly trying to prove that. How would Vasili fare? As pale as he was, he might wilt in the heat.

Another laugh rippled from the wagon. Yasir's this time.

What if Vasili did want him for something more personal? Yasir was attractive, his tanned skin and eyes—so southern, and so like Niko's—were highly alluring. But besides the rage-filled kiss Vasili had branded Niko's mouth with in the farmhouse field, the prince hadn't shown any physical interest in anyone. He might have, of course, during his last year without Niko inside the palace, but it seemed unlikely considering the disgusting rumors suggesting Vasili only fucked elves.

Julian had said Vasili didn't experience feelings like most people, and in another breath, told Niko how Vasili was desperate for attention. So which was it, and why the fuck did Niko care? Even if that kiss in the field had meant something—which it clearly hadn't—getting involved with

Vasili in any emotional or physical way would be tantamount to cutting his own throat.

Still, the way Yasir kept looking at Vasili made Niko grind his teeth. Vasili was either oblivious to Yasir's long looks or acutely aware of them and was using the man's interest for some hideous trap he'd spring later.

It was only right that Niko should warn Yasir. He'd do it later that evening when they made camp.

A dust cloud drifted across the open plains to the west, beneath the blazing sun. Niko raised a hand and squinted toward it. Did clouds often form on the ground in this exposed landscape? The dust shifted sideways, blown by the wind, revealing five dark marks hidden inside. Riders.

Niko whirled his horse and whistled through his teeth.

Yasir's sudden "Yar!" jolted his carthorse from its plodding walk to a canter. Vasili clutched at the seat's rails, planting himself in place. Niko hoped he had good reflexes; he would need them to stay atop the bouncing wagon.

Niko spurred his horse alongside the wagon. "Five riders!"

"Get to the canyon." Yasir produced a whip and cracked it in the air above the carthorse's head, making the animal lurch forward. "We'll lose them in the brush!"

The road ahead disappeared beneath a rippling heat haze. There was no sign of any canyon, but clearly Yasir knew the land. The wagon bounced and jostled, looking as though it might collapse on striking the next pothole. But it thundered on intact.

Adamo—still tied to the rear of the wagon—neighed hard and tossed his head. The rope snapped, and the charger squealed. Vasili whipped his head around, face anxiously searching for his faithful companion.

Damn horse. Niko galloped alongside the wayward beast and snagged the frayed end of the flailing rope, pulling Adamo into a gallop alongside.

The wagon veered to the left suddenly, the road dropped beneath the heat haze, and a rift opened in the ground. Niko's horse almost went plunging over the edge into the yawning canyon. He hauled on the reins, making the animal scream to a halt. Through the heat haze, the canyon had been almost invisible, but now it yawned ahead like Etara herself had torn open the earth.

The road continued snaking down one side. The wagon bounced and clattered dangerously close to the edge. One wrong twitch on the reins and the wheels would slip over the side. Nobody would survive the drop onto the jagged rocks below.

Niko hunkered down and cantered after the wagon, wincing every time the wheels strayed too close to the edge.

As the road leveled out, Yasir masterfully wove the wagon along the canyon bed, around skeletal trees, splashing through the shallow, nearly dried-up river. The river veered right, and Yasir angled the wagon around the bend at a reckless speed. The wheels along one side lifted, the wagon tipping. Niko's heart tried to choke him, and then the wheels slammed back down again and the wagon rattled on until, finally, Yasir slowed the sweating carthorse and trotted it among a small patch of brush that would surely do little to hide them from above.

"Stay here," Niko barked, tossing Adamo's rope toward the pair. Without waiting for a reply, he dismounted, freed both swords, and stalked back through the brush. The riders wouldn't be far behind, but he'd have a better chance of getting close on foot.

Niko crept toward a boulder at the bend and crouched behind it. Three riders atop their horses trotted down the road. Two waited at the top of the canyon, their silhouettes dark against blazing sunlight.

Niko could take one out by surprise, but the two others would be more difficult. Assuming they were armed.

Yasir crouched beside Niko, a small, slightly curved, half-wood, half-metal contraption in his hand. Unless he was going to throw it at them, Niko wasn't sure what good that little club-shaped thing would be.

"Varian's keeping the horses calm," he whispered.

Niko eyed the three approaching riders picking their way over the dried riverbed. They wore head coverings wrapped around the lower halves of their faces, leaving just their eyes exposed. Two were dark-skinned, like Niko, but another was fairer. They all wore light, layered robes. "Who are they?"

"Marauders. They roam the roads looking for easy pickings."

Talking their way out of trouble was unlikely then. They'd want the contents of the wagon, and if its owners put up a fight, they'd leave their bloody remains for the vultures.

Yasir switched his strange weapon to his left hand and wiped the palm of his right on his thigh. Sweat beaded at his hairline, and it had nothing to do with the heat. He wiped his forehead dry.

Now wasn't the time to get into it, but it was becoming

clear Yasir wasn't accustomed to battle. "Do you at least have a blade?"

He nodded tightly but lifted his little backward club. "Hoping it won't come to that."

Niko refrained from telling him he might want to turn the little contraption around to hit them with the heavy end, but he wasn't sure it would make a difference. There wasn't much weight in the thing whatever way he swung it. Walla help them.

The two riders atop the canyon had vanished in the sun's glare. They wouldn't go far.

The lead rider in the riverbed walked his horse around a scattering of larger boulders.

"Etara make my aim true," Yasir whispered, then the fool stood up.

Yasir straightened his arm, flicked the club's upward hook backward, pointed the narrow end at the rider, closed one eye, and pulled on the contraption's ring. The little thing barked louder than a firework and briefly lit up like one too, startling Niko from behind the boulder. Impossibly, the rider, still some distance away, jerked in his saddle like he'd been hit, and tumbled from his startled horse.

The two other horses shied, desperate to flee from the sudden light and noise. Niko saw his moment, bolted forward, and made it to the nearest marauder as he reached for his curved blade. Niko swung his blade, slicing into the man's arm. Blood splashed. The marauder cried out, pulling back. Niko yanked him from the saddle, then angled the tip of his blade against the man's exposed throat. Terrified eyes looked up at him from between his face wrappings.

All Niko had to do was push down and end it. He breathed hard, fingers twitching around the blade's handle. The lust for blood ran hot in his veins. Out here, nobody would know. Another body, and they'd attacked first.

Yasir's noisy weapon barked again, and the third rider galloped off, bouncing in his saddle, barely staying seated.

Niko held the marauder's blinking gaze. Niko bared his teeth. This man wasn't an elf. He didn't need to slaughter him, despite what his muddled heart and head were telling him. "A few rolls of silk aren't worth your life." He straightened and backed up. The marauder rolled onto his front and scrambled to his feet. Clutching his wounded arm to his chest, he staggered after his skittish horse.

Niko watched the riders until they were out of sight. The one Yasir's weapon had dealt with lay dead on the ground.

Yasir appeared to be hastily refilling his barking weapon with black powder, spilling most of it over his dusty boots.

Niko sheathed his blade and approached. "We'd best get back to Vas—Varian."

Yasir wiped his sleeve across his face and nodded, fumbling his strange little noisy club thing back into a custom-made pocket.

"What is that thing?"

"Pistol." Yasir's smile jerked, finding its place on his lips again. "I won it in a game of cards."

That *pistol* had killed a man at twenty paces. Such a thing would have been more than useful at the frontline, against the elves. "Will you show me how it works?" They headed back down the river toward the brush.

Yasir shrugged, pulled it from its pocket again, and

showed it to Niko. Up close, the weapon had a strange kind of compact elegance to it. Even the metal parts had been etched with decorative swirls. Beautiful, if strange. "It's fuelled by black powder?"

"The powder explodes and sends a ball down the barrel into the asshole arguing with you."

Niko frowned. "A ball?" Fire and noise and death in such a tiny thing. It sounded like sorcery. "Are there more of these?"

"Not many in Seran or Loreen. The few I've seen came from the lands across the sea—"

"Halt there!"

The two missing riders weren't missing at all.

One held Vasili as a shield against him, a blade at Vasili's throat and a hand over his mouth. The prince's glare burned through Niko, like this was *his* fault. The second remaining marauder, the one issuing orders, brandished another deadly, curved blade. "Back away," he said, eyes narrowing. "We're taking the wagon."

That damned wagon wasn't worth the trouble. "Take it," Niko said.

"What?" Yasir spluttered, fumbling with his pistol again. "No, you can't do that."

Niko sighed. The wagon, Yasir, it was all unnecessary. If it had just been Niko and Vasili, none of this would have happened. "Take the wagon and go. We won't stop you."

"No! Don't listen to him. That's my business in there!" Yasir lifted his pistol and pulled the hook, but it just made a hollow snapping sound, and the marauder frowned instead of dropping dead. He clearly hadn't seen what had happened to his friend.

Niko stepped forward, hands raised. "Let my friend go

and leave. There's been enough trouble already. It doesn't need to get any worse."

The lead marauder's eyes darkened. He likely snarled behind his face-covering. "Bring the blond." He backed up, and his companion did the same, dragging Vasili with him.

Vasili's eye flared wide. With his mouth smothered, he panted heavy breaths through his nose.

Niko lifted a hand and stepped forward again. "Wait... You don't want to do that."

"Stay back! Or the pretty one gets his throat cut!"

Vasili's breaths stuttered. His captor dragged him backward some more, headed for the back of the wagon.

That same anxious flutter he'd felt back when watching Vasili leave tightened Niko's chest now. These thieves were going to drag Vasili with them, probably beat him, or worse, and when they were done, they'd abandon him at the side of a road. Only, none of that was going to happen because Niko wouldn't allow it.

He lowered his arms, crossed them in front of himself, and freed both blades. "I said *let him go*."

The lead marauder nodded, and his companion dragged the struggling Vasili to the back of the wagon. Niko squared up to the man. Taller, broader, Niko had the strength and weight advantage, but the marauder's curved blade was a beastly looking thing. Not as vicious as an elf blade, but close.

This would have been a real good time for Yasir's barking pistol to work.

Behind the marauder, Niko saw Vasili bucking, the knife at his throat of little concern as he thrashed against his captor's hold.

Vasili stilled. His captor grunted at the rigid weight in

his arms, and then a horrible laugh crawled from Vasili's lips, behind his captor's fingers.

The fine hairs on Niko's arms rose, chased by a chill. He'd heard the same laugh a year ago when it had slithered its way out of King Talos.

Vasili jerked in his captor's hold, instantly dislodging himself. He spun, grabbed the man's throat, and plunged a previously hidden blade into his heart. But he wasn't done there. The man coughed blood, staggered against the wagon, and Vasili backward-slashed the man's throat open —each move elegantly precise and horribly accurate.

Niko choked on a shout to stop.

Vasili twisted, flicked his wrist, and the small blade flew, slamming into the lead marauder's back. The man fell forward into Niko's arms. With no choice but to catch him or topple with him, Niko grabbed him, holding him close in some macabre embrace.

Vasili was behind his victim suddenly. The marauder's body jerked, he gasped his last breath an inch from Niko's face, and as Vasili stared over the man's shoulder and through Niko, a swirl of black swam in his single eye.

The dark flame.

Its poison tainted the air, its chill like ice in Niko's veins. It was bigger than Vasili, bigger than this canyon, and it wanted out.

Was this the moment Niko was here for? Was this the part where Vasili lost his battle with the flame and Niko was forced to raise his blade to the prince one final time?

"Vasili?" he croaked.

Vasili blinked. The black vanished, making way for the return of the brilliant blue. The prince's gaze wavered, his pupil shrinking. He staggered, barely holding his balance, tilted his head, and lifted the bloodied blade in his hand as though he was seeing it for the first time. Then he saw the bodies and turned on the spot, staggering under the weight of his own actions.

"*Fuck*," Yasir said from close behind Niko. He'd seen it, seen everything.

Niko let the marauder's body slip from his arms. The prince looked up. Red speckles of blood had dashed his face, stark against his pale skin. Fear flickered in his eye. He'd lost control. Was this the first time, or had there been other moments? Niko tightened his grip on his sword.

Vasili straightened, ran a hand through his wild, knotted hair, and swallowed hard. "We've wasted enough time. We need to move." He strode out of sight behind the wagon toward Adamo.

Niko sheathed his blades for a second time and regarded the bodies. Perhaps the marauders had deserved to die. They surely would have killed them given the chance. But Vasili hadn't killed them. The flame had. Or maybe they were one and the same now?

"His eye..." Yasir whispered.

"You didn't see it," Niko snapped. "You didn't see any of this."

"Lycus!" Vasili's voice lashed. He emerged atop Adamo. "If you mention a single word about burying these bastards, so help me Etara, I will have you flogged. We're leaving. Now."

Yasir's face mirrored the confusion and distrust the man likely felt inside. He'd be wondering exactly who Vasili was and if anything he'd just seen was real. He tucked his pistol away, climbed onto the front of the wagon without a glance at either of them, and geed his horse on.

Vasili held Niko's gaze, daring him to question what he'd seen, demanding it even.

This was foolish. They didn't need to stay with Yasir. He'd already seen too much. Mention of a one-eyed man with darkness in his soul would soon travel from Yasir's gossiping lips to the rest of Seran. The smart thing to do would be to make sure Yasir couldn't speak of any of this, permanently. But he'd be damned if he was going to hurt an innocent man.

Niko strode past Adamo and muttered under his breath, "You're going to get that man killed, and I'll have no part in it."

"You'll do as I order."

Niko checked for Yasir and found him back driving the wagon, geeing the carthorse along. He turned to glare up at the prince atop his massive horse. "We're not in the palace now, Your Highness. You're alone, and I'm the only bastard stupid enough to stick by you because I know what you are. We should leave him. Right now. He'll forget what he saw. If we stay, he'll ask questions, and he'll keep watching you, and as soon as you think you're done with him, you'll kill him."

Adamo shifted, and Vasili tightened his grip on the horse's reins. He leaned down. "You think me a monster?"

"I know you are." Niko flung a hand back toward the retreating wagon. "Let the man go."

Vasili glanced at the wagon and back to Niko. "I have no intention of hurting Yasir. I find his presence refreshing." *Unlike yours*, the prince's unspoken words rang between them.

Niko threw his hands up, retrieved his wandering horse, and swung himself into the saddle. He trotted the animal alongside Adamo.

The prince's pale lashes fluttered, and some of his hardness thawed. Adamo leaned in toward Niko's horse, and Vasili reined him back, keeping his distance.

"Do you even care how three men just died?" Niko asked.

Vasili hadn't known about the third, but it didn't matter because he'd looked at the dead like they were no more interesting than deceased animals in a hunter's trap.

When he didn't reply, Niko trotted his horse on. Moments later, Vasili reined up alongside him but stayed quiet. As they approached the wagon, he said, "Yasir knows Seran. We'll need him once we're in the city."

There was more to it but arguing with Vasili was fruitless. The prince only gave up information when it suited him. Damn Vasili for dragging another innocent soul into his wretched world. "Just so you know, if it weren't for the flame, I wouldn't be here."

Vasili's cheek flickered. He stared ahead. "So you persist in reminding me."

"Lose control of it and I'll put you down."

"Of that, I have no doubt." Vasili clicked his tongue and trotted Adamo on to meet up with Yasir.

He'd effortlessly killed those men, but it had been self-defense. The moment it turned into madness, it was over. And now they both knew the truth they'd danced around.

Perhaps Niko's words had been harsh. Vasili had been about to be bundled into the back of wagon, and considering his past, the thought of captivity alone would have been enough to trigger him. But after Niko had seen him so callously dispatch those men, the prince had needed to hear the truth. They'd both needed to hear it. Niko couldn't afford to forget the vulnerable prince who had slept in his now-burned armchair was the same who had half a world-ending power running through his veins.

At least Vasili had appeared to wrestle back control. But for how long?

CHAPTER 9

The southern lands grew bitterly cold at night. Yasir had warned them of lighting a fire. It would be visible for miles. Shivering, they huddled in the back of the wagon, and Yasir took first watch. Vasili was supposed to sleep, but he sat by the wagon's opening, a knee drawn up to rest an arm on as he stared out into the starlit night.

Niko lay stretched out on a cover protecting the precious silks beneath. As beds went, it was probably one of the most comfortable he'd ever slept on. But sleep was elusive tonight. Every time he closed his eyes, Julian's easy smile and charming laugh haunted him. And when he wasn't seeing Julian's ghost, when sleep was beginning to lure him into its embrace, the chilling dark clutched at his chest, sucking on his soul and snatching him awake.

Niko startled himself awake for a third time, and Vasili cast him a cursory glance before returning to stargazing.

In starlight, Vasili looked like a ghost too. Niko rolled onto his side and propped his head on his hand, studying the prince. Several shades of grey made up his proud face. His lips were thin and colorless. But when he'd glanced back, his blue eye had shone its Caville defiance. This was one of those rare moments Vasili wasn't sneering or looking down on him. Niko could almost pretend they were just two unimportant men caught in strange circumstances. Vasili was a farmer and Niko a blacksmith, hammering out iron for a living. Life wasn't complicated. There was no dark flame, no looming war, and no elves.

Vasili, the farmer, was infinitely more likable than Vasili, the prince.

"Dare I ask why you're staring?" Vasili asked without looking.

Niko smiled, confident Vasili couldn't see the smile in the dark. "You should rest."

He finally turned his head and waved a hand toward Niko. "Yes, but you take up all the space, so..."

There was space beside him. Granted, it was tight. He opened his mouth to suggest Vasili was slim enough to fit and then promptly closed it when the thought of the prince lying beside him ignited a breathless skitter of nerves.

As stubborn as Vasili was, no man could go without sleep for days. Niko shuffled himself against the wagon's side, making more space. "There's room enough for two."

Vasili frowned—at least Niko thought he did. Hooded and with his face turned from the stars, he was all shadow. "No."

"A bed of silk not good enough for you?"

Vasili stared outside again, cheek fluttering.

Ah, it wasn't the silk. It was Niko. "Perhaps Yasir

would be more to your liking, Your Highness?" Niko drawled. "You can make him laugh some more."

"Nikolas—"

"I'll get him in here," Niko shuffled toward the wagon opening. "If I ask him nicely, maybe he'll bring a whip."

"*Nikolas.*" Vasili grabbed Niko's arm, jolting Niko's thoughts and actions to a halt. Niko glanced down at Vasili's tightening fingers, and the prince let go. "It's not you," he said. "It's too enclosed."

Niko glanced around the wagon's cramped interior. It was small, yes, but easier to keep warm and...

The cage the elves had kept Vasili in couldn't have been much larger. Suddenly the wagon didn't look so comfortable. Vasili avoided traveling inside the carriage, even in the rain. When he had to stay inside, he sat by the opening, exactly as he did now.

Vasili shifted back into his sitting position and stared out of the wagon, decidedly not looking at Niko.

And now Niko felt like an asshole.

"I, er..." He returned to his bedroll of silks and considered how best to take everything he'd just said back. "Sorry."

The soft starlight touched Vasili's jaw, sharpening its edge. "I don't want your pity."

Maybe it would be better for Yasir to join him. Niko's presence only made everything worse. The pair had ridden together all day, sharing water and chatting like friends.

"Where is Yasir?" Niko grumbled.

"He's been pacing the same spot for some time, building up to asking questions I have no intention of answering."

"If you answered, maybe he'll stop looking at you like

you're Aura's gift to men," Niko blurted. And immediately wished he hadn't.

Vasili stared. "He what?"

By the three, why couldn't he keep his foolish thoughts to himself? "How he looks at you sometimes," he hastily explained, feeling heat warm his face, "I just thought, he might have propositioned you."

Vasili blinked. "*Propositioned* me? In what way, Nikolas?"

"What fucking way do you think?"

"You think he wants to fuck?" Vasili's mouth twitched.

"No, he wants to paint you," Niko drawled sarcastically. He swallowed and was glad for the dark so Vasili didn't see the heat on his face. He side-eyed the prince and caught sight of his lips tilted upward in a shallow smirk. "You're screwing with me. You know exactly how he looks at you. Of course you do, you're you." Gods, it was time to stop talking before he buried himself deeper in the hole Vasili had dug for him.

A small, light laugh escaped the prince. "Of all the wonderful things you are, Nikolas, astute is not one of them."

May Etara rip open the earth and swallow him down. "Forget I said anything. Forget this entire conversation."

"How can I forget seeing you so flustered? Had I known the mention of sex would unbalance you so, I'd have made sure to discuss it before now. I assumed you were a man more... experienced."

The shadows were too thick for Niko to fully read Vasili's face, but he was definitely smiling. And damn if that little ache in Niko's chest didn't thaw into a strange kind of comforting warmth. Of course, Vasili was laughing at Niko's expense.

That was enough personal talk. Niko clambered by Vasili and out of the wagon before Vasili could talk Niko further in circles.

"Nikolas?"

"Yes?" Niko reluctantly turned.

The prince smiled, and this time genuine humor glittered in his eye. "Tell Yasir to bring his whip."

Niko showed Vasili his middle finger in a sign Yasir had taught him. When he turned his back on the prince, Vasili's thick chuckle followed him into the dark.

YASIR DIDN'T ASK his questions, and the night passed without event. At dawn, they wordlessly packed up and moved off, with Vasili on the driver's bench beside Yasir.

Strange, spiked plants peppered the desert, and the clouds were few and far between.

Early afternoon, Vasili switched to riding Adamo. Yasir had given Vasili his wide-rimmed hat, which Vasili donned with a flash of a smile. The hat shielded his face and neck from the worst of the sun, but sweat plastered Vasili's filthy white shirt to his back and shoulders.

Niko suffered too, wilting under the heat as he'd assumed Vasili would. Loreen's hottest day was half this forge-like temperature. The horses would need water soon.

Niko's mood soured with every plodding hour. He watched Vasili and Yasir share the water pouch and listened to Yasir's aimless chatter. Finally, in the late afternoon, the desert gave way to lush greenery. Trees with fan-like leaves frequently dotted the horizon, but the air dragged like water over Niko's lips, becoming cloying.

"There she is..." Yasir called. "The ocean, see her?"

Between the green hills ahead, Niko did see a turquoise splash of color. Only a few clouds dotted the sky. The rest was a wash of blue as far as the eye could see.

"Deceptive isn't it," Yasir added. "Looks close."

"How long until we reach Seran?"

"Ten days, maybe. The road gets tough from here on out."

Like it hadn't already been tough. Gods, Niko was saddle sore, hungry for something that wasn't rice cakes, and in dire need of a bath.

Vasili and Adamo plodded ahead. The prince had barely said a word to Niko since their conversation in the back of the wagon.

"I, er... been meaning to ask." Yasir wiped at his sweating face. "I tried talking with him, but Varian has a knack for talking around a subject."

Niko snorted. "You have no idea."

Rocking with the wagon, Yasir wet his lips and took a moment to continue. "How much of the south did your mah tell you?"

"She barely spoke of it."

Yasir narrowed his eyes on Vasili. "There's a story—a legend of sorts. A woman called Zarqa' al-Yamama could see the future, among other things." Yasir noticed what must have been an incredulous look on Niko's face. "There is a point to this tale."

"You are fond of fantasy tales, Yasir."

"Granted, a few might be fiction. Besides, you're half Seranian, aren't you curious about your heritage?"

"A little." There hadn't been much time for curiosity as a blacksmith's boy, and considering Mah's history was a taboo subject, Niko hadn't thought much of his family beyond the forge. The south seemed like a whole other world away and nothing to do with him.

"You'll like this one, and it's relevant to our *friend*." He inclined his head toward Vasili.

The way he said "friend" had Niko wondering exactly what Vasili had told him. "Tell your tale, Yasir."

"Zarqa' al-Yamama fought against the *nasdas*, a hideous being that could kill just by touch, as though it drew the very soul of a person out of their body and into its own, making it stronger with every death. Zarqa' and the nasdas warred for centuries, until Zarqa' tricked the nasdas into a human body, like a jinni in a lamp."

Mah had told him that one. "I've heard the lamp story."

"Your mah told you about its three wishes? Did she tell you the three wishes were, in fact, keys that locked the nasdas' prison?"

"No."

"Most myths don't say how Zarqa' was a sorceress, or how her eyes were black, but I've heard a lot of stories, made up a whole lot too. But what I saw in your man when he killed those marauders reminded me of that old tale. I asked myself why a man of high society—he can't hide his accent—would be traveling so humbly south, and why he needs such a formidable guard alongside him, and why, when he was threatened, his eye turned all-black, just like Zarqa's from the legend."

Niko pinched his lips together. This was exactly what he'd feared would happen.

Yasir side-eyed him. "The sorceress Zarqa' trapped the nasdas in human form, inside a mountain, locking it deep inside the stone with three keys. She charged her soldiers, *shirdals*, with keeping it there."

Niko squinted ahead at Vasili's back.

"Do you know what shirdal means, Lycus?" Yasir asked.

"No."

"Griffin. Like the Loreen King's banner. That's some coincidence, don't you think?"

"Uh-huh." Niko's heart thudded harder. So Yasir, after seeing Vasili's all-black eye, assumed he was some kind of sorcerer? Gods, if only it were that. The truth was more likely to be Vasili and his brother contained the split spirit of this nasdas—or as the Cavilles called it, the dark flame. "Out of interest, when did this Zarqa' trap the nasdas inside a mountain?"

"Seven centuries ago, so the legend says."

"Hm. Long time," Niko said.

"Of course, it's all fantasy," Yasir added. "Because if the nasdas existed, that'd be some serious world-changing shit people would need to know."

"We have enough trouble with elves." Niko forced a laugh. "It's just a Seranian story."

"Yeah, except... there's a family in Seran, known as the shirdals, among other names. I figured maybe your man might have heard about them, and given his... affliction," Yasir gestured at his eye, "thought he might be heading their way?"

Which would make this journey no accident on Vasili's part. If he'd read in his books about a people in the south who were aware of the dark flame, there would be no better time to visit them than now, while Vasili was temporarily free of the palace. "Interesting story."

"Yes, I thought so too."

"But what does it have to do with Varian?"

"Well, his eye, I thought. You don't see something like that every day."

"His right eye was taken by elves."

"Not that—fuck. I had no idea. But that's not what I meant, and you know it. I saw what he did, saw something inside him—"

Dammit, why didn't Vasili listen? He'd known Yasir wouldn't let it go. "I suggest you don't mention your stories to anyone."

"He killed those marauders like they were no more bothersome than leaves in the wind. I've seen men kill. What Varian did was—"

"Defend himself."

Yasir frowned hard. "His eye, Lycus. You saw it too. That's not normal. He has magic in him. You can't deny it."

"I don't know what you want, Yasir, but I'm suggesting you don't mention these tales to Varian—or anyone. I'd hate to think what might happen should your stories be taken for truth."

Yasir snorted. "So it's like that. And if I talk, what happens to me?" His glare burned Niko's face, and Niko silently cursed Vasili all over again. "And here I was, thinking we were friends."

Niko flinched at the man's tone. "You were mistaken."

"Clearly."

His gaze found Vasili riding ahead, rocking with Adamo's plodding motion, the reins loose in his hand. This was his fault. He should be the one warning Yasir to back off. "Don't talk, Yasir," Niko warned. "And don't touch Varian."

"Don't touch him?" Yasir spluttered a laugh. "Isn't that his choice?"

"I'm not protecting him," Niko met the man's eyes. "I'm protecting you." He'd said enough, and tightening his reins, he trotted his horse on, leaving Yasir to mull over the words of warning that had been long overdue.

He drew up alongside Vasili and opened his mouth to demand Vasili talk to Yasir when Vasili asked, "You hear that?"

"Yasir has some interesting theories about you."

"I've heard them. I can hardly not hear them when he fills every second with needless chatter." Vasili kicked his heels against Adamo and grabbed the reins "Yar!" He startled Adamo into a gallop, threw a grin over his shoulder, which was surely designed to lure men to their deaths, and then hunkered down, riding Adamo over the brow of a hill, vanishing in the heat haze.

"Dammit." Niko whipped his reins, launching his mount into Vasili's dust trail. He galloped over the hill toward the roaring sound Vasili must have been referring to. The lush landscape rolled back, revealing a narrow ravine split in half by a plunging waterfall. Cool mist spritzed the air. Water droplets scattered the sunlight, projecting a rainbow above the pool. After the dry heat of the desert, the waterfall oasis didn't seem real.

Niko pulled his horse to a stop at the high point on the bank. Near the pool's edge, Vasili had already dismounted Adamo. He waded, fully clothed, into the water, threw Yasir's hat back onto the stony riverbank, shook his hair out, and dove underwater, vanishing from sight.

Seconds passed.

The falls thundered. The pool's surface rippled and

churned. Vasili should have resurfaced. Niko's heart thudded hard in his chest. He couldn't hear it, not over the sound of the falls, but he felt it thumping against his ribs.

Vasili burst from the pool's surface, gasping. He ran his fingers through his platinum hair, turned, and appeared to be laughing, though the falls stole that sound too. A pure and carefree smile lit up his face, and Niko's wrecked heart raced for another reason.

Adamo had plodded to the pool's edge to drink. Vasili splashed water at the horse, called it a damned fool, and then stilled as he caught sight of Niko watching.

Niko expected the man's smile to die a quick death on his lips, but it broadened instead. He watched Niko, and Niko watched him back, and what was this because it seemed like Vasili might be waiting, but surely not for Niko to join him?

The prince's deft fingers loosened off the laces of his collar, gaping the shirt open. Water glistened on his face, and with his hair swept back, his stunning appearance was all the more striking. His clothes clung to his chest and arms in all the right ways, reminding Niko of the time the prince had stepped naked from his bathing pools at the palace. And by the three, he looked like some vision of desire deliberately put on this world to lure Niko into that pool and probably into some kind of trap.

The sudden clatter of the approaching wagon snapped Niko out of his reverie. The prince's smile slipped sideways, turning sly as he turned his back and dove under the surface a second time.

Niko released a breath and shifted uncomfortably on the saddle, trying to alleviate the awkward and damned inconvenient arousal. Apparently, he still wasn't over the kiss in the field.

"Ah, finally." Yasir appeared and tore off his shirt as he made his way down to the pebbled beach.

Vasili, drenched through, waded from the pool as Yasir unashamedly stepped out of his trousers and took a running dive into the water. Vasili's lofty gaze tracked the man's powerfully graceful plunge.

Niko swallowed the bitter taste of jealously on his tongue. Despite what his body thought, he didn't desire Vasili, so what did it matter if the prince happened to be drawn to Yasir?

Vasili gathered his messy hair in his hands and wrung it out. He lifted his gaze again to Niko and the prince's pink lips quirked, like he knew damn well how Niko imagined clutching the back of the vicious bastard's head and thrusting his tongue into that sharp mouth.

He recalled exactly how Vasili had tasted, all bitterness and sharp edges, and fuck if Niko's cock didn't throb at the memory.

Vasili had kissed like he'd hated him, and it might have been the most intensely passionate kiss Niko had ever experienced. He wanted that again. Wanted Vasili in his fists, wanted him sprawled backward on a bed, his mouth snarling, his eye ablaze with hatred, and gods, he wanted to fuck the prince until he lost his mind to the feel of him.

Niko tore his stare from Vasili's and swallowed hard. That damned half-sideways smile the prince was giving him... He fucking knew what it was doing to Niko. And Niko was caught. Hard as iron, there was no way he could hide his arousal. Joining them in the pool was absolutely out of the question. But he sorely needed a bath.

"Lycus!" Yasir called, treading water. "Join us."

Niko pinned a wooden grin onto his lips. "Right after I've tied up the horses."

Yasir said something lost beneath the sound of the falls. Probably some jibe at his expense. He made it to the wagon and painfully dismounted his horse, then adjusted his trousers and erection, willing the obvious arousal away. What he really wanted to do was take himself in hand, fix that image of a drenched Vasili in his head, and pump until he spent his seed, but by the three, he was a grown man and could control himself.

There was just something about Vasili that fucked with Niko's head. It'd pass. Then he'd go back there and wash up.

Maybe he'd wait to wash up until Vasili was far away from the pool.

Or maybe he'd get back on his horse and ride away.

Gods, if only it were that easy to escape Vasili. After everything the prince had done, and would do again, Niko should despise him. And he did. But there was also that other side to Vasili, the one who had wrapped Niko around his little finger. The Vasili who had folded himself into Niko's chair, the Vasili who doted on children and animals, the side who wanted a simple life with simple things, the vulnerable man beneath all that ice. Niko would be lying if he tried to deny he didn't feel something for *that* man. The rest of Vasili could go fuck himself, but the hidden prince—he was why Niko was still here, why he'd come this far and why he was still standing with him despite everything he'd done.

Niko straightened and breathed hard, filling his lungs, re-centering himself on the task ahead. Vasili did not control him. Vasili had no power over him. He was just a man with a curse who needed protecting until they could figure out a way of getting Loreen back.

The key to surviving this had to be staying detached, like he'd been on the front line. Block everything off. Fear. Anger. Loneliness. He had to forget all that again. He didn't need to go as far as being the butcher, but he did need to get the prince out of his head, or this would all end badly.

"Nikolas!" Vasili's shout rang over the rumble of the waterfall.

Niko bolted from the wagon and darted down the bank toward the beach, where Vasili knelt over Yasir's twitching body, trying to hold him down. "He collapsed."

Tremors wracked Yasir. Niko tore off his own filthy shirt, bundled it up, and propped it under the man's head. He grabbed a stick, pried Yasir's mouth apart, and wedged it between his teeth. "To stop him swallowing his tongue," he said, aware Vasili had backed off, giving him room to work.

"What's happening to him?"

Gods, he sounded genuinely concerned. "Seizures." The tremors were remarkably similar to those Vasili had experienced in the palace. Niko had known soldiers similarly afflicted. Lack of salt could bring it on, although Yasir had been careful to bring a bag of salt with them. Vital in the heat, he'd said. Some folks just had fits that were never explained. Yasir hadn't mentioned any such affliction, and he would have, seeing as he'd told them most everything else about his life.

Yasir groaned, his back arched, chest heaving. He

opened his rolling eyes, revealing a flicker of something that should not be there.

Niko's breath caught. He froze. That couldn't be right. He used a thumb to draw the eyelid back again. He had to be sure.

Black.

But...

Niko snapped his head around to find Vasili looming, his face artificially blank. Oh, the bastard knew.

Yasir thrashed again. Niko grabbed his flailing hand and clasped it between his own. "Hold on, Yasir. I have you."

Vasili had done this.

He wasn't sure how, or why, but the black smoldering in Yasir's eyes could not be denied.

And as soon as Yasir was safe, Niko was going to tear Vasili apart.

CHAPTER 10

Yasir's thrashing had ceased and his breathing slowed. Niko plucked the splintered stick free, scooped his remarkably light body up, and carried him up the slippery bank to the wagon. After tucking him safely inside, Niko carefully removed his own swords, and with them the temptation to run Vasili through, and clambered back down to the beach.

Vasili's brow pinched, his chin lifting.

Niko curled his right fingers into a fist.

"Stop," Vasili ordered. The princely tone did uncurl Niko's fingers, but only because he'd chosen another method instead of punching the prick.

He grabbed Vasili's wet shirt in both fists and shoved. Vasili staggered over the pebbles, tripping backward, but kept his balance.

Niko grabbed his shirt again, and this time he yanked the prince close. Fabric tore, the collar ties pulling free. "What did you do?! Lie to me and I will fuck you up, *prince*."

Vasili bared his teeth. *"Unhand me."*

Niko tightened his grip and pulled the prince face-to-face, as close as they'd ever been. "You fucking poisoned him."

Vasili merely gritted his teeth. He didn't fight, though he could have. Comparing Vasili to a snake was too good. This bastard was a fucking eel. For all his words about doing the right thing for Loreen, he was no better than his rat of a brother. Amir had poisoned the guards. Now Vasili was doing the same with some unsuspecting merchant whose only wrongdoing was happening across Vasili's path.

Niko shoved Vasili back again, freeing him, needing to push him away before the anger boiled over and he did something he'd regret.

The water pouch the pair had been sharing lay on the pebbles nearby. He scooped it up and tore off the stopper. It didn't smell like poison. Something else then... He recalled how Vasili had held the dagger in his lap that night in the rain, as though he'd been ready to use it. If the prince knew anything, it was how to bleed. He and Yasir had shared water throughout the entire journey. And Vasili had always been the one to refill their pouch.

And now the real reason Vasili had adopted a stray merchant began to reveal itself.

"My brother has a retinue of guards possessed," Vasili finally said, shouting the words over the roar of the falls. "He's turned Loreen against me. Every day, the flame gets louder in my head. All I have is a bastard blacksmith who despises me, who would have killed me already if not for the horror my death might unleash."

Niko upended the pouch, pouring its pinkish water onto the pebbles. Fucking Caville prick. "You saw what it did to Julian." He tossed the pouch at Vasili's feet and stalked closer, making the prince back up. "You've poisoned an innocent man."

Vasili held out a placating hand. "Nikolas—"

"You singled him out at the inn. Traveling alone, vulnerable. You knew exactly what you were doing. At the very best, your blood will make him mad. At the worst, you've got yourself a Julian all over again." Niko's vision spun. "Wait, did *you* poison Julian?"

Vasili snarled. "When was I supposed to poison Julian? While they had me tied down and drank from my wrists, or when they left me bleeding for days on end. No, I didn't poison your *precious* Julian. Elves did that."

Niko staggered and closed his eyes, trying to regain his balance in a world that was all wrong. He didn't know what to believe anymore. He stared at the empty water pouch between them. "You're the same as Amir."

"Nikolas, will you listen!" Vasili's voice cut through the roaring falls. He moved closer, not giving ground. "Yasir asked for it. He saw it in me when I killed the marauders, he knew the southerners' tales, and he asked for it. He calls it *magic*. He *wanted* it."

"So you opened a vein and gave it to him?" Niko spluttered, turning away, needing to *move*, but the rage wouldn't let him leave. He spun again. "And how is that any better? You took advantage of a man's ignorance, and I've no idea why I'm so fucking surprised when you've fucked me over countless times."

Niko marched forward until they stood just a step apart. "Amir bound me and Julian dosed me with spice and fucked me. They did *exactly* what you knew they'd do, so you could plot your escape. Don't fucking try and tell me

Yasir understood what he was getting into with you. Nobody has any fucking idea what it means to be used by Vasili Caville."

Vasili's brow pinched. His lips parted, words unspoken behind them. He even looked as though he were the one betrayed, like *he* was hurting. "You know who I am," he growled. "I don't care what has to be done. I can't afford to. I need allies. I need an army to rival my brother's if I'm ever going to get Loreen back. I'm alone. I have this... darkness inside of me, desperately trying to escape, and I don't have long before it burns me up, like every other Caville. So yes, I took advantage of Yasir. I gave him my blood to see if I could use him like Amir used the guards, and I took advantage of my brother's fascination with you to distract him, and I will use anyone and anything the same, time and time again, Nikolas, because if I don't, we all die. I have no choice."

"Choice?" He spat a cruel laugh. "I'm sure every Caville bastard thinks they're the fucking hero while the rest of us die for you. I'm done with it, with all of it, with you."

"Then go, Nikolas, walk away."

Niko started up the bank.

"Surrender then, you fucking coward," Vasili tossed out.

He stopped and worked his jaw around the filthy words he wanted to fling back at the prince. "How dare you... I witnessed good men and women die fighting elves because you wanted to play farm boy and left a fucking gate open! Call me a coward again and I'll—"

"Strike me? Do it."

Niko stepped face-to-face with the prince.

His damp hair was wild and messy, his clothes wet and

sticking to him, his face so full of Caville superiority that Niko wanted to shove him under the water and hold him there.

"I've lost *everything* because of you. Countless families lost it all," Niko said, "and you don't give a shit."

"I can't afford to care." Vasili spread his arms. "At least you had something to lose. What do I have? I'm the prince of ashes, the prince of madness. The only thing I've ever wanted is to not be who I am. I don't get to walk away or give up. My life is a cage. But you," he poked at Niko's chest, "Nikolas Yazdan, blacksmith's boy, don't see any of that. You see a prince, born into power and privilege, and you think I should have all the answers, that I should just be able to raise an army, defend Loreen from the elves and my insane brother, while at the same time wrestle the ancient curse that doesn't give a fuck about any of this. You hold me to some higher moral regard that even you can't obtain, and when I fail to reach your lofty heights, you judge me for it."

A sharp laugh snapped out of Niko. "Shall I pity you, prince?"

"No, you can help me."

Anger flared hotter in Niko. He stared unblinking into the prince's icy glare. Oh, Vasili was furious too. So furious, he breathed hard, hands clenched at his sides, holding himself back. Was he holding the dark flame back? "Help you? I've seen what helping you looks like. If I laid down and took what you gave, I'd be dead." Tremors rippled through Niko's rough words. "Just like all the others you've used up and discarded. I will always fight you because nobody else dares to. The second I stop fighting you, that will be the moment you stab me in the back."

Vasili's lips gave a telling twitch. "No, Niko. I'm not asking you to stop. I'm asking for help."

"I despise you, Vasili Caville."

"A man like you should."

And what did that mean? Niko felt it all come undone, felt the moment the anger and lust and confusion spiraled out of control. Mindless, he grabbed the prince's ripped shirt and hauled him into a savage kiss. Vasili's poisonous mouth parted, his tongue swept over Niko's, tasting, and all the rage and frustration and hatred boiled over, blazing through Niko's veins, turning the kiss desperate and raw. Gods, it was like before, hot and hungry and rough. Vasili's sharp teeth nipped at Niko's lip and then the prince plunged his tongue in, and Niko thrust back. The kiss ignited a mad, breathless desire to have Vasili writhing under him, gasping Niko's name, his thin fingers wrapped around Niko's cock. He wanted to *hurt* him, to make him feel something. Instantly hard, the sudden friction of Vasili pulled close stole the breath from his lungs and all remaining reason from his head.

Niko spread a hand against the prince's damp shirt, soaking in his trembling warmth beneath. He needed to feel Vasili's wiry strength, to touch every forbidden inch.

Vasili's right-handed slap came out of nowhere and struck his cheek so viciously, Niko staggered backward, ear ringing, face ablaze. Shock dumped ice water on the lust, instantly dousing it. "Fuck!"

Vasili stumbled over the stones, hastily retreating. He touched his fingertips to his lips, tasting, and looked at Niko as though horrified.

Gods, this was madness. How he was around Vasili,

that wasn't him. He hadn't meant... Niko shouldn't have touched him, but it had been more instinct than thought.

When was the last time anyone had *held* Vasili? But that didn't matter. If he didn't want to be held, then Niko had just forced a kiss on him, and that... that was wrong.

Niko swallowed the taste of Vasili on his tongue. "I'm sorry..." he grumbled, "I..." He turned away, leaving the prince on the beach.

The slap hurt, but that kiss... the emotion set free within it, the sensuous way in which Vasili had explored him with lips and tongue and teeth—gods. It had only lasted seconds, but it *had* been real, and not just on Niko's side. He'd give half his soul to feel his passion again.

But it wouldn't happen. Couldn't. The heat in Niko's cheek made it clear Vasili didn't want it.

Niko's heart was too fragile a thing for the prince's manipulative coils anyway. Only a fool gave their heart to Vasili because the prince knew only how to crush the life out of everything he touched.

Niko climbed into the back of the wagon and watched over Yasir until he stirred awake and blinked bloodshot blue eyes. "What happened?" he croaked, then swept his tongue around his mouth and grimaced. "The beach... I was..."

"You and I need to have a talk about Varian—a man whose real name is Prince Vasili Caville."

CHAPTER 11

Yasir had asked Vasili to share his *gift*, as he'd called it. And because Vasili was the kind of man who didn't need any encouragement to do the wrong thing, he'd agreed.

Niko didn't know whether to laugh or punch them both. At least Yasir wasn't summoning fiends. Yet. Julian's conversion had taken time. Months, maybe years. He hadn't said but gave the impression he'd been trying to get *the man in the cage*—Vasili—to trust him for a long time.

Niko promptly confiscated all the water pouches, dumped their contents, and refilled them with fresh water before they'd moved on from the waterfall to the night's camping area. The humid, lush landscape closed in around them as night fell. They sat around the fire, the only sound that of the crackling wood. They hadn't traveled far from the waterfall. Its roar still rumbled in the distance. The wagon had been pushed off the winding track for the night, and the horses munched on whatever reedy grasses they could find.

If any predators found them here, Niko contemplated feeding Vasili to them. He tried to recall what happened to the flame if it was set free away from the palace or another Caville, so it had no other anchor. He knew that should Vasili die close to Amir, the middle prince got all the power. But out here? The flame went free... and he was fairly certain that would mean chaos.

"I, er..." Yasir cleared his throat. "Would anyone like some tea?"

"*No*," Niko and Vasili both said in unison.

Vasili shook his head, caught Niko's eye, and looked away.

Yasir clattered about making hot tea for himself and mumbling curses. With his drink in hand, he sat back, pulled his hat off, scratched at his head, and sighed. "This is all my fault."

"It's not," Niko said.

"You can't blame Vasili—" Yasir began.

"I fucking can."

"Nikolas sees only in black and white," Vasili snapped. "Right and wrong are simple things in his naive world."

Niko snorted. "Tell me the flame is benevolent. Tell me that... to my face. Tell me it won't fuck Yasir up."

"If I could make him stronger, make you... stronger, Nikolas, give you power, make you into more than a blacksmith..."

Vasili trailed off, probably because he'd seen the look of horror and disbelief on Niko's face. "Go on, finish that sentence, Your Highness. *Make me a sorcerer*?"

Vasili looked away.

How long had he been thinking that little gem? It was a wonder he hadn't spiked Niko's water too. He probably would have if they hadn't happened upon a merchant traveling alone. Was that why he'd lured him south?

Niko's twitching smile was alive on his lips. "Poison me with your blood and I'll stab you in the fucking heart—if you have one."

Yasir glanced between them, and when the silence dragged on, he cleared his throat again. "It seems to me that you've both been dealing with something far larger than you are for too long. You clearly need help."

Vasili gestured and humbly dipped his head. "You're correct, Yasir. I was asking for help, but Nikolas saw fit to fling accusations instead."

Niko shot the prince a deadly look and then angled himself toward Yasir, deliberately not rising to Vasili's bait. Yasir was a victim in all of this. And what was done to him was wrong. "In the morning, pack up your belongings and leave—go home, somewhere safe, get away from us."

Vasili's glare turned icy.

Yasir knew too much, but Niko didn't care. "I've seen the dark flame," he told the merchant, watching his face tighten. "I saw what it did to Talos. I know Amir, the prince—*king*—it's corrupting now, and I know what it will do to Vasili. There's no way this ends happily. If you walk away now, you can escape it all. The effects of the blood, if there are any, will hopefully wear off. You can still get away, Yasir. Don't throw your life away for Vasili Caville's sweet lies."

Yasir mused on the words, occasionally glancing at Vasili. "I appreciate the thought, Nikolas. But I want to help."

"You'll die."

"Nikolas—" Vasili warned.

Niko glared at the prince, and Vasili glared back. "You gave me no choice when you threw me in your dungeons."

Yasir choked on his tea. "You did that to him?"

"I..."

"Oh, that's not all he's done," Niko laughed dryly. "Vasili, you claim to have no choices either. Yasir has a choice. Are you really going to take that from him like you took everything from me?"

Vasili pursed his lips and looked down. When he looked up again, his gaze slid to Yasir. "Nikolas is right," he said softly. "I was not forthcoming with the facts. You cannot make an informed decision if you are not informed. You were looking for magic in me, some... link to your myths, and I am not that. What I have given you *is far from good.* It was only a small amount, but I was wrong"—he flicked a glance at Niko—"to inflict it upon you. Nikolas is also right in that this will likely end badly for everyone involved. You are a good man, Yasir. Albeit one who talks far too much. You should not have to share the burden of this curse. It is mine to bear alone."

Niko wasn't sure—especially as Vasili looked at him like he wanted to stick a dagger somewhere vulnerable—but it had sounded as though Vasili had just apologized, in his own Caville way.

Yasir sipped his tea. "I understand." He considered the words and nodded, either to himself or Vasili. "I'll take a walk, I think." He stood and brushed his clothes down.

"Now?" It was dark beyond the firelight, and there would be predators out there.

"I need to think. Alone. It'll be fine. I'll stay close... I just... I can't think with you both staring at me."

Niko watched him head through the thick leaves and

disappear. He raised an eyebrow at Vasili's carefully measured expression. "If you haven't fucked him up for life, it'll be a miracle."

"Thank you, once again, for your startling honesty." Sarcasm dripped from the prince's words. "You told him who I am. If he talks, the repercussions are on you."

"If he talks, I doubt anyone will believe a word of it."

"Amir?"

"Is far away, probably staring at his own reflection while pleasuring himself."

Vasili's small snort alleviated some of the tension between them.

"You apologized. That must be new for you. Did it hurt?"

Vasili flashed him a hollow smile. "As much as the family dinner I once ordered you to attend."

Niko smiled. "Agony, then." Mention of the dinner pulled his mind back to how Vasili had collapsed after, the dark flame withdrawing into King Talos. Vasili had suffered. His whole life had been degrees of suffering as he'd watched the madness taint everyone around him. The prince never really had been free to choose anything, except when he'd pretended to be a farm boy, and Niko had flung that back at him when they'd argued. It had been a coward's blow, and he regretted saying it. Maybe he'd deserved that slap.

Perhaps Niko did try and force Vasili into some righteous corner, a place he was never going to fit. Because Vasili was not some distant prince atop a white charger, who could wield the power of the Cavilles. He was a man, full of weakness and fear and vulnerabilities, and he'd been battling the impossible alone for a long time. Even on the front line, facing elves, Niko had never been as alone as Vasili had been for years.

He didn't understand Vasili, his methods, or his way of life. Probably never would. But he was beginning to understand the weight of the responsibility resting on his shoulders.

"What happened at the beach, I—" Vasili began.

Niko's heart lurched. "When we reach Seran, will you seek out the shirdals Yasir spoke of?"

Vasili hesitated, and his face, usually so guarded, revealed thin lines of concern at the corners of his mouth. "I know where they are. I—we will need to tread carefully."

"Who are these shirdal people? They're dangerous?"

He rubbed a hand over his face. "In some of the old books, the shirdals were protectors, part of the old families, like the Cavilles, but they were charged with guarding what they call the nasdas—our dark flame. In other works, however, their motivations were not so honest. The shirdals fought for control of the dark flame. They... used it, instead of guarding it."

"There's a surprise," Niko drawled.

"They have influence and power. Both of which I am sorely lacking."

"Jumping into bed with the enemy, however tempting, is rarely a good idea." Niko realized how pointed his words were too late to take them back.

Vasili swallowed hard. He plucked a twig from the ground and snapped it in two, then tossed both pieces into the fire. "Whatever awaits us in Seran, the shirdals cannot know who I am until we're ready. I have someone there. She'll help."

"And you trust her?"

"As much as I trust anyone."

That wasn't comforting. But if he already had someone in the city, that would suggest this was no impromptu journey south. "How long have you been planning this?"

He looked up, like he was innocent. "Planning what exactly?"

"Going to Seran, finding the shirdals?"

"Since I learned of their existence—long ago, but I was a boy then and couldn't leave the palace without Talos's permission, and, of course, then the elves and the war came, and Julian..."

If the shirdals considered Vasili a threat or saw power within him, they'd use him. It would be best to tread lightly in the new city and quietly learn all they could before revealing too much. Perhaps, as Vasili had already said, Yasir could help with that. If he stayed. Niko was beginning to hope he did, even though he shouldn't. They needed help, and it was just a matter of time before Vasili snapped, or Niko did. As the beach had revealed, they could not continue as they were.

"Where is he?" Niko got to his feet, grabbed the short-sword—easier to swing in dense undergrowth—and headed toward the patch of undergrowth Yasir had vanished through. "Stay by the fire."

Thick leaves barred his way. He batted them aside and took a natural curve left around a wall of giant ferns. Yasir had said he wouldn't go far, but it would be easy to get turned around. Huge fronds and leaves blocked the light from the fire, allowing just glimpses here and there.

Hands grabbed at him. Niko almost jolted back,

bringing his blade up, only diverting the swing at the last second when he recognized Yasir's stricken face.

"Something's here," he hissed, clutching at Niko's arm. "Something big."

Niko froze. Water dropped from fat leaves above, some animal called far away, but there was no other noise to suggest they weren't alone.

"Come back to camp."

"But I heard it. Something breathing..." In the dark, Yasir's eyes glistened. He clearly believed he'd heard something, or maybe it was the Caville madness beginning to grip his mind.

"Beside the fire is the best place for us." Niko sheathed his blade, grabbed the man's reaching hand, and drew him back along their trampled path. Dancing firelight warmed the overgrown foliage, lighting the way. The sounds of the fire crackling spoke of safety.

Soon, they'd be in Seran and this wretched journey would be done with.

He pushed a huge banana leaf aside and jolted to a halt. Beside the fire, a huge, four-legged beast loomed over the prince, like a wolf, only bigger. Firelight shone through the wisps of dark making up the creature's mass, like a nightmare come to life. Beneath it, Vasili arched off the ground, arms flung out, mouth open. Black veins cracked across his pale skin and snaked down his forearms, up his neck and face, as though at any moment he would splinter into a thousand pieces.

The beast's jaws lay open. Ethereal smoke rose in wisps from Vasili's body and poured into the creature.

Fury shattered Niko's shock. Whatever that thing was, it wasn't damn well taking Vasili. Not while Niko was here.

He drew his blade and, with a roar, charged forward—and plunged straight through the beast. A shock of cold washed over him, snatching his breath from his lungs, just like the fiends had. But this beast was no fiend. It wasn't even solid.

Vasili jerked, all-black eye rolling.

Gods, no. That bastard thing wasn't taking him!

Niko swung the sword again, but it sailed through the beast unhindered, as though it were simply slicing through air. The creature continued absorbing the dark flame right out of Vasili's skin.

"Do something!" Yasir screeched. He bolted in, dropped to his knees, and grabbed at Vasili's arm. The beast snapped at Yasir, startling the man backward onto his ass.

Blades didn't work.

Metal had worked on the fiends, but this thing wasn't a corrupted elf. How could Niko fight a dream-creature?

Blackness throbbed off Vasili, the flame rippling higher, drawn from his body. Whatever was happening might kill the prince, and Niko hadn't survived the Caville palace and the prince's machinations for him to watch Vasili die and do nothing.

There had to be a way to get it off him, to stop it.

The beast focused again on Vasili. Vasili's back arched, rising off the ground, as though pulled by invisible strings.

Niko tossed his sword in the dirt and grabbed at Vasili's limp hand. The beast swung its huge head and snapped sharp teeth together inches from Niko's face. Ember-red eyes burned through Niko, scorching his soul, touching his heart with darkness. Unflinching, Niko stared back. Whatever this thing was, whatever it was doing, it would have to pry Vasili from Niko's cold, dead hands.

Niko pulled, but Vasili's rigid body didn't budge. He should have been able to heave him out from under the beast's stance, but the prince was stuck, and with every second, more darkness spread beneath his skin, bleeding from his veins, painting him with the dark flame's consuming touch.

The beast growled. Its lips rippled over jagged teeth.

"He's dying!" Yasir's cries weren't helping.

Niko swore, released Vasili's limp hand, and clambered to his feet. He scanned the camp for any weapon. Anything. There had to be something that would stop it. Yasir's small bag of salt caught his eye. He snatched it up and threw the contents over the beast. Pink, crystallized salt dashed the beast's side, sizzling into its smoky mass. It raised its head and let loose a haunting howl. The sound faded as its body dissolved into nothing but air.

The black veins were fading from Vasili, but he'd never looked paler. Niko dropped to his knees and cupped Vasili's cold face. Pale lashes fluttered, his lips gently parted. He still breathed. Relief had Niko gasping. He scooped Vasili into his arms and carried him to the wagon. "Yasir, get us on the road!"

Niko sat in the rear of the wagon, shortsword in hand, as Yasir quickly cleared the camp and drove the wagon and horses back onto the track.

Shadows blurred by. Niko watched for any sign of glowing eyes, listened for howls, and kept the almost-empty bag of salt within reach. Behind him, Vasili lay motionless, pale and cold.

He draped the silks over him and then lingered to watch him sleep.

A life in a prison of fear was no life. Niko did not agree with Vasili's methods, but he was beginning to understand how the prince believed he had no choice in them.

Maybe Niko could show him that choice was all he had, if he ever woke up.

CHAPTER 12

Vasili woke a day later. He didn't speak, just took a few rice cakes, drank some water, and when they stopped at a brook, he took himself off, returning later with his damp hair slicked back, his face still pale and glare defiant. He might even have been the typical Vasili Caville again if Niko hadn't seen the cracks in his emotional armor, or his slight hesitations and the way his fingers trembled.

Yasir chatted aimlessly, providing what was fast becoming a sense of normalcy, and eventually, the jungle gave way to more substantial roads as they passed carriages and mud-built huts and people tending the red soil.

The farther they traveled, the larger those huts became, until red mud houses lined the roads and Seran was upon them. The city spread for miles into the distance, abruptly meeting a vast swathe of glittering green ocean.

Exotic spices scented Seran's hot, humid air. Colored banners flapped from first-floor windows, zigzagging up the street above their heads. Traders at their stalls shouted their wares in a language Niko had never heard before. Yasir chatted back to them, the words smooth and rolling, then described the street to Niko as one of several main streets that led to the central hub of the city.

Noise and color and smells and laughter.

After their isolation, Seran was an explosion to the senses that left Niko stunned.

Yasir meandered his wagon alongside others overloaded with cargo of all kinds. Niko plodded his horse behind, keeping an eye on Adamo while Vasili rode him confidently through the crowds. The prince naturally had the big horse under control, but the crowds were thick, and one loud noise might spook the beast, and why did Niko even care?

This newfound worry for the prince was... unexpected. Vasili's withdrawn behavior after the attack was probably rooted in his previous capture. They hadn't spoken about the beast, just picked up and moved on as though nothing had happened. They hadn't spoken much since the attack.

At least when Vasili was snarling at Niko, he knew him to be well.

Yasir led them to a meeting place called the *Whispering Pearl* taverna, a drinking place with tables outside in a courtyard, alongside the bustling street. The swinging sign above the door depicted a massive clam with a blue pearl inside. Niko had never seen a clam before, but he'd seen Mah's pearls when she'd returned late from the lord's manor and set them aside in a velvet-lined box then hidden them beneath a floorboard. He fended off thoughts of why a lord might have given her pearls, or why she'd needed to hide them.

Yasir booked rooms at the taverna, then left to deliver his wagon. After checking the rooms, Vasili had promptly vanished among the crowd, saying he'd seen a clothes trader on the street. Niko worried every second he was gone. Which was ridiculous and unnecessary. Vasili was capable of looking after himself.

After washing the grime from every crack in his skin, Niko ventured into the taverna's courtyard and took a table by the street, where he could watch the people flow back and forth and watch for Vasili. Maybe he should have gone with him. But he'd been so quick to leave, Niko had been left on the back foot. Again.

People laughed and frolicked in the street. The drinking from the taverna had spilled outside. Even after the sun set, hot air still clung to the tightly packed streets. Strange, constant lighting placed high on poles buzzed to life at dusk, chasing off the dark and lighting up the streets as though it were almost daylight again. It was all noisy and colorful and close, and nothing like Loreen. It would take some getting used to.

Yasir slid into the chair opposite Niko. He'd rid himself of the traveler look and wore a gown of colored and layered silks that reminded Niko of Lady Maria's beautiful clothes. He'd also shaved off his beard, leaving a narrow goatee that enhanced his charming face, adding more roguish charm. His crooked smile completed the picture of a wily trader. He instantly looked as though he absolutely belonged.

"By the three gods, I must get you out of those old Loreen clothes." He grinned and raised his hand to summon a server who dutifully poured them both wine.

"Seran is busier than I expected."

Yasir picked up his wine, his movements as smooth and confident as they had been when they'd first met. "This?" He gestured at the packed street and its river of people. "This is nothing. You'll have to see the commerce quarter but watch your pockets. Thieves are rife." He downed half the wine at once and waved the server over again. "Leave the bottle and another glass. We're expecting a third." The server obliged. When he'd left, Yasir asked, "Where is Varian?"

They were back to fake names, which was a relief in such a busy place where anyone might overhear them.

"Purchasing clothes, apparently," Niko grumbled.

Yasir raised a dark eyebrow. "Well, he won't find much Loreen leather here. It's too hot and getting hotter. Summer in a few weeks." Yasir nattered some more about summer festivals, and Niko let him drone on as he scanned the constant flow of strangers. Anyone could be a threat. In Trenlake, all the faces were familiar, and those who weren't were instantly watched as outsiders. Here, there were too many people to know or recognize.

"You'll get used to it," Yasir assured. "Ah, here's the illusive man. By Aura, he makes a *fine* piece of work."

The pale-blond-haired man striding toward them demanded every head in the courtyard turn his way. A dark purple satin shirt—the kind that billowed at the waist and cuffs—complemented his lighter coloring. A red sash held up slim-fitting black linen trousers. His boots were laced all the way to his knees, silver hooks gleaming. But the real transformation had taken place in his face. He wore a hint of a smile, like it wouldn't take much to summon a laugh. A lace patch covered his right eye, drawing attention to it rather than hiding it, and a trio of small golden hoops hung from one ear. His hair, partially tied, lay in smooth waves over the opposite shoulder.

The startling transformation rerouted all the thoughts in Niko's head to exactly what it'd feel like to take him *out* of those beautiful clothes one careful satin layer at a time. His body eagerly responded, cock swiftly hardening and pulse so thick he could taste it.

"Lycus?" Yasir grinned knowingly.

He cleared his throat. "Yes?"

The man laughed. "Never mind."

Vasili pulled out a chair and poured his new sensual transformation into it. The delightful scent of rosewater tickled Niko's tongue, and heat swelled between his legs, making him fidget awkwardly.

"Lycus," Vasili greeted, tone light, "Yasir."

Gods, he looked like he was made for the vibrant streets of Seran, and Niko should probably say something, anything, but he'd forgotten how words worked, and if he didn't pull his mind out of the gutter, where it had firmly lodged itself on seeing Vasili wrapped in exotic clothing, then he was about to look like a fool.

"Give Lycus a minute to adjust," Yasir chuckled, earning a glare from Niko.

"I see you had fun while I was left worrying," Niko grumbled, reaching for the wine.

"You were concerned?" Vasili's brow arched.

Niko gulped the wine down without taking a breath. Any reply he gave, Vasili would no doubt use against him later.

"You needn't have been," Vasili said. "I've left you fresh clothes in your room."

He spluttered the wine. "You purchased me clothes?"

Vasili gestured at Nikolas's filthy attire as though that was reply enough.

Yasir had a sly, knowing look on his face. Gods. This felt like a trap. All of it. The city. The wine. The clothes. The prince being very... Vasili. A trap he had no hope of escaping.

Vasili slid his attention to Yasir. As they discussed more permanent lodgings, Niko's gaze snagged on how the artificial light caught in Vasili's earrings. Niko hadn't even known the prince had piercings. Not that he should have. And what did it matter anyway? There were more important things to focus on—like the beast's attack—than how his dark purple shirt, with its wide lace-lined collar, gaped open and inviting at the neck. A neck that demanded the lightest of kisses.

Niko poured himself more wine. He should probably eat something before drinking more, but Vasili and Yasir were deep in conversation about a woman Yasir knew who owned several houses. One, a townhouse, she could rent to them. Yasir even suggested Niko's talents as a blacksmith were sought after in Seran, where metalsmithing was rare. This was important information Niko should have been soaking up, but those damned earrings kept twinkling, and the way Vasili ran his fingers through his hair, deliberately sweeping it back to reveal the decorated eye-patch instead of hiding it, or how he stroked his wine glass, distracted him.

Niko swallowed hard.

The kiss in the field might not have been an angry, one-off encounter, and the kiss on the beach, well, that had clearly meant something too, before Vasili had knocked some sense into him. If Niko couldn't stop thinking about how the prince's soft lips had tasted so sweet and yielding and how he desperately ached to feel all of his tense, icy body yield beneath him, then he was going to make a fool of himself.

Seran would have pleasure-houses. Clearly, he was in dire need of a release. Maybe then he'd stop thinking of how easily Vasili's shirt laces would spill open under his fingers.

"Doesn't it, Lycus?" Vasili asked.

"Yes." He had no idea what he'd agreed to. There was a warmth in Vasili's face that hadn't been there before, flushing his cheeks a delicate pink. Probably the heat. Or the wine. Would he gasp or sigh under Niko?

Yasir had Vasili smiling, and the smartly dressed trader brushed Vasili's hand, like he'd done dozens of times, and it was time Niko left. He didn't need to see them getting overly familiar when Vasili shoved Niko away at every moment.

Niko's refreshed glass of wine went down all too easily. He stood to leave, and the courtyard spun some, making him grab the back of the chair. "I'll, er... see you both tomorrow—in the morning, sometime."

He had no coin and couldn't ask Vasili for some so he could pay an escort to go down on him. That left his own company and his hand, which, considering he couldn't get Vasili out of his head, would only make the need worse.

Vasili's hand landed lightly on Niko's.

Niko snatched his back, startled that he'd dare voluntarily touch.

Vasili's smile tightened, and Niko stammered, "Good night." He'd been so conditioned not to touch that it had been instinct to pull away. Vasili didn't *do* touch. But he didn't do color and life and look like sin walking either. Niko had to leave now before the sweet wine made him say all the things inside his head.

He retreated to his room, berating himself with every step. Vasili was forbidden. The slap on the beach made it clear he didn't even want intimacy. Niko was chasing the impossible. He had to push the man from his thoughts. They were in Seran. Here to find the shirdals. Niko had to protect Vasili from Amir and anyone else who would use him while he formed a plan to retrieve Loreen's crown. If Vasili still wanted that. He'd seemed pretty comfortable in Seranian clothing. With Yasir.

A shirt and trousers waited for him on his bed, each lined with a hint of lace, nothing too frilly but trimmed with just enough embellishment Niko could get away with it. With his southern heritage, he'd look good in the rich, dark colors, *dammit*.

He changed into the outfit and dampened his hair, combing it under control with his fingers. The man looking back at him from the taverna's gilded mirror belonged among the crowds on Seran's streets.

Clipping his shortsword to his belt, he left the taverna for the bustling streets. Night or day, the hour didn't seem to matter to Seranians wanting to trade or socialize. With their strings of colored lights and heaving crowds, the markets throbbed with life at night.

Niko wandered through it all, observing the people. Some were armed with blades or pistols, like Yasir's. Old, young, men, women, beautiful burgundy skin, rich ebony, pearly white. Seran was the kind of city where the three gods had tossed all their ideas together and left them to bake in the sun.

The street opened, and the salty smell of the sea washed the heat from Niko's face. Enormous ships were tied at a dockside, their masts as tall as houses, rigging stowed.

A young flower-seller appeared beside him, holding out a large oxeye daisy.

"I can't pay." There had been a few overeager traders trying to steer him toward their wares. He'd managed to avoid them, but this one wasn't as pushy.

She shrugged, tucked the flower into his shirt laces, grinned, and strode off, skirts swishing.

Bars lined the dockside, full of rowdy sailors. Niko ambled with no destination in mind. He drew a few curious glances, but none lingered like they might on a stranger. He felt settled, like this place, despite its noise and heat, was safe. Loreen hadn't felt safe since the war. The war clearly hadn't reached Seran. Yet.

His mood soured.

Loreen had been a glittering jewel once too. Now it had a poison festering at its center.

Amir.

The dark flame seemed a million miles away from these carnival-like streets. It would be easy to settle here, to forget, until the elves crept closer, saw the brilliance of Seran, and decided to destroy it. There was nothing they hated more than the beautiful.

"Lost, friend?"

Niko blinked back to himself and casually regarded the young man who had spoken. With just a thin, short-sleeved shirt hugging his torso, his well-defined arms gleamed under the warm bar lights. "Not lost, just finding myself," Niko answered smoothly.

The man's smile was broad and inviting, alluring. The man's hand lightly brushed his and beckoned him toward the bar, where a group of seamen caroused. "Can't have you drinking alone."

And then, inexplicably, Niko found himself among the group. Wary at first, he guarded his sword and had no coin to keep safe but checked for pickpockets all the same. As the night wore on and the sweet wine flowed, he stopped looking for threats in the shadows, for blades at his back, and let Seran embrace him, as though he were finally coming home.

CHAPTER 13

Niko woke to a pounding in his head, or was that the sound of pounding on his door? It ceased, so he let his eyes close again, drifting somewhere warm. The pounding started again, rattling the door hinges.

"Hold up," he grumbled.

The door swung open and Vasili was in his room. The prince's steps slowed as he followed the trail of clothes. His gaze trawled over the wilted oxeye daisy on the dresser and back to Niko sprawled on the bed, where he'd fallen after dragging his exceedingly drunk self back from the docks at dawn.

"Did you enjoy yourself?" Vasili asked, the venom in his voice rousing Niko from his wine-addled thoughts.

He seemed pissed, which was nothing new. Niko flopped a hand over his eyes. Luckily, he hadn't stripped off completely, or else Vasili would be getting an eyeful. Maybe he should have, then Vasili would learn to knock and *wait*.

"What do you want?" Niko reluctantly swung his legs over the edge of the bed and rubbed at his face.

Vasili clearly wasn't going to go away.

"For you to do what I brought you here for."

"And what is that, *Varian*?"

"If I were taken last night, you'd never have known it," he said, sounding like the Vasili who had tried to buy him in a pleasure-house.

It was too early in the morning for his shit. "*Were* you taken?"

"Clearly not."

"Disaster averted. May I sleep now, Your Highness?"

Vasili scooped up the shirt from the floor and flung it at Niko's chest. "Get dressed. You aren't here to *seduce* the locals."

Niko held the scrunched shirt in his lap and glowered. There hadn't been any seducing, just a great deal of enjoyment and too much wine. But Vasili could think what he liked, seeing as he probably hadn't spent the night alone. "Did you enjoy your evening with *Yasir*?"

"Speak your mind, Niko," he snapped.

Oh, he was pissed all right. Something had happened. Had Yasir finally acted on those long looks, or had Vasili just woken up and decided he hated everyone but mostly Nikolas? "I just thought that, Yasir and you—"

"Don't *think*, Nikolas. It does not become you." He marched from the room and slammed the door.

In one breath, he'd told Niko to speak. In the next, to be silent. Navigating Vasili's moods was like walking on cracked ice. But for all his sharp bluster, he had very little, if any, power over Niko. Maybe that lack of control had caused his ire. And they still hadn't talked about the beast.

Niko fell back onto the bed and huffed. He could have lost himself in sexual pleasures last night. The man who'd been the one to invite Niko into their group had made it clear he'd have willingly drawn Niko aside for some personal time. Niko had almost surrendered, but then Vasili was in his head. Vasili from the waterfall, with his hands sweeping through his wet hair. Vasili who lay cold and near-death in Niko's arms. Not the fiery, brat prince who'd just slammed the door on him—that Vasili aroused Niko's cock more than his heart. The soft, vulnerable Vasili who triggered more of an instinct to protect than to fuck—it was that bastard that had stopped Niko from indulging.

"Fucking princes."

He padded to the washbasin, cleaned up, dressed, and headed downstairs only to be told Varian had settled the fee for the rooms and was tending their horses. Niko braced himself for a day of biting his tongue around Vasili and found him outside, tacking up the pampered Adamo.

"Mount up, we're moving." Vasili hauled himself into Adamo's saddle, barely sparing Niko a glance.

Niko quickly mounted his horse. "Moving where?"

"A townhouse." He clicked his tongue, and Adamo trotted out of the courtyard.

"Wait. This house... Do you trust Yasir?"

"I don't trust anyone," he called back. As he turned Adamo, he added, "Except you." He pulled the horse back around again and trotted into the street, leaving Niko staring after him.

Vasili's distinctive figure almost disappeared. Niko had to fight his way through the crowd to catch up. Vasili trusted him? He almost broached the subject some more, but the crowd bustled, jarring the horses, and the ride to the docks required all his attention just to stay mounted.

The townhouse was a handsome, three-story, redstone-clad dwelling slotted in the middle row of neighbors. Large windows looked out over Seran harbor and the red earth of the headland beyond. After tying up the horses, Yasir unlocked the doors and swept through the building, explaining how pipes carried water to and from the property and how power fizzled down wires into wall lamps. It made Niko's cottage look like a mud hut and further reminded him of Seran's obvious differences. Vasili appeared to appreciate the high ceilings and grand staircases spiraling between the floors.

Yasir entered the room Niko had lingered in to admire the view. "The keys." He handed out a rattling set of metal keys. "First month's rent and bills are paid and your horses are stabled nearby, courtesy of Vasili's—*Varian's* jewelry. After that, there's a forgemaster up the street looking for someone to help expand his business. The wages should cover everything you need."

Niko took the keys. They weighed heavily in his hand, like commitment.

"You don't like it?" Yasir asked, noting Niko's hesitation.

"No, it's not that. Yasir, thank you. We would not be here without you, and I've not been kind these past few weeks. It's nothing personal."

He settled a hand on Niko's shoulder. "I understand. You've both been through a lot. It must be difficult to trust again."

"Yes." Any more of a reply felt awkward. How much did

he know about the more personal aspects of Vasili and Niko's relationship? Had Vasili opened up to him during all the days and nights they'd sat together on the wagon. It was difficult to imagine Vasili *talking* about anything personal, and the fact Yasir might have been the one Vasili opened up to made Niko scratch that aching spot over his heart.

"I'll check in with you over the next few days, but my ship's due to set sail at the end of the month. I'll be sailing the trade routes until autumn."

"Wait. You have a ship?"

Yasir swung open the window and leaned out. "You see her there, the beautiful lady with the blue hull and three masts? *Walla's Heart.* She and I, ah, what can I say? She is the love of my life. We don't always get along, but we love each other nevertheless. You know how it is with the temperamental ones."

"You're her captain?"

"She's all mine," he beamed.

Captain Yasir Lajani. A few pieces of Yasir slotted into place. The seafaring tales, the references to the ocean. Then Yasir did know how to keep some secrets close. Did he have any other surprises? "I'm impressed."

"Ah, if I'd known ships got you hot, I'd have mentioned her long ago." He chuckled and headed for the door. "Now get out there and get to know Seran."

"Yasir, wait..."

The merchant turned, revealing a crooked smile. "I'm all right," he said. "No ill effects from the... what happened."

"That's good." Slightly unbelievable, given how devastating the dark flame could be. "Just... be careful. If Vasili is offering you something, it usually means there's a whole lot of baggage as part of the deal."

The warning had the opposite effect Niko had been hoping for and made Yasir's smile grow. "He's in good hands with you."

Niko clenched his jaw. "He doesn't think the same."

"Oh, he does." Yasir smirked and briefly bowed his head in a farewell. "I'll visit in a few days."

"Yasir?" Now he'd begun to ask, he had to finish. "Did something happen last night... with Vasili?"

Yasir's brows lifted. "No. Nothing happened. Keep him safe, hm? I'll bring some more wine when I next visit. You can tell me how you're settling in. I want all the stories, don't spare the details, you hear?" He grinned, clearly happier to be home, and left.

Niko observed the street from the window. He listened to the man's boots strike the stairs and the door clunk closed behind him. Moments later, Yasir's colorful figure merged with the flow of people outside and vanished.

With Yasir gone, the house felt too big, too quiet. Despite guarding his heart, Niko had grown fond of the merchant captain. He really had been easy to like. Vasili had clearly felt the same. His mood would be foul now Yasir had left.

Niko climbed the stairs to the top floor, where Vasili had taken up residence, and knocked at the door.

"Enter, Nikolas."

The prince leaned against the wall by the window. He'd been watching the street too. The setting sun painted him in pinkish light, highlighting the vision of silk and masculinity that had Niko's heart racing. "Your keys." He set the keys on a sideboard. Niko straightened to leave, but instead, his gaze roamed Vasili's casually poised grace.

"Will you stay?" Vasili asked, still gazing out the window.

"Stay?" He almost choked on the word. "Why?"

Vasili looked down, perhaps considering his reply. "Why do most men seek the company of others?"

Niko's heart thudded too loudly, pounding its way up his throat. Was this a trick? Was he talking about company or *company*? He wasn't smiling. His face was a mask, unreadable. No tick of the lips meaning he was amused, no glint of slyness in his eye.

"Yasir left some wine." Vasili moved to the nearby sideboard and removed a dark bottle. "Share it with me." Two crystal glasses came next, pinched between his long fingers. He still hadn't looked over.

This was a terrible idea. Niko should leave. Now. "I'm tired..."

Vasili hesitated, the bottle poised over one glass. "Of course, from your evening carousing." He poured the wine for himself, scooped up the glass, and finally peered at Niko over its rim while drinking.

The lace-lined eye-patch gave him an air of mysterious elegance. That and the stare clearly designed to hook Niko in had Niko rooted to the spot.

In all the time he'd known Vasili, the prince had never asked him to stay. He'd never told him he trusted him either. Until today. Bizarrely, something else Vasili had said days ago came back to him now. About Niko not being astute, about him being many "wonderful" things. At the time, Niko had been too flustered to notice how the pertinent word in that sentence hadn't been *astute* at all. His occasional glances, like when he'd been alone in the waterfall pool and noticed Niko watching him. Maybe they'd been signs of a prince who was desperate for company but didn't know how to ask for it. What was he really asking for here?

Or was this something else? Something more insidious. Vasili was nice only when he wanted something.

Niko's gaze fell to the empty glass and back to Vasili's guarded face. Ah, now it made sense. "It's poisoned."

Vasili carefully set his fragile glass down. He spread both hands on the sideboard and bowed his head between his braced arms. "I swear you were put on Etara's earth to torment me." His shoulder blades flexed, like he was holding himself restrained.

"Torment *you*?" Niko blurted incredulously. "And you only have yourself to blame, Your Highness. You forced me into your service, remember?"

"How can I forget when you insist on bringing it up during every conversation?" He straightened but stared at the wall behind Niko, cheek twitching.

"We don't have *conversations*. You bark orders and I obey, like the dog I am—"

Vasili was in front of him suddenly, a wall of satiny shirt and untied collar. His pulse fluttered at the thin skin of his neck. His fingers danced up Niko's cheek, and all the words stalled on Niko's lips.

Vasili bowed his head. His mouth hovered so close that Niko forgot how to breathe.

"I have hurt you," the prince whispered, his usually smooth voice suddenly hoarse, "and I will never be sorry." His words teased over Niko's lips. "Because it brought you to me."

Soft, warm lips brushed Niko's. Fingers locked in Niko's shirt.

He shouldn't do this, shouldn't yield. Vasili was poison. He'd crush Niko's bruised heart. He'd hurt him again and again. It was who he was. But by the gods, Niko wanted to feel that hurt if it meant feeling Vasili come undone with him.

Vasili's lips teased his open. His tongue fluttered in, and Niko let it. The moment was brittle, easily shattered. There was no spice between them. No excuses. No denials. Niko gently slid his fingers over Vasili's hip, testing for the moment he'd snatch all this away, but he didn't.

Niko carefully returned the kiss, reining back the building urgency. The effort to restrain himself made him breathless, made him tremble. Vasili's hands pressed against his chest, as though to hold him back, but he didn't push.

The kiss heated, Vasili's tension unraveling as his mouth took everything Niko gave.

Oh, by the three, this was everything Niko had dreamed, everything he'd so desperately ached for. To feel Vasili surrender—not fight, not rage, just relax his guard and open up. This was the Vasili Niko couldn't think around, couldn't resist, the Vasili hidden from a world that would disparage and shun him for surviving.

Niko walked him back, and Vasili bumped against the sideboard, rattling the wine glasses. The sudden stop pressed his firm body into Niko, or Niko pressed into him. He wasn't sure. Couldn't think. A hard rod dug into Niko's thigh, evidence Vasili wanted this too. He'd been so sure the prince felt only hate, but his keen arousal meant everything.

Niko dropped his hand, cupping Vasili's cock through his trousers fabric.

Vasili gasped in his ear, and Niko had to pull from the kiss to bite his own lip to keep from groaning. Vasili's gaze caught his, and the moment stilled, stretched between them. If Vasili touched him, if those precise fingers brushed over his aching cock, like all the times he'd dreamed, he might lose his mind.

Niko skimmed his hand up Vasili's chest, rumpling his shirt. "You have no idea how long I've dreamed of this..." he confessed.

Vasili's fingers looped his wrist, holding him off. The prince averted his gaze, and the heat between them quickly turned cold.

The fucking scars. Dammit, Niko knew not to touch him there.

He brushed his jaw against Vasili's. "I'm sorry... I didn't... I don't have to touch you for this... for us to do this." Why wouldn't the right words come? He meant to say he knew Vasili hurt, he knew how touch reminded him of pain, but they could still do this. He clearly wanted to. And Niko could go slow. Whatever Vasili wanted—needed—to feel safe, he'd do it.

Vasili swallowed with a loud click.

Niko still had his hand on Vasili's cock, but its earlier hardness had softened.

"Leave," Vasili croaked.

"Vasili—"

He shoved Niko back and braced himself against the sideboard, turning his head away. "Leave, please."

Niko raised his hands and backed up a step, giving him space. If he'd just look over, he'd see he didn't have to fear what they had, what they could do. "It's all right. I won't hurt you—"

Vasili's mouth tilted. "It's not you." He closed his eye and sighed hard through his nose. "Just get out, Nikolas."

Niko turned on his heel, closed the door on Vasili, and paused at the banister, breathing hard. When Vasili was hurting, he lashed out. Or froze. Two extremes. If he could just let Niko in, he'd see how he didn't need to fear pleasure.

Niko breathed out a long, shuddering sigh and returned to his floor.

CHAPTER 14

Over the next week, Niko worked at the local forge, tended to the horses in the livery yard, and explored Seran's sometimes dazzling and always overwhelming nightlife. The old city hugged the docks, while the newer areas, full of proud redstone buildings, crawled into the distance, encroaching on the jungle. Strange animals were sold at the nightmarkets; even stranger meats adorned the menus of the countless eating houses. Coin and entertainment, heat and sex bloomed around every corner.

Why Mah had ever left for Loreen's restraint and grey-clad world was a mystery.

Vasili artfully avoided Niko. He needed space, and so Niko gave it to him. He'd open up when he was ready. Or maybe he wouldn't. Niko wasn't sure anymore. The soft, achingly gentle kiss had changed everything. Rage and sex, while fucking hot, were a flash in the pan. But that damned soft, hungry kiss Vasili had delivered... Niko found himself dwelling on that kiss more than was probably healthy.

All of this had to be at Vasili's pace. And that pace was killing Niko. He could show him how to love. Vasili would probably hate every second of it, until he stopped fighting. If he would just trust Niko enough to surrender to him, he'd show him what it meant to be lost in pleasure. It didn't have to mean any more than that if he didn't want it to.

Niko spent the evenings with the dockworkers, finding them easier company than the icy prince at home. The men and women of the dockside bars asked nothing of him. They clocked off late, long after the sun had set, and spent hours drinking, eating, and carousing at the outside tables.

A week after the kiss, he returned to the dockside again and spotted the flower-seller outside one of the eateries. With a pocket full of coin from his first week's work, Niko paid her for a long-stemmed thornless rose and the oxeye she'd previously given him.

"Ah, Lycus has fallen for Amala!" one of the workers jibed. The fun-loving, muscular man called Ehran waved Niko over. Wine sloshed into glasses, and Niko quickly fell into the habit of relaxing among them.

"She has nice flowers." He set the rose down and smiled into his glass.

The group snorted and laughed. "Picks them from her family garden and sells them," Ehran said. "Like she needs coin when everyone knows she'll never want for anything in her whole life."

He laughed along. "Why's that then?"

"The Yazdans look after their own."

A sip of wine lodged in his throat. Niko spluttered, wheezed, and earned himself several painful slaps on the back before he croaked out, "Yazdan?"

"Forgot you're not from around here," Ehran laughed. "You know the type, bred into coin. They own half the houses around these docks, all the old Seran town. The name is as old as dirt but glitters like gold."

The conversation drifted onto other topics, but Niko's mind spiraled around the discovery. There had to be more than one branch of Yazdans? Perhaps it was a common Seranian name. Besides, Niko took his father's name, and Pah had nothing to do with the south. Hated it, in fact.

Unless, because he was a bastard—as Amir had revealed—he'd taken Mah's name.

Yazdan.

As old as dirt but glitters like gold.

"You all right, Lycus?"

He needed to know. "Yeah, I... just... need to find something." He left the group and searched the bustling dockside for the flower-seller. Amala Yazdan. He caught sight of her dark, braided hair strewn with flowers among the crowd and fought the flow of people to catch up with her.

"Oh, hello again," she beamed. "Back for more?"

"Amala Yazdan?" he asked breathlessly.

"Yes?" She tilted her head. Dark blue eyes, so unusual with bronze skin. So like Niko's.

"Have you heard of Leila Yazdan? She would have lived here maybe thirty years ago? She would have been young then... Around nineteen?" He winced. Amala was likely no older than nineteen herself.

"Leila?" She frowned. "I don't think so. I can ask the family if you like?"

"Would you?"

"Of course. Who shall I say is asking?"

"Lycus. And I'll find you in a few days? Will that be enough time?"

"Of course." She grinned again and drifted off, her steps light as she smiled at the people bidding her a good evening.

Yazdans in Seran seemed like something Yasir should have mentioned as soon as he'd heard Niko's real name. He liked to talk, so why the silence?

He wandered the docks and found the groaning mass of ship, the *Walla's Heart,* docked against the harbor wall.

Dockworkers bustled about her deck, busy loading her with goods. Niko asked after her captain and was invited on. He climbed the gangway and spotted Yasir's distinctive hat among the workers. He approached, finding the captain counting crates and marking them off.

"Hello, Lycus." His grin faltered. "Everything all right? Is Varian well?"

"Fine." A deckhand muscled Niko aside. The deck wasn't the place for this. "Is there somewhere we can talk?"

Yasir waved him to the back of the ship, the stern, he explained, and opened the door into a low-ceiling cabin.

Yasir was already pouring wine at his heavy dark wood desk when Niko asked, "Yazdan? Have you heard that name before, Yasir?"

He smiled, but this time it fell flat. "Yes." No tales, no offering of information. Usually, he was difficult to shut up.

"You didn't think to mention it in all the time we were on the road?"

"It's a small world." He handed over the wine. "Lots of Yazdans about."

Niko frowned at the man, a man he'd come to trust, who was obviously hiding something. "Where do they fit within your story of the griffin and the dark flame?"

He clasped his glass in both hands and sat in the chair behind his desk. "They're one of the old families, like the Cavilles, charged with keeping the dark flame controlled."

"And you didn't think to say, '*Hey, Niko, your family name features in these tales too*' in all the time we were togther? With all the information you threw out, you didn't once say the Yazdans are tied up with the Cavilles in all this ancient bullshit we're dealing with now?"

"Well, I did mention it... to Vasili," He took a drink, wetting his lips. "He said not to speak of it again, so—"

Niko spread his hands on the desktop, leaning in. "You told Vasili."

"He already knew, Niko. And I didn't tell you because... well, he cut the throats of the last people who pissed him off."

Of course Vasili knew. Like he knew exactly who Niko was when he tried to buy him with a bag of coin and threw him in the palace dungeons instead, keeping up the Caville tradition of screwing the old families for control of the flame, no doubt. Cavilles and Yazdans, charged with protecting the flame, only the Cavilles got greedy and decided to take it.

And here they all were, dealing with that ancient fuck-up to this very day.

This was all beginning to reek of lies, and Niko was in the dark. Again. "That fucking snake."

Yasir winced. "Isn't that why he brought you with him, your family and the connection to the flame?" Yasir trailed off at Niko's glare. "I see this has all just occurred to you," he mumbled, hastily drinking more wine.

"He didn't *bring* me. I fucking chose to be here." Had any of it been a real choice? The palace fire, the guards at the cottage. A few nudges here and there and Vasili could have maneuvered those pieces into place. *You will return.*

Niko shoved from the table and rubbed at his face, trying to clear his thoughts. "The Yazdans are the shirdals? The people who protect the flame?"

"I, er..." Yasir's gaze darted.

"Fucking lie to me and you won't be on this ship when it leaves."

"Yes. I mean, they claim to be protectors of the dark flame and all that, but it's more family legend than actual practice. If they really did care, they'd be all over what happened at Loreen with Talos and er... his sons."

All that time on the road, Yasir and Vasili had been discussing the Yazdans and they'd had one right alongside them the whole time. That wasn't a coincidence.

"I brought half the dark flame to their doorstep." Gods, he'd brought Vasili here, right to the Yazdans, to what could possibly be an enemy. Was that why Vasili had dragged his own Yazdan along? Was Niko leverage? "I can't trust anything he says..." He paced as the past few weeks unraveled in his head. And that damned kiss. Was that a lie too? Vasili used everyone. "He brought me here for my name. To use me to get among them."

"Oh, the Yazdans don't know you're here." Yasir confidently waved a hand.

"How do you know that?" Niko stopped pacing and glared.

"I..." Yasir swallowed. "They purchase my silk and a bit of spice here and there. I see them... regularly."

"Regularly?" He veered around the desk and leaned against its edge, deliberately inside Yasir's personal space, making him tilt his head up.

He nodded tightly. "They have no reason to know about you or the prince."

Then if they didn't know, Niko could get the jump on Vasili. Everything he knew was filtered through the prince. He needed to get to the source first. "Can I meet them?"

"I... Maybe you can... I suppose."

"As Lycus from Loreen, not Vasili's Nikolas." Whatever the fuck *Vasili's Nikolas* meant.

"Yes, yes. I can do that. Tomorrow, the family is hosting a gathering. A summer event. You can be my companion?" His grin bloomed again. "A grand idea! Their gatherings are stunning. Free food and wine, and—"

Niko slapped Yasir's shoulder, making him jump. "Wonderful. I'm looking forward to it."

"Will Vasili be attending?" he carefully asked.

"Vasili doesn't need to know any of this." If Vasili was going to keep secrets, then so could Niko. "Where shall I meet you?"

"On the dock. We'll take a carriage up to the Yazdan house."

Good. This felt like progress. Niko would investigate the Yazdans and get the truth before Vasili could twist it. He was done being Vasili's puppet. Tomorrow, he'd meet his possible family on his terms.

CHAPTER 15

Niko used half his wages to purchase a handsome high-collared red-and-black-patterned satin shirt with hidden fasteners and the rest to hire a tailor to hastily create some flattering velvet-trimmed trousers.

After dressing in the fresh clothes and lining his eyes in kohl, as Yasir had suggested, he stared at the stranger in the mirror. That man looked nothing like the soldier who'd fought on the front line or the blacksmith who regularly went to bed with coal buried under his nails, but he did look like he belonged on the exotic streets of Seran.

Floorboards creaked above.

He should tell Vasili he was attending a gathering, a half-truth.

After making a few final adjustments to the clothes and tugging on the polished black boots, he stood outside the prince's door, trying to form the right words in his head. He hadn't spoken to Vasili in a week, not since he'd been ordered out of his rooms. They'd passed each other on the stairs like two strangers passing in the street.

The door abruptly opened.

Vasili froze at the threshold, eyebrow raised. He looked splendid again, better than he'd ever looked in Loreen. Shirt billowing, earrings glinting, mouth tilted in such a way that Niko had to root himself to the landing floor to keep from kissing him, making him gasp again, making the uptight prince lose his control.

"Going out, Nikolas?" Some odd note pitched his voice slightly too high. His glare rode over Niko before darting back to his face. "If you want my permission, you have it."

He just had to be a prick. "I don't fucking need your permission."

Vasili waved him off. Niko was leaving anyway, but now he'd been given permission to leave, he almost wished he didn't need to.

"Enjoy yourself," Vasili added. "The gods know you've paid for it."

The door closed again, sealing the prince inside his rooms.

Now Niko felt guilty for snapping at him. But he'd deliberately and regularly kept Niko in the dark. This was his fault anyway. "I will," he told the closed door.

"Good," the prince's voice slithered beneath it.

Yasir waited on the dock beside a two-person carriage. His eyes widened. "By Aura's wonder, you look good enough to eat," the captain purred, offering Niko his hand to guide him into the back of the carriage.

Yasir climbed in beside him and thumped on the roof, signaling the driver to leave. They jerked into motion, and Niko settled back. He reflexively moved to rest his hand on the pommel of the sword he wasn't wearing. He'd meant to smuggle in a dagger, but he'd left the house so quickly, he'd forgotten to slip one down his boots. Damn Vasili for distracting him.

"I take it Vasili doesn't know you're here with me?"

"He knows I'm here, but not with you."

Maybe he should have told him.

No, Vasili wasn't his *master*, and Niko wasn't his doulos. Niko owed the prince nothing. He'd paid more than enough. He could walk away right now if he wanted...

Which was a lie.

Because of that damned soft kiss.

And this was why kissing Vasili would always be a terrible idea. The prince had his claws even deeper into Niko, occupying more of his thoughts than ever.

"Have you ever cared for someone who doesn't give a shit?" Niko asked.

Yasir's hand deliberately brushed Niko's knee as he adjusted his position to angle toward Niko slightly. "Some people struggle to show their feelings. They can be difficult to crack, but worth it." He eyed Niko expectantly, waiting for the truth.

Yasir had spent weeks traveling with them. He'd be a fool not to notice the tension between Niko and Vasili. "It's complicated."

Yasir chuckled.

"It's not like *that* between us," Niko dismissed with a laugh. "A long way from that."

Yasir nodded sympathetically. "Then this gathering will take your mind off him."

"I'm sure it will." Niko wasn't even sure it was possible to ignore the specter of Vasili in his head. He'd tried and failed for over a year. "Tell me about the Yazdans."

"They do a lot for Seran. Help maintain the harbor, ensure taxes are paid and repairs are undertaken. They look after their interests. Ocean trade is their main source of income. That and property."

"The house we're renting is theirs?"

"One of many. Everywhere you look in Seran, they own some part of it."

"And the family. Who are they?"

"Shah Kasra Yazdan is the patriarch."

"Shah?"

"Lord. Although, in Seran, the shah is treated more like a king." Yasir grinned. "Handsome bastard, even in his sixties. The gods made the Yazdans too damn pretty." His hooded gaze lingered on Niko. "It's grossly unfair. So, I suppose, the shah might be... your grandfather?"

"Maybe." Niko shifted uncomfortably. He still wasn't sure his mah had anything to do with the Seranian Yazdans. He'd never even considered having an extended family. It had only ever been Mah and Pah, and they were his world. To think he might belong to a substantial, powerful bloodline didn't sit easily on his shoulders.

"The shah's wife, Sheran, is just as formidable. She oversees the schools and sits on the high council. They have something like... nine children? Most are older, moved abroad. The Yazdans own a fleet of merchant vessels. Most of the children went into business in manufacturing and distribution. Roksana is the eldest daughter and as formidable as her mother." Yasir's expression gained some of that southern mischief Niko had come to expect of him. "A privateer, she's well-known for leaving wrecked ships in her wake. You'll meet her tonight."

"A pirate?"

"Privateer," he repeated with dramatic emphasis. "Piracy with the shah's stamp of approval. Don't call her a pirate."

Was Yasir a privateer too? Legalized piracy seemed like the sort of career a fox like Captain Lajani might enjoy. "So what you're saying is my potential family is made up of ocean-going thieves and merchants?"

He laughed at that. "They're practically royalty."

Niko had been happy with the way things were before Amir had revealed his pah might not be his pah at all. Everything since then had gotten complicated. "And where were the Yazdans during the war?"

Yasir sighed. "Your mother never told you any of this?"

"When I returned from the front, she was gone."

Yasir frowned and straightened the creases in his gown. "Seran stayed out of the war until the last few years. We held the oceanfront. Elves aren't fond of big bodies of water, but that didn't stop them from launching their crude fire ships and seeding assassin boats among us. The Yazdans lost half their fleet. They built more, but it was like trying to plug a sieve with your fingers. Too many elves got through. The Seranians, armed by Yazdan weapons, held them at the harbor, but not without losses."

"Have the elves returned since?"

"We haven't seen hide nor hair of an elf since King Talos negotiated peace."

That would change. And soon, with Amir on the

throne. The moment the elves sensed weakness, they'd strike. If they hadn't struck Loreen already. Gods, Niko needed to focus on what needed to be done and not let Seran seduce him into thinking the world was a safe place. He'd need to keep Vasili focused too. The prince had taken to Seran like a snake shedding its old skin for a shiny new one. Prying him out of Seran and encouraging him to return to Loreen could be difficult.

The carriage rocked to a halt outside an enormous house carved from a cliff-face of red rock. A fountain burbled in the sunken center with the buildings built around a main courtyard, as though the central garden were an outdoor royal court. The only thing Niko could compare to its lavish splendor was the Caville palace gardens. But the colors here exploded. The water glowed green, the house blazed red, and enormous tropical plants sprouted out of the earth.

Yasir strode inside, passing the guards who nodded, clearly recognizing him. Niko stuck close by, trying not to stare open-mouthed at the circus of people and noise and light. People milled through columned walkways, chatting and laughing, dressed in their fine silks. An army of servers offered wine and food.

Gods, it was another world, a fantasy one, where the war and the dark flame didn't exist. To think of how madness and bloodshed had underpinned the Caville palace and spilled into Loreen's streets, and yet here, in Seran, life was untouched by darkness.

What a life to live.

Yasir introduced *Lycus* to various businessmen and women of Seran, all of whom Niko politely greeted, emulating how Lady Maria had gracefully moved about the

Caville crowd. He could play at being a lord, especially as he'd inherited Mah's Seranian looks. The crowd here assumed he was one of them, and he was happy to let them believe those assumptions.

Yasir found a group of seafaring folks and easily fell into their conversation while Niko sipped his wine and scanned the crowd. Yasir had pointed out a few of the Yazdan children, all older than Niko, probably aunts and uncles.

A striking woman caught his eye as she broke from the hubbub and approached. A silk sash swished at her hips, and her unruly mahogany hair was barely restrained by a tight braid. Rogue curls spilled free. Red-painted lips matched the full, long red shirt. Bangles adorned her wrists, jewels twinkled at her ears, and pearl-inlaid pistols decorated both hips. "Captain Lajani!" she boomed, making Yasir splutter his wine. "Where the devil are my silks?"

"Roksana." Yasir grinned and flicked spilled wine from his fingers. His friends quickly made themselves scarce. "I had some trouble on the route down from the north." Her mouth twisted, and Yasir adjusted, piling on the charm. "Of course you'll get your silks."

She huffed and finally noticed Niko. "Who's this? New paramour?"

"Ah, no." Yasir laughed nervously. "Lycus is a friend of mine. From the north. Lycus, I have the pleasure of introducing Roksana Yazdan."

Ah, the infamous privateer. Roksana's dark eyes sparkled with intrigue. "Well met, Lycus. You look familiar. Have we met before?"

"My lady," Niko carefully matched his smile to hers. "I can't imagine where."

She narrowed her eyes and nodded knowingly, then offered her hand. Niko took her fingers and raised them to his lips for a light, respectful kiss. The signet ring caught his eye. Not a griffin, like the Cavilles, but an obsidian flame set into a golden background. He carefully released her fingers. "Interesting crest. A family insignia?"

"You aren't familiar with it?" She was still openly scrutinizing him. "Good gods, Yasir, what backwater place did you rescue him from?"

"Loreen."

"Oh," she said, like that explained everything. "They don't even have electricity there, do they?"

"I don't believe so." Yasir fiddled with his collar. "Talos thought it dangerous."

"Ugh, so uncivilized." She shuddered. "Although, you sir, are clearly not uncivilized."

"This is my first time in Seran," Niko replied, neither confirming nor denying how savage he could be.

"You don't happen to frequent the Fortisque?" she asked, interest sharpening.

"I don't know what that is."

Yasir cleared his throat. "A coffeehouse in the commerce district." He said coffeehouse in such a way that Niko wondered if the word coffee could be substituted for pleasure.

He arched an eyebrow. "I haven't."

"Perhaps you should. Hm?"

He dipped his chin slightly, unsure whether this was an attempt to seduce him or something else. "And why is that?"

"I'm always interested in meeting Captain Lajani's new friends." She grabbed Yasir's shoulder and gave it a hearty squeeze. "Get me my silks, Yasir, or we're going to have a problem. And you know how much I dislike problems." She patted his shoulder and slid her dark eyes back to Niko. "Lovely to meet you, Lycus. Do you have a family name?"

"I do." He could have fabricated one, but Roksana seemed the kind of woman to go asking after him, and he'd rather she didn't. Not yet anyway.

She grinned. "Hm, a secret keeper. Well, I hope we meet again, perhaps at the coffeehouse, hm? Ah, here's Father."

The hubbub from the crowd rose in volume, and a beautiful senior pair emerged from inside the house, arms locked. Even without the crowd's reaction, Niko would have known them from their regal presence alone. Shah Yazdan and his wife Sheran. Aging in years, both wore their lifetime experience on their faces. He could imagine they were formidable, and, by the way the crowd dipped their heads, the people here respected them.

Was he truly related?

Did it even matter? He'd still be a bastard, born out of marriage to Lord Bucland, who had clearly wanted nothing to do with Niko. If only Mah had taken him aside and explained it all. If only the war hadn't happened. If only Vasili hadn't been taken from the palace garden and bled in a box for eight years. Maybe things would be different. The war wouldn't have happened. Mah would still be alive to answer his burning questions. She'd been gone years, but her loss still haunted him.

"Lycus?"

"Yes?" Niko blinked, bringing himself out of his spiraling thoughts.

Yasir's soft hand gently rested on Niko's hip. He leaned closer. "This must be difficult for you."

"No, it's not hard. I..." Everything in his head was all tangled up with war and family and Vasili, and the evening's heat made the crowds feel too close. The bright laughter and startling opulence, the sweet air and all of these strangers. Maybe it was difficult, dredging up a past he didn't understand, bringing it into a future he understood even less. He felt adrift, inadequate, an imposter—and suddenly, painfully alone. He didn't belong in these clothes, in this house; it was like he'd been brought here without having a choice in any of it.

Niko wiped the dampness from his forehead.

"Some air for you, I think." Yasir steered him through the corridors, and Niko let his legs carry him away from the crowd. The corridors opened into a tall, narrow hall ending at a balcony overlooking the moonlit sea. Yasir plucked Niko's wine from his hand.

Niko braced himself against the balustrade, bowing his head, letting the cool ocean breeze kiss the back of his neck.

"The Seranian people's spirit has always been with Walla, our ocean goddess. Do you feel her?" Yasir asked.

Niko snorted at the godly nonsense but lifted his head anyway and breathed salty air into his tight lungs. He'd never really believed in the gods. They certainly weren't at the front when he'd needed them the most. "It's difficult sometimes," he admitted. "I don't understand it. My body remembers how to fight at the wrong moments, and my head forgets I'm not in the midst of battle."

Yasir stared out to sea. "It's said emotional battles linger long after the war has ended. Every time I smell smoke, I remember the burning ships and feel like I'm choking." He stroked at his throat.

What he spoke of sounded familiar. Like the memories were suddenly present and real. He rested his arms on the balustrade and peered out at the silvery ocean. "There's nothing dangerous back there. I almost wish there had been."

"Well, then clearly you've never dallied with high society."

"I've dallied with the Cavilles. They make the Yazdans look like harmless kittens."

Yasir chuckled, finished his wine, and set the glass on top of the balustrade. "If you were mine, I'd take you in my arms, tell you you're not alone, and well..." he gestured loosely, "you can gather the rest." He handed Niko back his glass, his face sheepish.

The flirting... He'd assumed that was just how Yasir was. Not that he'd genuinely wanted a more physical connection. "Yasir, you're a good man—"

He laughed sharply. "Please don't apologize. It'll just make this awkward, and I didn't say those things to make your life more difficult, just to let you know that you have friends, if you'll let them in."

He downed the wine and leaned a hip against the balustrade. Yasir smiled back, albeit softer and pulled down at one corner with regret. "It's not personal. I'm having a hard time trusting anyone, even myself."

"I know. Vasili told me how you were both betrayed." He lifted his face to the evening sky. "Vasili should be here."

The balcony was a long way from the crowds, and mention of the prince wouldn't be overheard, but Niko's heart skipped at his name nonetheless.

Yasir sighed. "He'd look like a fucking work of art on this balcony."

"Hm," Niko grumbled, "I wouldn't trust myself not to shove him off."

Yasir barked a bright, carefree laugh. A chuckle bubbled out of Niko too, and all the weight from earlier fell away.

Yasir draped an arm around Niko's shoulders and led him back toward the gathering. "Shall we see if I can introduce the formidable Nikolas Yazdan to his potential grandfather and then you can get back to your prince?" Niko shot him a warning glance, and Yasir grinned back. "Watching you both dance around each other is pure entertainment on my part, but I do wish you'd just fuck already."

Niko opened his mouth to deny everything, but Yasir's comical look of *You're really going to argue this?* silenced him. Instead, Niko said, "I think you're mistaking sex for the desire to kill."

Yasir chucked. "Much the same thing."

The sunken gardens were as busy as before. The shah stood atop the steps, presiding over it. He had a warrior's physique and would have made a solid soldier in his youth.

Niko caught the shah's blue eyes as Yasir maneuvered him through the crowd. Blue eyes. Dark hair. Bronze skin. Niko could hardly hide his own resemblance, but there were plenty of other similar individuals in the crowd. They couldn't all be bastards.

"Shah Yazdan." Yasir bowed. Niko quickly echoed the

motion. "May I introduce a good friend of mine, Lycus Kazemi. He's recently settled in Seran. It would be remiss of me not to bring him to one of your wonderful gatherings."

"Lycus," the shah grumbled, his voice resonating honor and pride. He touched his forehead and offered his hand. Niko smiled, dipped his head, and took his hand. A ring glinted on the shah's finger.

"I hope you're enjoying everything Seran has to offer?" the shah asked, withdrawing his hand and folding his fingers and the ring into a loose fist.

"The city is a wonder."

"Where do you hail from, Lycus?"

"The north."

"Hm, you don't look it." The man who might be Niko's grandfather smiled. His eyes filled with warmth. "Means wolf, doesn't it?"

He hesitated, briefly scrabbling around to understand the question. This was beginning to feel like an interrogation. "Lycus? Yes."

"A dark wolf," the shah mused. "Aptly named. You have hungry eyes."

The nearby crowd had stopped chattering to listen, and Niko found himself the center of attention. There would be no better time to ask the shah about the flame. He might not get another chance, but all he could think of was how looking at the shah was like looking in the mirror at an older version of himself. "Can I ask, Shah, your family crest? It's interesting."

The shah lifted his hand to admire the ring. "The flame, you mean?"

"I wondered about it, having seen your family wearing it this evening."

The shah narrowed his eyes. "*Lycus*, you say?"

Subtlety never had been Niko's talent. The shah was not convinced. "I… yes?"

"An old northern name." The man's tone had hardened. "And a lie."

Niko swallowed. He couldn't possibly know the name was a lie just because of its origins. Could he?

"Why are you asking about the flame, Lycus?" All of the warmth and familial tone had vanished from the shah's voice.

More of the crowd fell silent. Niko wet his lips. "I meant no offense."

"Did the Cavilles send you?"

Shit. "I—"

The shah's wife appeared at her husband's side and snaked her arm in his. Through a thin smile, she said, "Captain Lajani, it's time you left with your companion."

"Of course, *farsi*." Yasir bowed low. "Lycus, I believe we've worn out our welcome."

Niko stared his grandfather in the eyes. Eyes so like his own. The man knew Niko was a Yazdan. He couldn't fail to. This was too good an opportunity to let go.

"Leila Yazdan?" Niko blurted.

The man's lips parted. "Leila?" His voice softened before he caught himself and the shutters came down over his expression again. "There is no Leila Yazdan. Now, best you leave of your own will. Or should I summon the guards?"

"That won't be necessary." Niko forced a smile. "A pleasure to meet you, Shah Yazdan. I'm sure we'll meet again very soon."

Yasir hastily steered Niko through the crowd and back outside to the waiting carriage. "Well, that was entertaining," he muttered. "You probably don't want to piss off the most important family in Seran if you want to keep a roof over your head."

Yasir chatted some more, but Niko considered how the shah's face had changed at the mention of Leila, Niko's mah. "He knew her."

"Her who?"

"My mother."

"Yes, well. The family connection was pretty fucking obvious, don't you think? You're a mirror image of the man."

"I had to be certain."

Yasir rolled his eyes. "Seems your mother kept a lot from you." He leaned against the carriage door and pursed his lips. "There were subtler ways to get your answers than come right out and demand answers of the shah in the middle of his summer celebrations." Yasir watched the window. "I bet you were a riot in the Caville courts."

"Something like that."

They fell into an easy quiet, lulled by the rocking motion of the carriage. There could be no doubt. The Yazdans of Seran were Niko's family, despite the shah's denials. But what did that mean? Vasili knew, he had to. He'd always known. So, what game was the prince playing now?

The carriage pulled up outside the townhouse. Niko climbed down and turned to bid Yasir a good night, but

Yasir's smile rapidly faded as his gaze caught on something behind Niko. "Your door's open."

Dread chilled Niko's blood. He climbed the steps, passing into the unlit hallway. Yasir sent the carriage off and hurried inside too.

"Vasili?" Niko called.

Nothing.

He glanced back at Yasir, finding the same dread echoed in the captain's eyes.

Niko bounded up the floors. Vasili's door lay wide open. Inside, the sideboard's drawers had been pulled from the unit, their contents strewn about. Shards of a smashed wine bottle glinted on the floor. A rug lay askew, and among its folds, Niko found the jagged neck of a broken bottle. "*Vasili*?" he growled.

What if he lay dead in the next room? What if the dark flame had been set free?

The bedroom was empty. No bodies. No signs of any struggle. All the rooms were empty. Yasir checked the rest of the house and returned grim-faced.

Vasili had been taken.

CHAPTER 16

"The Yazdans did this." Niko paced Vasili's main room, occasionally glancing through the window at the sparkling city docks, expecting or hoping to see Vasili's distinctive outline among those loitering on the nighttime streets. "They took him." He had to get Vasili back. If the Yazdans likely knew about his blood, the curse, the dark flame, all of it, then they'd restrain Vasili, probably bleed him.

"I found this..." Yasir had been tidying the mess when he straightened and handed a ring to Niko.

Niko's heart sank. The griffin ring. Gods, what did it mean? Had he thrown it there? Was it a sign?

Niko should never have left.

Vasili had said he'd brought him here to protect him, to stop him from being taken, and Niko had neglected that duty out of spite. This was his fault.

Niko's guts turned over. He reached for the dresser and slumped against it. If whoever had Vasili used force against him, one of two things would happen. He'd snap and lose control of the flame, or he'd freeze and suffer. Neither of those outcomes was acceptable.

Niko had to find him before that happened. He bolted for the door.

Yasir stepped into his path and blocked him with a hand. "Before you go charging off—"

"Get out of my way."

Yasir lifted his hands off but stood firm. "You can't march back into the Yazdan house all bluster and no evidence."

"The hell I can't."

"You don't even know they have him!"

"Who else would?" He stepped around him and opened the door.

"If Vasili were here, he'd tell you to stop!"

Niko stopped. He was right. Vasili would tell him not to be a fool, not to rush into something he didn't understand. Which right now, was everything.

Yasir's stricken face dampened some of Niko's frustration. If Niko were wrong, and he went charging into the Yazdan house, he'd expose Vasili. There still could be another explanation.

Niko slammed the door and braced both hands against it. "Fine. We do it your way."

"We need to think," Yasir said. "If we're going to go up against the Yazdans, we need to be smart. We need to be *certain*. So let's backtrack..."

Niko turned and watched Yasir fall into his habit of pacing when he was worried. "Did Vasili say anything to you before you left?"

"Nothing."

Yasir frowned. "I find that unlikely."

Niko thumped his head back against the door and briefly closed his eyes. "It was trivial. He and I… we argued. He was glad I was going out, and I was a prick about it."

"Was he glad you were going out because he had plans? Was he meeting someone?"

Niko opened his eyes and lowered his gaze to Yasir. "You think he planned this?"

"No, but—"

"There's blood on the broken bottle."

Yasir lifted a finger. "It may not be his."

Niko walked his thoughts back. His instinct had been that Vasili was taken, but that was because he'd assumed Vasili's innocence in this. The prince had never been innocent. "You think he attacked someone?"

"I saw him ruthlessly cut the throat of a marauder, so I'd prefer to eliminate the possibility before we go charging after him in some rescue he doesn't need."

It was more than possible Vasili had attacked someone. Even likely. Vasili was ruthless. He'd told Niko time and time again that he'd do anything to protect Loreen, including kill.

Niko considered the mess in the room again—since tidied away by Yasir. They only knew for certain that there had been a struggle and someone was hurt. Vasili could have entertained someone while Niko was out—taken advantage of being alone—and attacked them.

"He said nothing about guests?" Yasir asked.

"We haven't spoken in… a while." As Yasir's gaze grew

more interested, Niko waved him off. Telling him how things had gotten physically heated before Vasili had dumped ice water on that a week ago wasn't going to help now. "It's not relevant." Besides, did they ever speak? Vasili barked orders and Niko obeyed.

"Has he been meeting with anyone? Visiting anywhere? If we know who he's been with, we can ask around—"

"He said he knew someone in Seran."

"Good. That's a start. Who?"

Niko spread his hands. "I didn't ask."

"Why not?"

"Because..." Because Vasili was Vasili, and Niko never got a straight answer anyway, so he hadn't asked, knowing Vasili wouldn't tell him. It seemed stupid now.

Yasir's frown darkened. "Do you two speak at all or is it just grunts and snarls the whole time?"

"Vasili and I aren't friends, Yasir. I'm here to protect him because of the curse, and he's in Seran to find sanctuary and allies, if any exist. We don't talk, we don't share tales. He doesn't answer my questions. We aren't close, like he is with you. I'm here to keep him safe, and I've failed. This is wasting time. We need to go to the Yazdans."

"Look, I agree... I do. I just think we need to be prepared. What if it's not them, what if it's his brother?"

Niko's heart fluttered. Could it be Amir already? They'd never discussed the shadow beast that had attacked Vasili, what if it had been Amir's? But if this were Amir, he'd gloat. He'd make sure Niko knew it was him. The prick would have left a note. As much as he'd changed with the flame alive in him, he was still the self-centered attention-seeking asshole he'd always been.

Niko shuddered a sigh. The truth was, he had no idea

if Vasili had been taken or if the prince had done the taking. Vasili might walk back in at any moment, his steps light, his face blank, and he'd snarl at Niko for being foolish enough to think anyone could overpower him. But Vasili wasn't invulnerable, like most everyone believed, including Yasir. The prince was riddled with insecurities and fear, and if he *were* taken, then right now, he'd be reliving everything he went through with the elves, and that wasn't right, not even for a cruel prick like Vasili.

Gods, the ache in his chest had become a gaping hollowness. "I have to find him, Yasir."

"I know..." Yasir nodded. "We will."

"You don't know. You can't." Every second with Vasili absent felt as though someone were carving pieces off Niko's heart. And it wasn't just because of the threat from the dark flame. He and Vasili never talked because there was only the past to talk about, and neither of them wanted to go there. He'd seen Vasili afraid, seen him furious, seen him brave. Seen a hundred sides to him and knew there to be a hundred more, but by the gods, Niko needed to see him safe. He almost prayed Vasili *had* attacked someone because Niko could rage at him and they'd fight, and that would be normal because that's how things were between them. But this absence, this silence? It hurt more than any lashing whip.

Vasili was gone. Niko had failed him.

Yasir gripped Niko's shoulder and looked him in the eyes. "We'll find him. Whatever it takes. You have my word."

Niko covered Yasir's hand with his and leaned in. "At first light, I'm going back to the Yazdan house."

"Niko—"

"I have to."

Yasir sighed. "Then I'll come with you."

"Don't you need to sail at high tide?"

Yasir gave a troubled sigh, the kind that spoke of more concern than pity. "Whoever hurt you both is a damned fool. No, I won't be leaving friends in need. That's not who I am." Yasir turned in a whirl of motion, grabbed a pen and paper from the drawers he'd neatly tidied, and sat at the small table. "We'll make a list of all the people you've met or know in Seran, and tomorrow, we'll speak with them all, from dusk to dawn, if we have to."

Niko pulled up a chair to the table and sat. "I don't have many names. For all I know, you could have taken him."

He looked up. "Darling, if I'd taken Vasili, he'd be sleeping off a night to remember in my cabin. Besides, I was with you. You can check my ship if you wish."

"I will."

Yasir smiled sadly. "Very well, but assuming I don't have him, we'll need to ascertain who Vasili has been socializing with."

Niko managed to name two people he'd seen Vasili speak with, and both of those overlapped Yasir's list. By the time they'd scribbled down names and discussed the possibilities of Vasili's whereabouts, the sky—visible through Vasili's window—had begun to lighten.

"It's time." Niko stood. Taking the royal ring from his pocket, he slipped it over his little finger. The legend told of how griffins were protectors of the flame. Vasili would have forced the role upon him with blood if he'd found the nerve, but now Niko wore the mark willingly, like he'd worn the crest in battle. He never had escaped service to the Cavilles or the palace. His duty had followed him to Seran, and it had never felt more right.

He'd find Vasili today, even if he had to turn the city upside down to do it.

CHAPTER 17

Niko rode Adamo while Yasir took Niko's horse. The cool, early morning air nipped at Niko's face and hands.

A brief stop confirmed Yasir didn't have Vasili aboard his ship and allowed Yasir to change out of the lord's attire into garments more befitting a ship's captain than a silk merchant. He wore his pistol exposed at the hip and had gained a severe look Niko hadn't known he'd been capable of.

On the ride up the long road to the Yazdan house, Yasir spoke of their plan for the day and how they were going to track down the names on his list, but it wouldn't be needed because they'd find Vasili with the Yazdans. Niko was sure of it.

No guards flanked the entrance gates this time. The gates lay open, the way inside unbarred. The red rock house loomed against the cliff-face, its emerald fountains sparkling in the red-tinged morning sunlight.

Yasir turned his horse on the approachway. "It's quiet."

"It's early." Niko urged Adamo forward with a jab of his heels. The horse's huge hooves clopped on the road. A flock of colorful birds startled from a nearby palm.

"There should be guards." Yasir's hand rested on his thigh, near his pistol. "There are always guards."

In the stark light of day, the house had lost some of its fantastical allure, but the sprawling columned wings around its sunken gardens still spoke of paradise, albeit an apparently empty one.

The burbling fountains absorbed the sounds of clopping hooves. There should have been staff milling about, readying the house for the day ahead. The foreboding silence crackled against Niko's skin. He swiftly dismounted Adamo and followed the tiled walkways into the gardens. Perhaps everyone was sleeping off the night's merriment. But the silence didn't feel like the slumbering kind, it felt like the kind Niko had walked through after a battle. The silence that was left *after* the storm had passed.

He jogged down a set of steps, deeper into the garden, with its neatly trimmed hedges and tiled, intersecting pathways.

This wasn't right. Houses like this were never silent.

Niko reached the main fountain. Wine glasses and tankards sat on their sides, as though the people who had attended the gathering had merely stepped away for a moment.

Broken glass crunched under Niko's boots. He glanced down at the scattered glass twinkling in the sunlight. Yasir approached, his boots disturbing a thin layer of dust.

Kneeling, Niko clutched a handful of the grey dust and sifted it through his fingers. Ash. But what had burned?

His stomach dropped. Not *what*.

He bolted from the fountain, up the main stairs, where the shah and his wife had descended the previous evening to join their guests. Ash had gathered in corners, like sand blown in from the desert. It quietly shifted around Niko's passing.

He dashed through the columned hallways, checking chambers for signs of life.

"Niko?!" Yasir had his pistol palmed as he caught up. "What happened here?"

It couldn't be real, could it? All those people...

He checked doorway after doorway but was met with more silence and soot.

"We should leave..." Yasir said.

A motionless body lay facedown in the corridor ahead, his hand reaching toward a window overlooking the ocean. Niko knelt at the man's side and checked for a pulse at his clammy, cool neck. Fluttering touched his fingertips. He rolled him on his side and met his grandfather's veined, weeping eyes. The old man's pale lips moved, but no words escaped. His hand trembled, reaching for Niko's face, but then he dropped it and swept up Niko's hand instead, folding the Yazdan ring into it.

"Who did this?" Niko cradled the man's head.

The shah's gaze fogged over. His lips still moved, chanting the same thing over and over. Niko lifted the shah close. "Who did this?" he whispered into the shah's ear, clutching the frail man close. The shah paused and whispered a single, clear word.

"Caville."

The shah's body loosened, falling limp in Niko's arms,

becoming hollow as his life left him. Niko lay the man down—his grandfather—and staggered to his feet.

"What did he say?" Yasir scanned the gardens.

Ash-strewn corridors. The dead devoured.

The dark flame had washed through the Yazdan house, consuming everything it touched like it had that day in the Caville palace under Talos's control.

All those people.

Hundreds.

Gone.

"We need to leave," Niko snapped. "Now."

They retreated to the horses and galloped from the grounds, only slowing once the house was out of sight and Seran's busy streets embraced them once more. The color and noise and life didn't feel real, and Niko walked Adamo through it, his mind cold and quiet.

"Niko, what's going on?" Yasir reined up alongside. "Will you answer me?"

Amir. It had to be because the alternative was a thousand times worse.

They couldn't go back to the townhouse. If Amir had taken Vasili, the risk was too great.

"Your ship." Niko pulled Adamo toward the docks. "We'll talk there."

They tied the horses alongside the crates waiting dockside at *Walla's Heart* and climbed abroad.

"Dismiss your men."

Yasir hesitated but obeyed, giving his crew the day off as he cautiously eyed Niko. When they were finally alone on deck, Yasir turned to Niko, "What the fuck happened back there?"

He grabbed Yasir's arm and hauled him into the cabin. The ship rocked gently beneath his feet, or perhaps he was unsteady because of what he was about to reveal. "They're all dead."

"The shah is... Shit... If anyone saw us. We should report it—"

"No, Yasir." His head ached, the images swirling around and around. "*They're all dead.*"

"What?"

"The Yazdans. Everyone. It must have happened after we left."

"*What* happened?"

"The dark flame. It consumed them. I've seen it before with Talos, but not on that scale." He propped a hip against Yasir's desk and rubbed at the bridge of his nose.

Yasir snorted a laugh. "That's impossible."

"The ash, Yasir. You must have seen it. That's all that's left."

The color drained from the captain's face. He flopped into his chair, suddenly silent. "Why?"

"Because they were Yazdans, because it was pissed, because the person controlling it... lost control."

"But isn't it locked up inside the two princes?"

Niko rubbed at his forehead. He needed to think. Too much was unknown. Had Amir taken Vasili and eliminated the Yazdans? But that didn't seem like Amir's way. He was too flashy, too obnoxious.

So, what if Amir wasn't here at all...

What if Vasili had come to Seran—not to find allies, but to kill them? What if the prince was already lost to the flame and Niko had *helped* it get this far?

"We have to find Vasili."

"We will—"

"Not tomorrow, Yasir. Not later, we have to find him *now.*" *And stop him.*

Yasir poured himself a drink, fingers trembling, the decanter rattling against the glass. "Tell me how to find a man like Vasili in a city of hundreds of thousands of souls?"

Hundreds of thousands of souls.

All fuel for the dark flame.

Oh gods. He could only hope that this was Amir because if it was Vasili, then they were all as good as dead. Amir made mistakes, he was a brash fool, but Vasili... if he'd lost his battle against the flame, it would have the perfect vessel. It would consume everything in its path, including the prince.

Yasir handed Niko a drink. "Whiskey. Dark and hot. Like you." Yasir grinned, but the attempt at humor quickly died.

Niko stared at the glass.

If the madness had taken Vasili, then Niko had failed. He'd done nothing to stop the flame. He'd *helped* it. He'd lost Vasili and failed at the one vow he'd given the prince, to kill him if he ever lost control.

Were there clues? Had Vasili said anything to hint at losing control? He'd spoken of the madness, told him it was in his head, said it would consume him like it had the others and he didn't have long.

But the Caville madness, so obvious in Talos, hadn't been present in Vasili. Or had Niko just not wanted to see it? What if the flame was learning? Was it clever enough to be subtle, like possessing the palace guards and quietly building itself an army? Was it conscious?

Niko grabbed the glass and downed the drink, then spluttered and choked as the heat burned through his chest.

"Steady there."

He held the glass out for a second helping. "There must be a way to find him."

Yasir refilled his glass. "There could be. I mean, I did consume, er... some of his..." He cleared his throat. "Blood."

Niko looked up. "You said it had no effect."

"Well, that's not exactly true."

"*Yasir*."

Yasir waved him off. "There are dreams, and sometimes, I can make shadows move."

"By the fucking three, why didn't you tell me?"

"Because you don't approve and you're just as terrifying as Vasili." He swallowed hard. "After we arrived in Seran, I couldn't let it go. I did some digging into old archives. I found reference to sorcerers, men of magic."

Exactly as Niko had feared Yasir would. "You didn't think to mention this?"

"I was just dabbling." He cleared his throat. "Anyway, armed with my research and while you were out at the docks every night, I, er... I asked Vasili to continue sharing his,"—he circled his hand in the air, averting his gaze—"power."

Gods, did nobody listen to Niko? "Did Vasili tell you about Julian?"

Yasir's brows pinched. "A little."

"Julian was a sorcerer too, further along than you are. Vasili's blood drove him insane."

"He was the, er... the soldier you... were close with? Vasili said the elves killed him."

"Vasili is a fucking liar, Yasir. When will you see that? *I* killed Julian, right after he dosed me up with spice and tried to let the elves into Loreen. He had access to all the dark powers you're coveting, and he wielded them effectively. The dark flame ravaged his mind, Yasir."

"Vasili said the elves made him mad. That he was good once."

And that was probably true, at least half of the truth, which was where Vasili excelled. "Think about it, Yasir. Vasili was driven from his home by his brother, who has already begun experimenting with blood-possession. He meets you, a lone traveler, an adventurous soul. He's going to tell you what you want to hear. He's going to slowly poison you like the snake he is and use you time and time again, because that's what Vasili does. And don't assume I'm pissed at him because of our past. He's told me who and what he is a dozen times. What you're describing is Vasili all over. He will fuck you up and leave you broken and bleeding behind him."

Yasir rubbed at his face. "It's done. And if I'm screwed, so be it. Doesn't mean we can't use whatever tools we have at our disposal to find him."

Gods, when they found Vasili, Niko was going to kill the manipulative bastard. He stared at the Caville ring on his finger and had half a mind to throw it at Yasir. It suited him—the prince's sorcerer. Niko was just the prince's assassin.

Taking the Yazdan ring from his pocket, he placed it on the finger next to the Caville's ring. Maybe sometime soon, he'd pick a side. A family he didn't know, or the lying prince he did?

"You want to use the dark flame to find him?" Niko asked.

Yasir nodded. "What have we got to lose?"

Only your soul.

CHAPTER 18

Yasir cleared his desktop of charts and navigating equipment and replaced them with a beautiful hand-drawn street-map of Seran. The city's spiderweb network of concentric streets branched out from the old town and the docks at its southern edge.

Niko was admiring the elaborate artwork when Yasir lit a black candle and carried it to the table. "This may not work. It's just a theory at this stage... I haven't been able to do much more than shape shadows."

"Did Vasili show you how?"

"No, he told me the Cavilles rarely use their magic. They leave that to their sorcerers. He can, I think, but he doesn't like to."

Niko recalled Vasili telling King Talos that using the flame wasn't the Caville way. Had he meant it literally? It could be the more he used it, the more the flame tried to free itself from his grasp.

He glanced again at Niko. "The information I found

was penned by Yazdans. Their past seems to be inextricably linked with the Cavilles."

Niko snorted. "Of course it is."

"But from what I've read, it doesn't appear to have been a friendly relationship. The Cavilles and Yazdans have been at each other's throats for forever."

"There's a surprise," Niko drawled.

Yasir used another candle to light the wick of the black one. The new flame spluttered to life, tinged purple. "Do you think your mother had a reason for going to Loreen?" Yasir asked idly. "Something to do with the Cavilles?"

"Maybe." Niko thought of Amala, the flower-seller, and Roksana, the privateer. He'd only just found them, and now they were gone. Now he'd never know them.

Yasir dripped black wax onto the map, pooling a globule near the commerce district.

"Do you know what you're doing?" Niko asked.

"Vaguely." Yasir grinned. "No, not really."

"Then this is reckless."

"So is every time I go to sea, but I'm still here."

"Because you can only die once," Niko added.

Yasir half smiled. "I see why he listens to you."

"Who?"

Yasir chuckled, set the candle down, and spread both hands over the map with the hardening wax pool in the center. He focused on that pool, spread his fingers, and breathed out.

Niko inched back and rested his hand on his sword's pommel. Julian had learned to wield the preternatural forces of the dark flame well enough to summon fiends. Those encounters would forever haunt Niko's dreams. Willfully inviting the dark flame into being seemed like opening the door to all the nightmares best kept locked far away. But if it could help find Vasili, then perhaps it was worth it.

Yasir whispered harsh, hissing words Niko couldn't decipher.

The wax shifted, liquefying again into a shiny bubble. Yasir's whispers grew louder, and the wax shimmered, gathering itself together in a tighter nodule.

Niko leaned closer.

The wax rippled. A drip stretched out like a tentacle, following the twisting outline of Seran's old streets. It flowed around bends and through junctions, marking a pathway. Then it stopped and suddenly solidified again, freezing its jagged line rigid.

Yasir puffed a hard sigh and bowed his head.

Niko kept his hand on his sword. The captain's pistol was within reach. If Yasir went for it, Niko would draw. The possessed had burned his home, almost killed the prince, and had probably done a whole lot more Niko didn't yet know.

Yasir cleared his throat and straightened. "All right?" he croaked. The dark briefly swam in his eyes and was gone. He blinked and frowned at Niko's grimace. "Not good?"

"Something to keep an eye on."

Yasir shuddered, flicked his hands out, and regarded the map. "The Fortisque."

"The coffeehouse Roksana mentioned?"

"The same."

That couldn't be a coincidence. "Vasili's there?"

"Something clearly is." He straightened his cuffs and cleared his throat again. "Let's go and find out."

~

THE FORTISQUE WAS a grand building in Seran's commerce quarter. It looked more akin to a courthouse than whatever a coffeehouse might be, but the patrons passing through its door appeared to range from those dressed in rich silks to traders from the markets. Men and women alike.

Niko carved through the dawdling people, up the steps, and ventured inside. A few wary glances were tossed his way, but none lingered. People gathered around small tables, no chairs—and talked business. Money and trades. Not a pleasure-house, then, but something more official.

Niko was about to turn around and head out when he heard a rolling laugh, the kind so rare he wondered if he'd conjured it up. Yasir must have heard the same because he charged through a back door and out into a sheltered, private courtyard. And there, sprawled in a chair, laughing like he didn't have a single care, was Vasili.

Relief washed through Niko—he was alive and well! Then rage burned all that away. That slithering prick!

"Oh, Yasir! I hope you finally have my silks?!" Roksana's voice chimed, though it carried a slurring edge, as though she'd been drinking all night. She sat opposite Vasili. Several empty wine bottles stood on the table between them.

Vasili's laughter faded as he glanced over his shoulder. He raised an eyebrow at Niko's approach. Niko was almost on him when the prince's dagger flashed. The prince remained seated, but the point of the dagger was angled an inch away from Niko's heart. A knowing flicker sharpened the prince's blue eye. "What have I done to anger you now?"

This couldn't be real.

Niko backhanded the dagger from his grip. He'd have lunged in and knocked the bastard from his chair if Vasili hadn't moved like the snake he was and slipped out from under Niko's lunge to whirl, snatch an empty bottle from the table, smash its body, and brandish the jagged neck.

"*Where were you?*" Niko snarled.

Vasili frowned and adjusted his grip on the bottle. "Back down, Nikolas."

"Like your fucking dog? I don't think so."

"Shit," Roksana slurred and glanced at Yasir. "Are they always like this?"

Vasili didn't look wounded. He had the slightly glazed appearance of someone high on spice, but his clothes showed no sign of a brawl. He was still the same picture of sophisticated elegance that suited Seran so well, and now nothing made any sense. How could he be here, getting high and drunk with Roksana?

The privateer watched from her chair, barely fazed. She'd heard Vasili call him Nikolas but didn't seem surprised his name wasn't Lycus.

Yasir had plucked his pistol free but kept it pointed down. "Where were you both last night?" he asked.

Vasili slowly lowered the bottle. "Is this about the mess at our house?"

Roksana took the hem of her shirt and lifted it to reveal a thick gauze covering her lower belly. "Got me good, he did. I went there to tell you both to leave before Father got wind I was housing you. Unfortunately, it didn't occur to me how Cavilles don't take kindly to unannounced folks walking about their rooms."

She knew Vasili was a Caville. They knew each other... *She* was Vasili's woman in Seran.

"Roksana, you were at the ball," Yasir said.

"Yes, I was trying to get you both to come here without making it obvious, and then you went and insulted the shah, so I lost my chance to speak with you privately. I came back here shortly after, to check on Vasili."

"Vasili was here the whole time?" Niko asked, watching the prince's brow knit together.

"The whole time," Roksana confirmed.

"You know each other?" Niko asked, needing it confirmed.

"Vasili and I met years ago, after I went north, looking for Leila Yazdan."

She knew his mah? Wait... As important as all of this was, Roksana had left the Yazdan gathering early. She didn't know her family was dead.

Vasili set the broken bottle down on the table. "What's happened?"

Yasir glanced at Niko before beginning, "Roksana, your home, your... father. We were there this morning, looking for Vasili, and what we found... devastation." He moistened his lips. "There's nobody left."

She laughed, as though his words were a joke, but that laugh quickly faded in the face of Niko's grimace. "I don't understand."

"They're gone," Niko said. "Sometime last night, the dark flame consumed them all."

Roksana gasped. "What? No. The flame?" She stood

from the chair. "Yasir, what is this nonsense? What are you saying?"

Niko glanced to Vasili to check his reaction. Fear stole the color from Vasili's face. He staggered and reached for the table. It seemed genuine. But how could Niko possibly know what was real with him?

"It's true..." Yasir confirmed. "You should... I can take you there, if you like, I—"

She bolted from the chair and out of the courtyard.

"I should... go after her," Yasir said. "She's going to need help. Are you both safe here?"

Vasili stood with his hands gripping the back of a chair, his head down. It all seemed so real.

"Are we safe, Vasili?"

The prince lifted his face. The dark didn't coat this eye; he was still Vasili. But he'd slipped before. "Go with her, Yasir," he said.

"Meet us on your ship," Niko added. Yasir nodded and left, and now the small open-air courtyard sheltered just the two of them, an oasis of quiet in Seran's center.

"Amir..." Vasili said the name like spitting something foul. "He's in the city."

"You were here the whole night?"

Vasili looked up. The fear had vanished like it always did, buried beneath layers of Caville misdirection. Did Vasili make them all think he was in this coffeehouse, when in fact he'd been the one to sweep through the Yazdan house and destroy everyone inside?

"You're wearing my ring." He sauntered toward Niko.

"I'm wearing two." He lifted his hand. "I was with the shah when he died. He gave me his ring. Do you know what name he said with his dying breath?"

"By the way you came at me moments ago, I can certainly guess." Vasili's hand slipped into his slim waistcoat pocket. His fingertips came out coated in blue powder. He raised it to his lips.

Niko caught his wrist, the same wrist he'd broken a year ago, the bones so brittle now. "Don't."

The prince blinked slowly. "Why not?"

"We need you clear-headed."

He smiled and stepped closer, closing the distance between so they almost touched. "We or *you*?"

"Vasili... I have to know. Were you here all last night?"

The lashes of his left eye fluttered. "If you discover the answer to that question, will you tell me?"

Oh gods. He didn't know. He wasn't lying, he just didn't have the answer. That was so much worse than the truth. He could have killed those people. He was more than capable.

"I have to get you somewhere safe." Niko twisted his grip on Vasili's wrist, controlling the hold.

"Hm, then you'd better let go." Vasili inched closer and leaned provocatively against Niko. "Unless you plan on dragging me out of here," he purred.

He should let go, but his fingers stayed loosely clamped enough to feel Vasili's pulse lightly tapping against his fingers. "Did you kill them?"

His pulse quickened, and Vasili yanked his wrist free. "No." His fingers fluttered to his forehead. "I don't know. Perhaps I did? I truly don't recall."

If he hadn't been so damned high, he'd have known. "What *do* you recall?"

"Lashing out at Roksana. Coming here with her, then going back... for my ring, for you." His cheek twitched.

"Of course, you weren't there, because you're never where you're supposed to be. And then..." His brow pinched. "I don't fucking know, Nikolas. Does it please you to know your disgust at my continued existence is correct? I'm everything you hate, and soon, you'll kill me to stop me, just like you've always wanted. Will that finally make you happy? Will you smile over my grave or spit on it?"

"You don't disgust me—"

"You've hated me since the moment you saw me."

"No, I hated the ring and everything it stands for."

"*You hate me*," he jabbed a finger at Niko's chest, "because in your simple life, I should have fixed everything. You believe me to be a failure. You believe I'm weak. I see it in your eyes every time you look at me. I let the elves in. I killed your parents and the thousands of others I failed. I'm the source of all this madness. It's my fault Julian hurt you. You taunted Amir to no end, but it's my fault he fucked you—"

"He didn't—"

"This whole fucking war is my fault." He pulled from Niko's grip and stalked away. "Gods, you're so damned righteous. So fucking right about everything." He stumbled and fell against the table, then shoved it away, sending the chairs crashing to the floor.

"The spice..." He'd seen him like this before. Spice amplified everything. The moods, the manic behavior, the madness behind it all, trying to tear free of him. It was all part of who he was, but not all of him. Vasili lashed out when threatened.

Niko glanced at the door behind him into the coffeehouse. They hadn't drawn much attention but would soon. "Vasili, let's go somewhere—"

He whirled. "I suppose you despise me for not telling you about the Yazdans?"

Niko stilled.

The prince grinned, his teeth white behind his ironic smirk. "I didn't tell you about the Yazdans because you would have come to Seran. And I…" He looked up and blinked into the sun. "I would have lost you." His shoulders fell, the weight of his words suddenly upon him. When he finally looked at Niko again, rage and fear made him snarl. "You left me with a brother I no longer recognize and this thing in my head that *won't fucking shut up*!"

Niko grabbed him by the arm and yanked him close, jarring the prince hard against him. "Listen to me!" Vasili's snarling mouth burned so temptingly close. He twitched in Niko's grip, tensing to fight. "I'm not leaving you now, even though every instinct is telling me to, so get your shit together and be the prince Loreen needs." Niko locked an arm around Vasili's lower back, trapping him. Vasili, taut and fierce, fumed back at him. "We've come this far. I need you to be better than this."

"And what if I'm worse?" His gentle touch landed on Niko's cheek. Face-to-face, with nothing between them, Vasili's layers came tumbling down.

"Then I'll deal with it." Niko tilted his head. Vasili's breath fluttered against his mouth. He looked into his eye, the blue so brilliant it blazed like the ocean under the sun. "I'll do whatever needs to be done. I'll stop you if I must. But until that moment, I'm here, protecting you from everything that would hurt you, even yourself. Do you hear me? A griffin must forever hold the flame. I'm holding you. I *am* your protector. If I weren't, I'd have killed you a hundred times already."

"No..." Vasili sank his fingers into Niko's hair and twisted, holding him rigid. "You'll be my assassin," he snarled, then slammed his mouth into Niko's.

He tasted of heat and spice, and Niko's body burned where Vasili touched. This was so wrong. Vasili was high and hurting, but by the gods, the need to have him stole all the wrongs and made them right.

Vasili tore free with a gasp but clutched Niko's face between his hands, preventing him from retreating.

Color touched Vasili's cheeks and lips and his eye shone with lust. He was beautiful and fierce and utterly mad, and Niko knew he could never tame him. He'd always be this man of wild contradictions, impossible to predict, dangerous to contain. Lightning in a bottle.

Niko reluctantly pried himself from the prince's grip. "You'll regret all this once the spice wears off." A small, tentative smile played on Niko's lips. For all the rage, Vasili looked at him now with a rampant heat in his gaze, like he wanted to ravage Niko and didn't care they were in public.

Vasili brushed his thumb across his own lips, tasting Niko or spice. He breathed too fast, but delight made the pale, cold prince glow with warmth. "I regret nothing."

Niko laughed despite himself and shook his head. "Come then, to *Walla's Heart*, Your Highness. May Yasir's ship give us sanctuary until we figure out what the fuck to do with you."

CHAPTER 19

By the time Yasir boarded his ship, the spice had worn off, and Vasili was once again aloof and untouchable.

"Ah, the palpable tension between you both," the captain declared. "I have *not* missed that."

Vasili, propped against the wall of the cabin, gave Yasir a dry look.

Niko stood at the edge of the captain's table. The map of Seran lay open. Vasili had seen the black wax's zigzag path and barely lingered to examine it.

"One of you must stay with me at all times," the prince announced.

Yasir immediately looked at Niko, making it clear whose job that was.

"If more bodies are found," Vasili continued, "in the same fashion as you saw at the Yazdan house, and my whereabouts are known, then we'll know I'm not to blame."

"And if no more bodies turn up?"

"They will." Vasili pushed off the wall and approached the table. "The dark flame wants freedom. It will ruin and wreck everything in its path to get it. In the past, that meant destroying everything and everyone close to the Caville it possessed. Since Talos harbored it and killed my elder sister as sacrifice, it appears to be strengthening. It's reaching beyond the Cavilles, seeking to eradicate old families, probably due to their link in the past." He looked down at the map. A few thin lines appeared between his brows. "The Yazdans notoriously fought the Cavilles for superiority over the flame. Although I suspect it was more complicated and my ancestors altered the history to suit themselves."

"The Cavilles stole the flame and its power, and the Yazdans tried to stop them?" Niko floated the theory he'd been considering.

Vasili looked up and nodded. "That seems likely. The Yazdans are well-known for being righteous assholes."

Niko pinched his lips together.

Yasir cleared his throat. "Roksana has sent out messengers to recall the rest of the family. The shah will be given a funeral fit for a king. But all the other guests and the shah's wife vanished. There are many questions and not many answers." Yasir pointedly lifted his gaze to Vasili.

"It will get worse," Vasili said ominously. "With the Yazdans weakened, Seran is vulnerable." He glanced up at Niko, his gaze heavy with foreboding.

"Elves?" Niko voiced what he must surely be thinking.

"They will be observing from afar. If they sense weakness, they'll take advantage of it."

"Where do the elves fit with the dark flame?" Yasir asked.

"Like everyone else, they want the power but will settle for unleashing its chaos. They are creatures born of the era of the dark flame. They survived when the flame was doused and bottled inside the Caville bloodline. Their numbers began small, but they've been growing in strength these last few decades. Loreen hasn't had accurate numbers for months now. Not since Talos brokered peace."

"So there could be hundreds of thousands of them? Oh, well, that's... terrifying." He set his pistol on the table and loosened his jacket. "What do we do now?"

"We?" Vasili asked.

Yasir blinked at him. "If you think I'm going to sea with this threat hanging over Seran, you don't know me at all." He stood straighter.

Vasili ran his hand over the map of Seran, his light fingers tracing the old streets. He looked up, straight into Niko's glare. "What are you thinking, Nikolas?"

"Truthfully?"

"Is there any other way with you?"

"I'm thinking you took advantage of Yasir. You made him believe he had a choice when he was already too caught in your coils to ever be free of you. I think, Your Highness, that Yasir is too good for you and you're lucky to have him as a friend. I think if Amir is here, he'll be at the shah's funeral because he's an attention whore, and if he isn't, and this is all you, then I'll have my blade sharpened and ready to take your head the second you lose control. I think the three of us have a chance at stopping all of this from getting worse if we're careful and clever."

Vasili folded his arms.

"What he said," Yasir whispered, "about the too-good part. I'm not sure—"

"Niko is right." Vasili gestured at the map. "I wanted a sorcerer, someone to control. You are that."

"Put like that," Yasir said, "you really are a manipulative bitch."

The prince's unremorseful smile slithered onto his lips. "When is the shah's funeral?"

"Three days," Yasir grumbled.

"Then we have time to further explore your capabilities."

Niko might have felt sorry for the captain if he hadn't warned him about Vasili weeks ago. Back then, Yasir might have been able to wriggle free, but he'd sealed his fate the second time he went back to Vasili. Now, he was one of them, for better or worse. At least he wasn't working for the elves, and at least Niko hadn't given him his heart.

That lesson had been learned the hard way.

"This is fascinating..." the prince said, relaxing enough to admire the map. "How did you know to do this?"

"Seran's archives. There are books there on sorcery."

The prince's interested piqued. "I'd like to see those books."

"I'm sure you would, Your Highness," Niko interrupted, "but until we know you're not the source of the flame, you're staying right here."

Vasili's attention reverted to the map. He asked Yasir again about the magic involved, apparently impressed the spell had worked on water. The pair would be lost to their *dark flame* discussions soon.

"I'm going to get some air." Niko retreated onto the ship's large deck. The stowed rigging clanged softly in the breeze, combining with the sounds from the dockside bars. He leaned against the side rail and watched the people some distance away. Nobody had any idea about the possible nightmare stalking them.

Seran was loud and colorful and exactly like the middle prince. If Amir were among the crowd, he'd blend right in.

If Amir was here.

Niko wasn't sure he didn't have the mass murderer in the cabin right now.

He also couldn't trust Vasili not to further corrupt Yasir. The prince would absolutely push his new sorcerer to keep trying darker and more dangerous things, which would require more blood, more poison, and nothing about that sat easy with Niko.

Yasir left at dusk, touching his hat and smiling as he passed Niko on the deck. Seran's twinkling waterside streets soon swallowed him up.

Niko was back at the rail, absently watching the docks come alive at night, when he sensed he was no longer alone. "Yasir cares," Niko said.

"Then he has much to lose." Vasili stopped at the rail beside Niko and admired the dockside.

Raucous laughter bubbled up from the crowds. Men and women loitered outside bars, their merriment spilling into the streets. It all felt surreal after last night and the morning's massacre.

"Do you think he's out there?" Niko asked, searching for Amir's royal blue coat and short blond hair. The rat-bastard hadn't been much more than a dangerous nuisance before, but now he was something else entirely.

When Vasili didn't reply, Niko checked to see if he was even listening. He watched the crowds too.

"No... I don't." The prince swallowed softly. "I can't account for the hours lost last night."

"Spice takes memories."

"That is true."

Niko faced the revelry again, grateful it was far enough away that the lights didn't reach the ship's deck. The quiet aboard the ship, softened by the gentle lapping of the sea against the ship's hull, lulled Niko's ragged mind. "We'll surely know soon enough."

"You met Shah Yazdan at the gathering?" Vasili asked, sounding interested.

"He threw me out."

"Understandable."

Niko huffed, then leaned a hip against the rail and faced the prince. The shifting light from the docks illuminated the small smile on his lips. He didn't look over, which was probably a good thing. It certainly made it easier for Niko to admire his face in profile. The kind of proud face you'd expect to see on a coin. But then Vasili bowed his head, and the regal poise vanished behind an almost shy glance. It must have been the light because Vasili wouldn't know modesty if it looked him in the eye. "I sometimes struggle to speak my mind, while you have it down to an art. I was silent for years."

Niko kept the wince from his face. Julian had told him of Vasili's silence while he'd been caged. It must have been a way to keep control of some part of himself while the elves took from him.

"When I returned, my silence kept everyone away. I used that to my advantage, but it also cost me."

"Made you lonely."

The corner of his mouth ticked, giving him away. "Of course, you'd see straight through that."

"I didn't, not at first. I thought you were a vicious, frigid, icy Caville prick. It took me a long time to see anything else under all those layers."

"What do you see now?"

"A vicious, frigid, icy, Caville prick... but someone else too. You hide him well. You guard him because he's the most vulnerable and probably the most honest part of you."

Vasili gripped the rail beneath his hands and pointedly stared at the drunken revelers again.

"It's all right to be vulnerable, Vasili. It makes you human."

He'd fallen still, like he did when threatened, right before lashing out, but it was fear holding him firm, not rage.

Niko ached to touch him, just offer his hand, but touching Vasili usually resulted in a slap to the face, and after seeing the ashes of his family scattered in the breeze, he wasn't sure he could handle another blow. "Where did Yasir go?" he muttered.

"To get supplies."

Vasili placed his hand on the rail next to Niko's. His thumb brushed Niko's finger in a small, fleeting touch. He'd surely startle and pull away, but the touch lingered, becoming deliberate. And suddenly, Vasili's thumb against Niko's finger was all he could feel.

Did Vasili even know what physical comfort was? Had anyone ever truly loved him? His mother perhaps. He'd spoken of her in warmer tones, unlike the rest of his family. "Do you ever think of the boy—?"

"Alek? No."

Yet he'd instantly known who *the boy* was.

Vasili added, "I try not to." He trailed his long fingers over the back of Niko's hand and lightly rested his hand over Niko's. If it had been anyone else, Niko might have taken the touch as the beginnings of some deeper want, but Vasili seemed content to stand beside him and stare at the city. His hand on his felt more real than anything Vasili had given him before, even the heated, fury-fueled kisses.

It felt like an acknowledgment of some kind, but Niko couldn't guess at what. Whatever he guessed, he'd likely be wrong. For now, the touch was no more or less than a touch. And that would have been enough, but then Vasili's fingers trailed suggestively up his sleeve, eliciting a thrill in Niko's blood that went straight to his cock.

When Vasili leaned a hip against the rail, fixing Niko in the middle of all his attention, the heat in Vasili's gaze hinted at where this might go.

Niko tasted his own pulse on his tongue, his heartbeat suddenly thick and loud.

Vasili danced his fingers across Niko's chest, over a shoulder, and up his neck, and it was all Niko could do to hold himself back from grabbing the prince by the hips and thrusting a kiss on him that would probably earn another slap.

He shifted closer, a hand on Niko's chest, adjusting Niko's stance to walk him back against the rail. Niko had no desire to stop this, even as half his sense told him to. The last thing on Etara's earth he needed was to get further involved with Vasili. But he'd never been very good at resisting temptation, and the prince was definitely that, especially when he leaned in and his light fingertips stroked Niko's jaw. Vasili was close enough to kiss now, but the prince held back, lifting his gaze as though assessing or waiting or judging. Niko didn't know which. He tipped Niko's jaw up, his mouth so close that the sizzling promise of a kiss had Niko's cock rapidly hardening.

Niko brought a hand around and captured Vasili's hip, needing leverage to hold him in place.

Vasili tilted his head. "Don't."

Niko removed his hand and braced both against the rail instead, but he added a twist of his top lip as he did, not entirely comfortable relenting.

"Good." As a reward, Vasili bowed his head, brushed his cheek against Niko's and lower. The prince's hot, vicious mouth suckled at Niko's neck. His tongue flicked, so devastatingly light that Niko's groan was out before he could stop it. Rough-and-wild-and-fast Vasili, he could handle that whirlwind. But this slow and gentle, teasing and light Vasili was fucking torture. The wicked gleam in the prince's eye revealed he knew it too.

Vasili shifted his hips, deliberately grinding close. Friction sizzled all the way up Niko's spine.

"Ah," Vasili warned. "Hold the rail, Nikolas."

He hadn't realized he'd grabbed the prince's waist again and quickly returned his grip to the rail. The angle meant Vasili leaned into him, plastering his hard body close. By the three, it was like being handed a feast while starving and not being allowed to sample the bounty.

Vasili's mouth teased Niko's open, subtly convincing Niko's lips to part. He darted his tongue in. Soft and warm and made to unravel the most restrained of men. The teasing kiss left Niko gasping.

Vasili's left hand gently clasped Niko's neck while his

right slipped lower, carving between their pressed bodies to find Niko's cock. His palm brushed roughly through Niko's trousers fabric, finding its goal.

"Fuck," Niko spluttered. His body responded, hips tilting, angling his need deeper into Vasili's hold. Vasili had his cock palmed, and all rational thought abandoned Niko's head. "Let me touch you?" he growled out, only adding the question at the slight tilt in the final word.

"No."

Niko panted through gritted teeth. Need simmered through his veins, lighting him up, building to a painfully bottled ache, and Vasili held the tap closed. Held his cock in his grip and wasn't fucking moving. "You're killing me."

Mischief glittered in the prince's eye. He knew exactly what he was doing, and by the three, it was horrible and wonderful at the same time. Vasili's talented fingers molded around Niko's cock as much as the trousers fabric allowed, and he began to rub. It wasn't enough. Niko needed more.

Vasili plucked on Niko's shirt laces, spilling them open. His wet lips and tongue swirled along Niko's collarbone. Blunt teeth nipped, his fingers squeezed, and Niko gasped at it all, the stimulation coming too fast. And he still couldn't get past the fact Vasili was doing this. Forbidden Vasili. The man he didn't dare touch. He gripped the rail harder, squeezing so damn tight his knuckles ached. Vasili's hand rubbed and squeezed and kneaded, and Niko was about to lose his mind and his load.

Vasili kissed him suddenly. He sucked on Niko's lower lip as he withdrew just as quickly. Niko chased the kiss, even as he pulled away. He needed to taste him, to sink his teeth into Vasili's skin and thread his fingers with Vasili's.

He wanted to slide his fingers into his hair and hold him still as he fucked Vasili's hand—needed to make Vasili moan and cry out and make him *feel*.

"Do I need to restrain you, Nikolas?" he purred.

"Fuck!" Niko slammed his wandering hands back on the rail. Frustration strummed through him. He wasn't sure he could do this the way Vasili clearly wanted.

Vasili's lips brushed Niko's, and again, when Niko leaned in to capture that kiss, Vasili withdrew like the tease he was. "Touch me without my permission again," the prince whispered, "and this ends." His hand squeezed the head of Niko's cock, punctuating the threat with a sharp dart of pleasure that made Niko's back arch and his balls ache. He was going to spill in his undergarments if Vasili didn't ease off. But would that be so bad a thing? This didn't have to mean anything. It changed nothing, and by the three, Niko desperately needed it.

Vasili tugged roughly on Niko's pants ties, jerking Niko's hips in urgency. His quick hand plunged inside, his warm, lithe fingers encircled Niko's flushed erection, his thumb brushed the damp slit, and Vasili's tongue plunged into Niko's mouth. Niko moaned into his mouth. It *was* an attack. He couldn't think to breathe. All he could do was ride the blinding onslaught of pleasure and kiss him back so savagely that Vasili couldn't fail to feel his desperation. And it was desperation. He'd wanted this horrible, vicious prince bent beneath him for so long, since the kiss in the farmhouse field, since he'd woken among damp sheets, with the dreams of fucking Vasili haunting him. He'd even thought of Vasili while he'd fucked Julian.

Gods, it had always been Vasili.

Pleasure snapped, uncoiled, and rolled up Niko's spine,

his seed pulsing free. He arched, moaning out his release against Vasili's hand. The prince sighed in his ear, glided his hand up Niko's hard length, and deliberately brushed the sensitive tip. Sparks of too-sharp after-pleasure bucked through Niko, and it was a fucking miracle he still held the damn rail.

Vasili stepped back, his gaze sultry, leaving Niko breathing hard, cock exposed and leaking the evidence of Vasili's attention.

A glimpse down and Vasili's own hardness upset the line of his fine trousers. But if he didn't tolerate touching, he wouldn't tolerate Niko going down on him either. He was about to offer when Vasili lifted his hand to his own mouth. His pink tongue licked Niko's cream from his fingers, and his scandalous mouth tipped into a crooked smile.

He hadn't expected... *that*. Or the salacious look he was getting now, or the way Vasili knew how much it had killed Niko to hold back, but also how much hearing Vasili snarl orders had absolutely made Niko need to obey them. In those moments, hands gripping the rails, he'd have done almost anything to keep Vasili's hand on his cock and his tongue against his skin.

And that was a damned terrifying thought.

Do I need to restrain you, Nikolas? No. Vasili wasn't ever having that much control over him, like he'd once had Julian begging on his knees.

"This changes nothing," Niko growled out, roughly tucking himself away.

The prince flicked his fingers, took a slim piece of silk from his back pocket, and wiped them clean. "Why would it?"

Gods, the bastard's attitude should have turned him off, but there was something in Niko that delighted in hearing that sniping tone. He wanted to hear it more, wanted to see Vasili snap and rage and lash out, and he wanted to hear him tell Niko to get on his knees—because the outline of his hard cock inside his trousers meant he was alive and that he felt *something*.

Niko shoved from the rail and crossed the deck to Vasili in three strides, stopping so close Vasili's chest brushed his own with every breath. The prince stilled, lifting his chin. He never backed down, but he did glower at Niko. If Niko unlaced Vasili's trousers and dropped to his knees to swallow the prince's cock deep, would he let it happen?

"Someday soon, I'm going to take you in my mouth, *prince,* and I'm going to milk you until you cry my fucking name."

Vasili's stillness thawed. His sly, knowing smile returned. He opened his mouth to speak, but then his gaze skipped over Niko's shoulder and his smile locked in place, turning wooden.

Niko turned to see Yasir approaching along the dock. Damn that man's timing. He turned back, but Vasili was already making his way inside the cabin.

And maybe it was over. Maybe that was all it would ever be between them, a quick hand job and nothing more.

Yasir tossed him a grin, and Niko nodded back, watching the captain head into his cabin too.

Nothing with Vasili was simple. Niko didn't trust him, probably never would. Two cities relied on Vasili to do the right thing, but he didn't do anything by what was right and wrong, he followed his own set of morals, and those did not always align with the rest of the world. It was Niko's responsibility to keep him in line, to keep him true, and to keep him safe. Fucking Vasili would complicate all that because Vasili was already rooted deep inside his head. He'd let Julian inside too, and the damage done was still a gaping wound.

It couldn't happen again.

Even as the thought of Vasili's hand on his cock perked his eager member right back up again.

He sighed hard, ran a hand through his hair, and breathed in to level his body and thoughts. Only when he was sure he was composed and his cock had lost interest, he headed inside the cabin to observe Vasili train the other man he'd manipulated into their lives.

CHAPTER 20

Vasili and Yasir discussed foreign words, their rhythmic order, and what shadows they could summon, while Niko watched from the back of the captain's cabin. Left to his own devices, Vasili would have Yasir performing dangerous rituals within a week. Yasir needed little encouragement, and Vasili knew exactly how to tempt him.

The more Niko listened, the more the sense of wrongness grew.

When Vasili's blade appeared in the prince's hand and he rolled up his sleeve, Niko's stomach turned over. Vasili pressed the tip to his wrist and cut diagonally. Clenching his hand, he held the bleeding wound over a glass.

This was wrong. It felt wrong. It looked wrong. The results were wrong.

"Nothing to say, Nikolas?" Vasili asked without looking up. It was the first time he'd addressed Niko since he'd gotten Niko off on deck hours ago. It was now approaching dawn, but it felt like weeks had passed, or like

Vasili's hand on his cock had never really happened, like Niko had dreamed the whole thing.

Maybe he'd delivered an unprovoked hand job to unbalance Niko, to distract him from how his scarlet blood spilled into the cup. Niko stepped from the gloom. "You don't need to do this." The silvery ladder of old scars running up the prince's forearm shimmered cruel reminders of his past. "You've bled enough."

"I don't have a choice." He didn't snarl, but it wasn't far from his lips.

Niko spread his hands on the captain's desk and leaned in, ensuring Vasili met his stare. "That was true before, but not anymore."

Vasili flicked him a look. "The damage has already been done." More blood dripped into the glass.

The damage had been forever etched into Vasili's skin. His torture was a substantial part of his past. It would be almost impossible to see beyond it. The past was always in the present, if you let it be. Vasili's mind would always go to the worst scenario to protect himself.

"Stop," Niko urged.

"Blood fuels the flame. Yasir must consume it if he's going to grow in proficiency, and there isn't time—"

Niko backhanded the glass off the table. It shattered spectacularly against the floor.

Vasili stabbed his blade into the desktop, left it jutting up, and grasped the cut, clutching it closed. "This must happen."

Niko pointed a finger at Vasili. "No. And don't fight me on this. You will not win."

The prince's glower chilled the room.

"I've listened to you both for hours. You've read a few

books, learned a few chants, and now you're spilling blood in the desperate hope you can turn Yasir into a Julian you can control. It's bullshit. All of it. Nothing good ever comes from the flame. You know this, Vasili. And you know what it will do to him. Maybe you don't give a shit, but I do, and I won't stand by and watch you both fuck yourselves up over the slim chance the dark flame won't turn on you."

"Then leave." And there was his snarl.

"You know I can't."

Vasili reached for his blade.

"Pick it up and we have a problem," Niko warned. His hand hovered.

The bloodletting had to stop. Vasili thought there was no other way because it was all he knew, but there was always another way, a better way. The right way. "We'll stop this without spilling your blood."

"How?" He left the dagger embedded in the desk and turned away, snatching up one of Yasir's silk scarves from a chair to tie around his wrist. "How do I stop Amir, who by now has probably poisoned the entire Caville palace? How do I stop the flame from consuming me and everything around me? Tell me your plan, Nikolas. Tell me how to claim victory for Loreen when all I have is a horse, an overeager merchant captain, and *you?*"

"That's not all you have," Yasir interrupted. "There's Roksana Yazdan."

Vasili laughed. "She's more interested in her ships than fighting a new war."

"You clearly don't know the Yazdans." Yasir laughed, like everyone should get the joke, but his laughter faded beneath Niko's stare. "They'll not let the massacre rest.

She'll be back. And she won't be alone. Nikolas is a Yazdan. Nobody can deny that. Maybe the Yazdans will fight alongside you if you let them?"

Niko wasn't sure of the Yazdans loyalties, and from Vasili's frown, neither was the prince.

"You have my ship," Yasir added. "I know you think I'm here for the magic, and admittedly, it's seductive, but that's not the reason. I've drifted my whole life, lived on the fringes, until the war, until the elves threatened Seran. I'm not a soldier or a royal, but I have connections, and now maybe a little magic too. You don't have just a merchant captain. You have access to all of Seran's information. Amir doesn't know this city like I do. He's made an enemy of the family who rules this city. This isn't Loreen. We don't wilt here—we fight!"

Vasili tied off the silk bandage with his teeth and silently held Yasir's gaze, then slid his attention to Niko. He was afraid. Niko wouldn't have seen it before, hidden beneath all the prince's layers. Hidden in his tightness. Afraid was good. Afraid meant Vasili finally cared.

"You're not alone," Niko said.

The prince turned his face away and ground his teeth. He didn't trust easily. He could only rely on himself, but months ago, he'd told Niko he couldn't do all this alone, and he was right. One prince wasn't going to save the world from the elves or the flame. He needed allies, and he had them. If he'd just let them in. Just as Yasir had tried to tell Niko.

It was time to ask for help.

"The funeral," Niko began, an idea forming. "You should attend as the Caville prince."

"Doesn't that defeat the purpose of my coming to Seran in hiding?"

"Show Amir you're not afraid. Show the Yazdans you respect them. Be Vasili Caville, but be the Vasili Caville you've always wanted to be, not the beaten tool your father made you out to be."

Vasili breathed in so hard his nostrils flared, and Niko was sure another verbal lashing was coming his way. Instead, Vasili asked, "And if Amir attacks?"

"He'll do that whether you're there or not. But if you are there, if you have visible allies, it will unsettle him. He won't expect it, and when caught off guard, Amir fucks up. Once he's on the back foot, we disable him and figure out what to do with him once he's restrained. He can't be that hard to bring down. He's still Amir."

Vasili glanced at Yasir.

The captain spread both hands. "It's either brilliant or stupid."

"A truly fitting description of Nikolas Yazdan," Vasili acknowledged, almost smiling.

"I suppose we won't know which it is until after the funeral," Niko added, "if we're all still breathing." He grinned and grabbed the blade, freeing it from the desk. He showed it to Vasili. "I'm keeping this until you can both be trusted."

"I'll find another," Vasili said.

Of course he would. He probably had multiples knives shoved up his ass. Niko pursed his lips, keeping the numerous insults locked behind them. "We all need sleep. It's been a long day and night. No more sorcery."

Yasir nodded obediently while Vasili glowered at having his blade taken away. Niko tucked it into his belt.

Vasili might hate him, but having the prince not open a vein felt like a breakthrough. Now, all he had to do was ensure Vasili wasn't the source of the flame to begin with.

"We'll sleep here," Yasir said. "I have a cot. I'll sling up some of the crew's hammocks. Agreed?"

"Agreed," Niko confirmed before Vasili could slither away. "You're staying right here," he ordered the prince and smirked as Vasili's tight lips twitched to argue.

Yes, this felt like progress. Vasili was finally listening. It felt good and right. And finally, it felt like they might have a chance against forces far bigger than any of them.

A DAY LATER, Yasir produced clothes fit for the Loreen Prince. He'd also purchased clothes for Niko in the Seranian higher-class style. Niko eyed the trim pants and lace-embroidered shirt with curiosity. The trousers and shirt were a contrasting mix of glossy silk and matte linen. The dark purple and black enhanced Niko's southern attributes.

"Funerals are always at night," Yasir said. "I'd try to prepare you, but... it's best you just experience it."

"Can I take my swords?" Niko asked.

Yasir grinned. "It would be unusual not to."

The day passed without event. Vasili observed the docks from the ship, lost to his thoughts, and Niko observed him, waiting for the dark flame to assert itself.

When the night of the funeral came, the prince was dressed in white with golden trim. Delicate gold thread glistened artfully at the seams. It should have been hideous, but wrapped around Vasili's figure, the ensemble enhanced his natural elegance and air of superiority. On deck, he tugged at the loose cuffs and buttoned up the high collar. His remaining rings caught Seran's multicolored lights.

Niko remembered the Caville ring he'd taken and promptly removed it from his finger, handing it over.

Vasili looked at the ring as though considering not taking it. "I threw it away. I suppose it's only right that a Yazdan brings it back to me." He slid the ring on and lifted his gaze. For a fleeting moment, the man inside the prince looked out from behind his cool blue eye, and it seemed as though he wanted to speak, to say whatever was on his mind. Instead, a sizzling arrow shot into the sky over Seran and exploded with a thunderous clap.

"Ah! The festivities begin!" Yasir announced, emerging from his cabin and rubbing his hands together in glee. He also wore dark colors and finished off the outfit with a pink feather in his hat. "Food, drink, laughter, dance, and love! Death is no somber event in Seran." He jogged down the ship's gangplank toward the waiting carriage. "Come along!"

Niko gestured for the prince to go first and followed behind like Vasili's deadly shadow. Perhaps that was fitting. If anyone tried to hurt Vasili at the funeral, they'd have to get through him first. Unless Vasili was the one needing to be put down. His blades had been sharpened in preparation.

Another flaming arrow launched into the sky over the city and exploded into a wash of red sparks.

Niko winced at the boom and watched the red light burn through the night sky. Hopefully, it wasn't an omen. After settling in the carriage beside Vasili, he glanced at the prince staring out of the small window. He'd never looked more regal or more like he loathed every second of being inside his own skin. To anyone unfamiliar with Vasili's ice, it all appeared to be directed at those around him, but in truth, the walls he erected were to keep the real man safe inside.

It had taken too long for Niko to realize that. To realize a lot of things.

I would have lost you.

He hadn't forgotten Vasili's words at the coffeehouse, although they'd been fueled by spice. After all this time, all the hurt, had Vasili learned to care? And did he truly care about losing Nikolas, or was it all some elaborate game? Experience told him the latter, but he was still trying to understand the complicated man that was Vasili Caville, and he had a long way to go yet.

"Ready, Your Highness?" Niko asked.

Vasili breathed in and held that breath until his thin, infamously shallow smile crawled out of its hiding place. "Are you?"

CHAPTER 21

Yazdan flags—a black flame on golden silk—fluttered in the cool night breeze. Torches thrust into the ground led the way through extensive tropical gardens, but they seemed more ceremonial when paired with Seran's colored lights. Fireworks occasionally boomed above, raining color. Color was everywhere, in the streamers hanging from thick-leaved trees, in the guests' attire, in the feasts of fruit and wines.

Yasir led Niko and Vasili into the gardens, found wine for them both, and left to look for Roksana.

The occasional weapon caught Niko's eye, pistols and shortswords worn by both men and women. They could be guards placed among the crowds, but they weren't alert in the same way guards should be. Seranian custom appeared to dictate that funerals were loud and colorful, and guests were armed.

"Death appears to be celebrated here," Vasili noted, raising the wine glass to his lips.

He'd been quiet since the carriage ride. That razor-sharp mind of his was probably thinking up all the ways he could manipulate the next Yazdan he met.

"Hm," Niko mused, eyeing another lordly character walking by with a dagger at his hip. If the crowd turned hostile, fleeing would be the only option.

A few figures parted down a wide pathway to reveal Yasir in a heated exchange with another man. He had a parted mop of chestnut hair and typically luscious, dark Seranian looks. Yasir reached for the fellow's elbow but was quickly shaken off.

"A lover," Vasili said.

Niko looked again at the exchange. There was some passion in it, more than was worth a business disagreement. "I suspect he has many."

"But not I, if that's what you're alluding to."

"I wasn't." He hadn't been, but considering Vasili's tone, he wondered if he should have.

"You've accused me of it in the past, nonetheless."

Niko stared at the exchange, keeping Vasili in his peripheral vision. The prince watched Yasir too, his expression locked in nonchalance. Yasir was close to Vasili in a way that was different to what Niko had with him. It wouldn't have surprised him if they'd been *closer*. Yasir flirted and Vasili was... Well, he had ways of making men beg. "You were close enough to share blood, so why not a bed?"

"Like Julian?"

This was rapidly veering into territory Niko would prefer to forget.

"I didn't bed Julian," Vasili added. "And I did not feed his desire for Caville blood."

Niko glanced about them to make sure nobody was

within earshot. "No, you just fucked with his head and whipped him instead."

Vasili faced Niko, demanding Niko return the stare.

"He was the enemy," Vasili said. "Through pleasure, I was able to control him—" Vasili's silvery brows pinched and his pert lips thinned into a grim line. "I don't owe you an explanation. It was before you and I met—"

"There is no *you and I*." Niko's heart thudded in his throat. He stared at Yasir and his companion again. Their argument was faring no better. Clearly, Yasir's companion was angry about something, and Yasir was trying to fix whatever had gone wrong.

Vasili loomed, as he did so well, and Niko desperately wanted to take those six words back. He wanted them to be the truth but wasn't sure if he'd just lied to them both because there definitely was a "you and I," but the details of that relationship were too complicated to think on.

"Because you're too *good* for me?" Vasili slid his glare back to Yasir.

"No." Niko snorted. Was that what Vasili truly believed? "I've never been good."

"Because the poison in my veins might contaminate the infamous Yazdan honor?"

"Vasili..." Niko faced him, inching closer, but not too close. There were too many eyes observing them for anything more personal. "I didn't even know the Yazdans existed—"

"Because I cannot tolerate touch?" The prince blinked. His tone was icy, but Niko heard its cracks. He lifted his chin. "Yasir returns."

"I'm sorry..." Yasir blustered. "I got... a friend... waylaid."

Niko cleared his throat. He'd have to talk with Vasili alone later. "We saw."

"Ah, yes." Yasir pulled on his sleeves, straightening the silk. "I've found Roksana. She's asked you both to join her with the Yazdans for formal introductions."

"Of course," Vasili said. He blinked at Niko. "Let us officially meet your esteemed relatives."

Vasili left his wine behind on a wall, and Yasir led the way through the extensive grounds toward a columned portico carved into rockface that must serve as the family crypt. The closely crowded people outside all shared the same familial traits, with Roksana among them.

She broke from her companions and muttered, "Let's get the formality over with, shall we, so we can move on to more pressing matters." She turned on her heel and announced in her timbre voice, "*Vasili Caville of the Royal House Caville.*" The crowd's chatter quickly fell away to near-silence.

Vasili dipped his chin. "My heartfelt condolences. The death of your father and beloved shah is a terrible blow to all."

He went on to flatter the city and its people in that smooth, charming way that he did, but Niko was barely listening. The people gathered at the portico ranged from mid-thirties to late fifties in years. At least two generations. Amala was here, an oxeye daisy in her hair.

A shimmer of light slid along a blade, catching Niko's eye.

A man who had been standing to the right of the group sprang forward. Niko freed his shortsword and parried the man's dagger off its trajectory toward Vasili.

Shouts went up. The man locked gazes with Niko and

took a barefisted swing that would have knocked Niko out cold if he hadn't signaled the swing in the heave of his shoulder first. Niko ducked and refrained from plowing headfirst into the fight, rooting himself between Vasili and the threat.

Someone wisely grabbed the Yazdan fool and dragged him backward.

"It was him," the man yelled and tore himself free of the hands holding him. "That Caville coward killed the shah!"

"Alissand," Roksana snapped. Although younger than him, her voice held more authority. "Stop it, brother."

Niko freed his second blade in warning.

"And you!" Alissand pointed a rough-skinned finger at Niko. "Protecting a Caville. Who is this man?" he asked Roksana, disgusted at the idea that someone might defend a Caville.

"Nikolas Yazdan, *Leila's* son," she announced.

Another hush fell over the Yazdans, but this time Niko sensed more nervous trepidation in their glances than curiosity.

This was not how he'd planned to officially out himself and Vasili.

Vasili's touch on his arm gently guided Niko aside. "We came here amicably, and this is how you greet us?" Vasili's voice had gained its dangerous Caville edge.

"*Amicably*?" Alissand spat. "It is no coincidence you're here and our father is killed."

Niko lowered his blades. "We didn't come for blood. We came for peace." He glanced at Vasili, and the prince's stance softened again, as much as it ever could.

Vasili nodded. "My advisor, Nikolas, is right. I have no

wish to disrupt your mourning. We have much to discuss, but this is not the place nor time. We came out of respect. An alliance can be—"

"Yazdans allying with Cavilles?! I see the insanity has filtered through Talos's balls to his pathetic offspring." Alissand laughed and then gestured with flair. "Escort them off the grounds."

"Excuse me a moment." Roksana grabbed the man's arm and hastily pulled him away from the scene. They continued to bicker, but the chatter and the breeze drowned them out, and as no guards came to march Vasili away, it seemed Alissand was more bluster than bite.

"I see now where you get your bullishness from," Vasili muttered so only Niko could hear.

Amala stepped forward, took the flower from her hair, and handed it to Vasili.

"Welcome to Seran, Prince Caville."

The look of alarm on Vasili's face quickly vanished, replaced by warmth as he took the daisy. One of his rare, soft smiles made it to his lips. "Thank you."

Amala gave Niko a raised eyebrow and a look that told him she didn't appreciate being lied to but she'd let it go. "Leila was your mother?"

"She was."

"She was my great aunt, I think. I'd have liked to meet her." She handed Niko a daisy too.

"I'm sure she'd have liked that."

Amala drifted off, leaving Niko staring after her until he realized the crowd had swelled as other guests tried to see the prince.

Vasili politely dismissed himself and drew up alongside

Niko. "Well, that could have gone worse." He twirled the daisy between his fingers.

"We're alive—it's a win."

"The evening isn't over yet."

Word was spreading that a prince was among the crowd, escorted by a new Yazdan. Niko heard his and Vasili's names whispered on the lips of those around them. "We're being watched."

"Princes generally are."

He sounded thoughtful. Niko glanced over. He'd tucked the daisy behind his ear, and behind his sly hint of a smile, the hidden prince looked back at him. The daisy complimented all his white and gold. The sudden desire to pull him behind a palm tree and taste his lips again, to feel him pressed close, had Niko tripping over his own feet.

He hastily stared ahead and willed his eager cock to promptly forget the fuckable prince beside him before it got him in more trouble.

"No sign of my brother."

"No." If Amir were here, he'd be the center of attention. But if he wasn't, then what did that mean? Had the dark flame used Vasili to murder the shah and others? If so, then surely being among them again would spur the flame into action once more. Niko looked more closely as Vasili meandered ahead, through the crowd parting for him, their gazes pinned to the prince.

A sudden urge to bundle Vasili up and whisk him away almost had Niko crowding close again. They could return to Yasir's ship, maybe sail somewhere far away. On board, he'd have time to try and understand what these feelings for Vasili meant, if they meant anything at all. Or maybe he'd just get him back to the ship to hear him sigh in

Niko's ear again, to feel his soft mouth yield, his fingers dance down Nikolas's cock.

Roksana's approach interrupted his unruly thoughts. "Ah, apologies Niko," Roksana beamed, falling into step. "There's one bullheaded male in every family. In fact, I'm sure we have more than one." She glanced at Vasili and watched him take an offered wine glass from a passing server. The flower in his hair softened his Caville iciness, and even Roksana couldn't fail to notice how at ease he appeared.

"He likes Seran," Roksana said.

"Do you think so?"

"I've known him since he was a boy. He rarely left the palace. He wrote me occasionally."

"He did?" That seemed unlike Vasili. Whatever would he put in a letter? Demands and denials?

Roksana's grin hinted at some internal joke. "You don't know him very well, do you?"

Niko bristled a little. He thought he was beginning to know Vasili, but every time he got a grasp on the man, he slipped through his fingers. Like now. Writing letters to Yazdans?

"He's always been keen to unite our two ancient families. He saw what the flame was doing to Talos and knew the Cavilles needed allies. Of course, this was before the war, before his... absence."

The way her tone dropped suggested she knew a great deal about Vasili and his eight-year absence.

"Our families were allies, long ago. The Yazdans ruled the south and the Cavilles the north, and the land prospered." She must have seen the disbelief on Niko's face and chuckled. "It's hard to believe, especially after one of your uncles just tried to stab the prince. I've tried smoothing the way over the years, but I'm at sea more than on land, and family politics is not where I'm most comfortable. Put a blade in my hand and point me at a ship to plunder, and I'm invested, but during these events, among family, I don't have the smooth-talking skills that Vasili clearly does."

The prince had been drawn into a conversation with two guests. How exactly, Niko had missed, but he seemed quick to smile. The smiles weren't all fake either. With the flower in his hair, the flutter of his hand, and the way the colored lights warmed his face, he could almost be a very different person to the one who had ordered Niko whipped. But that was half the problem with Vasili. He changed his behavior to suit the moment. Would Niko ever discover who he really was inside? He'd surely have to get him away from the flame, from the palace, from everything he knew for that to happen. And such a thing was unlikely.

Roksana snatched up some wine and handed a glass to Niko. "He likes you."

"You're not the first to tell me that, and I still don't believe it."

"He wrote me last year, told me about the Yazdan living in Loreen. Told me how you were Leila's son. He said you're a foolish brute, too honest for court and too righteous for Loreen."

Niko laughed over the shock of hearing Vasili had mentioned him.

Vasili glanced over his shoulder. His smile stayed. Even grew a little, and it was like being back at the waterfall again, with the prince knowing exactly how he looked and exactly how Nikolas would drop to his knees to hear him whisper orders in his ear.

"There's a great deal he doesn't say with words. You just have to look closely for it."

"Hm."

"You like him?" she asked.

"No." He slowly shook his head. "*Like* isn't... that's not it."

Roksana chuckled. "Yazdans are brilliant defenders. We'll stand up for what's right until our dying breaths, but we're absolutely shit at anything personal." She thumped him on the shoulder hard enough to make it ache. "Welcome to the family, nephew."

Niko's sense of warmth and belonging grew. He brushed the ring on his finger and lifted it for Roksana to see. "The shah gave me this. I'm not certain I deserve it..." Her smile had wilted some, and he trailed off, fearing he'd have to return it.

"Don't let Alissand see you with that."

"Why?"

She winced. "Just... keep it hidden."

"If I shouldn't have it, take it back." He began to pull the ring free.

"No, keep it on. He gave it to you. It's yours now. And keep Vasili close. Can you do that? I think we'll all be working together soon. Caville and Yazdan, like it should be. We just need to get a few of the family on board—"

A firework exploded over their heads. Sparks rained over the crowd, eliciting a chorus of *oohs* and *aahs*. Red light spilled over the gardens.

The sound of glass shattering pulled Niko from the light show, and as he turned his head to check on Vasili, a man dressed in dark blue approached up the path, his lopsided grin broad across his lips, his stride absolute, and his eyes all-black.

Vasili's wine glass lay broken on the path in front of him, and the prince stared at his brother.

Niko tossed his own glass, drew his blades, and launched forward, but Vasili was several strides ahead, and Amir was gaining.

"Who—" Roksana began. Niko didn't hear the rest.

Another firework whistled overhead and exploded like a clap of thunder. Blue light rained. Blue for Cavilles.

Blue light hollowed Amir's cheeks. He raised a pistol and pinned his aim on Vasili.

Niko wasn't going to make it. The pistol would fire its lethal shot and Vasili would fall.

Amir pulled the arming hook on the pistol back. He closed one eye, tilted his head.

A shot barked. Niko flinched, expecting Vasili to fall, and by the gods, he'd gut Amir where he stood. But Amir spat a cry, dropped his pistol, and clutched his hand to his side. His glare scythed left, to where Yasir stood, smoke spiraling from his drawn pistol.

Vasili raised his hand, but not to Amir. "Nikolas, *stop*."

Niko slowed, the order sinking into old soldiering muscles, making him hesitate.

The prince approached his brother. His pale hand tenderly pressed to Amir's snarling face, drawing him up from his hunched position. He whispered something lost in the noise. The young king's all-black eyes widened. His face fell, and Amir grabbed for his brother's arm in desperation, as though Vasili were his only safe place.

Vasili withdrew a dagger from its hidden sheath at the

small of his back. A dagger Amir, standing in front of him, couldn't see.

If Vasili killed Amir here, what happened to the flame? Did it escape, or did it all funnel into Vasili? Niko recalled something about the Cavilles needing to be close to the palace to keep control, but all the information he had came from Vasili. What if the flame was too much? What if it tore through Vasili and devoured him mere feet from Niko?

Was this the moment he'd choose whether to save Vasili or kill him?

Amir tore free of Vasili and staggered backward, seeing the dagger in his brother's hand. "You'd have killed me?" he asked, and he sounded small, like they were boys again.

"Amir," Vasili reached out. "It must be controlled."

Amir's head tilted awkwardly. His lips parted in a macabre smile, and then the laughter began, deep and rolling. The sound boiled out of Amir, just like it had his father.

Niko was done waiting. He spun the blades in both hands, reversing his grip, and plowed in. Vasili barked another order, but this time he let it roll off. The dark flame glared out from inside the king, using his eyes to see, his body to move. Amir lifted his bloodied hand. Dark flame sparked alive in his palm, quickly consuming his hand. It danced up his arm. Amir flicked his wrist, and the flame lashed, cutting through the air toward Niko.

But the move was obvious, as obvious as the man wielding it, and Niko ducked, stepped aside, and bolted off his back boot. He slammed into Amir's gut, tackling him clean off his feet. He'd never been heavy, but he was fast.

Niko just needed to pin him down. The king slammed into the ground with Niko sprawled over him.

He still laughed, and madness flashed in his black eyes.

A horrible, hungry cold crawled over Niko, its touch spilling from Amir's body.

"Look out!" Roksana yelled.

The shimmer of fireworks on a blade to Niko's right. He ducked, but a stinging heat still zipped across his shoulder. Roksana's right hook smacked across the attacker's jaw, rocking him on his feet. A stranger, just someone from the crowd. But his eyes... "He's possessed!" Niko yelled. And he wasn't alone.

Others broke from the crowd, their eyes empty and soulless. Six, eight... more... everywhere.

Amir's laughter suddenly ended, cut off like a candle snuffed out. *"You cannot fight me."* The voice was warped and twisted, sounding like it had been wretched up from the king's soul.

"Niko! *Vasili?*" Roksana yelled. *"Where's Vasili?!"* She kicked another possessed guest aside but more swept in. Not all in the crowd were turned. Some had freed their weapons and joined the fight.

Niko swung around at Roksana's warning. Vasili wasn't where he'd left him. He searched for white and gold among the heaving bodies and clashing swords.

"Poor dog, lost his master?"

That voice he knew.

Niko snarled and slammed a fist into Amir's cheek. Bone crumpled, but the king grinned through blood bubbling between his lips. He spat in Niko's face, and cool blood splattered across his cheek. Its coppery taint sizzled on Niko's lips. *Caville blood. Poison.*

Niko scrabbled backward and wiped the blood and spittle from his lips.

"Do you believe you know my brother, dog?" Amir climbed to his feet, chuckling. His eyes were clear again; he was back in control. "Do you believe he doesn't want this power? He's a Caville. Power is in our veins." He lifted his arms, and his sleeves slipped down, revealing ladder-like scars where he'd bled himself to feed his army. "He's always desired it. He's not the man you believe him to be." Amir's gaze locked with Niko's. "You already know this... you know inside, *Nikolas Yazdan*. Vasili is the worst Caville of all."

No, it was lies. Vasili was bad, yes, but not like Amir, not like Talos. He was different. From the prince pretending to be a farm boy to the man who'd saved Niko from the elves. Vasili Caville wasn't like the others. He couldn't be, because for all his faults, Niko cared for him.

The sounds of metal clashing and people crying out filled the night. Sounds of war that stalked Niko in his dreams. So like the front line, where the ground had turned to bloody mud and bodies piled up. He looked down now, expecting the paths to run red. This wasn't the front, but he tasted blood and heard the cries. Sweat broke out across his skin. His heart raced too fast.

"He's always known who you are." Amir cocked his head. "He's used you from the day you met, and so masterful is his lie, he even told you the truth, and still you protect him."

His approach stumbled Niko backward.

The possessed were all around, emerging from shadows and cutting down innocent people. Heat flushed through Niko, making his head throb. He had to stop Amir, to disable him, but Vasili was missing, and what if... what if Amir was right? "You're the damned liar, Amir!"

For all the darkness in his eyes, when he spoke, he still sounded like the prick who'd taunted Niko in the palace bedchamber—the wretched middle prince who had tried to fuck Niko and failed. "I was the one who told you about your whore mother, about your bastard blood. Me! Vasili has revealed *nothing* to you. I've only ever told you the truth." Amir laughed softly and stopped with just a few strides between them. "He has you on the end of his leash, Nikolas Yazdan, and you're too dumb to see it."

Niko's grip tightened on the sword handle. He had to raise his blade and cut the king down, but... "Did you kill the Yazdans in their home? Was it you, Amir?"

Amir's lips twitched. "Who hated the Caville palace enough to burn it to ash? Who used you and Julian and everyone he's ever met for his own nefarious means? Whose blade killed Talos? Vasili has made a fool of you, like he makes fools of us all. I'm here to *stop* him."

By the three, Niko couldn't listen, but he couldn't bring himself to cut Amir down either. Everything he'd been told about the burning palace, the possessed guards, it had all come from Vasili. Vasili was more than capable of lying to twist the facts. Every breath was a game to the prince. He did nothing without a motive. He lived to stop the elves, whatever the cost, and if that meant possessing all the flame, there was no doubt in Niko's mind: he'd do it.

Gods, he didn't know what was true anymore.

Too many possessed carved through the crowd. Too many to fight. And Vasili was missing, after telling Niko he should not leave his side.

Amir laughed. "Run, dog. Run back to your master."

Niko turned and plunged through the scrabbling battles.

"He'll kill you!" Amir called. "He'll kill us all!"

Where was Vasili?

A flash of white and gold, that was all Niko needed to find. He had to be here. Niko had only turned his back for a few moments. If he could find him and see he wasn't the cause of all this, it would be enough. But he had to know. For sure.

A slash of a dagger swung in. Niko parried it aside and kicked the possessed man back into the fray.

What if this was all smoke and mirrors? What if Vasili had deliberately drawn Amir here? He needed the rest of the flame, and for that, he had to kill Amir on Caville ground. He'd take him home, to Loreen.

Vasili would need a carriage.

Another possessed launched herself at Niko, screaming like a banshee, blade raised. Niko thrust his sword in, cutting her down, leaving her rocking on her knees. So many... Vasili couldn't have orchestrated their attack? He'd been with Niko and Yasir on the ship.

Rage and confusion whirled, fueling every step.

Who to believe? Who to trust?

There was too much at stake to be wrong.

More possessed lunged in, and Niko dispatched them all, barely losing his stride.

A flash of white ahead. Someone moving fast. The fleeing crowd flowed around Vasili while he battled a possessed. Two already lay on the ground at Vasili's feet. The prince slashed the third's throat and flung his dagger to impale a fourth Niko hadn't even seen bearing down on him. A fifth barreled in. Vasili tackled him against a low wall, and they both tumbled over into the grass.

Vasili fell onto his back *and froze*.

Niko's heart leaped into his throat.

The possessed guest knelt over Vasili, his grin oddly detached from his expression, just like the guards who had attacked Niko in his cottage. The guest raised his shortsword.

Vasili flicked his hand, and a lash of dark struck the possessed in the chest, arching him backward, mouth gaping. The dark flame coiled around him, covered him, *devoured him*, until there was nothing left but ash blown by the wind.

Was that how the Yazdans had all died?

Niko dashed forward, but Vasili's all-black gaze pinned him still.

The prince bared his teeth in a snarl and slowly, he began to rise.

"Vasili, damn you!" Niko tightened his grip on his blades. "Did you play me this whole time?"

The prince's mouth tilted. He raised his dagger. "Are you going to kill me, Nikolas?"

By the three, no. It couldn't be true. He knew Vasili was a fucking snake, but not like this. He couldn't believe it, he wouldn't. What he saw now, that wasn't Vasili—it was the flame. "Fight it."

Vasili climbed over the low wall and stalked forward. "You vowed you'd stop me."

People fled and fought and cried and screamed, but there was only room in Niko's thoughts for bringing Vasili back from the dark. Or he would have to kill him.

A manic grin tore across the prince's lips. "You're here

for this, so kill me." Vasili lowered his left arm and pressed the tip of his blade to his skin, spilling his blood. "Or is it this you want? A Yazdan sorcerer, just like your hungry ancestors. Always taking. Never enough."

No, this was the flame. For all his wickedness, his lies, and his entrapment, Vasili couldn't lie about the kind of man he was, hidden deep inside, and Niko knew that man existed. He'd seen him in the small moments, the quiet moments, the soft kiss, his gentle touch, and his rare laugh.

"I make a better assassin." He thrust his shortsword low, forcing Vasili to parry, and when he did, Niko thrust in with the heavier blade. Vasili danced back. The swing missed, but now Niko was close, and as Vasili brought the dagger back in, aiming for Niko's middle, Niko dropped his sword, caught the prince's wrist, and twisted. The old break fractured anew. Vasili cried out, and Niko yanked him in close, trapping him in his arms. His next words brushed the prince's cool cheek. "I will be the death of you, but not today, my prince."

He didn't fight. He'd known he wouldn't. A few stuttering breaths and the tension melted from Vasili's body. He sighed, like he had when they'd been this close before. Surrendering, but only to Niko.

"Vasili! Niko!" A carriage clattered through the grounds, Yasir atop the driver's seat. He reined the twin horses to a halt. "Get in!"

Niko grabbed Vasili's chin and forced him to look up. His blue eye blazed with all the fury and indignation he'd come to expect from the prince. "There you are."

"Unhand me," Vasili seethed, but the threat had vanished, leaving his demand weak.

Niko pulled Vasili along and shoved him toward the carriage. "Get in."

Vasili's scathing glare said the prince was back in control, but for how long? Cradling his right wrist, he used his left to haul himself into the carriage. Niko clambered in behind, wedged himself in a seat, and clutched the sword across his lap.

"Hold on!" Yasir yelled. "Yar!"

The carriage bounced and skipped. Vasili clutched at a handle, his glare pinned to Niko.

"Why didn't you stop Amir?" Vasili demanded, shouting over the carriage's clattering.

"Why did you run?" Niko glared right back.

The prince's cheek fluttered. The carriage jerked, rattling them both. Vasili narrowed his eye, and Niko had seen that look right before the prince had killed a doulos.

Niko didn't see a dagger, but Vasili would have one. If he lunged, he'd be fast, and in the small carriage, Niko's sword would be unwieldy.

"Are you going to use your sword on me, *Niko?*"

"Do I need to?"

"Niko!" Yasir's cry rang out. Something huge and heavy slammed into the carriage, knocking Niko from side to side. Horses squealed, but the carriage kept on bouncing forward, its wheels screaming against stone.

Niko grabbed at the door and opened the cracked window. Seran streets blurred by. The carriage was surely racing too fast through them.

A shadow beast just like the one in the jungle galloped alongside, trailing inky smoke, and behind it, a second gained.

"Shit." If the carriage stopped, the beasts would tear inside and...

Vasili continued to glare at Nikolas, his jaw locked and eye fierce.

"Did *you* summon these?"

Had he summoned the one in the desert? Was *he* feeding it? Were they Vasili's wretched experiments gone wrong?

"Gods-damn you, Vasili, tell me the truth!"

CHAPTER 22

Another impact sent the carriage skidding across the road and knocked Niko back into his seat. Jarred from his grip, his sword clattered to the floor. Yasir's yell and the crack of a whip pulled the carriage from a dangerous swerve, but they were still racing along. Either the beasts would get them, or a sudden stop would.

Niko lunged for the sword.

Vasili kicked it from his grasp and slammed his left hand up, under Niko's chin, driving him backward against the seat. Vasili was on him suddenly, a knee in his gut, a hand at his throat. Niko jerked his elbow up, impacting hard with Vasili's chin, knocking the prince's head back. He grunted, and Niko shoved, slamming him back into his seat. But the small, bouncing carriage kept jerking and jumping around them, and when Niko made a grab for Vasili, the carriage tilted, Niko's reach sailed wide, and Vasili's kick landed hard in Niko's middle, instantly wrenching the breath from his lungs.

"Niko! Get up here!"

Niko heard Yasir at the same time as Vasili's fingers wrapped around his throat and squeezed. Niko kicked out, but his knee struck the side of the carriage, and Vasili was crouched over him, pinning him down.

His chest burned, lungs screaming for air.

He plucked at Vasili's fingers, trying to lever them off.

Dark spots swam in his vision. He kicked uselessly again.

"Amir turned you, didn't he? Turned you like he turned all the others!"

Niko shook his head, as much as Vasili's vise-like grip allowed. He shoved at Vasili, but the prince twisted, and Niko's fumbling efforts to push him back slid off.

A beast slammed into the door, the carriage bounced sideways, and Vasili fell, hitting the opposite door. The door swung open onto a blurred street, almost dumping Vasili outside. The prince snagged a handle and caught himself. Niko snatched his blade off the floor. Vasili saw, disgust pulled on his mouth, and then he clutched the outside of the carriage and vanished from sight.

The beast saw Niko through the swinging door, still inside the carriage, and locked on.

"Shit!"

The creature was easily the size of Niko, and if it got inside, there'd be no escaping it.

"*Yar*!" Vasili shouted from above, now in the driver's seat. The whip cracked, and the carriage lurched, the horses finding more speed from somewhere.

Maybe Vasili had tossed Yasir from the carriage?

Niko wasn't sure about anything anymore.

The beast galloped up to the swinging door. Its red

eyes fixed on Niko. It would get inside, and then what? Death, surely. What else could it want?

Niko rocked on his feet, sheathed his blade, and kicked open the opposite door. Seran's rows of tall, redstone houses spooled by. If he fell, the carriage wheels would kill him as surely as any beast.

He reached around the open doorway and grabbed a hold of a piece of protruding trim. A beast galloped closer, teeth bared, eyes ablaze with cold, inhuman intelligence. It would kill him. Probably kill them all.

Niko clutched the exterior trim and climbed onto the roof. The wind rushed by, flicking dust into his eyes. He laid flat, fingers digging in, and caught his breath from Vasili's kicks.

Vasili's white hair flailed wildly. Yasir *was* beside him, but when the captain glanced back, the flame lived in his eyes.

Then the beasts were his? They were together. Caville and sorcerer, just as Vasili had planned. Did that mean the beasts were for Niko?

After everything he'd done for Vasili, this was how the prince repaid him?

Niko was done being his dog.

The carriage skipped and danced, the streets rushed by, people fled from its path, and ahead, the many masts from docked ships thrust upward like beacons.

Niko crawled forward, one solid handgrip at a time.

The carriage swooped down a steep, narrow street, scattering traders in its path. The beasts were out of sight behind, but they'd be close. The sound of the horses' hooves hammered on stone. The carriage rattled and groaned, jarring Niko with every jolt and bump.

The old road tilted downward. The carriage picked up speed. Niko lifted his head to see between Vasili and Yasir, where the road plunged, ending in a sharp left turn *around* the dock. The carriage wasn't going to make that turn.

"Yar!" Vasili cracked the whip using his unbroken left hand while Yasir mastered the reins.

They weren't slowing.

They were speeding up.

Vasili glanced behind him, hair lashing, his blue eye glittering with the knowledge of what was about to happen.

"Don't!" Niko cried.

Vasili's lips ticked. He faced forward, and the whip cracked again.

This was insane.

Niko scanned the rushing street for a place to jump. The shadow beasts lunged and snapped, desperate for their prize.

The horses screamed.

No time.

Niko stared ahead. The road veered to the left suddenly, and for a few precious seconds, the carriage plowed on. The horses screamed again and pitched over the dock edge. And then the world was falling. Vasili dove to the side. Yasir jumped. But Niko clung on. Brackish waters rushed up. The horses hit first in an explosion of water. Niko jumped. Water slammed into his shoulder first, making it pop and blasting a wave of heat down his side. He thrashed, gasped air, then saw the carriage roll midair and plunge toward him.

A gasp and he dove down. A hard and sharp *something* stabbed into his side. Water spilled into his mouth and down his throat. He choked around it, desperate for air. His heart was a drum, beating down every dying second.

Smoky light rippled above. He kicked toward it. His heart thumped so hard it threatened to hammer its way out of his chest. Just a few more kicks. He reached out a hand, grabbing at a length of thick metal chain, and hauled himself to the surface.

Small waves tried to dash him against the enormous black wall. He breathed. In. Out. In. Out. He lived. Agony helped remind him he was alive by washing up his arm and trying to empty his guts into the harbor.

Debris from the shattered carriage drifted in the water. The horses were gone, pulled down by their tack. But so were the shadow beasts.

The dark harbor waters bobbed.

"Haul the anchor!"

The chain he clung to clunked and began to rise. Niko kicked off from the ship's hull and swam to the harbor wall, dragging his damned burning arm with him. He'd dislocated the shoulder. Bastard thing hurt like one of Vasili's kicks to the gut.

Walla's Heart.

Niko scanned the dock for her distinctive blue hull and spotted her still safely moored. Between him and the ship, the dock waters churned. Still no sign of Vasili and Yasir.

Vasili wouldn't be dead. It took more than a plunge off a dockside to kill the prince, but Yasir was a concern.

He hauled his battered body from the water, took a few moments to catch his breath, and limped toward *Walla's Heart*. If anyone saw him, he really didn't give a shit.

Lamplight shimmered inside the captain's cabin. "Vasili, you fucking eel, face me!"

The door flew open, and a wet, ragged Vasili stormed out. He lifted a finger and pointed it at Niko, protecting his wounded right wrist against his chest. "One word from Amir and you turn on me?!"

Niko reached for his sword and found it gone—lost somewhere in the harbor. Vasili saw the gesture. His nostrils flared, and he stalked forward, stepping so damned close Niko could feel the anger radiating off him. "I trusted you."

"But I can't trust you. I don't know if you killed the Yazdans—you could have. You came at me, Vasili, opening a vein, ordering me to kill you."

"You know that's not me!"

Yasir emerged from the cabin. "Niko, stand down. We don't have time—"

Niko flung him a snarl. "You don't get to tell me to stand down."

He lifted his hands. "I'm not your enemy. Neither is Vasili."

"You have no fucking idea what *he* is." Niko jabbed Vasili in the chest. "If I was still inside that carriage, I'd be dead."

"But you weren't, and you aren't." Vasili stepped back. "It was the only way to see off those beasts."

"Would it have mattered if I were dead? Do you give a shit about any of this? Yasir? Me?"

"You've asked me that before." He ran a hand through his hair and flicked the excess water from his fingers. "You know the answer."

"That was then." Niko lifted his chin and backed up a step. "All of this... Trying to buy me in the Stag and Horn, because of my name, making me think you're some trapped victim in a life you don't want. Is it all an elaborate plan to claim all of the flame for yourself and use it to destroy the elves?"

Vasili's soft lips parted. He blinked slowly, almost seductively, and hesitated, searching for the right words. Niko had no idea what was taking so long because the answer was clearly fucking *yes*.

"You son of a bitch." He stepped back again. "You lying, manipulative, poisonous fucking snake of a man."

"Nothing has changed."

Niko held a hand up and went back to cradling his limp arm. "*Everything* has changed."

"Just your understanding of it all."

"And to think I *cared* for you." Niko turned away and squinted at Seran's shining lights.

"You don't."

"Don't fucking tell me how I feel, Vasili, when you're incapable."

Vasili sighed. "Did you learn nothing from loving Julian?"

"Mention him again and I'll kill you with my bare hands." He made a step toward Vasili and caught sight of Yasir tensing up. Shadows swam in the captain's eyes. Damn them both to Etara's deserts.

Niko barked a shrill laugh. And to think he'd been a part of this, he'd *helped* Vasili.

"Was that why we came to Seran, so you could kill the Yazdans, gain their strength for the flame, lure your brother into unfamiliar territory, overpower him, and take the flame all for yourself? You had Roksana, someone who knew the city and the family, someone who could get you inside. Gods, the more I think on it all, the more it all falls into place. You hated your palace and everyone in it. You set the fire, freeing you up to abandon it, just like Amir said. You don't care about being king. You never have, so you let Amir claim it. The guards were your experiment, and so are the beasts. That one in the desert wasn't attacking you, it was feeding from you. It's always been about the flame, using it, controlling it, doing anything and everything to manipulate it to do your bidding, just the same as you do to everyone you meet. The Yazdans had no idea you had them in your sights. They couldn't have prepared for you. Nobody can."

Vasili wet his lips. He cradled his broken wrist against his chest again and waited, letting the words settle around them. "Eight years, Nikolas. Eight entire years and every day, they cut me open and took more of me. If you think I won't do everything in my power to stop them, then you really don't know me at all."

Niko closed his eyes. It was true. Amir had been right about all of it. And the worst of it was, Niko had somewhere in all of this learned to care for Vasili. He'd fallen for the lie *again*.

"I can't..." *I can't do this, I can't be here, I can't survive you.*

"Gentlemen, we need to set sail," Yasir said. "I have to ready the ship or risk the Yazdans sinking her after that shit-show we just escaped. I need your help to do that. I can't sail her alone, and my crew is scattered."

Niko opened his eyes and headed for the gangplank.

"Don't leave." Vasili's words almost stopped him, they tripped him, but he kept on walking.

"Nikolas, if you leave, I can't control it."

His boots thumped down the plank.

"Nikolas!" Vasili snapped, wielding his name like a whip crack. "I need you."

Niko pulled up short at the end of the plank. Nothing had changed. Vasili was still the prick who had beaten and manipulated Niko every day since they'd met, but that wasn't new. He'd lied and used people. He was dangerous and vicious, sly and callous. None of that was new. Vasili was still the man he'd always said he was. The mistake had been Niko's, in trying to make him out to be something he wasn't. Just because he had a glimmer of kindness in him, that didn't make him worthy of any part of Niko's heart.

"I need you." Vasili stood at the top of the gangplank, looking a wreck in his sodden clothes and knotted hair. "I can win this war, but I need you beside me to do it."

"You have Yasir."

"Yasir isn't you."

"The way you do things—"

"Is the only way."

"No." Niko retraced his steps up the plank and met Vasili face-to-face again, this time with the prince standing on higher ground, the way onto the ship barred through him. "You have been through terrible things, Vasili. Things that would change any man. Your past has made you who you are. You can't see another way, but there always is one. It may not be the easiest or the most obvious, but it's there."

"If I can't see your way, Nikolas, how can I follow it without you?"

"I don't know if I can find it in me to care." He turned away, and this time when he walked down the plank, there were no words strong enough to stop him. "I'm done with you, with the Cavilles, with the flame, with *all of it*. I'm fucking done with you."

"Nikolas."

"No, Vasili."

"Nikolas! You can't walk away from me!"

He walked away from *Walla's Heart*, away from the merchant captain, and away from the prince who was too far lost to darkness to save. Whatever happened now, Niko's part in it was over. He was done being his master's dog.

CHAPTER 23

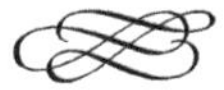

The Yazdans took him in, asking few questions about Vasili, because—as he was learning—Yazdans looked after their own. Seran's vibrant atmosphere had faded some since the two attacks on its beloved family, but within a few weeks, and with the help of the Yazdans coffers, life quickly returned to its vibrant normalcy. The Caville King, last seen at the shah's funeral, had not resurfaced, but the Yazdans were recruiting those who could wield a blade, or wanted to learn. Niko, at Roksana's suggestion, fell into the role of recruitment and training and focused on that instead of the lingering threats circling the city and his own thoughts.

News from Loreen was scarce and unreliable, passed by word of mouth via traders. The city was on its knees, the palace in ruins, law and order non-existent.

Elves would claim it soon, if they hadn't already.

Loreen's people had begun to load their life-long belongings onto carts and make their way south. But, as

Niko had discovered earlier in the year, the passage was rough and marauders rife.

As summer faded into autumn, Niko created patrols as far north as he dared send the men, often joining them himself, policing the main road so the few Loreen's who made the trek had safe passage to settle.

Nobody had heard from or seen the *Walla's Heart* in months, not since the ship had left the docks with a minimal crew on the night of the funeral massacre. A massacre blamed on the Cavilles and poison. Technically, true.

Vasili was out there, plotting.

Amir was biding his time.

Elves would be watching.

And Seran had become the hot, noisy, colorful center of it all.

Perhaps the new war would pass Niko by? He tried not to think of it when he visited the docks and spent the nights among the workers, like he tried not to think of Vasili or Yasir after drinking too much wine and fucking around with a few willing partners. He tried not to think of Lady Maria and what might have become of her, or his loyalty to the griffin, of his honor as a soldier to always fight for what was right and not turn his back on defending Loreen.

He'd been burned too many times.

The blacksmith from Loreen, a lord's bastard son, the Yazdan boy—that man was a different person to the man he'd now become in Seran. Nikolas Yazdan, master at arms for the grieving but formidable Yazdan family. Not better than he was before, not that, but he was getting by. Even if it felt like a charade.

Until the note came. His name written in Vasili's free-flowing handwriting and the paper smelling like rosewater.

Roksana handed it over as Niko stumbled in late at night, or early in the morning, he wasn't sure which. Niko took one look at the writing, smelled the familiar scent, and tossed it in the smoldering fireplace.

Roksana grabbed a poker and flicked the singed envelope out again, then stamped on it to crush any embers. "Idiot." She blew off the ash. "If you don't open it, I will."

Niko dropped into one of the grand chairs beside the fire and huffed a sigh. His head rang from all the noise in the bars and his body ached from all-day trainings. And according to the spinning walls, he was also devastatingly drunk. "There's nothing in that letter but trouble."

"I've watched you Niko, this past month. You work like a mule, you're at the docks until dawn, you rarely sleep, and then you start all over again. I worry you're going to find trouble anyway."

"I'm fine," he groused back, pinching the bridge of his nose. He had been at the docks most nights, spending what coin he'd earned training new recruits. Sleep didn't come anyway, so he'd given up on that weeks ago, and only last night, he'd contemplated taking the spice being shared among the men, just to hollow out the guilt gnawing on his insides.

Roksana tore the wax seal off the envelope. Niko sprang from the chair and snatched it from his aunt's fingers. "Damn, now I have to read it."

In reply, Roksana scooped up two glasses from the sideboard and produced a bottle of dark rum from somewhere—she usually had a stash at hand. She handed Niko a glass as he dropped back into the chair. "It had better bloody mention Yasir Lajani," she said. "I paid that urchin true. He owes me silks! If he dies on some adventure, I want my damn coin back."

Snorting at Roksana's brutal honesty, he reluctantly pulled the thick paper from inside the envelope, breathing in the faint smell of roses.

Nikolas,

I suspect you'll burn this letter on arrival, but Yasir will not stop speaking of you, and with his voice added to the others in my head, writing this will be cathartic, if nothing else. You're a stubborn, righteous fool. I hate that about you. I hate how you believe there's a right way for everything. There isn't, but of course, somehow, you find one.

A Caville must forever hold the flame. That was how it was sold to me by my mother. But she was wrong, because as you said, Cavilles are not the protectors we make ourselves out to be. The truth is, a griffin must forever hold the flame. You were my griffin. For all our differences, I trusted you. But it was more than that. It was something I did not understand or allow purchase until I watched you walk away. You were more than my protector, more than my griffin, more than I cared to acknowledge because to care is to have something to lose. And I'm afraid to lose any more of myself.

I care about you, Nikolas. I hope you're satisfied. I would prefer not to acknowledge it. You're a distraction. One I cannot afford. I had hoped, in your absence, these feelings would fade. They have not, and now Yasir—astute and relentless as he is—demands I write this. Hopefully you'll never read these words, and thus our last meeting will be the end of it. But if you do happen upon this letter, well then, I suppose something has changed.

I did not do all the things you suspect me of, but many I did, so what does it matter? You believe me capable, and I am. Thus, they may as well be true.

In many ways, I wish Julian had been the man you fell for, not the traitor he was to us both, because you deserve someone with a good heart. Perhaps you have already found that someone. I hope never to meet him, for I fear all good things I touch turn to ash.

Loreen is dying.

Yet, for the first time in my life, I feel very much alive.

I wonder if those two facts are related.

And I wonder if I hadn't met you, whether the flame would already be free.

I have a path now. I do not know if it's the correct one.

I once told you how I regret nothing. I was wrong. I regret not restraining you. It would have been... memorable.

Now, I pray this letter is burned, or perhaps I will tell Yasir it has been dispatched and toss it into Walla's ocean.

If you do receive this, then by the time you read these words, I will already be in Loreen. It must end where it began.

You had a choice, and you chose to walk away.

I envy you that.

V

"Well?" Roksana asked.

Niko screwed up the note in one hand and threw it to the floor, then tossed back half the rum, coughing lightly as it burned all the way through.

"That bad, huh."

"Read it if you want."

She hesitated, then picked it up, unfolded it, and read silently.

Niko closed his eyes and let his head drop back. The letter sounded sweet, but every line was another twist of the knife. "That prick."

"I don't see the problem," she said, once finished. "And you must tell me about the restraints sometime."

Niko cracked an eye and caught his aunt crossing her legs and leaning back in the chair, her smile contagious. She shrugged, "Call me curious. He seems the sort to have all manner of kinks. What? It's always the quiet ones who surprise you."

Niko groaned, wishing he'd burned the letter.

She had a lover in Seran. A woman whose identity she fiercely protected. She'd only told Niko because he'd seen the pair late one evening, engaged in a *heated and very physical* conversation outside a bar. Men didn't interest her. It was part of the reason Niko found her so easy to speak with. He'd told her most things—maybe everything—on warm and quiet mornings when his head was fuzzy and the past too close, like this morning.

"He signed it off telling me exactly where he'll be because he thinks I'll go to him."

"Will you?"

"No," he said firmly. He finished the rum and leaned forward, accepting more from his aunt's bottle. The room spun some more, a warning to back off the alcohol, but now Vasili was in his head again, like a snake, always slithering around Niko's defenses. "No," he said again, catching his aunt's long, unconvinced look. "I'm not snapping to heel."

"All right."

"I'm done with him."

"So you said."

"Did I tell you how he had me whipped to prove a point?"

She shrugged. "You also said Amir would have killed you otherwise."

Dammit, he had. "That's... different." He was sure he slurred that last word. "That man is poison."

"Saved you from elves too, right? He's the reason you still have two ears?"

Niko screwed up his nose. He'd forgotten he'd told her that. "He... Yes, but that doesn't erase all the shit I had to deal with around him."

"No, of course not. But..." She leaned forward. "Let's turn this on its head— Just hear me out." She gestured with her glass, cutting off Niko's protest. "Vasili Caville has to maneuver his insane family, the threat of an invasion, and the madness in his head. He was tortured for eight years and shouldn't have survived. The only reason he did was because the elves let him go, sending him back with someone he trusted, someone he maybe cared about, to infiltrate his home. But that someone turned out to be his enemy. Now he's alone again. He has nothing but his name. He's hurting, but he doesn't get to give up. So what does he do? He knows of one man, one chance to take back control. A blacksmith soldier with a knack for killing elves. Someone as straight as an arrow, someone true, someone who has seen a whole lot of shit too." She pointed at Niko.

Niko pressed the cool glass to his cheek. "He could have asked for my help instead of throwing me in his dungeons and treating me like a slave."

"If he'd asked, you'd have told him to fuck off. You broke his wrist, remember?"

He snorted a dry laugh. "Twice now."

"He's in pain, he has nobody, so he brings you in, and he uses you to distract Julian while he maneuvers the pieces on the chessboard, buying himself room to move and think. And do you know what happens? He begins to appreciate you. He wrote me... told me about you."

"Called me a brute."

"The fact he bothered to mention you at all tells you everything you need to know."

"It's all bullshit. He lies like he breathes."

"Vasili doesn't know how to care. He didn't even know he was capable of it until you entered his life. He made you a distraction for everyone else, but you became one for him."

"You can't know that."

She shrugged. "Maybe not, but I've found people are more honest in their letters than they are in person. What he can't say to you, he can write down. Maybe that letter isn't all bullshit. Maybe it's all true. He regrets your leaving, he hates that you've distracted him, and he needs your help."

"And what if he killed your family, your father... What if that was him?"

"*Our* family. Well, if he did, you'll be right beside him to deliver the justice he deserves."

"I'm not going back to Loreen."

"Niko, look me in the eyes and tell me you can forget him, forget everything, and let whatever happens in Loreen happen without you. Tell me that."

He leaned closer, meeting his aunt's gaze. "I'm not going back. If he wants me to go back there, he can come and ask me himself."

Roksana sighed and conceded with a nod. "All right. Then I suppose I'll have to go."

"Why?"

"Because it's who we are. We've always protected the flame. That ring on your finger, that means you'll keep the flame safe."

Niko tore the ring free and tossed it at his aunt. She caught it with a frown. "I've given enough."

She turned the ring over and flicked her dark gaze up to Niko. "Your grandfather gave you this for a reason. He loved Leila. He loved us all, but he loved her more. She tried to convince him to go north, to stand beside the Cavilles in a war she was adamant was coming. He refused, claiming the Cavilles should beg for his help, and then she was gone. She left her ring too. It broke his heart. When it was clear she wasn't coming back, I went after her, met Vasili, who was interested in forming an alliance, but we couldn't find Leila. And then the war did come... the rest you know. Leila would want you to have her ring, and she'd want you and me to help Vasili, because she cared."

She handed it back.

The ring shone in his palm once more, seemingly heavier for all the history it carried. "It's not fair that she's not here now."

"Life isn't fair."

Niko rubbed his face, trying to clear his thoughts. "He gets inside my head. I can't think around him. I know what he is... but I still..." He swallowed. "There's parts of him I hate, and then there's this part of him I'd do anything for. I think..." He shuddered a sigh. "I think that's the part that scares me. I don't understand why I'm so wrapped up in him.

He's an asshole. I hate him, I just..." He slumped forward, burying his face in his hands. Most of the time he wanted to wrap his fingers around Vasili's throat and throttle him, and mean it, but there was that small need to protect him, to keep him safe, to fight the whole world for him. It was *that* need which terrified Niko. "Roksana, I hate how he lies *all the time*. I hate how he measures people by how useful they are to him. But by the three, I can't stop thinking about the real Vasili, the man he keeps hidden, but it's not even just that. The dark side of him—it ties me in knots, and gods, I need that too. I thought I loved Julian, but it was Vasili in my head the whole time. Do you know how fucked up that makes me?"

When Niko finally lifted his head, Roksana was close enough to look him in the eyes. "For what it's worth, I may not have known you long, but hiding isn't you. You need to go to Vasili, tell him everything you just told me, and see what he does."

"He'll laugh, and we'll fight, because he's a cruel son of a bitch."

She tipped her glass and chinked it with his. "That letter is an open invitation to go to him, if you want. It's up to you what happens next. But you need to draw a line under it, either way, or it'll drive you out of your mind."

If he went back, it would all start over until he killed Vasili or Vasili got him killed. He still wasn't entirely sure whether the suicidal carriage ride had been designed to finish him off or if the beasts were Vasili's creation.

Vasili's world wasn't Niko's. It never had been. It never could be.

He sucked in a deep breath and shoved to his feet, then grabbed for the chair as the room spun again.

"Here." Roksana held out the rum bottle. "You'll need it."

Maybe he'd find answers at the bottom of it. Or maybe he could replace Vasili's poison in his head with the rum instead. Tomorrow, he'd decide. Tomorrow, he'd make a choice. The Yazdans or the Caville prince.

CHAPTER 24

"Elves! Niko! *Elves*!"

He tore from his bed, stumbled into a pair of trousers, and was out the door, throwing on a shirt, head still dizzy from drink and lack of sleep. Roksana met him in the hallway. She thrust a pistol into his hand and his new sword with its slightly recurved blade and a nasty backward hook at the tip, designed to rip off armor.

"Where?"

"In the grounds... Come!"

"Inside?" That didn't seem... possible.

"A small force, scouts maybe." She ran ahead.

The sounds of ringing metal and pistol-fire echoed down the open-sided corridors.

"We assume they came by ship last ni—"

A cloaked figure sprang from a window, lunging at Roksana. She lifted her pistol, but the cloaked mass slammed into her, driving her backward against a column. A small blade flashed at her throat. Roksana brought her arm up to lever the attack away.

Niko freed his sword and swung it with practiced ease, lodging the blade into the elf's upper spine. It bucked. Roksana kicked it off, and Niko tore the blade free. The elf fell in a motionless heap. Blood oozed from beneath it. Red eyes gazed up, unseeing. Gnarled skin and sharp teeth. There was no mistaking it.

His mind clicked, instincts kicking in.

Niko switched his sword to his left hand and freed the pistol Roksana had been teaching him to shoot. "Lead the way."

Roksana cast him a grateful nod and they dashed toward the sounds of battle.

Elves swarmed the gardens in the early morning light. All thoughts of *why* were shoved aside. With no time to strategize, all he could do was cut them down. The pistol barked, but the weapon was too slow to reload. Niko tossed it aside and let his blade sing.

Elves moved like shadows, smooth and fast. They dropped from windows above the courtyards and spilled in from walkways, swarming like ants. Niko swung and parried and slashed and cut through them. Too many to be a scouting force. Years on the front line came rushing back to him, his muscles remembering how to dodge, to swing, to *fight* like there was nothing else. Just him, his blade, and the elves at the end of it.

Slowly, the sounds of battle began to fade and the elves stopped coming. Niko stood among the dead and wounded. It was over, almost too soon. He spotted an elf crawling through the dirt and made his way to its side. He still crawled on, thinking only of escape.

Niko kicked the elf over onto his side and the elf stared back. If he had a weapon, he didn't reach for it.

"A live one?" a Yazdan soldier asked, coming up behind Niko.

The elf was bigger than most of his kind, his skin a light green, mossy color. He wouldn't speak, they rarely did in any language Niko knew, but he bared sharp teeth either in a threat or a grin.

Niko backed up a step as more soldiers approached. "Tie him and take him somewhere secure."

All around the trampled gardens, the men and women of the Yazdans' newly trained guards tended the wounded and the dead. Under the blazing sunlight, with the stink of death rising into the air, it still didn't seem possible that elves had so brazenly attacked.

"Send all available scouts into Seran," Niko ordered the soldier. If the elves were here, they could be sacking Seran. "Report back immediately."

He fell into the role of organizing the aftermath of battle. The day passed in a blur, ingraining into his clothes and skin, the smell of blood baking under the sun.

A rider sent word that Seran was safe, no elves. It should have eased his mind but only cemented the concern. Why attack the Yazdans and not the city itself? Why now? Yasir had said elves weren't fond of the ocean. If they'd come by sea—a direction nobody would expect—then they had a damned good reason. It bothered him more than the blood under his nails.

With the house clear and the bodies burning, Niko descended into the cool caverns honed into rock beneath the house, to the prison where the elf had been kept.

One flame torch flickered in a wall sconce outside the prison cell, making the shadow of the bars dance across the lone elf. Male, muscular, and heavy. Blood had dried on his face. Red eyes held no emotion. He stared back at Niko like a wolf eyeing a rabbit.

Few elves were successfully held for long. They had a knack for escaping, or killing themselves. They endured torture like the soulless creatures they were. But Niko knew how to make them scream.

He nodded at the guard to open the cell door and stepped inside. The elf lifted his chin and bared sharp, jagged teeth in warning. This one had deliberately knotted its long hair, threaded the long oily locks with leaves and twigs for camouflage. Red paint made from Seranian dirt marked his cheeks and neck, helping him blend with the earth.

His tattered cloak was a ragged patchwork of animal hide. The guard should have removed it. Elves liked to keep blades hidden in the seams of their clothing.

Niko crouched outside his reach and held the creature's stare. He had probably killed hundreds of men, the same as Niko had killed hundreds of elves. There was no reasoning with them, no truce. They had no honor, no respect. They killed, and they burned, and they destroyed. It was who they were. And this one looked at Niko like it had already won despite being chained in a cell with no way out.

Asking him questions wouldn't work. They only understood the language of pain.

Niko pulled his cleaned blade from its sheath and rested its tip against the floor. The elf's gaze flicked down to it and back to Niko's face. The chance of him knowing Niko's reputation as the butcher was slim. The war had been almost two years ago now, and the front had been miles upon miles of battle lines.

The elf sprang, fingers outstretched, nails gleaming. Niko held fast. The chains yanked it back. He thrashed and bucked, snarled and growled, desperately pulling at the shackles around his wrists. He'd known elves to gnaw off their own hands to escape. They were strong too, but the shackles were thick. He wasn't escaping anytime soon.

Niko straightened, watching him thrash like a wild animal caught in a snare. He bludgeoned him with the handle of his sword, knocking the creature out cold. The elf's cloak came away easily, leaving the creature clad in a patchwork of dark leather. Niko dragged it free of the cell and tossed it at the guard's feet. "Check the seams. Be careful. Their blades are poisoned. Burn it when you're done."

"And what do I do with him?"

"For now, nothing."

NIKO RETREATED TO HIS ROOM, where the Yazdan staff had left a steaming bath and lit the fire. Hot evening air drifted in through the open windows, bringing with it the smell of the sea. He stripped off and climbed into the bath, sinking his shoulders beneath the waterline.

He'd briefly caught Roksana on his way back to his room, finding her as troubled as he. She'd been the one to tell him to come back here and rest. But they'd both known he wasn't sleeping tonight. He'd discuss the attack tomorrow with Alissand and the rest of the family.

If the elves hadn't come from the sea, then they'd come from the north, which meant Loreen had fallen.

Niko's hands trembled. He watched the tremors,

turning his hands over. After battle, the shakes came. Every time. He clutched the roll-top edges of the bath and rested his head back. If Loreen had fallen, did that mean the war had been for nothing? Did that mean Vasili was dead?

Guilt writhed low in his belly.

He should have gone.

Vasili thought one man wouldn't be enough, but a blade was a blade. Niko might have been able to make a difference if he'd been beside the prince. Instead, he'd walked away. Maybe it had been the right choice, but if it was, why had he regretted it every night since leaving him?

His chamber door rattled open. Sharp boots struck the floorboards.

Niko twisted, about to remind whoever it was that the room was occupied, but the words fell unspoken from his lips.

Cloaked from head to toe in silvery grey, with boots riding up to his knees, there was no mistaking his long, lean gait or the shimmer of the Caville ring on his finger. He pushed his cloak's hood back.

Vasili.

Relief almost tore a sob from Niko's lips. Not only was he alive and here, but the prick was also *smiling*.

How? His heart drummed too loud. Had he not been naked in a bath, he might have crossed the floor and punched that smile off the prince's lips. "Still haven't learned to knock?" he drawled instead.

Vasili regarded the room, with its roaring fireplace, fine rugs, ornate furniture, and vast window. "It didn't take you long to live like a lord." He strode toward the window and swept the rippling silk drapes aside to admire the ocean view. "You always had it in you."

Niko had a thousand insults ready to speak, but all of them had lodged in his throat. He just walked right in like it hadn't been months since they'd seen each other, like he hadn't written a letter confessing his feelings?

He pulled the tie at his neck, and the cloak slipped from his shoulders. A loose ponytail, tied off with a simple strip of silk, over the crisscross laces of his grey-and-white lace-lined corset. He looked... good.

Shifting firelight glinted in his three earrings.

He looked more than good.

Niko blinked. Had he fallen asleep and this was another one of the Vasili fantasies that had haunted him since leaving the palace? "How did you find me?"

"Roksana told me which room was yours." He turned to face the room and, folding his arms, leaned back against the sill. The breeze teased his hair.

Niko swallowed hard and hoped the prince stayed by the window because there were parts of him that were more than substantially pleased to see Vasili again.

"I thought you were in Loreen?"

Vasili's lips parted and his brows inched up slightly. "Ah... you received my letter."

"Roksana fished it out of the fire."

The soft laugh that rippled from the prince did nothing to soften Niko's cock.

"I was high when I wrote it." He fluttered a hand. "Make of that what you will."

Of all the raging demands needing to be answered, the questions to be voiced, the lies and deceit and betrayal, there was one thing that was absolutely true between them. The one thing Niko was struggling to think around. Need.

Vasili's gaze lingered, unblinking. He'd stilled, as though waiting.

Niko wet his lips, and Vasili might have tracked that movement, though it was difficult to be sure from across the room. And then Vasili was approaching, boots striking the floor with precision. He moved with smooth seduction, as though he was absolutely aware of every inch of his body and how to use it to steer Niko's thoughts deep into the gutter.

He rested on the side of the bath and stroked his fingers through the water. When his gaze drifted lower, his eyebrow lifted at Niko's obvious desire beneath the water.

"Why are you here?" Niko asked. His voice had gained a gravelly undertone, the kind that dragged.

"Why do you think?" His fingers swirled, his gaze low, lashes hiding his eye from Niko's attention. Gods, he wanted to tip his chin up and taste his lips, to feel the prince soften beneath his kiss.

"Will you ever answer truthfully?"

His lips ticked. His gaze flicked up, locking with Niko's. He lowered himself to his knees, still meeting Niko's stare, and sank his hand beneath the water. Strong fingers effortlessly wrapped around Niko's hard cock, and the sudden thrill stole Niko's breath. He gritted his teeth to keep from groaning and clutched at the sides of the tub. The prince's fingers stroked, finding just the right amount of friction to splinter Niko's thoughts. His body quickly forgot every terrible thing Vasili had done.

There was no use in begging to touch him, he'd refuse, and so Niko stayed rooted in the bath, pleasure sparking in his lower back with every single one of the prince's rhythmic strokes.

He breathed too fast, giving himself away. Vasili watched his face, reading, assessing, controlling the pace with every twitch Niko gave him. The intensity was both the worst and best part. Pink heat bloomed across Vasili's cheeks. His soft lips parted, so ripe for Niko, and by the three, if this was a dream, he didn't want to wake up.

Gods, he was going to come.

Then Vasili—prick that he was—let go and stood up. He casually made his way across the room to the bed, dripping water from his fingers. His absence left Niko gasping, desperate to take his cock in hand and finish all the good work Vasili had started.

Vasili reached behind and unlaced his corset, letting it slip down his arms. He turned on his heel, facing Niko again, and discarded the garment on the floor. His fingers popped his shirt fastenings open next, exposing his lean, pale abs beneath, like an invitation.

What was this? Some trick to have Niko salivate for something he couldn't have?

Vasili—half-undressed—leaned against one of the bedposts, folded his arms, and waited.

By the three, the temptation was going to kill him. But if Vasili was setting him up just to push him away again, he wasn't sure he could take it. He closed his eyes and bowed his head, willing his thoughts from his dick and into common sense.

"Rest assured, this means no more or less than it appears to," Vasili said smoothly, his voice like silk through the fingers.

It was all the excuse Niko needed. Spurred into motion

by the prince's invite, Niko climbed from the tub. The only thing that stopped him from crossing the floor and devouring Vasili was the prince's raised, speculative eyebrow. How could he be so fucking nonchalant and indifferent while Niko's heart raced, and his body raged, and his mind screamed at him that whatever this was, he'd pay for it.

"If you want me, my prince, *then you can fucking come to me*." Soaked and gleaming in front of the firelight. Erect and eager. Scarred and rough. Niko smiled and waited. Vasili was just as hungry, but Niko was not his pet who answered when his master called. Vasili could come to him, or this wasn't happening.

Vasili glanced at the window, where he'd left his cloak, weighing the options, and then he pushed off the bedpost and crossed the floor, stopping so close that Niko smelled the sea on him. His earrings shimmered under the same light shining in his eye. He tilted his head, snaked a hand around the back of Niko's neck, and pulled him into a soft, yielding kiss. The kind of kiss not meant for Vasili. A real kiss. And Niko folded his arms around his lean body, careful to avoid pulling him too close and putting pressure on the scars.

Vasili softened in his arms. His tongue swept in, taking and giving, but not too much. The prince's soft fingers skimmed Niko's jaw, and Niko was damn well lost.

He pulled free of the kiss and brushed his lips over Niko's cheek, whispering, "My griffin."

The words unleashed some part of Niko that had been waiting for the prince's acceptance. Niko was naked and in his arms, but Vasili was the vulnerable one.

Vasili's fingers skimmed down Niko's chest, freeing a

riot of shivers that had Niko's cock raging and needy for touch, and then Vasili's cool fingers closed around him again, and the prince thrust his tongue in to meet Niko's. Niko had surrendered too much of himself already, and he'd surrender more.

He kissed his beautiful jaw, nipped his neck, and listened to Vasili's rapidly shortening breaths. Vasili wanted this, *needed* it, maybe more than Niko, and Niko would do anything so Vasili could feel again, like maybe he had with Alek. He desperately needed to see Vasili lost to desire, to see him free in those blinding moments of ecstasy.

"Tell me what you need," Niko whispered in his ear.

Vasili gripped Niko's shoulders and turned him, then pushed gently. "On the bed." The snarled order was not as gentle as his hands had been, but it elicited a sharp dart of desire in Niko, making his cock twitch. He sat on the edge of the bed and parted his legs to allow Vasili in close. The prince pushed between his knees, cupped Niko's jaw, and kissed him harder, his urgency like a fire to Niko's touch-paper. Vasili needed control, and Niko was both alarmed and thrilled to realize he'd let him have it.

"Lay back." He pushed down on Niko's chest.

Niko propped his elbows on the bed, and Vasili brought his knees up to straddle Niko's thighs. Errant locks of the prince's long hair framed his face, and all Niko could see was Vasili's broad smile and the bright delight in his eye. So beautiful... like a marble statue, made to be admired. Niko brushed the smooth line of his cheek.

"Don't touch." But this time, the prince said it with a sly smile. "Lie back. Raise your arms above your head."

A flutter of nervous excitement shortened Niko's

breath. He obeyed, skin tingling beneath Vasili's stroking hands. The prince's soft, wet mouth teased over his bare chest, toward a nipple. Niko swallowed audibly.

The prince's tongue swirled around Niko's nipple. His hand encircled Niko's cock at the same time as his teeth pinched.

"Fuck." Niko bucked, igniting Vasili's warm laugh, and by the three, Niko's heart melted at the sound. He wanted to haul Vasili up and kiss him until there was no more breath left in his body, but Vasili's free hand clamped down, pinching Niko's wrists together above Niko's head.

"Stay," Vasili said.

Niko growled out a warning but kept his hands held high.

Vasili straightened, running both hands down Niko's chest, and pulled the silk strip from his hair, freeing his long locks. He pulled the silk tie through his fingers, and all Niko could think was how those fingers really, really needed to be on his cock.

Niko panted too hard, too fast. He couldn't deny the desire his body was revealing with every breath or the way his heart quickened at what use Vasili had for that silk.

Vasili fell forward and looped the cool silk around Niko's wrists, tying them together above his head. The lick of silk and the dance of Vasili's fingertips against his skin summoned a moan. Vasili's open shirt revealed his chest within licking distance, his scars gleaming. Niko bit his tongue. His throbbing cock leaked in want.

Then he realized what the silk was for. "You're tying me?" It made his heart skitter, but the tiny bite of fear did something else to Niko too—made everything more immediate. Made his skin burn with anticipation.

"Pull hard enough and it will loosen," Vasili said. His mouth hovered over Niko's. "If you wish it to."

Oh gods, Vasili had tied him... he was fucking restrained. His heart thudded hotter and louder. He didn't trust him enough for this. But he had said he could pull free... But he didn't want that. Not yet.

Vasili's hand pressed against Niko's chest, holding him down. The prince looked into his eyes, and it was like seeing him for the first time. There had been glimpses—Vasili asleep wedged in a chair, Vasili enjoying the simple pleasures of chopping wood, Vasili at the waterfall—but not like this. Vasili, open and honest, his smile bright and alive, his barriers abandoned. Because he felt safe.

Vasili's smile tilted, and his fingers skimmed Niko's chest, circling around a spot below his right nipple. "This scar?"

The scar Vasili had found was tiny. Little more than a nick. There were bigger, more obvious scars for him to focus on, but the play of Vasili's fingertips, circling tighter and tighter—gods, his mouth was dry. He wet his lips. "Elf dagger."

Vasili tilted his head. His light touch skipped lower, over Niko's abs. "This one?"

Oh, by Aura, the prince was going to kill him by teasing alone. Niko swallowed and looked at the ceiling while Vasili's fingers danced around the deeper, more ragged scar at his hip. Suddenly, soft, warm, wet lips sealed over the scar. "Fuck!" He arched under the prince, barely containing the moan. This wasn't fair.

"Tell me."

"Elf. Ambush."

"Hm." Vasili pushed both hands up Niko's chest and

tongued a trail behind them, veering below Niko's left pectoral. "This one?" His tongue flicked over a patch of rough skin, and Niko loosed a growl.

"Fell from a horse." He couldn't do this. His cock was leaking, his body ablaze, and Vasili was too damn calm and controlled. "Kiss me, damn you."

And suddenly, he did. Vasili's mouth was soft and gentle at first, his tongue a tease, but as Niko tasted more of him, he wanted more, needed more, and Vasili answered those silent demands, shoving his tongue in and rocking into Niko. This had gone different in Niko's mind. He'd have grabbed the prince and flipped him onto his back, then made him writhe as he lavished attention on his cock. That's how it had gone in his dreams. But Vasili clearly had his own way.

Straddling Niko's hips, he straightened and tore his loose shirt over his head, then shook his hair out and grinned. Niko had never seen him so... unbidden. Vasili kissed him again, and his cruel mouth found all the wicked ways to torment Niko as it traveled down his neck and chest, tongue flicking.

Niko's cock twitched against his lower belly, silken strands of precum cooling on his skin. Vasili's fingers skimmed the wetness, and his mouth followed, chasing down, over his hip.

Vasili was going to suck him off, and, by fucking Walla, he wasn't ready for this. But gods, he needed it.

A quick puff of air cooled the head of Niko's cock, and Niko thrust his hips up for more. "Fuck, Vasili..."

A soft chuckle filled the room, and fuck if Vasili wasn't going to kill him from desperate need alone. Warm, soft lips sealed over Niko's crown, and his tight, sucking mouth stole him in deep. Tingly desire raced down Niko's back and all reason vanished.

Niko tossed his head back, arching his spine, seeking more of the perfect tightness. Vasili took him to the hilt then withdrew, and the whimper Niko freed was nothing like any he'd made before.

Vasili's weight briefly vanished. The bed rocked as he climbed off, but by the time Niko could see straight again, Vasili crawled back up the length of him, naked head to toe and breathtaking. Firelight licked over the lattice of scars on his chest. His bare thighs gleamed, the scars fewer there but still present. And his cock, so erect and thickly veined that Niko swallowed hard, wishing he could swallow *him*. By the three, he was a vision of grace, of slim masculinity, and everything Niko desperately wanted to sink his fingers into in all ways.

Vasili struck in a kiss, both messy and raw. Niko tasted his own salty seed, then Vasili clasped both their erect lengths in his fist and stroked as one.

Niko growled into Vasili's mouth and nipped at his lips, needing more, shoving his cock into Vasili's pumping hand, losing himself to everything Vasili gave. Pinned, tied, and thoroughly caught, he should have despised the prince's control, and maybe a small piece of him did, but the lust and mindless need overrode any fear.

Niko gasped free of the kiss, his lower back tingling, pleasure cresting. He groaned out nonsense words, maybe begging to come. He was close.

Vasili sat upright and granted Niko the perfect sight of the prince riding him, mercilessly working his hand around their cocks. His smile, the gleam in his beautiful eye, the curl of his wicked tongue as it touched his top teeth, and the strength in his grip—it was all too much, too Vasili, and Niko came with a shuddering cry. Creamy seed dashed his chest in spurts. But even as the sensitive comedown made him twitch, it was Vasili poised above him, cock still in hand, who held Niko entranced. The prince threw his head back, bit his lower lip so hard it would surely bleed, and gasped aloud. His abs rippled and flexed, body shuddering, and then his seed pulsed free, spilling warmly onto Niko's belly.

Niko had never seen anything so fucking beautiful in all his life.

Vasili's eye fluttered open, his lashes light. He smiled, and the rest of Niko's heart cracked wide open. He was doomed. He'd follow this fucking asshole anywhere, do anything for him, probably die for him, and none of it made any sense, but understanding anything in this moment was beyond him.

Vasili kissed him with swollen lips, then peeled off and sashayed toward the bath, displaying a fine, tight ass that Niko couldn't tear his gaze from. Niko knew all the ways to make that ass work for the both of them, but Vasili wasn't ready. He tossed his hair like a fucking tease, then glanced over his shoulder, and the prince's sideways grin struck like an arrow to Niko's heart.

That was it. He was fucking dead. Vasili had killed him with lust and want and impossible things. Niko flung his head back to stare at the ceiling and heard the bathwater slosh. Gods, he was doomed.

Arms aching at their awkward angle above his head, he tugged on the silk and felt it unravel, just as Vasili had said.

Concerns tried to creep back in—why was he here, why now, where had he been, what had he been doing—

but Niko refused them purchase. Instead, he rode the glorious post-sex high, content to stay right where he was and watch Vasili's smooth hands stroke his arms in the firelight.

After washing, Vasili toweled off and padded back to the bed to casually lay on one side, head propped on a hand as his gaze roamed up Niko's thighs, over his belly and chest, to his face. "I should have gone to Loreen. I should be there now."

"Why aren't you?"

"Must I spell it out for you, Nikolas?"

"Please do, Your Highness."

Vasili cupped Niko's cheek, keeping him from looking away. "Day and night, you occupy my thoughts."

Niko's smile grew, and Vasili's eye narrowed, like this was not the good news Niko seemed to believe it to be. Vasili let go and rolled on his back, maybe to stare at the same spot Niko had and hoped to find answers there. "Tomorrow, we talk," he said. "Leave tonight as this and nothing more."

Niko heard, *leave tonight as perfection*.

It almost sounded like a question, and when Vasili looked over again, Niko nodded in reply. Under Vasili's gaze, he left the bed for the rapidly cooling bath, washed clean, and tossed a few more logs on the fire. When he returned to Vasili, the prince lay sprawled on his side, naked on the top sheet, breathing softly, deeply asleep.

Niko retrieved his cloak and lay it over him, then climbed in on the opposite side, not daring to touch, despite aching to fold him into his arms.

CHAPTER 25

Niko half expected Vasili to be gone like a dream when he woke. He'd even tried to resist sleep, but exhaustion had taken over.

He blinked awake with early morning light spilling into the room and found the prince lounging in a chair by the window, his shirt back on but loose, laces untied, and cuffs trailing free. Even his trousers rode low on his hips. He looked as though he'd been poured into the chair, and Niko wondered if he was still dreaming. Because none of this felt real. Distrust began seeping back into his thoughts, but he pushed it aside in favor of enjoying the view.

The prince's fingers tapped on the chair's arm. He smiled coyly, then pushed to his feet, grabbed Niko's clothes, and tossed them on the bed. "I should greet the Yazdans in a more official manner." He shrugged the tailored corset over his shoulders and loosely into place, then reached behind him and pulled the dangling laces to tighten the garment, instantly accentuating his lean figure.

Did he know his every motion seduced? Probably not. When it came to his own body, Vasili seemed oblivious.

Niko grabbed the shirt and trousers, concentrating on dressing instead of how easy it would be to stand and pull the prince back into his arms. "More official than sleeping with one?" He tied off the trousers fly and looked up to find Vasili moving in.

His smile was sharp and hungry. He gave Niko a small shove in the chest, dropping him onto the edge of the bed, and maneuvered between Niko's knees.

Yes, this was what Niko wanted. He almost opened his mouth to ask for the silk tie, but Vasili slipped his fingers through Niko's hair, tilting his head up. Niko gladly kissed the smile from his lips. His heart fluttered, coming alive beneath the prince's obscenely gentle touch. Someone like him shouldn't be allowed to be so fucking gentle.

Too soon, the kiss was over. Vasili turned his back to Niko, managing to make even that small step seductive. Flicking out his hair from beneath the corset, he reached behind him, offering the laces. "Tighten me, Nikolas."

With the taste of the prince's sweetness lingering on his lips, he took the laces between his fingers and stood. Vasili's proximity filled Niko's head with all the ways he could make the prince gasp and shudder.

Niko's heart lodged once more in his throat. How Vasili's hair could still smell like rosewater after being at sea for weeks was beyond Niko, but it did, and the urge to breathe him in made Niko tremble. He hooked his fingers into the corset's crisscross pattern and tugged lightly, tightening the silk laces from the back of his neck, between his shoulder blades, and down to his lower back. One final tug and the corset cinched closed. Vasili loosed a small, sharp intake of breath, and Niko's fingers stilled.

His heart pounded, mouth dry. His cock pressed uncomfortably against the inside of his trousers. He'd clearly only sampled what Vasili was capable of. He should sweep the prince's hair aside and kiss him softly on the back of his neck, and then one thing would lead to another, and Vasili would tie him up again, his teeth pinching Niko's nipples, his hands effortlessly stroking him.

Vasili turned his head, his face in profile, lips teasing a smile. If Niko touched him, he'd be punished, and the thought alone made Niko's cock throb with need. Would he tie him harder this time? Did Niko truly want that?

Now was not the time to indulge. Elves had attacked, and there was still work to be done on the clean-up. Roksana would be looking for him. Not to mention the family would need to know about Vasili or else he risked being discovered, and that likely wouldn't go well with Alissand.

"The family will be nervous after the attack yesterday," he said, stepping out from behind the prince. The cool breeze from the window helped soothe the desire some.

"Attack?" Vasili asked, brow tightening.

"Elves." He pulled on his boots and looked back at Vasili, finding him all tied off and buckled up in his exquisite attire. Concern shadowed his face.

"A sizable force. We barely dealt with them."

He glanced at the window behind Niko. "By land or sea?"

"Sea, we think."

Vasili straightened his cuffs, ran his hands through his

hair, and headed toward the door. "Then Yasir was correct. Their presence here is no accident—"

"Wait." If Niko let him leave without discussing last night and what it meant, the opportunity would be lost and they'd go back to the way things had been before. Distant. Icy. Was that what Vasili wanted, after that note? Niko couldn't stand that. Not now. Things had to be different, didn't they? He wanted them to be. But did Vasili want them to be? "Vasili. This. Us..." Gods, he was shit at words. "Last night—"

"There's no time, Niko. If elves are he—" He opened the door.

Niko saw the pistol too late—heard the shot before understanding what was happening. Vasili reeled, his left hand going to his right shoulder. Blood rapidly bloomed through his fingers.

Guards poured in. "Get down! Down!" One kicked Vasili's legs out. He went down onto his hands and knees. The guards grappled with him, holding him down between them.

"Stop!" Niko lunged forward and was met with a pistol between the eyes, freezing him rigid. Alissand glared from behind the weapon.

His uncle jerked his chin. "There's only one place a Caville should be and it's not a Yazdan's bed."

Niko lifted his hands. "You don't understand. Vasili isn't here to fight us—"

"Oh, I understand. Vasili Caville is harboring half the flame, a power that should never have been freed. That freedom is over."

Freedom? What freedom? He wasn't making any sense.

The guards manhandled Vasili to his feet. Blood dribbled from the corner of his mouth, and a pink flush burned across his cheek. They'd struck him. Fury blazed in his eye. And not just fury, but a swirl of darkness. "Unhand me, damn you!" Vasili pulled on the guards' grip, baring his teeth in a sneer, but they held firm.

He knew Alissand hated the Cavilles, but this was absurd. "Alissand, stop this... Let Vasili explain."

Alissand shook his head as though disappointed. "It's not your fault. You're ignorant of our ways. Leila didn't teach you. The Cavilles must be dealt with."

"Dealt with?" Niko glared back. "This is a mistake. It's you who doesn't know what you're dealing with. Vasili doesn't just contain the flame. He can and will wield it. Let him go, or you risk the lives of everyone in this room."

Alissand frowned. "Then you do know and you willfully engage with it? You are no Yazdan." He raised the pistol again, this time with intent to kill.

"*It?!* What exactly do you think he is?"

A dangerous gleam shone in Alissand's eyes. "A curse and a tool."

Whatever was happening here, Alissand was wrong, and Niko wasn't about to stand by and let them hold Vasili. His blade lay against the far wall, too far away. His pistol was on the dresser, but even if he could reach it, he hadn't re-armed it since the battle.

He considered tackling Alissand. The man was in his middle years but far from weak.

"Don't try me, boy. I will put you down, Yazdan or not."

His uncle wouldn't kill him... would he? "Where's Roksana?"

Alissand snorted. "Readying the cells."

"No..." She wouldn't. She knew Vasili—she'd never turn against him like this. Against Niko. "Don't do this."

Vasili's laugh rippled out of him and instantly sucked all of the heat from the air, leaving it chilled. Inky darkness flooded his eye. "The Yazdans and their relentless righteousness. I should have known. *Nothing* changes."

Alissand nodded at the rightmost guard. He drew back his fist and struck Vasili in the jaw, whipping his head to the side and splitting his lip. Vasili spat blood, staggered in the guard's grip, and smiled.

"Stop!" Niko took a step forward.

His uncle's pistol dug against his skull. "One more step and you're a dead man."

They struck Vasili again, and this time he went down hard. He tried to push onto his arm but collapsed, unmoving.

While all eyes were turned to Vasili, Niko snatched his uncle's pistol out of the man's hand and turned it on him. But a guard plowed in and tackled Niko. His back struck the bedpost. Hands clawed at his grip on the gun. A punch landed in his middle, and he could do nothing but buckle over and breathe. The gun was gone, snatched from his fingers by the same people he'd damn well trained. This wasn't right. They weren't like this. Roksana would listen... Something heavy and hard struck him in the lower back, and Niko blinked, finding himself facedown on the floor, spluttering.

"Stay down," Alissand barked.

Niko had made a mistake. Somewhere... sometime... he'd chosen the wrong side, the wrong ring. Damn them.

"Hurt Vasili and I'll kill you!" Niko's arms were yanked behind his back. A knee dug into his spine. Gods, no. This couldn't happen. If they touched Vasili, if they restrained him, hurt him—it wasn't right. It couldn't happen. "Just... let us go, just listen. He came to help, he came for peace, *gods-damn you*, he's not the enemy!"

Alissand loomed. "He came ashore with *elves*."

"No, he didn't," Niko spluttered a laugh, "and if you knew him, you'd know why that's impossible." Alissand must have assumed Vasili was corrupted. Because of his past, perhaps. Or the rumors. Eight years as a prisoner. The rumors Amir had spread. Damn that rat for his lies! "He was on a ship, yes—*Walla's Heart.* Find Captain Lajani. He'll tell you everything, but trust me, Vasili would never work with elves."

"You chose the Cavilles, Nikolas. We took you in, and this is how you repay us? There is no room for traitors among Yazdans."

"I don't give a fuck about the family. If you so much as cut Vasili, I will hunt you down, *uncle*, and rip your gods-damned—"

Alissand's boot came down, delivering silence.

WRACKING coughs dragged him from unconsciousness, dumping him onto the very real and cold floor of a prison cell. Breathing hard, he groaned and rolled on his back, waiting for his lungs to settle and the all-over throbbing to ease. Clearly, the beating hadn't stopped after the boot to the face. His chest ached. He poked at it and found a few ribs moved in directions they shouldn't. At least they hadn't tied him.

Where was Vasili?

Besides himself, his cell was empty.

Alissand had caught them both unawares. And now they'd taken Vasili to gods knew where, which was exactly what they'd tried to avoid since arriving in Seran. Niko swore. The cold stone walls bounced the curse back at him.

Roksana would end this insanity. She'd learn of Vasili's capture, come get Niko, and this would be some hideous error of his uncle's.

He grabbed the cold iron bars and pulled himself onto his feet, then rested there a while, forehead pressed to the bars, to catch his breath. Then he heard breathing—and not his own.

The elf in the opposite cell had shuffled closer to his own bars, as close as the chains fixed to the floor would allow. His red-eyed glare skimmed over Niko in wordless assessment.

Niko bared his teeth, but the elf continued to stare.

Putting Niko in here with an elf was probably Alissand's idea of irony.

He looked around for anything he could use to make some noise and found a tin cup. He sniffed the water it contained, tasted it, found it fresh, gulped it down, and then rattled the empty can against the bars. "*Hey*!" The coughing started up again, but he kept rattling the can between the bars until the torch on the wall had burned low, and someone finally opened the door.

Roksana appeared, a fresh torch in her hand. He watched her replace the burned-out one on the wall.

"You're just going to ignore me?"

"Nikolas..." she sighed. "We couldn't wait any longer

for you to see the truth. It's clear you're emotionally entangled with the prince."

"Truth? What truth was I supposed to see? The fact Alissand is an asshole, verging on dangerous? Will you unlock this door? Have you seen Vasili? Is he all right?"

She blinked back at him like she hadn't heard a damn word.

"Roksana?" He stared through the bars. "I'm with Vasili to help control the flame. That's why we came here. Nothing else. You know this."

"He's turned you." She shook her head. "A Yazdan."

"What?" This was ludicrous. "What does that even mean?" The blood. Yasir. "Wait, you think he gave me his blood?" Niko snorted.

"Did he?"

"Fuck no."

"But he did with Yasir." A statement. Not a question.

Why wasn't she opening the damn cell? "Roksana, you know Vasili. He wrote you. You know he's not like the rest of the Cavilles. He comes off as vicious and manipulative but—granted, he is that—but that's not all he is."

She approached the bars. "Yes, I know the prince. He's calculative, manipulative, and powerful. He killed his father, his brother, my father, and our guests. He has to be stopped. I had hoped you'd stop him, but I was wrong."

"You have it all wrong." Niko's grip tightened on the bars, making them groan. "Gods, why does everyone think the worst of him?" Hadn't Niko done the same? His heart ached to think on how he'd fought him, how he'd instantly believed Amir because it would have made Vasili everything he'd feared. And it would have meant he didn't have to care for him anymore. Because wasn't that what Niko was afraid of more than anything else, more than this cell, more than elves? He feared loving someone who could never love him back.

"Where is he?" he asked.

"Safe."

"Safe for you or for him?" She blinked, like the answer was obvious. "Don't hurt him, Roksana. You know what he's been through. Please... just... don't hurt him."

"Niko, he's not who you think."

Niko grimaced. Amir had said the same. But they were both wrong. "I know exactly who he is. He's a monster, yes, but not the one you're looking for. All he's ever done is try to stop the elves and protect his people. You even said so yourself. You told me to go back to him. You said Leila would want that."

Her dark eyes were sad, perhaps even understanding. "I told you to go to Loreen because you'd lead us right to him, and Leila was a fool who'd lost her way, the Yazdan way."

Niko slammed his hands into the bars. "I'm ashamed of this wretched name, of you... All of you, if this is what you do with people who need help. All he's ever wanted was to be nobody. He fucking knows he's the last line of defense against the dark, and you... you do *this* to him? Everyone he's ever trusted has turned on him." Oh gods, that was the terrible truth. But he'd admitted to trusting Niko, flung the words at him because he hated that too. He didn't want to trust, didn't want to care, and Niko couldn't blame him when it had always been thrown back in his face. "Just tell me you haven't restrained him?" he asked quietly.

"He is... comfortable."

He obviously wasn't that. "Roksana." He gripped the bars again. "Elves put him in a cage for eight years and bled him, please—by all the gods—please tell me you haven't done the same. Please, just..." Her face fell, and he knew... he knew they were hurting Vasili. Maybe bleeding him. He moaned out the sudden, horrible ache and pushed from the bars. "Gods."

"His blood is a potent source of the flame."

He laughed and didn't care that it sounded thin and strained. He despised her, despised them all, and shot her a look that cut her excuses off. Did nobody have any good in them, did nobody have any honor?

"Niko, he killed your grandfather, my father—"

"We don't know that," Niko snapped. "Amir is just as capable. Amir is more likely to have killed everyone here to spite me." Oh, that was it. Amir would absolutely have killed the Yazdans if he knew Niko was getting close to them. Maybe it hadn't been anything as complicated as the flame eradicating the enemy. Maybe it was just Amir being the vicious, relentless asshole he'd always been but with access to a horrifying power.

He thrust his hands into his hair and paced. He couldn't let this happen. They couldn't hurt Vasili again. "You have to let him go. He's controlling it. He knows what he's doing, but if you restrain him, if you bleed him... he'll lose control. If we lose Vasili, we lose any chance at stopping it."

"Nikolas!" she snapped, whirling him around like a slap to the face. "It will happen eventually anyway, don't you see? Vasili was always going to lose that fight. It's in his blood!"

"But you don't have to damn well force him to surrender to it!"

Backing up, she shook her head, as though Niko was the failed one. "We have him contained. I'm launching a raid on Loreen to secure the king. We'll contain it, as we always have."

"Or set it free."

"It's not your fault, Niko." She turned away and made for the exit.

"Roksana, I trusted you. Vasili trusted you. He does bad things, gods know he's a prick, but deep inside he's not a bad person."

"I know," she replied without stopping, "but it changes nothing. We're doing the right thing, like we've always done. It'll be over soon."

Niko grabbed the can and tossed it through the bars at her, but she was already gone. The can struck the door and bounced back. Damn them all! Niko loosed a roar and kicked at the wall. He couldn't let this happen. It wasn't right. Vasili... Vasili should not have to endure the same torture again but from people he trusted this time.

The elf in the opposite cell was standing now. He peered through the bars, watching Niko pace.

"What are you staring at?"

The elf blinked slowly, then knelt, reached through his bars, and picked up the can. He eyed Niko, as though making sure he watched, and discreetly tucked the can inside his clothes. He smiled, backed away from the bars, and tucked himself against the back of his cell where the shadows were thickest. There the elf stayed, staring back at Niko, mouth displaying a satisfied grin.

CHAPTER 26

Niko didn't fully sleep, but he did dream, and in those waking dreams, a wolf circled the Yazdan house, larger than natural wolves and made from shadows. It circled around and around, looking for a weak point.

Niko snapped open his eyes. Still in the cell.

The elf stared through the bars. He sniffed and snuffled, tasting Niko's scent.

Niko turned away and stared at the ceiling.

It was no mystery why Leila left. Perhaps she'd hoped to find more sense in the Cavilles, only to discover they were equally as twisted. It would explain why she didn't make herself known to her sister when she came looking and why she'd never told Niko any of this. If only she was alive to speak with him, to tell him all the things he didn't know. If only elves hadn't killed her.

The elf tapped the bars with a nail, drawing Niko's eye. He produced a twisted piece of metal from under his shirt and grinned like he'd won a prize.

The creature had fashioned a lockpick from the can.

He raised his chains and set to work gouging the metal pick into the lock. By Etara, he was going to escape. Niko slowly crawled toward his bars, watching the elf work. A few twitches and jerks, and the elf's chains clunked and fell free. "Shit..." Niko mumbled.

The elf set to work on his cell door lock.

By the time Niko had hauled himself to his feet, the door swung open with a creak, and the elf stepped free. He was taller, taller than Niko, heavier too. Niko looked the creature in the eyes and wondered, if it came to it, whether he'd be able to fight him off. Niko had no weapon, but he was safe inside the cell.

The elf stepped up to Niko's cell door and worked his metal pick into the lock.

Well shit...

Niko backed to the rear of his cell, keeping his hands loose at his sides. He'd wrestled many elves, driven their faces into the dirt, pounded bones to splinters, and beaten them into a bloody mess. But none as big as this one.

The cell door clunked and swung open.

Niko readied his stance for attack and cleared his head of everything but what he needed to do to kill.

The elf jerked his chin, then stepped back, out of the cell. He grunted a low noise and gestured at the empty doorway. Niko wasn't falling for that bullshit. The elf sniffed, slid his gaze away, and approached the main door.

What the fuck was this?

Niko approached his open door and leaned out.

The elf was working on the lock for the main door. His back turned.

Niko stepped from the cell. The elf glanced back,

checking his location before concentrating on the lock again. Niko could rush him, wrap an arm around his neck, and choke him from behind.

He flexed his fingers.

But not before the elf got that lock open.

The lock clunked over and the door swung inward.

"Hey!" A guard appeared. The elf grabbed the man, hauled him into a brutal headbutt, and shoved him sprawling into Niko. It was almost too simple a thing to grab the unbalanced man and shove him into the empty cell, then slam the door closed.

"Escape!" the guard barked, dabbing at his cut forehead. "*Guards*!"

A smile lifted Niko's lips, and when he glanced back at the elf, a similar lift of the lips was echoed on his face, then the elf dashed out the door. He was gone when Niko walked free, vanished somewhere inside the Yazdans' sprawling house. A loose elf wasn't Niko's problem, not anymore.

The house was quiet, its corridors almost empty but for a few passing staff. Niko slipped into a few side rooms, avoiding any attention. He made it to Roksana's room, and with no sign of her, he checked various tables and dresser-tops for any clue as to Vasili's whereabouts. They'd surely keep him near the house. Somewhere close. He hadn't explored all of the house but had heard of more rooms hewn into solid rock. There'd be tunnels too. But how to find them without being seen?

Voices rumbled from the closed door. Niko pressed himself against the wall beside the door. Roksana's drawl was instantly recognizable. The other voice was a stranger's.

The door swung open and Roksana strode in. Niko slammed the door behind his aunt, making her whirl. "I don't want to hurt you," he said quickly. "Where is he?"

The shock on her face honed into fury. "Don't be a fool. Even if I told you, you won't leave here alive."

He stalked forward. "Where the fuck is he?"

"You can't save him, Niko." She backed up, hands out, trying to calm him.

"Whatever he is, whatever he's done, you don't fucking restrain him and bleed him like an animal! Even the Cavilles don't go that far."

"They don't have to!" she snapped, the same Yazdan rage burning in her eyes. "They have all the power, Niko. It's in his blood to free that power. It's in ours—in *yours*—to contain it! It's the Yazdan legacy."

Niko was tired of being told who or what he should be. He knew what was right, and this wasn't it. "Fuck legacy."

"You are a Yazdan. That ring proves it."

He pulled off the ring and threw it at her. It bounced off her chest and rolled across the floor. *"Where's Vasili?"*

Her hand casually slipped behind her back. "It doesn't have to be this way."

"No, it doesn't."

She swung a pistol up, but Niko had already launched off his back foot. He grabbed her wrist, twisted her arm hard behind her back, and drove her to her knees. She barked a sharp cry. The pistol clattered to the floor.

"You have no idea what I'm capable of," he pushed the words through his teeth and against her cheek. "Tell me where the fuck you're keeping Vasili, or by the three, I'll break every bone in your body. Don't think I fucking won't, *aunt*."

"I don't know—"

He leaned in, twisting her arm higher up her back, making her gasp. "Wrong answer."

"I don't know! It's the truth. I readied a cell, but Alissand didn't use it. I don't know, Niko. I swear. Alissand took him."

Dammit.

She blinked dark, glistening eyes. "Niko... You could be greater than this. You could be a true Yazdan."

He'd heard enough. After he briefly released her, she mumbled her thanks, adding, "You're a good man, Niko."

He scooped up the pistol. "I'm really not," he said and struck her under the jaw. She flew backward and hit the floor hard. And there she lay. A small shard of guilt tried to wiggle into his resolve, but his snarl soon denied it purchase.

HE MADE it to the docks as the sun began to bathe the city in early morning heat. *Walla's Heart* had her gangplank down, but Niko only needed to climb a few steps to realize the ship had been gutted. Its hold doors lay open, the expensive silks strewn about the deck, rippling in the salty wind. He checked the cabin and below deck, but the ship had been abandoned.

The docks had always been his refuge, and he lingered there now, drifting along the waterfront to the sound of clanging rigging and the workers unloading their ship's cargo. The air smelled of salt and seaweed, like it always had, but its sweetness felt like a joke. He couldn't go back to the house. Didn't have a home or a friend he could turn to. There was only one place left to look.

He stumbled into the open doors of the Whispering Pearl. The early morning hour ensured the taverna was quiet, its only patrons those who had lodged overnight. He almost turned around and left again when a figure seated in the yard outside caught his eye through the window, his wide-rimmed hat unmistakable.

Yasir.

As Niko entered the courtyard, Yasir looked up and beamed, but his smile quickly fell away. He'd shaped his goatee, making his face thinner, or perhaps the last few weeks at sea had thinned him some. He shot from his chair and took Niko's arm.

"They have him," Niko growled.

Yasir steered Niko back out onto the street. "Can't talk here." They threaded through early morning traders setting up their stalls. "Keep moving. We need to get out of sight."

"They have Vasili."

"I suspected as much when they tore through my ship. Luckily, I wasn't aboard or they'd have me too." His lips turned down in a severe grimace. "The Pearl was the only place I thought I might find you."

Relief rolled over Niko. He wasn't alone. He hadn't even realized he'd feared that until now. He gripped Yasir's shoulder. "It's good to see you."

A grin brightened his face. "And you. Navigating Vasili's moods was a nightmare without you. Come, I know someone we can trust."

A maze of narrow back alleys snaked through Seran's tightly packed backstreets. Yasir stopped at the door of a small, narrow flat-roofed redstone house. It was one of many similar houses strewn along the street, each leaning against the other like dominos about to fall.

Yasir's knock had barely rattled the door when it swung open. Yasir smiled nervously at the young man who had answered. "Liam... I—"

Liam reeled off a string of words in Seranian, ending with a vicious slap across Yasir's cheek. But that didn't slow his verbal tirade. He ranted some more, flung a hand at Niko, and stormed back inside the house, leaving the door open.

"Friend of yours?" Niko asked, eyebrow raised.

Yasir rubbed his cheek. "He said to go in."

"That's not all he said." He followed Yasir into the narrow corridor. Liam was the same man Niko had seen arguing with Yasir at the Yazdans' gathering. Clearly, they had some heated history.

"It's fine," Yasir said, seeing Niko's frown. "We're just... I'll explain inside."

The small interior spaces opened into a larger open-air courtyard area, shaded from the sun by the larger building next door. The little rooms and make-do furniture reminded Niko of his own cottage.

By the sounds of clattering coming from a kitchen area, Liam was either finding a knife to stab them both or making tea. He emerged moments later with a tray topped with a steaming silver teapot and quaint little cups. The thunder on his face hadn't eased, especially when he gave Niko a once-over.

Niko winced. "I'm sorry—"

"It's not you," Liam said, dumping the tray on a small table. The cups rattled. "Mint tea. For guests. The proper way to greet friends." Liam shot Yasir a scathing glare.

He'd removed his hat and coat and rolled up his sleeves. He looked more like the silk merchant Niko had first met months ago and less like the captain persona he'd lapsed into in Seran. He also looked like he wanted to crawl inside a hole and stay there.

"Liam, this is Nikolas—"

"I know who he is, precious." Liam tutted and flicked his gaze up to Niko. "He thinks I'm an idiot." Liam poured the tea and clanged the teapot back down. Then with a huff, he sat back in a chair, crossed his legs, and cradled his tea, staring at Yasir as though waiting for... something. Niko assumed that something would be an apology for whatever Yasir had done to clearly piss him off.

"I had to leave quickly," Yasir began. "There wasn't time—"

"You up and vanish, with no word. Again! And then you come here, with this piece of Yazdan meat,"—he flung a hand at Niko again—"no offense."

Niko kept his head down and sipped his tea.

"Then show up at the funeral with a Caville prince, no less! Half the time, I don't know where you are or who you're with, but why should I?"

"It's... difficult." Yasir helped himself to some tea and settled awkwardly in one of the chairs. Niko had never seen him so wooden.

Liam huffed again and rolled his eyes. "It always is with you."

A moment of awkward silence sucked all the heat out of the room. Yasir cleared his throat. "We just need somewhere to stay for a few days, somewhere safe."

"It's fine." Liam's tone had softened some. "Really. It's always fine, you know that. I just... A letter, something?"

Yasir nodded. "I'm sorry. I promise. Next time I'm delayed, I'll send a letter."

Liam's lips thinned. It was clear Yasir hadn't always kept his promises in the past but also that Liam cared deeply for him, deep enough to forgive.

The silence was back, as heavy as ever. Maybe they needed some alone time.

"The tea is lovely," Yasir said, taking a polite sip to emphasize his point. He cleared his throat. "Well, anyway..." He set his cup back on the table and stroked his goatee. "Niko, tell me what happened. Liam won't repeat anything we say. I trust him with my life."

Niko nodded, trusting Yasir's judgment, and told him all of it. How Vasili had appeared and apparently walked straight into a trap. How Alissand had sprung that trap, and now the prince was missing. "Can you perform the spell you did before with the Seran map? Find Vasili that way?" Niko asked.

"I—"

"Spell?" Liam tucked his chin in and raised his brow.

Niko winced. "I'll get some air, let you two..." He promptly left the room for the courtyard, catching only the occasional raised voice from inside.

Leaning against the sunbaked wall, he folded his arms and tilted his face to the sun. Wherever Vasili was, it was unlikely he felt the sun on his skin. Was that why he'd so often tipped his face to enjoy it?

Niko would find him, whatever the cost. This thing between them, slippery as it was, it mattered. His letter had made that clear.

He cared. And by the gods, Niko cared in return, and it had nothing to do with stopping the flame and everything to do with saving Vasili from everyone and every*thing* that had betrayed him.

~

YASIR COLLECTED Niko a while later and brought him into another small room, this one set up with a candle and map already in place. “Liam won’t be joining us.” Yasir waved Niko’s concern away, clearly not wanting to discuss it.

“He has you figured out.” Niko smiled lightly, hoping to alleviate at least some of the tension.

Yasir smiled sheepishly. “He’s kind and good and wonderful and deserves better. Which is why...” He picked up a candle. “Why I tried to distance myself. That clearly didn’t work. Anyway, let’s get this done.”

As before, Yasir dribbled wax onto the map and said the words, but this time with fresh confidence. When he’d performed the spell before, there hadn’t been any certainty it would work, but this time Yasir knew exactly what to do. He’d been with Vasili on the ship for months. More than enough time for the pair to explore what it meant to be a sorcerer. What other spells had they discovered together?

Feeling any kind of jealously was pointless, but like a fool, he felt it anyway. Although, had Niko spent weeks trapped aboard a ship with Vasili, he’d have probably shoved him overboard.

The small pool of wax shimmered on the map, near the dock, and as the cadence of Yasir’s tone changed, a tendril stretched from the pool’s edge and snaked through Seran's streets, but instead of wiggling around bends toward the Yazdan house, it veered into the main arterial streets, quickly racing ahead until it crawled from the map and trickled over the side of the table to the floor.

Yasir's murmurings stopped. "I don't understand. It should have worked. I'll try again." Yasir picked up the candle again.

Niko spread his hands on the table and eyed the waxy trail zigzagging across the map. "We're missing something..." The line taunted him. "Before he was taken, Vasili said the elves weren't here by accident. He mentioned you. Do you know what he meant?"

"We saw them at sea, at least we thought we did. One of the deckhands spotted a flotilla along the coastline. Just a handful of ships. Vasili wanted to get a closer look. We watched them a while..."

He trailed off, and Niko prompted, "Was that unusual?"

"It was more the..." He clutched a fist to his chest. "More a feeling inside." He laughed dismissively. "Sounds like crazy talk, I know, but I felt them watching us, like I sometimes feel Vasili watching. Like there's something bigger and hungrier than us out there."

Niko knew that feeling well.

"Vasili didn't say what he was thinking, but I saw the change in him," Yasir said. "That's when he said to go back to Seran... to you."

"He didn't say to come back to me, though, did he?"

"Well, no. Because the both of you have convinced yourselves you hate each other when it's clear to everyone else the opposite is true."

"I do hate him," Niko grumbled, looking again at the map. "He's a pain in my ass."

"Hm... If only *that* were true." At Niko's glance, Yasir grinned. "You walked right into that one."

He ignored that comment and Yasir's faux innocent expression, tilted his head, and eyed the wax trail from a different angle. "There's nothing personal going on between Vasili and I."

Yasir laughed.

Niko felt a small smile try and tug at his lips but quickly focused on the trail again and finding that royal *pain in the ass*.

If the wax didn't have a direction, why follow the streets? Why not just run off the map? He circled around the desk and knelt where the wax had dribbled from the table. The line continued across the dusty floor, veering in places, and then it disappeared under a door. He tugged open the door and followed the trail down the hallway, through another door, and into the kitchen.

Liam squealed, almost dropping the mixing bowl cradled in the crook of his arm.

The trail stopped abruptly in the middle of the floor.

Yasir stepped into the room behind Niko and stared at where the trail had terminated. "It worked?"

"What *is* that?" Liam grimaced. He grabbed a cloth off to the side and threw it at Yasir. "*You* clean that up. I'm not touching your magical *yudu* shit."

Niko glanced back, along the wax line, and leaned out, visually following it through the hallway and back into the other room, where the trail had begun. The line was almost perfectly straight. "It worked."

"So where's that supposed to be?"

"North. Look..." Niko returned to the previous room and showed Yasir the compass mark in the corner of the map. The wax had tracked northward.

"Loreen?" Yasir asked.

Alissand is taking him home. "If we take the horses, we can track them down." The Yazdans would have a cart or carriage, something secure to keep Vasili restrained. That would make their progress slow. Adamo was ten times as fast.

Niko made for the door.

"Horses? Niko... Wait!"

Niko turned to find Yasir grabbing his coat and hat while Liam stood back, his expression breaking into concern. "You should stay," Niko said.

It was Liam who shook his head. "Don't worry, Nikolas. I've tried to keep him here in the past. He's not made that way. Nothing will keep the fool from seeing whatever this is through to the end. Just damn well make sure he comes back to me?"

Yasir whirled and scooped Liam into his arms, planting a passionate kiss on his lips. "Don't wait for me." Yasir grinned, almost earning himself a second slap. Instead, Liam smudged baking flour across Yasir's cheek and shoved him off.

"I always do. Go. But you'd better write me, you *jendeh*."

Yasir winked, donned his hat, and scooped up his cloak. "Let's go rescue a prince."

CHAPTER 27

Adamo trotted over to the stable, snorting derisively at Niko, clearly not impressed with being abandoned at a stranger's yard.

Niko threw a saddle on him, while Yasir did the same with the smaller chestnut Niko had ridden to Seran months ago.

Niko swiftly mounted Adamo and gathered the reins, keeping the flighty charger under control. The animal already felt like it was ready to gallop off the edge of the map.

Trotting out of the stables into the dusty, heat-scorched field gave them a panoramic view of the city's bay and Seran's glistening harbor. The city looked like paradise, and it was a wrench to leave it now. They'd be back, but with Vasili.

"Some hard riding and we'll catch them. They can't have gotten too far with a wagon."

Yasir adjusted himself in the saddle. The supply packs

hung equally on either side. They'd tried to load them onto Adamo. He'd refused in a haughty fit. Yasir shielded his eyes and scanned the distant bay. "I'm going to miss home."

"Home or Liam?"

The captain blushed. "Both."

Niko turned Adamo toward the field gate. "We'll be back."

"Wait... Niko, look." Yasir stood in his stirrups and stared down at the bay in the distance. "Those ships?"

Niko scanned the view again, gaze lingering on the tightly formed group of ships approaching the docks. Eight, all with irregularly shaped dark sails. What was it Yasir had said, something about seeing a flotilla?

The city bells chimed, the alarm spreading on the wind.

"Oh gods... elves! Those are the ships we saw."

A boom sounded, and the horses shied. Adamo threw his head, twitching to break free. Black smoke rose from the harbor, staining the blue sky.

"Liam..." Yasir breathed. "I have to get down there!"

"Go." Niko scooped one of the traveling packs from Yasir's horse and hooked it onto his saddle. "Go get your man." Niko couldn't fight the elves, not this time. Vasili's safety was too important.

Yasir held his gaze, and there was something raw in that stare. Fear, for himself, for Liam, and for the city he loved, his home. Niko ached to go with him, to defend against the elves, but this fight wasn't his. "I have to find Vasili."

"I should go with you." Yasir looked at the city again, his heart in a small house in the backstreets of Seran.

"Get Liam to safety, then come."

A second boom sounded. More black smoke billowed from the dockside. Niko offered his hand, and Yasir grasped his wrist, gripping fiercely.

"Find Vasili, Niko. Make those bastards pay."

Niko gripped back, swallowing the emotional knot caught in his throat. "Get your man somewhere safe, and I'll see you soon, friend."

Yasir nodded, let go, and dug his heels into his horse's flank, bolting out of the gate and out of sight.

The dark ships spread like shadows through the turquoise waters of Seran's harbor. Seran would not be an easy target. The soldiering part of him wished he was galloping down there with Yasir. But his battle was elsewhere.

He patted Adamo on the neck. "Now, let's go get *our* man." He angled Adamo toward the gate and kicked the horse into motion, leaving the thundering sounds of attack far behind.

ADAMO DIDN'T WAVER. They rode through the days and into the nights, stopping only for water. Jungle turned to desert and then back to the wetter, colder climate of the north. There was only one road north suitable for wheeled wagons. The same road Yasir had navigated south along. Eventually, Niko must come upon Alissand's caravan.

He'd traveled in three days what Yasir and his wagon had traveled in weeks. But not without a cost. Saddle sore to the bone, Niko dismounted Adamo beside a creek and let the horse drink. He took some rice cakes from the pack and tucked himself against the roots of a large tree. Moonlight bathed the burbling creek in milky light. Moths fluttered in the still air. He watched them dance, knowing he couldn't stop for long, but also that he needed to rest, or he'd be useless when he eventually did catch up with Alissand.

Seran was either lost or saved by now. The city had staved off an elf attack before but only under the Yazdans' leadership. The elves had successfully managed to weaken the family. The initial attack had been a strategic one, clearing the way for a larger force.

But Niko wasn't there, and there was more at stake than the southern city. All cities would fall if Vasili wasn't found soon.

He wondered if Mah would approve of his actions, if Pah had ever known about any of this. He wondered about the lord he'd never known—the man who was his real father—and if that man had ever thought of his bastard son. Did he still? Assuming he and Lady Bucland were still alive. He wondered about a lot of things while resting beneath the tree by the creek, but mostly he wondered how long it would be before Vasili's resolve broke and he surrendered to the curse in his blood.

Adamo whinnied softly at the creek's edge, his ears going flat.

Niko stilled and quickly reached for his blade.

An owl hooted somewhere far off. The creek continued its burbling. All was quiet.

Adamo splashed backward through the water. The horse's nostrils flared, its sights fixed on something behind the tree Niko leaned against. Niko heard it then: deep, heavy breathing.

He slowly pulled his sword closer to his leg, tightening his hold. The blade hadn't done a damn thing to the creature before, but without any salt, it was the only protection he had.

A huge, hulking mass of wolf-like muscle and shadowy wisps stalked around the tree. Claws glinted beneath the moonlight. It lifted its maw and sniffed at the air. Red eyes focused on Adamo. The horse backed up again, stamping its hooves against slippery pebbles.

Unnoticed in the roots of the tree, Niko held his breath.

He couldn't fight this creature, and running would surely trigger it to chase.

The beast stalked toward Adamo, so close now that Niko smelled its cool, damp odor, like still air in forgotten places. He exhaled slowly.

The beast swung its head and locked Niko in its glowing glare. Its lip rippled, revealing curved teeth meant for tearing flesh from bone.

Niko stared, falling into the vastness of its gaze, seeing more than shadows, seeing life and intelligence, seeing something deep and dark and hungry. Something not of this world but not rabid.

The beast's snarl settled. It sniffed at the air, then lowered its head and ventured closer.

Maybe if Niko could bolt and mount Adamo before the creature tore into him, he'd be able to gallop free, but in the dark, through the trees, it was unlikely.

The beast's gaze slid to where Niko had hold of the sword. Its snarl bubbled at its lips again like it recognized the sword as a threat.

Niko slowly withdrew his hand—the sword was useless

anyway—and the beast's snarling faded. He pulled his hand all the way back, deliberately resting it in sight on his thigh.

Every instinct demanded he flee. The beast would smell fear. But if it were going to attack, wouldn't it have done so already?

It ventured closer still, fur coat leaving smoky trails, and then sniffed at Niko's knee, its red eyes watching his.

Niko willed his heart to slow.

This creature, it wasn't here to hurt him.

Satisfied Niko wasn't a threat, the beast lowered itself to its belly beside Niko's leg and planted its massive head between its front paws. Then, this *thing* made of smoke and shadow huffed something that sounded remarkably like a sigh.

The creature's heavy breaths slowed. By Etara, was it... *sleeping?*

Niko released his stalled breath.

The beast opened its eyes, fixing Niko beneath its penetrative stare again, and perhaps it was Niko's own imagination or wishful thinking, or maybe he was exhausted from traveling, but he was sure recognition sparked in those eyes. Then its eyes closed again and the beast *dozed*.

Niko glanced at Adamo. The horse drank from the creek, alert ears flicking, but he appeared content enough to let the beast be. That seemed like good advice. Niko rested his head back against the tree and waited for dawn.

Bright morning sunlight chased away the shadows and his company.

The next time Niko stopped to rest, he looked for the beast's eyes in the dark, but no beast arrived. It was another six days before he spotted fresh carriage tracks in the mud and another night before he caught sight of a distant flickering light. A campfire. Yasir had been right, firelight was visible for miles, and Niko had found his target.

After leaving Adamo loosely tied to a tree stump, Niko crept closer to the camp and crouched behind a boulder. Firelight illuminated at least eight figures seated around the camp. The same shifting light danced along the glossy black paint of a large carriage. No windows. The black-and-gold flame insignia marked its barred doors. The mark had never looked more insidious.

Yazdans.

Vasili was inside that carriage.

Acidic anger burned his tongue and blurred his vision. He bowed his head and squeezed his eyes closed. He needed to think clearly for this. Charging in, swinging a sword, would get him cut down in seconds. Outnumbered, he had to go about this differently. What would Vasili do? Poison them all, probably. Cut their throats as they slept. But Niko wasn't Vasili.

They'd have to sleep. They'd leave one or two men on watch. That would be the time to get a closer look at the carriage.

Niko settled in to watch them. The chill crept up on him as their fire burned lower. One by one, each of the men took to their bedrolls. Two guards stayed awake, sitting together outside the reach of the firelight, to keep their night vision. The carriage horses had been tied to one side to rest and feed. They dosed. The camp settled until just the guards' soft murmurings interrupted the quiet. They weren't looking at the carriage.

Niko rose from his crouch and crept around the outside of the camp until the carriage was between him and the guards. Soft earth muffled the sound of his approach. The carriage was bigger than he'd realized, more stagecoach than wagon. He quietly tried the handle, felt it click, and carefully swung open the door. The darkness hit him first, then the bitter scent of spilled blood. Grey smudges blurred and combined, slowly forming a recognizable shape.

Niko's breath caught.

Vasili. Bare-chested. On his back. Arms spread and tied to either carriage side with long lengths of rope, a bloody rag rammed between his bruised lips. He didn't look like Vasili. A part of Niko's mind tried to tell him this prisoner wasn't him. He couldn't be Niko's Vasili because this man was too broken, too bloody and bruised, and Vasili was always so strong and perfect. But then, as his eyes further adjusted to the dark, fresh, uniform cuts on Vasili's forearms caught his eye. Blood. The sheets he lay on were dark with it. Dried rivulets ran down Vasili's arms and chest, as dark as the veins it had spilled from.

Niko's mind ticked. Emotionless ice quenched his scorching rage.

He'd kill them all for this.

He reached for the ropes tying Vasili's left wrist. The frayed hemp rope had torn into his skin. Vasili had fought. At first.

Niko dug thick fingers into the knots, but blood had

glued them rigid. He freed his sword and slammed it down on the taut rope. Vasili's arm fell limp, his body limp too. Fresh blood dripped from his fingers.

Niko brought his sword up to slice through the second rope when a gun barked and light flashed. A bite of sudden heat tore into his thigh, buckling his leg under him. With a roar, Niko swung for the figure in the carriage doorway. A wall of smoky ice swamped him, poured between his teeth and down his throat, instantly choking off his air.

He gagged, stumbled, reached into the great mass of dark that flooded his vision for something to fight, but his fingers sailed through. Panic slammed his heart against his ribs. Hands gripped him, hauled him from the carriage, and flung him choking facedown in the dirt. He gasped around the choking invasion. A kick to the gut rolled him onto his side. He spluttered, wheezing, and then the suffocating mass withdrew, leaving him gasping into blurred firelight.

Alissand's rich voice rumbled, "Leila's son."

Niko blinked up at his uncle. Darkness swam in the older man's eyes. Did the flame possess him, or did he possess it? "This would have been so much easier if you'd just taken the flame like the Yazdan you were supposed to be."

Words wouldn't have come even if he'd had any. The touch of icy darkness had scorched his throat. It was temporary. He'd felt it before with the fiends, but right now, he needed to breathe, needed to fight. Gasping, he reached for his Yazdan blade, fallen a few feet out of reach beside him, and managed to slip his fingers around its handle.

Alissand pressed his boot onto the blade, pinning the sword and Niko's hand into the ground.

His uncle peered closer, as though searching for Niko's soul through his eyes. "You'd have made a fine sorcerer."

"*Fuck...you*," Niko wheezed.

Alissand laughed and straightened. "It's time you became one of us." He nodded at his guards. They swooped in, scooping Niko off the ground. His back hit the carriage. Hands pinned him there. Fingers pinched his nose and dug into his cheeks, forcing his jaw apart. He bucked, tried to kick, tried to focus, to *breathe*, but the assault was too fast, too strong.

A cool, thick, bitter liquid poured over his tongue. Not spice. He knew that much.

His lungs burned, chest heaving. He couldn't hold out.

Not spice... Blood.

The second he let it in, it would poison him. He'd never be free of it.

"Take it!" Alissand's fingers dug harder into Niko's cheeks. "Consume it, let it become you. Become who you're meant to be!"

His heart pounded in his ears, his body a riot of heat and pain. If he passed out, they'd pour it down his throat.

He knew now why Leila had left. He knew why Vasili hadn't tried to poison him when he'd had every opportunity. He knew what had happened over seven hundred years ago. The Cavilles bore the flame in their blood, but the Yazdans *used* it. The sorcerers who stood beside the Caville royals weren't slaves—they were masters. Cavilles were their victims. Just as Vasili had said.

His body and soul screamed for him to breathe, to drink. *To surrender.*

Never.

A surge of fury ignited his veins. He tore free of his uncle's grip and spat the blood into the bastard's face, hoping to momentarily blind him. A vicious backhanded blow rattled Niko's skull and flushed the world black for a few heartbeats. Only the guards holding him kept him upright.

Head throbbing and blood in his mouth, he glared at his uncle. "I will... never... be like... you."

Alissand wiped the blood from his cheek with his sleeve. "Kill him."

A punch landed in Niko's gut, buckling him over and stealing what remained of the air in his lungs. The world spun, the firelight suddenly too bright. He crumpled to his knees and dug his fingers into the dirt. It couldn't end like this... but he had nothing to fight with. No weapons, his body clinging to consciousness. He'd come this far, Vasili was so close, but he hadn't been able to free him.

Someone laughed. Alissand maybe. Gods, when would this world stop punishing him?

A heavy blow burrowed into his ribs. He coughed blood and rolled onto his side. A great beast made of dark flame and seething red eyes walked through the firelight. Niko blinked. He'd conjured the beast from his dreams, surely.

But then the screams began. Gunfire flashed across the camp, lighting up the gruesome evidence of the beast being real.

Niko buried his face into the dirt and heaved his hands under himself. He swayed on his hands, listening to swords clashing, pistol shots, and smelling blood and spilled bowels in the air.

Head spinning, Niko groped for his sword. He stumbled to his feet, sure a blade would run him through or a pistol shot would tear out the back of his skull. Grabbing the carriage handle, he swung himself inside. Vasili still lay there. Unmoving. He couldn't carry him out of there—he could barely carry himself.

Think... think Niko...

Gods, he just wanted to lay down beside him and let the world have them both. But Vasili wouldn't give up. He never had. Even now, wherever he was inside his head, he fought.

He had to get him away—just away, anywhere.

Adamo...

Niko whistled for the horse and stumbled out of the carriage. The beast's furious growls and snarls painted a picture of the bloody carnage nearby. He didn't look, didn't want to see or alert the creature to his presence.

He staggered to the front of the carriage and whistled again.

Come on Adamo...

Unconsciousness tried to steal him away again. He shook it free.

Adamo thundered from the night. Niko grabbed his reins, almost falling into the horse. Unsure of the carriage's straps and bindings, he did his best to tie Adamo to the gear and hoped it would be enough. "Sorry, boy... but you're all we've got." He clambered into the seat, took up the reins, and snapped them in the air.

Adamo dug his hooves in and heaved the carriage into motion, gathering speed the more Niko snapped the reins.

Go, Adamo... and don't stop, not for anything.

Howls and gunfire filled the night behind them, but as

Adamo galloped hard through the darkness, the noises faded under the beat of his hooves.

"*Faster, boy*," Niko begged. "Faster."

The carriage shuddered and rattled, and the night pushed in, but Adamo galloped fast and true, leaving the chaos behind.

CHAPTER 28

Adamo went to his knees as dawn broke across an unfamiliar valley framed by the beginnings of a vast mountain range. The overgrown road had snaked into a gulley and came to an abrupt end among huge ferns. It had probably been an old mining route once but had long since been forgotten. The carriage wheels dug in and lurched to a halt.

Niko stumbled from the seat. Fire shot up his wounded thigh, seizing it rigid. Heat thumped through his leg. He'd deal with it later. Limping, he climbed into the carriage and finally cut the last rope holding Vasili's left wrist. The prince was free, but he hadn't woken.

"Vasili?" Niko touched his face, smearing dirt across his cool cheek. "Vasili." His open wounds—pink slices in his pale skin—wept blood.

So much blood... So many wounds.

Niko swept his hair back from his face. Cool sweat glistened on Vasili's forehead and neck. His lips were blue, his skin grey.

Niko said his name again, maybe hadn't stopped saying it.

The cuts on his chest gaped and oozed, like countless hungry, pink mouths.

The hard knot in Niko's throat threatened to break free as a sob. He swallowed it, dug his hands under the prince's limp body, and scooped him against his chest. "Hate me for touching you later."

He staggered from the carriage, almost dropping them both. Gods, he didn't even know where to go with him or what to do. The landscape was strange, overgrown, and surreal, with enormous trees and rocky outcrops, valleys and peaks. The road had delivered them nowhere.

Yasir would have known where to go.

But Yasir wasn't here.

Niko staggered into the ferns with no direction. Anywhere was better than that bloody carriage.

The gentle burble of a creek lured him forward until the ferns finally gave way to a riverbank, the river's flow down to a trickle. Niko lay Vasili down on a soft area of thick moss at the river's edge. Dappled sunlight danced over the fresh wreckage of his chest and arms. He looked worse in daylight, like a corpse left by elves to rot in the sun. Was he breathing? If he was, it was too light to see.

Bloody fingers trembling, Niko reached out and touched the prince's neck for a pulse. There, a delicate flutter.

His sob finally broke free. He slumped against a nearby tree, clutching his hot, throbbing leg with one filthy hand. He'd need to bandage himself up, but what was the point if Vasili died here? It was too much. Everything was too much. He dragged his free hand down his face, trying to wipe off despair.

The prince was dying beside him, and he had no idea how to save him.

He should have done things differently.

Should have sent Vasili away from the Yazdan house instead of indulging in his foolish desires. Alissand wouldn't have captured him and they wouldn't be here now. Maybe if he'd never gone to Seran, Vasili would have succeeded alone. He was too clever to be caught by the Yazdans. But Niko hadn't known the truth, not all of it. History had lied. The Yazdans—blood drinkers, sorcerers—they'd never been good.

He checked Vasili's heart rate again, this time at his thin wrist, and listened to it patter. Faint but steady.

The next few hours were a numb blur. He found a blade in the carriage—probably the one used to cut Vasili's veins—and dug the pistol shot out of his own thigh, then wrapped the wound and set to work on a fire to boil the water he'd need to wash Vasili's wounds.

With every gentle stroke of a damp cloth, Vasili bled anew, like his body knew only how to give up its blood, not keep it. Niko meticulously cleaned each deep slice on his arms and chest. His breaths were shallow, like the next might be his last. Wherever he was inside his own head, Niko hoped he found peace there. He wouldn't blame him if he chose never to come back.

With Vasili's wounds cleaned and wrapped with strips of mostly clean cloth torn from the carriage fabric, Niko fed the fire and occupied his mind with building a shelter.

The prince didn't wake.

Adamo didn't fare much better. The horse had stumbled to the creek bank and rested at its edge, head drooped.

As night fell, Niko wondered about Seran and about Loreen, about Amir and Julian. He'd failed in all of it, hadn't he? He was just a man, tossed about like a ship in the storm of a past he didn't understand. He'd tried to do the right thing, but it wasn't enough. In every direction he looked, enemies lurked in the shadows. Was this how Vasili felt every waking moment?

Rain started in the night. The shelter kept much of it off Vasili, and the fire provided warmth. Niko wedged himself against the tree out of the rain and listened to the thick droplets fall from fat leaves. There had been nights like these he'd waited and listened for the sounds of elves stalking him and his men. That man in his memory didn't seem like the man he was now. He'd been full of fire and rage and the knowledge that he fought for what was right, for a cause worth fighting for.

Now it felt as though whatever he did, the cause was already lost.

VASILI'S THRASHING tore Niko from a dream. Shudders wracked the prince's body, locking his muscles and arching him off the ground.

"Shit." Niko gripped Vasili's arms, pinning him down, but it did little to ease the relentless assault running through Vasili's muscles and bones. The prince threw his head back, mouth thrown open in a silent scream. Niko's vision blurred. This wasn't fucking fair. "Etara, leave him be!"

Vasili fell limp, open eye rolling, infected by the dark. Niko clutched him tightly to his chest, forgetting the wounds and the orders not to touch. He cupped the back of his head, holding him through the aftershocks. "Come back, you stubborn prick."

He deserved to be free. Maybe he was the only one in all of this who did.

When Niko next woke, he reached for Vasili on the moss-bed, but his hand fell through the air.

"Vasili?"

He was gone.

Niko shot to his feet, grabbed his sword, and staggered down the creek-side. "Vasili?" It was still early. Dew coated the grass and a soft mist hung over the creek bed. He couldn't have gotten far.

Niko rounded a small bend and saw him then, crouched near the water's edge, hands out to balance himself as he stared back at Niko. His blue eye shone wide with raw fear. He bared a snarl, like a wild animal caught unawares.

"It's me." Niko gently lay the sword down. "Just me."

His gaze darted, chest heaving.

Niko stretched out a hand. "You're safe."

He bolted.

Niko launched forward, chasing the ripple of knotted white hair up the bank and into the trees. "Wait... Vasili. Gods, wait!" If he lost him in the trees, he might never find him again. He wasn't thinking right. He was terrified. If Niko didn't get to him, something else might.

Vasili fell, scrabbled forward, and was up again, thrashing through the ferns. Niko grabbed his hair—hating that he had to do this—and yanked. Vasili whirled, swinging an open-handed attack that would probably have knocked Niko on his ass if he hadn't snagged the prince's wrist and used his momentum to slam him into a tree instead.

Vasili writhed and hissed under Niko's hands, bucked and thrashed.

"Stop!" Niko pushed in harder, plastering himself against the prince. *"Vasili, stop."*

Vasili pushed, trying to lever him off, but Niko leaned all his weight in. The prince's eye flashed, but it was still blue, not black. He was still in there, just so fucking afraid he couldn't see how Niko was trying to help him. "Vasili, it's Nikolas. I won't hurt you."

The prince closed his eye. His mouth twisted, turning downward. Slowly, his hard tremors faded, then all the fight drained out of him. He slumped, dropped his head back against the tree's trunk, and panted through his clenched teeth.

"You're all right. I have you. It's just you and me. No one else. We're alone, you hear? We're safe." He pressed his cheek to Vasili's. "We're safe..." he whispered again.

A shudder ran through him, and a harrowing moan pealed from his lips, ending in a sob that made Niko want to fold him into his arms and keep him there.

"I've got you. All right? I've got you. You're safe." He told him all the things he surely needed to hear. "It's over."

The prince's trembling fingers clutched at the back of Niko's shirt. Vasili pulled him close and bowed his head, burying his face against Niko's neck, and sobbed. And by the three, it hurt to hear.

"I've got you." He said it over and over, as many times as Vasili needed to hear it. He'd say it a thousand times more if he could. He said it as the prince collapsed and Niko had to lift him into his arms again, and he said it as he lay him back down in their tiny shelter. It would take more than words for him to heal, but for now, words were all Niko had.

CHAPTER 29

Niko gathered thread from the carriage blankets to make a fishing line, keeping another for warmth. The rest of the blankets he burned, sending black smoke into the blue sky above the tree canopy.

He harvested a few more useful tools from the carriage, made a lure, and took a chance at fishing one of the deeper pools. He didn't want to walk too far from the camp, but at the same time, they needed food. A few hours in, he caught a trout, but the true success was returning to find Vasili sitting up at the fireside, a blanket wrapped around his shoulders. He was awake, and he hadn't run.

Vasili didn't speak as Niko prepared the fish to roast. He didn't look up, just stared into the fire. His silence was his way. Niko had no intention of forcing him to speak.

They ate the fish in silence.

Vasili's strength came back quickly during the next few

days, with more fish and roasted squirrel in his belly. Alissand probably starved him to keep him weak. If he were fed at all, it would have only been enough to keep his body from shutting down.

Niko steered his thoughts from that dangerous territory. Imagining all the horrors that had taken place inside the carriage was bad enough, and he hadn't lived through them.

On the fourth day, Niko put a burning torch in Vasili's hand and told him to follow him back through the trees.

The carriage had lost its shine since their gallop through the desert. Covered in dust and leaves and stripped of anything useful, there was only one final thing to do.

Vasili had the blanket hitched around his shoulders and the flaming torch in his right hand. He looked at the carriage, his face pained.

Niko backed off but stayed nearby. This was for Vasili.

The prince didn't wait long before tossing the torch through the carriage door. Flames quickly took hold, reaching high. The carriage snarled and crackled, coming undone inside the fire, and Vasili watched it burn until there was little more left than a pile of ash scattered with metal fixings. Then he dropped to his knees.

Niko rooted himself to the ground, fighting the urge to go to him. He needed this. But it was more than that. The symbol on the door, the dark flame on gold, it was the Yazdan symbol. Niko's family.

He didn't think he could hate a family more than the Cavilles. He'd been wrong. And Vasili must have seen the Yazdans in Niko every time he looked at him. Did he hate him now too?

More days went by. Now that Niko's thigh wasn't prone to cramping, using the small axe he'd scrounged from the carriage, he cut down some smaller trees and extended the shelter, turning it into a hut, with four solid walls and a roof.

Vasili still didn't speak.

Each day, he took himself down to the creek where Niko knew there to be a wide, slow-moving pool, and came back with wet hair. Vasili always went alone. He needed it. The fresh scars over the old would haunt him for a long time.

Niko hammered a log into place along one of the hut's walls, replacing a rotten one, when he spotted Vasili walking up the creek. He'd hacked off his hair to jaw-length.

Niko swung his hammer, missed the log, and struck his thumb. "Fuck!"

Vasili spooked, freezing still, ready to bolt.

Niko emerged from the hut, shaking the pain from his hand. "I like it," he said, hoping to relax him. "Your hair, I mean."

Vasili's mouth tilted into a lopsided smile. In the sunlight, he looked better than he had in days. Cheeks warmer. His stride more confident. More like his old self but still jittery, like cracked glass. Niko's heart ached every time Vasili winced, or when the prince lost himself staring into the fire and the memories hidden there.

He couldn't bring himself to suggest they leave. Vasili wasn't ready. He might never be ready. But a few more days rest would do him good.

Niko fixed up the hut, fished, foraged—all things he'd done on the front line, and Vasili watched and healed.

Returning from foraging late in the afternoon, he veered from his usual path to stop at the river to drink, but as he approached the river's edge, he'd forgotten to avoid the deep pool Vasili had claimed as his and found the prince shoulder-deep in the water, his hands running through his hair, washing it clean.

A twig snapped under Niko's boot, and Vasili jolted, twisting to land his fearful gaze on Niko.

"I, er..." Niko ducked his head. "I didn't mean to interrupt."

"Wait," the prince croaked.

Hearing him speak after so long jolted Niko to a stop. The one word had been deep and rough, like he'd pulled it from its hidden place.

The frown that made his face complicated came with a whole lot of hurt that he either didn't want to hide or he'd forgotten how to. "I don't..." He cleared his throat. "Will you stay?"

Niko set his bag of foraged food down. Vasili still stood in the pool like he was lost. He worried his bottom lip between his teeth, and Niko's heart lurched. To Etara's hell with it all... He tore off his shirt, kicked off his boots, and stepped up to the pool's edge. Vasili's wary gaze held him there. He looked like he might bolt again, and now Niko was stuck between trying to ease his mind and wanting to just go back to their hut and leave him be.

Vasili dipped his chin, which seemed like an acknowledgment, and Niko slowly waded into the water. He wobbled over some of the more slippery stones and caught

Vasili's tiny smiles. If he could make him smile again, really smile, then getting wet would be worth it.

Then Niko was chest-deep in the pool and facing Vasili. Water lapped around Vasili's pale shoulders. He stared at Niko, so raw and open, utterly unarmed. Gods, he looked young.

Niko raised his hands, lifting them out of the water so Vasili could see them. The prince frowned.

"Trust me?"

Vasili sucked on his bottom lip again and nodded. And if this was what Vasili was like when Julian had found him, then fuck that bastard for taking advantage of him. Blood or no, nobody had the right to hurt a man so thoroughly broken.

"Turn around," Niko said, nodding encouragement when Vasili's gaze flicked to his.

The prince slowly turned but quickly glanced over his shoulder, checking Niko's location.

"I'm just going to touch your shoulders. Do you want that?"

A short nod came a second later, and Niko brushed his rough hands together to warm them. His skin was rough from working, but right now, he figured Vasili could do with some feeling. Slowly, he settled his hands gently on the prince's shoulders. Vasili let out a short sigh, as though he'd been holding his breath. Niko gently rubbed his thumbs against Vasili's neck, massaging in light circles. The scars were fewer on his back, which was why Niko had asked him to turn. This wouldn't have been possible anywhere on his chest or arms, where most of the damage lay.

"How's that? Good?"

A low groan sounded through the prince, which Niko took to mean he liked it. He circled his thumbs lower, spreading warm fingers across Vasili's smooth shoulder blades, and then ventured lower, molding his touch to the prince's narrow waist. "This is all it is. Nothing more." Niko could do nothing to stop the deepening of his voice from giving the truth away. This meant everything but had nothing to do with how fucking hard his cock was—that was easily ignored. This wasn't about sex. Far from it. Vasili needed an anchor. He needed someone, anyone, so he could find his way back again.

He needed to know he wasn't alone.

And when had anyone just held his hand? When had anyone just touched him to offer comfort with no strings attached? Since Alek? All those fucking years ago. Since then, all anyone had ever done was cut pieces off him.

Niko worked his hands, kneading Vasili's lower back muscles, avoiding his ass, because Niko was only so strong, and if he started kneading him there, he'd probably spill his load and embarrass himself.

"Good?"

Vasili didn't reply, not with words, but he did lean back, trusting Niko to hold him. Niko stopped his hands, resting them gently on either side of Vasili's waist, and when the prince rested back against his chest, skin to skin, he lowered his head and brushed his chin against Vasili's shoulder. "This means no more or less than it appears to," he said, repeating Vasili words back to him, reminding him who he was and who he would be again.

They'd stayed like that a while, listening to the water burble and Vasili breathing, but it couldn't go on forever.

"I'll go stoke the fire." Niko withdrew then and waded from the pool. Vasili was watching when he turned, and he smiled the most true and honest smile he'd ever seen on him.

Back at the hut, Niko kept the fire blazing and put the finishing touches on a new extension he'd been building. It couldn't really be called a hut anymore. More a cabin, with two cot beds lifted off the ground on stakes, plus a stone-backed fireplace.

When Vasili returned, the prince arched an eyebrow at Niko waiting by the door. "It's no Caville palace, but..." He opened the door and let Vasili venture inside. "It'll keep us warm and dry if the weather turns."

Niko ducked through the doorway behind him and stood inside the smoky warmth. The fire crackled, water bubbling in the cans they'd salvaged. It wasn't his cottage, but it was a pretty damn fine shelter for however long Vasili needed it to be. Niko was damned proud of it.

Vasili stumbled and reached for the wall.

Niko swept in but received a scathing look, more like Vasili's princely glares he'd gotten from the icy Caville prince than those he'd seen earlier in the pool. He lifted his hands and backed off.

Vasili doubled over, arms crossed over his middle. He groaned, went to his knees, and when he looked up, the dark swam in his eye, trying to devour him from the inside out.

It hadn't shown itself in weeks, not since the seizure.

"Vasili..." Niko knelt in front of him, not touching, but close enough that Vasili would feel his next words. "You're not alone."

Vasili squeezed his eye closed and fought, like he

always fought. Even when there was so little strength left of him, he fought, because it was the only choice he had. Fight or surrender.

His hand shot out and grabbed Niko's. His fingers squeezed. Niko squeezed back. There was nobody in this world who fought like Vasili. Niko watched him fight with that thing inside of him, squeezing his hand, and gods, he was so fucking brave. Braver than Niko. Braver than all those in the past who had succumbed to the flame. Braver than the cowardly Yazdans who'd long ago given in to its siren call.

There was no use denying it. No use lying to himself.

"Stay with me," Niko said.

Vasili's hand gripped his tighter. A sign, an acknowledgment, or just holding on because it was all he had left. He fell limp, and Niko folded him close, listening to his soft breathing until the fire burned low.

NIKO LEFT the cabin to check on Adamo. The horse had taken to wandering through the forest, grazing on anything he could find before returning at night. Niko regularly checked up on him. When Niko returned to the cabin, a fresh pile of logs had been stacked outside the cabin, and a fire roared inside, freshly stoked and fed.

Vasili sat on the floor by the fireplace, his messy hair scruffy about his face. Firelight caught in his eye, making it sparkle like a jewel. He poked absently at the base of the flames, sending sparks rising.

"We can't stay," he said.

It had been so long since Niko had heard him speak,

he'd almost forgotten how luscious he could sound. His velveteen purr was deeper than before and scratchy in places, but all Vasili Caville.

"I know." Niko sat beside him as he'd done every night for what felt like forever now.

So this was it then.

There was a visible change in Vasili. He sat upright, his speech, his glance. It was all stronger and full of confidence. Did that mean their stay in the wilderness was over?

The sword he'd stolen rested by the door, like it had in his cottage. Much of the cabin reminded him of home, but having company was new. He'd liked it—not being alone. Being with Vasili. He'd liked it a lot.

"It's tempting." Vasili tossed the stick into the fire.

He didn't need to reply. Only a fool would miss how Niko had fallen into this life like it had always been waiting for him. And Vasili had fallen into it too. The thought of leaving it made him ache. The world outside had never held much appeal. The only thing that truly mattered in Niko's life was the man beside him now.

Gods, he didn't want this to end. Vasili must have seen it on his face because his own expression turned thoughtful. "This life wasn't meant for people like us."

But it could be. He was surprised to taste anger on his tongue after the past few weeks of living in peace with himself. Why couldn't they make this their life?

Vasili shifted onto his knees and held Niko's gaze. Maybe he wanted Niko to tell him to stay, to argue for this life, but what use was it? He knew Vasili was right. They could not stay.

Niko sighed. "This is the only time in my whole life I've felt as though I'm doing something right."

"Building a hut in a forest on the edge of nowhere?"

"No." He laughed softly at the absurdity of *that* but quickly fell serious again under Vasili's gaze. "Building a life... with you."

Vasili's brow pinched into a frown. He leaned forward, braced himself on an arm, and caught Niko's clenched jaw, holding him firm. Vasili's fingertips were light, but the intent was not. He drew Niko close. His mouth skimmed Niko's, and the promise of more simmered between them. If Niko did this, if he surrendered to him, here and now, he'd never get his heart back. He might have already given it away, out here in the wilds.

"Don't," Niko whispered. "My heart can't take another break."

Vasili's mouth smothered Niko's, tearing down the bars around his heart, and Niko surrendered to everything Vasili freely gave. He tasted that same bitter sweetness on Vasili's lips as he had in a farmhouse field so long ago, but this time there was no hate fueling their passion. This kiss was true, it was real, and by the three, it hurt, because they couldn't ever have the life they both so desperately needed.

Not tomorrow, not anymore, now Vasili was well again, but maybe they could tonight? Just tonight?

The kiss ended softly. Niko already mourned its loss.

"Did you come for me or the flame?" Vasili asked.

At the blazing palace, months ago, he'd raced into the fire to stop the flame from being freed. If Vasili hadn't been cursed with the flame, Niko might not have saved him from the flames. But now?

Niko touched Vasili's cheek and ran his fingers down his stubbly whiskers. "For you."

Vasili pushed lightly on Niko's chest, urging him to lay back. Vasili straddled Niko's hips and braced over him, until they were eye-to-eye. Delight had the prince smiling. He seemed freer in that moment, poised above Niko, playfully pinning him down. He wouldn't have said Vasili Caville had a playful bone in his body, but this was the secret Vasili, the Vasili only Niko knew.

Niko reached up and tucked Vasili's short hair behind his ear, then trailed his fingertips down the man's jaw, making Vasili's lashes flutter and his soft lips part. He leaned into Niko's touch, seeking more, then captured Niko's hand and pinned it to the floor above Niko's head.

He grabbed Niko's other hand and pinned that one too, so that Niko was trapped, both arms pinned high. He smiled against Niko's mouth.

"You truly came for me?" Vasili asked, as though still not believing it, despite all the evidence around him. And it was only then that Niko realized nobody had ever rescued Vasili. Until now.

"Like you once came for me when Julian turned and the elves tied me."

Vasili's tongue darted out and flicked against Niko's lip. "I had many reasons for saving you from those elves. Your name, for one. Don't mistake my motives as good, Nikolas."

"There's no chance of that, my prince."

A fresh kiss quickly became messy and breathless. Niko twitched beneath Vasili's tight grip, so desperate to touch him, hold him, taste him. He hooked a leg around his as a sign he wasn't letting him escape, but then Vasili dug his knee in-between Niko's thighs and spread his legs, opening him up while holding him down.

Vasili's teeth nipped at Niko's lower lip and then the prince freed Niko's left hand. Niko instantly plunged it into his hair, pulling him down, mouth to mouth, the kiss unyielding until Vasili's hand roamed over Niko's thigh and rubbed against Niko's rigid erection.

Vasili broke off, gasping. He pressed his forehead against Niko's, breathing hard, his gaze fixed on Niko's. "There is nothing else in this world that frees me like you do, Nikolas Yazdan."

There was no answer he could give, no words that would match that startling admission, and so Niko kissed him like he was a treasure all Niko's. This cabin and who they were inside its walls wouldn't last, but that didn't mean it couldn't happen. Niko needed this. He needed to feel again, like he hadn't in so long, like maybe he hadn't felt since Marcus at the front line, when he'd thought he'd found love and lost it the very next day. Since Julian, when, still reeling from Marcus's death, he'd hoped for love again and had it cruelly thrown at his feet.

After seeing Vasili near-death, after feeling him sob in his arms and watching him wrestle with the darkness alone, Niko needed to feel *him* again. And by the way Vasili rocked into the kiss, his hand desperately stroking Niko's cock, Vasili needed it too.

This night, in this place, they could be two humble men, a blacksmith and a farmer, not a soldier or a prince, and nothing could stop them.

Vasili withdrew, moistening his lips, and rolled to Niko's side on the cabin floor.

Niko waited for the prince's next move, but as his breathing slowed, Niko brought his arm down and tucked Vasili in close against his side. He was soon asleep, and to have him so close and so thoroughly relaxed enough to sleep in his arms, it was enough. It was everything.

CHAPTER 30

The fire had burned down to a humble glow and the air was cooling, but Niko couldn't bring himself to move from the bed. Vasili was sitting on the floor, resting back against the edge of the bed, angled toward the fire, with his long legs crossed at the ankles. His arm lay along Niko's thigh, and Niko absently ran his fingers over the back of Vasili's hand, drawing invisible loops on the prince's pale skin—one of the few places unscarred. The fact Vasili let him so casually touch his hand was some kind of revelation to Niko's hungry mind.

He was dressed in the crumpled and frayed shirt and trousers, having reapplied all the layers they'd gradually shed over the weeks in the wilderness. Earlier, Niko had watched him dress, admiring the way warm firelight had stroked over smooth skin, wishing he could kiss those narrow hips. He'd give anything to hear Vasili hiss in pleasure again or moan out his name. Each of Vasili's kisses was a gift. Each moan summoned from his lips was priceless because he gave them away so rarely.

He'd lose this Vasili again soon, but at least this time, with no distractions, no war or elves or terrible responsibilities, he knew what they'd shared was real.

"I need to explain some things," Vasili began.

Niko stopped drawing patterns on the back of his hand. "Walla fuck me. Vasili Caville is about to speak the truth? Surely not."

"Hush." The prince tossed him a coy smile. Twisting, he folded an arm over Niko's legs and propped his chin on his fist. With his hacked-at hair falling in front of his scarred eye and his creased clothes, he looked careless. He looked content and *happy*.

But soon his smile faded and his eye lost its gleeful shine. "I underestimated your family."

"The Yazdans are not my family."

"Regardless, I made a mistake in trusting Roksana and paid for it." His voice hitched.

Niko shifted onto an elbow. "What they did to you, that wasn't your fault."

Vasili turned his head away. His cheek pulsed, and it was all Niko could do not to capture his mouth in a kiss again and pull him back into bed, where he'd teach Vasili what it meant to be loved, one long, leisurely kiss at a time.

"The books I'd read. They painted the Yazdans as protectors of the flame, as people who could be reasonable. I believed they'd help."

"Were those books by any chance written by Yazdans?"

Vasili rubbed at his forehead, perhaps seeing off an ache brought on by painful memories. "I should have known they are just as touched by the dark as my own family."

"But they aren't born with it, like the Cavilles. It's a choice for them."

"They covet it, all the same. They were always sorcerers. They use the flame. All but you." His smile tried to return. "You defy everyone and everything, including me."

"I try." Niko jerked a brow.

Vasili laughed softly. "You succeed."

Niko twisted onto his side, still propping his head up, and watched the fire's embers throb. He hadn't escaped the flame's use entirely. Alissand had almost gotten his wish. He could still taste the bitter tang of Vasili's blood. He hadn't told Vasili what had almost happened and didn't feel the need to. "Alissand was behind all this. Now he's dead, perhaps they'll return to Seran and stay there." He doubted the Yazdans were just going to give up, but their numbers were greatly reduced, and Seran had been in dire need when he'd left.

"Dead?" Vasili asked.

"A shadow beast attacked their camp. That's how I was able to get you away. I didn't stay to count the bodies, but the attack was vicious."

Vasili smiled a reptilian smile.

"What?" Niko growled.

"There were eight of them," Vasili said. "The beast killed five. Alissand fled on horseback."

Vasili had been out cold the entire time, and Niko hadn't said a damn thing about any of it. "How can you know that?"

He hesitated a beat, gaze falling to where he leaned against Niko's leg. "Did the beast sit with you one night?"

Niko pushed upright in the bed and studied Vasili's expression. Mention of the beast hadn't surprised him. If anything, he smiled like he knew all the answers and was waiting for Niko to catch up. "That beast was yours?"

He looked up and swallowed hard. "Amir isn't the only one able to shape the flame."

"Vasili, that's," *fucking brilliant,* "reckless. The more you invite the flame in, the more it will assert control."

"And you're suddenly an expert on the flame, Nikolas?"

"No, I just..." *I care.* He let the end of that sentence trail off, unspoken.

"Yes, well." He tugged at a thread dangling from his sleeve. "Stuck as I was, I was out of options. It clearly worked."

"If you can do that, then why not have the beast attack Alissand earlier?"

"I could have. I wanted to. I..." He swallowed again, tasting the words before voicing them. "It's not easy to control, and had I killed them all, I'd still have been tied in the carriage. I needed someone left alive to free me."

He'd summoned a shadow beast. He was using the flame more and more. One day soon, it would eventually use him. But damn, his beast had saved them both. "You sent it to me that night?"

He huffed a light laugh as though *that* was ridiculous. "No, it found you. As I said, it's difficult to control. How my brother controls multiple beasts, I've yet to understand." Vasili caught Niko's heavy gaze. "He sent those beasts after our carriage and the one in the woods to me. Although, interestingly," he added, filling the heavy quiet, "the beasts can't be summoned at sea. In fact, the dark flame is blessedly silent at sea. Yasir had to dock his ship up the coast to experiment with his developing skills."

"Were you free of the voices on his ship?"

"As free as I can be."

That silence must have felt like freedom. "Yet you returned?"

"I told you, I cannot choose to walk away." His gaze drifted about the cabin, and the smile faded again. "I have never wished for freedom more than I do now. You make everything seem possible."

Julian had said the same of Niko. His words on Vasili's lips brought the past into the present.

"This hut you've built with your own two hands, it's remarkable. I wish..." Vasili swallowed the rest, probably because wishing changed nothing. "I must go back to Loreen, to Amir, and stop everything from spiraling out of control."

"Didn't we leave Loreen to escape Amir?"

"Yes, but his appearance in Seran, the beasts, everything he's done... He's revealed a weakness I should have seen before, one I can perhaps exploit."

Talk of Amir rapidly soured Niko's mood. He threw the cover back, planted his feet over the side of the cot bed, and grabbed his pants from the floor. He'd rather stay in the forest forever than see that bastard's face again.

Vasili trailed his fingers along Niko's bare thigh, tickling the fine, dark hairs, screeching Niko's thoughts to an abrupt halt. Lounged on the cabin floor, Vasili looked like a half-unwrapped gift. The appearance of his coy smile coupled with his lazy touch had Niko's cock rising in interest. Everything about the prince triggered Niko's desire and anger, frustration and the desperate need to protect. His whole world had become Vasili and that thought was fucking terrifying.

"There's something he wants," Vasili said. "It's

consumed him since he was denied it. It was there when the flame took him, when he attacked Seran, but every time he's close, it slips through his fingers. In his madness, he's fixated on it."

"Sounds like the perfect way to trap him. What is it?"

Vasili blinked. "You."

The desire tumbled away as Niko's suspicions rose. "I'm his weakness? And you want to *exploit* me?" Oh, they'd been here before, and it ended in Julian and Amir drugging him up and *raping him*. Niko brushed Vasili's touch from his leg.

"But this time you're complicit," the prince said.

Niko stood and tugged his trousers on. "And that makes it acceptable?" Vasili wanted to use him to get to Amir? It was like Seran hadn't happened, like they were back at the palace and Vasili was going to dangle Niko in front of Amir to distract him. "I foolishly thought you'd changed."

"Changed?" Vasili frowned. "Why would I?"

"Oh, I don't know, maybe because you'd learned that fucking people over is always wrong." He gestured at the cabin. "Maybe because of all this?"

Vasili shook his head and blinked up at Niko. "You're being unreasonable."

"*I'm* being unreasonable? You want to hand me over to your shit-weasel of a brother."

"Will you listen?"

"I am listening, that's the problem."

Vasili pursed his lips, his glare turning sharp.

"Was last night all lies? Or does it go back farther than that? When you got me off on Yasir's ship? You thought you'd... what? Fuck me, thinking once I'd gotten some cock, I'd roll over and let you fuck me another way?" Niko laughed hoarsely. "That's it, isn't it? You said you used pleasure to control Julian. You whipped him because he fucking got off on it, needed it even. And now you're doing the same to me because I'm stupid enough to think you might actually care? That we might actually have something?"

Vasili dropped his head. "By Etara, you're so gods-damned stubborn."

"No. I'm right."

"Amir learned about the Yazdans, the same as I did, and about you. He wants a Yazdan to control. He went to that funeral, not for me or for them. He went for *you*, Nikolas. The flame to him is just a means of getting what he wants, and he wants you, because you're—" he cut himself off.

"Say it."

"Because you're mine."

At least he'd hesitated.

Niko crouched, level with Vasili, and stared into his eye. Oh, he was angry too, barely restrained, still sitting against the bed, like he'd spring forward at any second and wrap his fingers around Niko's throat. "Maybe you'd like to whip me into submission, Your Highness? I honestly can't deny how I might fucking enjoy it."

Vasili's mouth twisted. He leaned forward, close enough his hot mouth almost scorched Niko's. "Whatever you think of me, the fact remains, you are Amir's weakness." He wet his lips. "The same as you are mine."

Niko's racing heart stuttered at that last word, and the rage quickly crumbled away. Gods, why couldn't he stay pissed at this bastard? Vasili would throw Niko to the wolves, and Niko—fool that he was—would willingly go every damn time. He thrust a hand into Vasili's hair, holding him firm, eliciting a tiny, restrained gasp from the prince. "Sometimes, I fucking hate you."

Humor sparkled in his eye. "Only sometimes?"

CHAPTER 31

Vasili steered Adamo back onto the unfamiliar roads with Niko tucked too damn close against Vasili's back. Although, the distraction of having him pressed close soon wore off with every passing day and the more Niko's body ached from the saddle.

Eventually, the meandering track grew busier, filling with folks dragging cartloads of goods south and messengers riding back and forth. Vasili stopped a messenger for news on Loreen. From his expression when he'd finished speaking with the woman, the news wasn't good.

The road delivered them to a village near Loreen that Niko had vaguely heard of. They traded a few of the tools they'd no longer need for food and a room in the village's only coaching inn. Their disheveled and unkempt state kept the village-folk from looking too closely.

Vasili's silence grew thick the more information they gleaned from the inn's paying guests. The king hadn't been seen in weeks. With no guards patrolling the streets, the city had become lawless and unsafe, driving all the good people away. Loreen was full of thieves, killers, and probably elves. If elves weren't already in the city, they'd be watching.

Knowing Vasili, he blamed himself.

After dinner, Vasili wordlessly left via the back door, probably to check on Adamo. Niko let him have his space and lingered in the lounge area for a few hours, listening to the local farmers and tradespeople talk of the harvest and raids, hoping for clues as to the state of the city they'd find when they arrived. He returned to their room long after night had fallen and found Vasili at the washbasin, shaving off his beard by candlelight. The soft light painted him in wonderfully seductive hues, and given how they were both safe and dry for the first time in days, Niko unashamedly admired the prince's figure.

"That would be better done in daylight."

"I grew bored waiting for you." He washed out the straight razor and applied its edge to his soapy cheek.

Niko stopped at his back, not yet touching, but fingers twitching to. Even after so long pressed against Vasili's back atop Adamo, the desire to touch hadn't faded. The long journey north had been practical and rough, with no heat between them. But now, the needs came roaring back, tingling through Niko's cock. "You were waiting for me?" He reached up to slip the razor from Vasili's fingers, hoping the prince would yield. His light fingers surrendered the razor without hesitation.

Niko stepped in, close enough against Vasili's back to feel his breath hitch. Vasili tilted his head, inviting the blade's edge against his skin.

They hadn't touched like this since the cabin. Days on the road, and with every mile that had passed beneath them, the memories of the cabin had begun to fade, dreamlike, into something that had happened to someone else.

But standing close again, Niko breathed him in and burned to hold him... More, he yearned for Vasili to hold him down and do all the wonderful things he so effortlessly did with his wicked tongue.

Niko drew the razor's edge down Vasili's cheek and glided it over the curve of his jaw, leaving the skin smooth and clean.

Admittedly, his focus wasn't all on the shave. Much of it was on how the press of his erection nudged Vasili's ass through his trousers fabric, and how Vasili occasionally shifted back, deliberately frustrating Niko. The reflection of the prince's blue-eyed gaze flicked questioningly to Niko.

Niko brought his right hand around to hold the front of Vasili's throat while he brought the razor in his left hand around to smooth off the stubble. The prince's pulse beat against Niko's thumb. Niko had him pressed against the basin, trapped in his arms, and so thoroughly caught. Not so long ago, this would never have been possible. The fact Vasili trusted him enough now made his head spin, made him breathless, made him want to scatter kisses down his neck, make him writhe and moan and gasp.

Vasili leaned his head back against Niko's shoulder. So free, just like he'd said. Niko set the razor down, never taking his eyes off Vasili's reflection. He bowed his head to Vasili's neck and placed a soft, open-mouth kiss on his clean, damp skin. He smelled of soap, and a smile upset Niko's kiss. These little moments, these tiny fractures in

Vasili armor, letting him see the man inside, these were so fucking precious.

"My turn." Vasili extracted himself from Niko's embrace and came up behind him, pressing in close, their positions now reversed. Vasili's warmth pressed against Niko's ass, his chest against Niko's back. They were both still fully clothed, but not for much longer if Niko had his way. He reached around Niko and lathered the soap in one hand, then applied the suds to Niko's unruly beard, catching Niko's gaze in the mirror.

"Do you trust me?" Vasili asked, picking up the razor.

"Rarely," Niko grumbled, voice rough.

Vasili shifted his hips, and the hardness of his cock nestled between Niko's ass cheeks, tearing a small hiss from between Niko's teeth. He hadn't even considered whether Vasili would want to fuck him like this, from behind... Lust tightened Niko's balls and made his cock ache.

"Wise." One hand gripped Niko's jaw while the other dragged the cool blade down Niko's cheek. Vasili's pink tongue moistened his lips. Niko gripped the edge of the washbasin to keep from turning and devouring him.

In the mirror, the marvel of Vasili stood behind him without his barriers. Beautiful, seductive, alluring. And before Niko could stop himself, he whispered, "I wish I could take you away somewhere."

"I'd stop you." The blade swept a fresh line clear of soap and whiskers.

"I know." A foolish confession. But true. Lady Maria, so long ago now it felt like a lifetime, had told him to take Vasili away. Back then, it would have been to bury his body in the woods. But now? He knew how much the prince ached for freedom, and he knew the man he'd be once he was free, and that man was full of laughter and color and light. That man made Niko's heart soar.

The clean edge of the blade returned to Niko's jaw and slipped easily under his chin, gliding down his neck. "When all this is over," Vasili whispered, gaze flicking up again, "give me your word you'll find someone. You'll take *him* to a cottage you've built somewhere far away from all this. And you'll live there, you and that good man, the man you deserve." The blade stilled, its edge pressed tightly against Niko's throat. Vasili's reflected gaze looked deep into Niko's. "Your word, Nikolas."

Niko's mouth dried. He should swallow, but the blade was too tight against his neck. Did Vasili care that Niko might one day find the ending the prince wanted for himself, or was this something else? Was he afraid to hope for such an ending? "When I find the man I deserve, I'll rescue us both." Whispering, he added, "You have my word, my prince."

A carriage clattered loudly to a halt outside. The sounds of boots on cobbles drifted in through the window. Noises Niko distantly registered but promptly forgot.

Vasili stroked the razor down Niko's neck, taking off the final suds. He tossed the razor into the bowl, dug his fingers into Niko's right ass cheek, and shoved him forward. Niko barely braced himself before Vasili's teeth nipped at the base of his neck.

"You must understand," Vasili said breathlessly against his skin, his hand sinking around the front of Niko's trousers. Fingers grasped Niko's solid length, briefly dumping out all the thoughts from his head. "It's all real. The cabin, what we have, *all of it, Nikolas.* It's real, and I wish I were different, Niko. I wish it didn't have to be this way."

Why did he sound desperate, like he was hurting? "Vasili, what way—"

A fist thumped on the door. "Open up!"

Niko jolted at the intrusion. He shifted, tried to rise, but Vasili's hand shoved harder, pinning him down. He swung his glare behind him and caught the raw look of fear on Vasili's face. But that didn't make any sense. Who was out there that he'd fear? And why wasn't he damn well letting Niko up? "*Vasili*—" he hissed.

The door burst inward.

Vasili's weight vanished.

Guards thundered in. Suddenly so loud and so many that it felt like an entire regiment had arrived.

Palace guards, Niko saw.

His blade, where was his damn blade? He scanned the room. His gaze snagged on Vasili. Why wasn't he reacting, why was he backing away, why was he standing in the middle of the room like none of this was real, like the guards weren't peeling around him, coming straight for Niko.

Because they weren't here for Vasili.

Dread drove a cold, iron rod through Niko's soul.

He knew what this was.

Vasili hadn't stopped the messenger to ask for news, he'd sent a message to the palace.

Gods, no...

He kicked out at the first guard, sending him sprawling. A second swung for Niko. Niko ducked, snatched the razor from the bowl, and lunged—*for Vasili.*

The shock on the prince's face was a wonderful thing.

He didn't move, didn't lift a hand to defend himself, just stood still, as though he expected nothing less, as though he welcomed Niko's wrath. Because he knew he deserved it.

A figure darted in. A fist struck Niko's jaw, making the room spin. Cold hands snatched Niko's wrist and twisted his arm up behind his back, dropping Niko to his knees, from where he saw only Vasili's scuffed and filthy boots. It had happened so damn fast that none of this felt real.

Betrayal. Again. Oh, how Niko knew its familiar sting.

Grief clogged Niko's throat, choking him. No, no... He'd given the prince the pieces of his broken heart, and Vasili had crushed them, exactly as he'd feared he would. But it couldn't be true. He'd said it was all real, the cabin, the Vasili he'd held near-death in his arms, the prince that came alive in Seran's heat-soaked streets. The cabin... what had he said? Something about Niko being Amir's weakness. Vasili did this because he thought he had no other way. "Vasili, don't do this!"

"Drop the razor, you beautiful fucking bastard," Amir hissed in Niko's ear. He punctuated the order by pulling Niko's arm in a direction it didn't want to go, forcing a cry up Niko's throat. Fingers tingling, the razor slipped from his grip and clattered to the floor.

Amir patted him on the head. "There's a good pet. *Now fucking hold him!*"

The guards swarmed in, hauling Niko back to his feet, and there they stood: the Caville princes. Amir next to Vasili, his smile slick and wicked, while Vasili's looked wooden, tacked to his lips because it was all the armor he had left.

"You bastard son of a bitch!" Niko spat at Vasili's boots. "You didn't have to do this!"

Amir sank his fingers into Niko's hair and gripped firm, yanking his head back. "No, dog, the son of a bitch is you." Amir's thick, wet tongue stroked up Niko's cheek. "Oh, you and I are going to have so much fun."

Niko bucked against those holding him, but it was no use. Even if he got free, there were dozens of guards, all with flickering black eyes, all possessed.

Amir thrust Niko's head back, letting go as he did. "Take this Yazdan bitch to my carriage."

"Vasili... *why*?" They could have found another way together.

"Elves have taken Seran," he flatly replied, voice as hollow as his gaze. "They're approaching Loreen's borders from the south and east. A simultaneous attack on two fronts. I cannot fight them as I am. Alone."

Niko let out a breath that sounded too much like a sob. "You weren't alone."

Vasili's light lashes fluttered, but he gave no indication the words had gotten through. "Now I have Amir's forces. Only with the flame can the elves finally be defeated."

"No... No." He was going to surrender to the flame. "Vasili, don't do this. This is exactly what the flame wants. It will consume you, Amir, Loreen, all of it." He bucked in the guards' grips. "There's another way!"

Amir snapped his fingers. "Gag him." A cloth was rammed in his mouth and tied off. It didn't matter anyway because there were no words left for what Vasili had done.

The guards tried to manhandle Niko from the room, but by the three gods, Niko had no intention of making it easy for them. He kicked and yanked, but there were too many, their strength too great and their eyes all-black.

"Wait!" Vasili's order boomed.

Panting behind the rag, Niko brought his glare up to watch Vasili approach. He'd take it back, he'd tell them to let him go, and they'd fight, they'd fight together, because this was wrong.

Vasili held Niko's blurring gaze. "You told me once how a blacksmith's blade was better than none. You were right. One blacksmith's blade has bought me an army, and all it cost me was you. I'm out of time, Nikolas."

No... Niko made sure Vasili witnessed the betrayal in his eyes.

Vasili nodded at the guards, and they hauled Niko backward, toward the door.

"I'm sorry," Vasili said, and those two words sank like daggers into Niko's heart.

CHAPTER 32

The more he struggled, the more the ropes bit into his wrists. Didn't matter. He twisted his legs, eventually managing to kick free of the ropes tied loosely around his ankles. For all the good it did him. He was still tied at the wrists and gagged so damn tightly he couldn't yank the cloth over his chin.

The carriage bounced and clattered, jarring Niko's spine. There were no seats inside, just plain boards. When the carriage occasionally stopped, he listened to the guards outside, expecting Amir to open the door and climb inside and gloat, but nobody came.

Vasili was out there, riding atop Adamo like the cold-hearted Caville prince he'd always been.

The more time that passed, the more his rage dangerously simmered in his veins.

He'd said the cabin was real—he'd said *they* were real.

And the worst of it was, Niko knew who Vasili was. He knew everything the prince was capable of, and he'd known Vasili would do this. What had he thought? That his dick was so fucking perfect that Vasili would suddenly become good after sampling it? By Etara, he was a fucking idiot. A stupid, blind fool. Again. And that was the worst of it. He hadn't seen it with Julian because the bastard had been so good at hiding his lies within himself. But Vasili... The truth was all over him, in every glance, every word. He fucking told Niko what he'd do, and still Niko had been surprised when the snake had turned around and sunk his fangs in?

Niko thumped his head against the side of the carriage hard enough to summon an ache.

After everything they'd shared, the heartless viper hadn't changed.

Fuck him.

Fuck them all.

Fuck Vasili, fuck Roksana, and fuck the Yazdans. Niko didn't need anyone but himself.

He kicked again at the door. Its panel dented some. He kicked again, then backed up and threw his shoulder into a lunge. The door flung open, he fell for a heartbeat, then hit the ground hard enough to stun the breath out of him.

Shouts rose.

He didn't dare look to see how close they were, just staggered to his feet, focusing on getting away. Scorching pain ignited in his shoulder—the same damn shoulder he'd dislocated before. Didn't matter. Didn't care. He was damn well getting away from them all if he had to drag his sorry ass from the road with his fucking teeth.

Horses circled in, blocking every angle. Their riders were dark silhouettes against the full glare of the sun.

The sound of a whip cracking was all the warning he received before agony tore down his back. He cried out around the cloth and whirled, squinting at the figure haloed in sunlight. Vasili... No, he wouldn't.

Niko staggered. The man atop his chestnut horse raised the whip again.

"Run, Lord Nikolas. Please run for me." Amir. His voice full of laughter.

The whip's crack came down on Niko's arm, zipping open a bleeding line.

Niko swayed on his feet, his body fighting to drop in the dirt. He fixed the rat prince in his sights and took a step forward. He'd pull that fucker from his horse if it were the last thing he ever did.

The whip cracked again, catching Niko's sore thigh. He barked a cry and went down to a knee.

"Get back in that carriage or I'll flay all the skin from your bones right here and leave your body hanging in a tree."

Everything ached and trembled. Blood dripped down his leg, or maybe it was piss. He couldn't tell. Didn't care. He got his trembling legs under him and stumbled toward Amir's horse, making the animal shy enough for Amir to fight to get it back under control.

"Oh, you want some more? Hm?" Amir laughed. "You like it, *dog*?"

None of the guards intervened, they just looked on like the puppets they were. Men and women who had lost their will to the flame. Niko couldn't see Amir's eyes in the sun's glare to know if he was truly lost, but he suspected not. The flame didn't care for any of this. It was Amir's doing.

The whip cracked again, slicing across his chest, leaving a hot, wet line in his skin.

He saw him then, saw Adamo pawing the earth, and saw Vasili coolly observing from his saddle.

Amir's gaze tracked Niko's, finding his brother at the end of it. He grinned at Niko and leaned forward in his saddle. "You're all mine now. Isn't that right, Vasili?"

Vasili narrowed his eye but stayed silent.

"Get his ass back in the carriage and tie his fucking legs properly this time!" Amir snapped.

Vasili's words, if he had any, were lost when the guards swooped in and manhandled Niko back inside the carriage.

They tied his ankles again, harder this time, and slammed the door closed.

THE NEXT OPPORTUNITY TO escape would come when they took him from the carriage into whatever building Amir would eventually tie him up inside. Niko was ready. If he failed again, if Amir got him somewhere secure, there wouldn't be another chance.

The carriage's jostling seemed to last a lifetime, but eventually, it rocked to a halt. The horses clopped away, their tack chinking, signaling the end of this journey. And finally, the door opened.

Two guards ventured inside to haul him out into a courtyard at night. The palace courtyard. Niko played at stumbling and made himself awkward to handle, as though weak.

"Loosen his ankles," one of the guards muttered. "Unless you want to carry him?"

"Carry him? He's twice my size."

Niko slumped over and mumbled nonsense.

The smaller guard pulled his ankle ropes loose. Niko brought his knee up, slamming it into the guard's nose. He flailed and screamed, alerting every damned guard in the area.

The other guard fumbled with freeing his sword. Niko ran at him and tackled him shoulder-first against a wall. The guard's head flung back, striking the stone. He staggered and dropped like a felled tree. His sword skittered across the cobbles, right into Niko's path. Niko gingerly angled his tied wrists behind him and ran the ropes against the edge of the blade. It took some fiddling, and any second, more guards would appear, but suddenly the ropes gave. Niko tore the rag from his mouth and bolted out of the stables, stolen sword in hand.

"Halt!"

The new guard's eyes weren't black, like the other two. Niko ran at him all the same, using surprise to shove him off his feet. He tried to get up. Niko struck him on the back of the neck and was running again.

"*Nikolas*."

He jolted to a halt at the familiar woman's voice and whirled. Lady Maria jogged toward him. She tossed him a cloak. "Quickly, put that on and follow me."

He blinked at her.

"Hurry, darling. Once the bells ring, I can't get you out."

He threw the cloak on and jogged alongside her. "What are you doing here?"

"I had planned on freeing you, but it seems you're already halfway there. There are too many guards by the main gate. They'll overpower you. Quickly, hide the sword inside and follow me."

He tucked the hood down to hide his face. "Did Vasili send you?" he asked, hating how hope leaped into his head. Vasili had planned this. He was always one step ahead. He'd planned for Niko's "escape" and sent Lady Maria to do his bidding like she'd done in the past. It had all been a ruse.

"No," she replied, and Niko's heart sank. "Come." She led him through the quiet palace grounds and out a side gate, bribing a guard with a silent exchange of coin. The transaction was so seamless she'd clearly done it before. The city of Loreen's curving streets unfurled in the night. A few hulking figures loomed in doorways, looking like they might stab a man for the contents of his pockets. Loreen had already been suffering since the war, but now half the houses they passed were boarded up. Slop blocked gutters and the ripe stench of decay hung in the stagnant air.

"Here." Maria opened the stained-glass door Niko vaguely recognized, but it wasn't until he was inside that he remembered its dark beams and long bar. The Stag and Horn pleasure-house. All its tables had been shoved to one side, and the windows were boarded like those of its neighbors.

A man in a heavy riding cloak emerged from the back room, his wide hat glistening with fresh rain. "Yasir?"

Yasir flung his arms around Niko and thumped him hard enough on the back to set all his wounds ablaze all over again. "Nikolas! I thought you'd died in the desert!"

Niko held Yasir at arm's length and grinned at the captain. He looked almost sheepish under the scrutiny. If

Niko had known what to say, he doubted he'd have been able to speak.

"Walla, look at you," Yasir grunted. "You're bleeding all over my silk shirt."

The man's smile almost brought him to his knees. He was afraid his legs might give out and gripped Yasir in a harder embrace, grateful when he subtly pulled away and guided Niko to the dusty bar.

"Get that in you." He busied himself behind the bar, producing an old bottle of something dark. "You clearly need it. Not too much, mind. We need it to clean whatever wound is producing all that blood."

Niko downed the drink, then spluttered from the heat and braced himself against the bartop, head bowed. He wiped at his mouth, gasping from it all. "Are we safe here?"

"Yes," Maria replied, appearing at his side. "The pleasure-house closed weeks ago. Although I can't stay long. I'll be missed." She placed a comforting hand on Niko's back. "Rest. We'll talk tomorrow."

"Be careful," he told her as she headed for the door.

"Careful is how I've survived this long, darling."

She left. Yasir locked the door behind her with a satisfying clunk, and the weight of what might have come to pass with Amir fell from Niko's shoulders. If it hadn't been for the bar holding him up, he'd have sobbed on his hands and knees. "Yasir—" A fresh drink appeared in front of him.

"It'll take the edge off."

Niko wrapped his fingers around it. "He gave me up to Amir." Saying it aloud made him want to throw the glass at the wall, and then the bottle. Instead, he swallowed the dark liquid down like the first, needing its heat to numb the pain.

Yasir nodded grimly. “Let’s get you cleaned up and, like the lovely lady said, we can talk tomorrow.”

Niko lifted a fresh glass to his lips but hesitated, the consequences of his actions only now catching up with him. Amir wouldn’t react well to his escape, and Vasili was alone in whatever was left of that palace. “*You didn’t have to do this*,” he’d whispered, but deep down, buried beneath all the hurt and pain, he began to wonder if there had ever been another way.

CHAPTER 33

The drink sat heavy on his empty gut, but it helped chase away the pain, both inside and out. Later, Yasir helped Niko strip out of the filthy clothes and clean the fresh whip burns, while explaining how he'd gotten Liam to safety before Seran had burned. Elf forces had sacked the ancient city. It was lost. He'd choked as he'd said it, and Niko almost wished he'd stayed with Yasir instead of chasing after Vasili.

The Stag and Horn's water still ran, so Niko washed clean. Yasir helped pour the alcohol, either into the wounds or drinking glasses. It became a blur of hurt that ended with Niko passing out cold alongside Yasir in one of the few beds left in the building.

He woke alone and stared at the old timber beams crisscrossing the ceiling.

Damn Vasili. May Etara take his soul. He'd known Niko had refused to play his game, and he'd played it anyway.

If only Niko could hate him like he had before. Things

had been simple between them then. Now, he wondered if he'd ever untangle the mess Vasili had made of his head and his heart.

Dressing in fresh clothes Yasir had provided, Niko descended the stairs to the bar and found Lady Maria already seated with Yasir at the single table in the middle of the vast bar area.

"Goodness, you look terrible, my lord."

Niko grunted a reply and ran a hand through his messy hair. Now the alcohol had worn off, everything ached again. His head throbbed in time with his bruises and the beat of vengeance. "Don't call me that."

"Lord? It's technically true," Maria said. "Although, your title is Lord Bucland, not Yazdan, but a title is a title."

"My lady, forgive me, but I've no idea what the fuck you're talking about." Weary and sore, he was struggling to keep up. Lordships were the last thing on his mind.

"Lord Bucland and his lady were found hanged from a tree."

Niko pulled out a chair and dropped into it, then dragged both hands down his face. "What?"

"As his bastard son and with no other blood relatives, his estate is yours."

Niko closed his eyes and sighed hard before opening them again. His mah's family had been more than enough to occupy his thoughts. The last thing he needed was more familial drama. "I can't deal with any of that now." He propped an elbow on the table and rubbed at the ache across his brow. "Hanged from a tree?"

"Not elves, if that's what you're thinking."

Niko's parents, Mah and Pah, had been found the same

way. Or so he'd been told when he'd returned from the front. "Were they killed or did they hang themselves?"

Lady Maria arched a dark eyebrow. "Nikolas, what's done is done."

Killed then. Killed in the same manner as his parents. "Which tree?"

"Surely, that doesn't—" Yasir cut off as Niko raised a hand.

"Which tree, Maria?" Niko asked.

"The old oak by the lake," she said, and by the way she lowered her gaze, she knew exactly what it meant.

The same tree his parents had been cut from. That couldn't be a coincidence. Or maybe it was and he was looking for connections where there were none because lately his whole life had been one long string of lies and betrayal.

"I can't deal with this shit..."

Yasir slid a glass of bronze liquid across the table. "Breakfast."

Lady Maria cleared her throat. "Names have weight, so don't be too quick to discard it. I've discreetly taken care of the necessary legalities for you—the Manor house is in a bad way and boarded up, but it's there—for when you're ready."

He nodded but quickly pushed the revelation aside. There were far more important problems to deal with.

A thin book lay open between them, its edges singed.

"Vasili doesn't know I have it," Maria said, turning the book toward Niko.

"You've seen Vasili?" Niko ran his fingers down the thick paper, over beautifully scribed words, keeping Maria from seeing any emotion on his face.

"He's furious. Amir is demanding you're found. If you aren't, he's not quiet about what he'll do to Vasili. They're avoiding each other, for now, but one will eventually attack the other. I fear it's never been worse. Amir is..." She waved a hand. "Well, he is what he is. I've mostly managed to avoid him since his return. Helped by the fact he's largely forgotten I exist and much of the palace has collapsed. Easy to disappear in."

"Thank you," Niko said, forgetting if he'd already thanked her. "You're taking a great risk in helping us." If Amir were to discover her treachery, the best she could hope for was a quick death.

"I'm not the sort to sit back and let events unfold around me."

It took someone far braver and more intelligent than he to survive the palace for as long as she had. Someone like Vasili. The prince would despise being back and being alone, but this time with the flame simmering in his veins and with only his murderous brother as company. It was only a matter of time before he or Amir let loose.

"My capture kept Amir controlled," Niko said absently, half his thoughts on the book, the other half inside the palace.

The page lying open detailed some kind of sorcerer's ritual for *binding*, the act of pulling a creature from the shadows and giving it form. Like the shadow beasts both Amir and Vasili had summoned.

Yasir had tilted his head and was snatching a few glances at the pages.

"Can you bind these creatures?" Niko asked him, tapping the roughly drawn image of a beast.

Yasir snorted. "I tried with Vasili when we docked up

the coast. I'd have more luck pulling a parrot out of my ass."

"Good to know." Niko huffed a laugh.

"Colorful," Lady Maria commented.

"Apologies, milady." Yasir reached over and captured her hand, then lifted her fingers to his lips for a chaste kiss. "I've spent so long in Niko's company, I've forgotten what it means to be civil."

She laughed, and it was clear Yasir hadn't lost his ability to flirt with anything that moved. "How did you both come to find each other?" Niko asked, flicking through the book's many pages. There was more than enough potent information in there to hopefully find the flame's weakness. It had to have one.

Yasir cleared his throat in the way he did when he was about to dive into a long tale.

"The short version, Yasir."

"Once Liam was safe and Seran was lost, I performed our little wax trick," he glanced at Maria's curious expression, "and when the damned line went up a wall, I realized I had no idea what I was doing, so I came to Loreen asking after you. I was making my way north anyway and there can't be that many Yazdans in Loreen."

"The captain is not subtle," Lady Maria said.

"No, he's not."

"With all of this to work with," Yasir gestured at himself, "it would be a shame to stay quiet, no?"

Gods, it was good to have him back. "You're lucky Amir didn't find you first," Niko said.

"Amir's mind is elsewhere," Maria added. "I have a few spies left in the city. They alerted me to a flamboyant southern man throwing the Yazdan name around."

Niko smiled fondly. “You are a woman of infinite surprises.”

“I’ve had to be.”

“I’m glad to see you’re safe.”

“Likewise, darling. I am, however, sorry to see Vasili back again. Did I not tell you to take him away?”

“Vasili listens to nobody.” Niko closed the book and frowned at the insignia on the front. A black flame on a gold background. Yazdan. Of course. And this was likely the book Vasili had salvaged from the fire. Had he deliberately dropped it in the grass that night, hoping Niko wouldn’t notice? “He recently reminded me exactly who he is.” He turned the book toward Yasir. “Read it. Every page.”

“I thought you didn’t like my using the, er...” He glanced at Maria. “Flame?”

“She knows everything. And the damage is already done. You need to be able to protect yourself.” He straightened and met Maria’s keen gaze. “Vasili mentioned there were more books like this one. Can you get them?”

“Some. Most were destroyed in the fire, but Amir has some. I may be able to remove them from his chamber for a few days while he’s distracted.”

“We have to find a weakness. Something that will end this. There must be a way.”

“The keys?” Yasir asked.

Niko frowned. “The what?”

“Well, they were called wishes in the old tales. You know, I mentioned it.”

“You’ve mentioned a whole lot of things since we met.”

“The jinni and the lamp and its three wishes. Only the wishes actually strengthen the jinni’s prison, not the other way around, like the tale suggests. Go back far enough and the wishes become keys and the jinni is the nasdas, the flame."

"Do you know what or where these keys are?"

"No idea. I mean, I thought it was all just a folktale until I met you and Vasili."

"We don't want to trap it again. We need to snuff it out forever. Find those books, Maria. We'll have to hope the information we want wasn't destroyed in the fire."

"What of the elves?" Yasir asked, looking up from the book. "They have forces moving north from Seran."

"And from the east, if Vasili is to be believed," Niko said. "Whether the flame wins or the elves do, we have no choice but to fight with what we have." Vasili would fight the elves. Alone if he had to. Niko could trust him in that, if nothing else. But he'd use the flame to do it. He'd kill Amir and take the flame to defend his city.

He wasn't sure who would be the more terrifying as the flame's only vessel. The mad Amir or the calculating Vasili.

Niko sent Maria back to find the books. While Yasir researched the book they already had, Niko threw on a cloak and took to Loreen's tired streets. He passed families carting their belongings along behind them, homeless or just wanting to be free of Loreen. His own passing garnered a few opportunistic looks from men and women who were, at best, thieves, at worst, looking for a lone passerby to take out their frustrations on. Loreen's downfall was worse than he'd feared. Worse than when he'd returned from the war. He wasn't even sure if there was anything good left in Loreen worth saving.

He homed in on the sounds of hammering and came across several spiked barriers, blocking off wide streets.

Defenses. Vasili clearly expected elves to spill into the city.

Niko drifted back to the pleasure-house, thoughts plagued by doubts. Vasili's betrayal was an open wound, but the more Niko thought on it, the more he tried to find another way, the more he began to realize controlling the king and his forces was likely the only way to defend Loreen.

And all it cost me was you.

But that way was wrong.

What they'd had together, Niko had foolishly believed in it.

He wished the weeks in the cabin had never happened. He wished Vasili had stayed at sea, and he wished the Yazdans weren't all righteous assholes on a crusade to control the flame and the Cavilles it lived in.

Niko found a bottle of wine among the many left behind when the Stag and Horn's proprietors had vacated and sat with it at the empty bar. Yasir wordlessly appeared and sat on a stool beside him. He handed over a salt mill. Niko regarded the salt warily and then raised an eyebrow as Yasir began to murmur and focus on his cupped hands. Trails of dark smoke drifted from between his fingers. With a grin, he tossed a black and slithering thing onto the bartop.

Niko froze. The black snake knotted into itself, red eyes fixing on his. There was a knowing in its eyes, just like that of the beast's Vasili had sent. Were these creatures conscious? Did they have a will of their own that the sorcerers corrupted?

Niko reached out a hand.

The snake lunged, mouth open, fangs exposed.

He sprang from the stool, snatched the salt, and tossed the powdery granules at the damned thing slithering across the floor. It bucked and twisted, shriveling like a slug caught in the sun, and puffed into smoke.

Yasir winced. "Clearly I haven't gotten the control part down yet."

Niko waited for his heart to settle. "All we need are a million more of those things and the war will be over."

"Yes, well... one is my limit." He sighed and flicked out his fingers, shaking off whatever residual power clung to him. "I'm afraid I'm not a very good sorcerer."

Niko reclaimed his stool and slid a glass of wine to Yasir. "I reckon that's a good thing. All I've ever seen the flame do is corrupt. I sincerely hope that doesn't happen to you."

They settled into an easy silence, the bleak prospect of the next few weeks weighing down on them. "The city is a shithole, but Vasili is preparing defenses," Niko said.

"That's good." The note of doubt probably came from having seen his own city fall and what it would take to fend off an invading force of elves.

"It's a fucking waste of time," Niko added. "If they're in the city, we've already lost, doesn't matter how many possessed guards Vasili has."

"What happened between you and him? You don't have to answer, I just... I know he cares for you. He didn't say it, but it was obvious."

The cabin, the real Vasili. He wished he didn't have those memories. "Nothing happened." He raised the glass to his lips and tasted the sickly, sweet wine. "Everything happened."

"You remember the night you thought he and I... thought we might have fucked?"

Niko snorted. Vasili had barged in the morning after and ranted at him for having a good time at the docks. He remembered it well.

"That night, he and I talked, a lot. There was spice, you know how it is?"

"Not really."

Yasir chuckled. "He talked about you. Said a lot of things, most of which were derogatory, if I'm honest, but what stands out to me is how he said you make him a better person."

"Vasili can't change. None of us do, really. He wears a lot of skins, Yasir. It's all lies."

"Yeah, I see that, but there's some goodness in him too." He sighed. "I'm sorry it didn't work out."

"You've got nothing to be sorry for. He dragged you into all this the same as he did me."

His gaze drifted to the salt scattered on the floor. "I should get back to work. Maybe I can produce something useful instead of a handful of angry worms."

"I'll get the salt."

MARIA CAME LATER with an armful of books and promptly left, concerned her regular excursions from the palace weren't going unnoticed. Yasir gathered up the books and took them off to a room they'd set aside for studying. Short of Yasir binding an army, there was little he could do to stop the inevitable battles ahead, but at least he would be able to protect himself.

That night, Niko dreamed of the wolf again, but instead of it circling the Yazdan ancestral home, it stalked him through Loreen's barren streets. He woke before dawn, sweat dripping down his back, and gave up on sleep. After a quick wash, he quietly padded downstairs in loose trousers and an unlaced shirt and brewed some tea in the scullery. With a mug of the steaming drink in-hand and his head still full of nightmares, he headed into the bar area to check the door locks.

The front door was ajar. He froze, hot tea still in his hand. The door was always locked. He'd checked it himself the night before.

A growl bubbled from the shadows to his right.

Ember-red eyes glowed in the dark.

"Nikolas," Vasili greeted calmly.

He leaned against the bar. His grey Caville cloak draped from his shoulders to his boots. The large hood hid much of his face. He looked almost exactly as he had the evening they'd met. He could have been the same prince who had tried to buy Niko with a bag of coin, but this version simmered with power. It couldn't be seen with human eyes, not yet, but Niko tasted it on his lips and felt its weight in the air like a thundercloud.

The beast's growls bubbled louder.

Yasir had brought Niko a sword. It was stashed behind the bar, but Niko had seen how fast the beasts moved. He'd never make it.

"It won't hurt you unless I command it to," Vasili said, face still hidden in the hood's shadow.

Salt.

The mill sat on the bar. Salt might see the beast off, but not Vasili.

Vasili turned his head and the soft light coming in through the windows stroked over his smooth jaw and soft mouth, leaving the rest of his face cloaked.

"Niko, do I smell tea?" Yasir jogged down the stairs.

Niko thrust out a hand, freezing him on the bottom step.

Vasili's lips ticked. "How domestic."

Yasir's hands dropped to his sides, his fingers rippling, *binding*.

Niko opened his mouth to warn Yasir against trying to use the dark against Vasili, when Vasili said, "Continue along that route, Yasir, and I'll rip your soul from your body before you draw your next breath."

Yasir gasped. His hands shot to his neck and his eyes blew wide. He staggered backward and fell against the stairs, gasping for air.

"Vasili!" Niko took a step forward, and the prince's head jerked, readying to fight. "Stop."

Vasili pushed his hood back. No eye-patch, not this time. Niko only knew he was furious because he'd seen that carefully measured expression of indifference too many times before. His eye sparkled blue, the pupil blown wide but not with the dark. He was still in control.

"Do you care for Yasir, Nikolas?"

Yasir gasped and gagged and clawed at his neck, boots scraping the floorboards.

"You know I do. So do you. Let him go, Vasili."

Vasili flung a gesture toward Yasir, freeing whatever hold he had on him. Yasir gulped air and coughed it back up again. He wretched and heaved and stared at Vasili as if only now realizing who and what the man was truly capable of.

The beast was silent now too, sent back into the shadows until needed.

Vasili took his time admiring the room as he approached the single table. He rubbed absently at his wrist. Did he remember meeting Niko here and how Niko had broken his wrist the first time? Probably. It wasn't a meeting likely to be forgotten.

"Yasir, leave," Vasili ordered, his tone typical of a royal. Gods, it was like Seran hadn't happened, like the cabin was a dream, like Vasili was about to order they both be whipped as though he had every right to control them.

"No." Niko approached the table too, his hot drink still cradled in his hand. "You made him a part of this. He stays. And you don't fucking dismiss him like he's your property." He set the cup on the table instead of giving in to the urge to launch it at Vasili. "It didn't take you long to become a Caville again. How did you find me?"

Vasili lifted his chin. "Your cottage is gone. Where else would you be? And my aunt isn't as subtle as she believes." His fingertips skimmed the tabletop and came away rubbing salt between his finger and thumb. He glanced at the floor, seeing it there too, and knew they'd been experimenting.

He was different. His clothes weren't as perfect as they'd always been, and his shorter hair still hung wild and free about his face. The more Niko saw of him inside the cloak, the more it seemed as though Vasili was unraveling at the seams. The dilated pupil suggested spice, a dangerous but familiar crutch and a sign he was barely holding himself together.

A pang of regret and fear tried to muddy Niko's anger. Fear that he was losing him to the palace all over again.

"Everywhere I look, I see enemies." Vasili settled his gaze pointedly on Niko.

Niko carefully straightened. "I'm not your enemy."

"Your actions speak differently."

"My actions?" Niko echoed incredulously. "My *fucking* actions?! You gave me up to your sick fuck of a brother. You—" Niko swallowed the rest and unclenched his fists. If this devolved into rage, nobody would win. Vasili was obviously here for a reason, and it wasn't to hurt them, despite his behavior. "What do you want?"

"You." He flicked a wrist. "Obviously."

Yasir approached from Niko's left, rare anger simmering off of him. He had his own strengths, and he would stand for what he believed in. Niko was sure of that. And right now, he stood on the same side as Niko.

"You will return with me to the palace," Vasili ordered.

The idea was so ludicrous that Niko couldn't stop his laugh from bursting free. "You'll have to get your guards and shackle me because there isn't a fucking chance I'll ever go back there willingly."

"For fuck's sake, Nikolas," Vasili hissed, finally revealing his frustration on his face, like the man in the cabin who'd wished for simpler things, "your stubborn selfishness will sink us all. Elves are a week away. I need Amir's forces, and if you do not return, he'll turn those forces on me, leaving Loreen vulnerable to attack. Seran has already fallen. If we do not stand, Loreen will be next. I did not suffer—*we* did not suffer for all those years to let elves take our lives from us. Thousands dead, countless soldiers slaughtered, families torn apart, and you're upset because I used you as a bargaining tool to buy the only army available to me?"

Disgust made his guts turn over. "No! Fucking... no. I'm... I'm upset because you're surrendering to Amir... and to the flame."

Vasili ground his teeth. "I surrender now, or tomorrow, or ten years from now, what difference does it make? It will always win."

"I told you I'd stand with you so long as you never surrendered."

"And it was a nice dream, while it lasted, but I live in the real world, Nikolas."

"There's a way..." Yasir croaked and cleared his throat. "The keys. I don't know where they are, but the books say the keys can stop it—"

"What books?" Vasili snapped.

"*Your* books," Niko said. "Taken from Amir, who likely stole them from the library before it burned. Go on," he urged Yasir.

"But in the Seranian language, the stories translate as the keys being close to the palace. Perhaps there's something within its walls that can stop the flame... Perhaps for good?"

Vasili blinked and briefly looked afraid, but then quickly shuttered his expression. "Or perhaps it's not literal. Whatever the case, *perhaps* is not enough. I cannot fight a battle with *perhaps*." His gaze slid back to Niko. "You will return to the palace, and you'll do whatever Amir demands of you. You'll be his fucking doulos, just like he wants. If that means you have to bend over and let him fuck you, you will do it. I need my brother to give up control. If he does not do that, if he kills me, which he will, given half the chance, all of the flame becomes his, and you have no notion of the chaos that will be wrought upon this land if that happens."

"You can't ask Niko to do that," Yasir said.

Vasili's eye flashed. "I'm not asking."

Niko drew in a breath and closed his eyes. "I can't—"

"You are a soldier, Nikolas. You vowed to protect this city. You fought and gave everything to stop the elves. The war never ended. It's here now, and your service is needed again."

He sighed and opened his eyes. "I can't fucking submit to that prick. I'll kill him or he'll kill me."

Vasili closed his eye and sighed hard. "Do you think I don't know that?" He opened his eye again, and his next words trembled. "Do you think I don't hate myself, hate everything I have become, and everything I've done and will do? You should never have shown me another way. Now every second of every wretched day in that palace is another drop of blood from my veins. *I don't want this either*." He cut himself off, his face so raw suddenly that Niko almost reached across the table to pull him close. "It must be done. If I do not return with you, either by force or under your acceptance, my brother and I—" He choked on the words. "Only one will remain, and whether it's he or I, the full force of the dark flame will consume whoever is left standing."

If Niko didn't return, the brothers would fight, and only the flame would win. With Amir's forces, Vasili would deter the elves. He might even drive them back. He *was* fighting, even now, just as Niko had demanded of him when they'd first met.

He didn't want the flame, never had. And he certainly didn't want it all.

Vasili stood rigid, but his fingertips trembled against the tabletop. He looked furious, spoke like he was too, but Niko knew him. Vasili Caville was terrified.

Niko spread his hands on the table and bowed his head. "I don't have a choice."

Outside the palace, Niko was nothing more than a blunt blade, but inside its walls, he could fight a different battle. Amir was dangerous, but he was also riddled with insecurity, and while the flame was split between the brothers, it *could* be controlled. If Niko could get close to Amir, there was a chance he might be able to distract and hopefully control him, just as Vasili had controlled Julian. Maybe it would buy time for Yasir to find answers in those damn books.

Cold, hard dread armored his heart, as though he were facing the battlefront again. But this battle would be different. It wasn't at the end of a blade, not this time. This time it was in his head. "I have to do this."

Vasili's cheek twitched.

"Very well. I'll go with you," Niko said.

"Good." Vasili sighed.

Yasir looked between them, his face pained. "This isn't right."

"No, it's not." Niko's emotional barriers slammed into place. "But it's the only way."

CHAPTER 34

He walked beside Vasili, through the palace gates and onto the grounds. He wasn't bound, wasn't forced at the point of a blade. Not on the outside, but inside, duty shackled his will.

Every step was weighted with lead. The palace loomed, its white walls charred and crumbling. The grounds had fallen into neglect. No staff came to greet them. There were no signs of life at all. The once-shimmering palace had become a mausoleum.

Vasili simmered beside him. He spoke only to tell Niko which way to turn. They approached the banquet hall, the same room Vasili had killed Talos in over a year ago. Guards stood at the doors as still as stone plinths.

Vasili walked ahead, meeting the guards' stalwart glares. "Allow us entry."

The dark swam in their eyes.

The guards measured Vasili with their flat stares and stepped aside.

As Niko stepped through the doorway behind Vasili, a

blast of icy wind rolled over him, sucking the heat from his bones. The last time Niko had been inside this room, Talos had been dead at his feet, killed by Vasili, and both princes had lain, out cold. He'd left them there, walked away and had never planned to return. Now, all the windows were thrown open. Torn drapes fluttered. Leaves rustled around the columns, and on the raised dais, the Caville throne loomed, supporting the prince-turned-king.

Niko's heart thudded harder.

Every step behind Vasili felt like a mistake.

Amir was thinner than before. His dark-eyed glare skimmed over his brother to land on Niko. He tilted his head, his brow pinched. A thin smile lifted the corners of his mouth, but that smile stayed far from his eyes. The dark withdrew from his eyes, revealing their brilliant Caville blue.

"Brother, you brought back my gift." The words were hollow, like the man. He got to his feet and met Vasili eye-to-eye at the foot of the dais. His full-length royal blue coat, always so artfully applied, hung off his thinner frame. Loose silver threads trailed from his cuffs. He absently picked at them now, slowly unraveling the stitching.

"Your new doulos, my king." Vasili swept a hand and stepped aside, revealing Niko.

"Hm." Amir looked at his brother as though expecting a trick, but when none came, he stepped in.

Vasili snatched his wrist. The brothers were briefly locked, like two crossed swords. "He's yours, but your guards are mine. The defense of this city is mine. You are king in name only. I control Loreen. Do you understand, *little brother?*"

Amir yanked his arm free and rubbed his wrist. "The city is dead anyway."

"Because *you let it die*," Vasili seethed.

Amir laughed and stepped away. "While you ran away with your blacksmith? How did that work out for you? Wasn't what you thought, was it? The Yazdans use us. It's always been that way. I showed them. ME!" He stabbed a finger at his own chest. "I took the fight to them and they were so stuck up their own asses they didn't think a Caville could touch them. It was too easy. I had the flame devour them one by one."

"You left Seran defenseless. The city has fallen to the elves."

"Fuck Seran. They never cared for us, so why should we for them? And fuck the Yazdans. You can't *love* one, brother. Hating us is in their blood." His salacious gaze fell again to Niko, undressing him with his eyes.

Niko's guts squirmed.

"Are we agreed?" Vasili asked coolly.

"Fine! The guards were a bore anyway." Amir slithered his way up to Niko. His eyes narrowed as he inspected Niko's forced expression. "Where to start with you, hm?"

Niko folded his fingers into a fist behind his back.

"I'll fuck that mouth first." He licked his lips, venturing closer. "There's no Julian this time. Just you and me, and I'm going to make you howl—"

Niko jabbed the bastard square between the eyes. Amir's nose buckled, bone crunched. The king's hands shot to his bleeding face.

A surge of satisfaction raced through Niko. He'd fucking kill the bastard, right here and now, flame be damned—

Vasili slammed a hand into Niko's chest, shoved him back, fear sharp in his eye. Fear for who? A sudden, savage lash of cold struck like a whip to the chest, but instead of landing on his skin, the lash poured down his throat to claim his lungs. Niko choked, stumbled—gasped at the dark, but all he saw in the swarming shadows was Amir's twisted face.

~

He came around slowly in a room with bars on the windows and rows of cot beds. The doulos chambers, but the beds were empty, stripped of sheets and belongings, and the air smelled stale.

Vasili sat on the edge of one of the beds, elbows on his knees, face in his hands, and fingers threaded into his hair. "A minute with Amir and you almost got yourself killed," he said into his hands.

Niko's knuckles throbbed. "It was worth it." The assault made his voice hoarse and his chest ache. Still worth it.

He sat up on the bed and waited for the room to stop spinning before meeting Vasili's fresh glare.

"Where are all the other doulos?" Niko rubbed at his throat, trying to soothe the croak.

The small laugh that slipped from Vasili wasn't entirely sane. "He killed them all."

"Shit. You could have mentioned that before I agreed to this."

"Would it have mattered?"

He knew Amir was mad, but he was only now beginning to understand Vasili's desperation. Niko winced and tried to reorganize his thoughts around where he was and what had to be done.

Vasili's gaze burned with fresh intensity. He was walking the edge too, just like Amir. But he wasn't exactly like Amir, that much had become startlingly clear. In those last moments before Niko had blacked out, he'd seen Amir for what he truly was now, and he wasn't in control.

"By the three, he's fucking nuts," Niko grumbled, still rubbing at his neck.

"He's embraced the flame," Vasili said, with a mocking flourish.

"You're not like that?"

"Oh," his laugh cut, "I'm not far off. I..." He licked his lips and stared at the floor. "Nikolas..."

The way he said his name, it wasn't like any way he'd said it before, and it made Niko's chest ache with guilt. Niko opened his mouth to explain why he'd hit Amir, but Vasili held up a hand, stopping the words.

Vasili sighed and rubbed at his face. This Vasili... He was bone tired, maybe even a little lost, like the last drop of strength had been wrung from his body. "This isn't going to work."

Niko half laughed. "I'm here, aren't I?"

"I can't protect you."

"I can protect myself."

Vasili's dry look dashed those words. "I have three thousand men and women to control, using a power I don't fully understand, and—at most—a week to master it before the elves arrive in force."

He'd do it. Whatever Vasili put his mind to, he'd accomplish. "You'll master it."

He smiled softly and gave his head a small shake. "I'm afraid."

"That's never stopped you be—"

"For you."

Niko's thoughts stalled. "Why?"

"You're too honest. You can't help yourself. You'll say or do something to trigger Amir. If I'm to master his possessed, I must focus. I can't have half my mind on whether you need saving or not."

Niko felt his smile growing. Vasili wanted to protect him? "I don't need saving."

Vasili's gentle smile grew too, and all that was missing was an oxeye daisy in his hair. He didn't want to be here with Vasili. He wanted to be back at the cottage, where he'd go to his knees and kiss that smiling mouth until he moaned Niko's name. But those dreams didn't belong here.

Vasili stood, crossed the floor, and as Niko tilted his head back, Vasili stopped so close he had to lean back to look up at his face, but it was worth it, because Vasili's expression was open and warm, and everything Niko would never have believed he'd see on his face.

Cool fingers skimmed along Niko's jaw. "You're impossible," Vasili whispered.

Niko caught his hand, daring to touch. He waited for Vasili's expression to tighten, but it softened instead. He couldn't remember the last time anyone had ever looked at him like Vasili was now, like he was their whole world in that moment. And he'd never expected to see that warmth from Vasili.

"You deliberately make yourself difficult to love," Niko said, peering up at the man who had consumed his mind and body for so long it had become the way things were now. "You push everyone away. Because anytime you've gotten close to someone, they've suffered. But it was never your fault, Vasili."

Vasili tilted his head back, showing Niko the underside of his jaw, and sighed. "Do you know me, Nikolas?" he asked, looking down and meeting Niko's gaze again, but this time his beautiful eye was glassy, as though he fought his emotions back into their box.

"I know you like nobody else dares." He straightened, putting himself chest to chest with Vasili. The prince's fingers still played lightly at his jaw, stiffening him with desire. "I know you love the sun on your face." He stroked his knuckles down Vasili's cheek, and when the prince leaned into the touch, he fought to keep his heart from hammering out of his chest. "I know you love the simple things."

"Such as?" Vasili asked. His voice had grown rich with the same desire that strummed through Niko.

"My hand on you now. This kiss..." He brushed a painfully light kiss against Vasili's lips, resisting as he tilted his chin up for more.

Vasili's breaths fluttered into Niko's. His steady hands pressed against Niko's chest, forcing space between them, but it was reluctant. A step back, and he was slipping through Niko's fingers. "I won't provoke him," Niko vowed. "I'll do everything you want me to."

"I don't want this," Vasili denied, his vehemence quickly returning. "I don't want any of this. What I want is a cabin in the woods with the man I fear I've come to care for, despite all my efforts not to. But what I want has never mattered." He turned suddenly, quickly retreating to the door. "Amir will offer you spice. Take it."

Care?

"Vasili, stop!"

Vasili opened the door but stayed, gripping against its edge instead of passing through.

"You can't..." Niko started forward but stopped again, leaving space between them so as not to push him away. "You can't say *that* and leave."

Vasili peered over his shoulder, only half turning, his escape a step away, but the sly look on his face wasn't an accident. "Get high, do whatever you need to, but don't provoke my brother."

"Fuck Amir." Another step. "I don't want to talk about him. Stay. Talk."

"If Amir finds me here, your suffering and mine will be worse. There is nothing else to say." He stepped through the doorway and pulled the door shut behind him. The lock snicked over. Niko swore, crossed the room, and pressed his hands to the closed door, knowing Vasili was on the other side.

Bowing his head between his braced arms, Niko asked, "Did you say you care to keep me here?"

"I said it because it's true," came his muffled reply.

Niko splayed his fingers and stared at the grain in the wood. "How long?"

The quiet dragged on, but he was still out there. "Some time between the kiss at the farmhouse and you saving me from the fire, but mostly in the woods, after you built us a life. It... surprised me." His voice had deepened, like he'd stepped closer to the door. "It's probably a phase," he said haughtily. "You're really not my type."

Niko laughed softly and thumped his forehead against

the door, imagining Vasili on the other side. "You have a type?"

"Hm."

"Submissive and obliging?"

"Something like that. I cared for you and you despised me in return, so there was no use dwelling on it."

"I didn't hate you," he replied softly.

Vasili's laugh was like liquid honey. "Liar," he purred, so close to the door that if Niko closed his eyes, he could imagine Vasili beside him. "You hate me still."

"Sometimes—most of the time—but then you're the real you, and I..." Niko wet his lips and wished he'd open the door. "Well, there was no saving me then." He curled a hand into a fist and thumped it lightly on the wood. "Tell me you plan to survive all this?"

The quiet dragged on. When he did speak, it was almost too soft to hear. "You will."

"Vasili," he warned, knowing that careful reply for the misdirection it was, "What of you?"

"I'll do what's necessary to stop the elves."

The sounds of his footfalls faded into the palace corridors until there was nothing left of the prince but his confession in Niko's head.

CHAPTER 35

D*on't provoke my brother.*

Niko paced, then sat on the edge of the cot bed, listening to Vasili's voice in his head.

The man I fear I've come to care for.

Gods, he didn't want to be here, didn't want to be Amir's plaything, didn't want any of this. He just wanted their real dream again; the cabin and the man who had just told him he *cared*. He might have thought it lies if Vasili hadn't tossed him that wicked little grin, the real grin that said he knew what he was doing to Niko and delighted in every torturous admission.

Vasili genuinely cared for him? This wasn't some spice-addled written fantasy letter, but startling reality. What did it mean that the prince had confessed such a thing? Too many questions, and until Vasili returned, there would be no answers—if he ever planned on having any. Knowing Vasili, he'd never mention it again, and Niko would be left wondering if he'd imagined it all.

But damn... Niko smiled at the empty room. Damn. Vasili cared and Niko cared right back?

But no, he couldn't dwell on that. Considering what came next, it would be better to forget Vasili entirely.

Amir should be his focus.

Niko's service had bought Vasili an army and Loreen a last chance against the elves. There was no other way.

He was a soldier. Fucking Amir, surrendering to that bastard's desires, was just another battle.

If he could think of it like that, he'd get through it.

Late afternoon light spilled into the room by the time the door lock rattled, and two guards entered. "The king is ready. Come along quietly and we won't have to restrain you." The guard who spoke showed Niko his iron shackles, emphasizing his point.

"You won't need those."

They escorted him through scorched hallways, passing crumbled holes in the ceiling where water streamed through. The palace was barely habitable and echoed the city's decay. Soon, there'd be nothing left of Loreen worth saving.

The new bedchamber they took him to was untouched by smoke or fire. The guards left him alone inside, closing the door behind them. Niko eyed that door. He hadn't heard a lock, but he couldn't leave. Couldn't walk away. Not from this.

He'd done some terrible things at the front line, given in to that monstrous part of him that had enjoyed slicing a blade through elf flesh too much, but he'd never submitted and never surrendered.

Vasili had better win his damn battle while Niko fought his.

Amir strode in near sunset, neatly closing the door behind him. He instantly stopped at a sideboard to pour himself a drink. Niko's only acknowledgment was a twitch of Amir's eyebrow.

He downed the contents of his glass and sighed like he'd already had enough of the day. "He finally got you to heel."

Niko clenched his jaw and locked his hands behind his back.

He leaned back against the sideboard and pressed the glass to his cheek, rolling it across his skin. "What did he tell you, hm? That this was for the good of Loreen? Did he appeal to your need to be heroic?" Amir's gaze drank Niko in. He was firmly Amir in this moment and untouched by the flame, probably because the dark had no interest in his carnal affairs.

"You look different." He set his glass down and moved to stand close. "Rougher, definitely. These last few months can't have been easy. Learning you had a whole other family, how it's in your ancestry to shape the flame. Oh yes, I know all about the Yazdans. I know all about you."

"If we're going to fuck, let's get on with it. You might learn a thing or two."

Amir's lips twitched. "There's that infamous mouth of yours." He reached up and dragged his fingertips down Niko's cheek. It was all Niko could do to stand rigid and not take a swing at him. He gritted his teeth and willed the disgust from his head. This wasn't going to get any easier.

"Do you really think that's all I want you for?" He smiled as he backed up. "Interesting." Refilling his drink, he took a medicine bottle from the cupboard beneath the sideboard and removed the stopper, pouring a few sprinkles of spice into his glass. "It's unlike my brother to be so short-sighted, but then I suppose, if he'd told you the truth, you wouldn't be here."

Whatever the bastard was talking about, Niko was done listening. Maybe he planned to bore Niko to death with the sound of his own voice. Gods, he'd almost prefer the sex.

"Where do you want me?" He didn't even bother to try and hide his impatience. At least nobody expected him to enjoy this.

"Right where you are."

That smile, there was something very wrong with it. Vasili had his own version, and it had nothing to do with happiness and everything to do with having caught his prey in his trap. Just what game was Amir playing?

"You clearly know about the flame, but I'm going to assume Vasili hasn't told you all of it."

"I know enough. I know it has you where it wants you."

Amir poured a second glass, spiked it with spice, just like his own, and, approaching Niko, he handed it out. "It'll make what happens next a lot more enjoyable for you."

A large part of him wanted to take the glass and throw it in Amir's face, but Vasili had said not to provoke him. He'd said to take the spice. And Niko knew from experience the vile drug would take the edge off whatever was about to happen. Niko couldn't fight, and he couldn't leave. There really was only one way he got through this, and that was to accept it.

He took the glass and tasted the drink. Woody and potent, like some of the harder drinks served in the Stag and Horn. It wasn't unpleasant. He gulped a few mouthfuls under Amir's watchful gaze.

"Your colorful friend... What's his name?" Amir gestured, reaching. "Captain Lajani—"

How did Amir know of Yasir? From Seran, perhaps? The carriage he'd had his beasts chase. He must have seen Yasir then. "Leave him out of this."

"An interesting threesome. A blacksmith, a silk merchant, and a prince."

"It's not... We're not involved... like that." Why was he telling him anything? Oh, the spice. He'd have to watch for it loosening his tongue.

"His lover should probably be aware of his infidelity, no?"

Niko gritted his teeth. Amir couldn't know about Liam. Yasir had kept him a secret from almost everyone. He was fishing, waiting for Niko to bite.

More of the drink went down smoothly, filling that empty spot inside from Vasili's leaving. "It's strange how the Caville smarts skipped you, huh? I mean, and what did you get Amir? It certainly wasn't the personality. The art of looking pretty?"

Amir's tongue darted across his lower lip.

He wasn't supposed to provoke him. But that hadn't been provocation, that was just... a fact. "I'm surprised Talos didn't drown you at birth instead of your elder sist—"

The backhand landed with a loud thwack and enough force to throw Niko against the bedpost. He dropped the glass, spilling the rest of the drink across the bare floorboards. His face was ablaze, but it had been oh, so worth it.

Amir's fingers locked around his throat and hauled him upright. "There's the Yazdan fire." He grinned. "This really would be very dull if you'd stayed obliging."

He produced some kind of glass cylinder with a metal spike on the end. Niko shoved at his chest, but Amir drove in, edging his forearm under Niko's chin.

Spice muddled Niko's reflexes, making him slow. Amir's palm slammed over his face, forcing his head back.

A sharp, jabbing sting burned at his neck. He got a knee between them and kicked Amir off, then clutched the strange cylindrical container and pulled its needle from his neck. "What the fuck?!" He threw it back at Amir but missed. It struck the wall and exploded, splashing red up the colorful wallpaper.

Gods, his neck burned. He dabbed at it and found more blood. Did Amir put something *inside* him?

"Gods, that look on your face... it's too fuckin' precious." He laughed again. "You're still catching up, aren't you? Best hurry, you don't have long."

Niko shoved off the bedpost and made a lung for Amir, but his legs felt like lead. He stumbled, pitched over, and dropped onto his knees and a hand. His chest burned hotter with every breath, like his heart pushed broken glass through his veins and it had all gathered there. "What—"

"What, what, what," Amir crooned.

Amir crouched, within reach, but Niko couldn't organize his thoughts enough to reach for him. "What did you do?"

"What Vasili couldn't."

Every vein felt hot and heavy, weighed him down. Not spice. Something else ravaged him.

"Your captain friend, he's not very good at binding the dark, is he?"

Niko crawled forward, desperate to keep from falling, but the room was spinning, and Amir was there, grinning down at him like he'd won.

"He's never going to be a sorcerer, for a very simple reason. He's not a Yazdan. He doesn't have the key in his blood, like you do."

"A... key?"

"Three keys. Three bloodlines. The Cavilles, we bear the flame, we're the lamp from the tales, the one always tossed away after it's been used. And the Yazdans—the sorcerers—they use the flame, shape it, destroy with it. And the Buclands, now they were supposed to stop it, kill it, snuff it out. There's not many of them left. None... actually, except whatever dregs are in your blood."

"Buclands...?" That name seemed relevant if he could just think around the fog in his head.

Three keys.

Three families.

It was all there, but Niko's damned thoughts couldn't grasp the pieces and slot them into place.

Amir's fingers locked in Niko's hair and yanked, dragging Niko back onto his feet. "The Yazdans bled us of power for their own personal gain for generations. They made us their slaves. So now I'm making you mine."

Niko reached for Amir's leering face and missed, falling into his embrace instead.

"I have you now, dog. Forever at the end of my leash."

Blood.

It was blood inside that cylinder.

Amir's blood. Caville blood. Infected with the dark.

And now it was *inside* Niko, ravaging his will, *binding* him to Amir, making him into something he despised. No, this was worse than surrendering, worse than enduring Amir's sick appetites. He could feel it, the flame... spreading, feasting, infecting. And it laughed in Niko's head, the sound so much like Talos's laugh in his final moments.

"I don't need an army," Amir whispered, "when Nikolas Yazdan is all mine."

CHAPTER 36

He drifted. Somewhere not awake and not asleep, somewhere *between*. In the *between*, the wolf from his dreams stalked him like it had before, circling around and around, coming closer.

And there was no escape.

"—My own concoction... with added spice—"

He recognized the voice as Amir's, but he was so far away that his words couldn't be important.

"He'll offer you spice, take it."

Vasili, yes. He knew that voice too. "I don't want this." Were those his words or Vasili's? The prince had told him he cared, but in his dreams, he had laughed and made Niko a fool for believing it.

"I've never lied to you, Niko." Amir again. "I'm the only one who's always told you the truth. Not all of it. Because where's the fun in that? But more than my brother ever has."

The *bastard Yazdan boy*, Amir had told him that. Told

him the truth. That he wasn't his father's son. He was a dirty secret. A hidden mistake.

A sharp jab of heat and tingling radiated from his neck, down his spine, and spread from chest to limbs, lighting him on fire with darkness. The pain plucked him from the dreams but just as quickly submerged him in them again. He saw Vasili in a starlit field, heard him rage that Niko had failed them all. He followed him through a gate, and behind them, a sea of elves poured in. Then the dream shifted, and the wolf was back, so close he could make out its rippling fur and dark, hungry eyes. Niko looked into those eyes, and his own reflection looked back.

That was when he knew: he *was* the wolf.

THE *BETWEEN* BEGAN TO FADE, and the edges of the room sharpened, coming into painful focus. His limbs were made of lead, his body of stone. A small voice at the back of his mind demanded he fight, but other voices were louder. Voices that told him this was right, that this was the way it should always have been, this was the purpose he'd been searching for, that the poison in his blood *belonged to him*.

Sunlight flooded the room, blurring his vision. Thunder rumbled. Dark and light, storms and sunlight.

Something was very wrong with *everything*.

The world had shifted sideways beneath him, and now he didn't fit within it.

The weight on his wrists lifted, freeing his arms.

Soft lips touched his own. "Take it," a familiar voice whispered. "Take it all."

Vasili.

Niko plunged a hand into his hair, needing him like he needed to breathe the prince into his soul, but the kiss was all wrong, the taste sweetened by spice, the mouth too hard.

Amir.

He didn't want this.

The king's rumbling purr shuddered through them both. His mouth took and gave, and that small voice screamed at him to stop, but he wasn't stopping, because there was something else in the king, something heavy, something powerful, and Niko *wanted* every last drop. More than want, he needed it. It belonged to him. Always had.

Thunder shook the world.

Niko pulled, gasping from the kiss. Shadows devoured the light in the room.

What... was this? He plastered a cool hand to his face. Gods, he was burning up. Who even was he?

"No, you don't get to stop." Amir's hand grasped Niko's impossibly hard cock, making him gasp. The king's tongue thrust into his mouth again.

His thoughts spun, body ablaze.

This wasn't right.

He didn't want this.

Didn't want Amir.

Didn't want this weight slowly suffocating him.

Or the voice in his head, telling him to surrender.

A vast clap of thunder struck the palace walls. Plaster crumbled from the ceiling.

"Dammit!" Amir's weight vanished.

Breathless, thoughts spinning, Niko tried to capture

them, make sense of them and this and everything, but every thought slipped through his fingers, desire scorched his veins, and by Etara, he'd never felt so fucking *alive*.

"Hm," the king grunted from the window, "I suppose it will have to be enough." He cinched his silk gown closed and returned to the bed. "Get up."

Niko's body immediately lightened and, without thought, he was sitting up and staring at Amir as though the king had all the answers and all he had to do was hang on his every word.

"You're going to kill all those vicious creatures, and when we're done with them, anyone who has ever stood against me will fall, including Vasili." Amir caught Niko's jaw and leaned in. "He'll understand then," he said intimately. "He'll see me like he used to, he'll know I'm worth his attention, right before you cut his throat."

Yes. Yes, Niko could do that. Heat swelled through muscle and flesh. Threads of dark flame bridged between his body and Amir's. Dark flame rippled down his arms and pooled in his hands. From the shadows, countless eyes burned like red stars. Waiting to be bound.

Power.

So much.

All of it.

He'd make all the monsters dance for him... for Amir.

No, not all the power was present. Fragments were missing. The other half of the whole was nearby—outside, his darkness bright in the Loreen streets, a shadow beast at his side as he commanded the souls of thousands holding back a wave of elf forces. A beacon in an ocean of dark. His other half.

Vasili.

I don't want this.

I fear... come to care for.

Amir's hands brushed over Niko's chest. Armored clothing was draped across his sizzling skin and buckled firmly into place. The king stepped back, pride in his eyes. "The first true Caville sorcerer in hundreds of years, and you're mine." He draped an arm over Niko's shoulder, pressing close to peer deep into Niko's eyes. "Obey me."

"Yes." He heard himself speak but the word wasn't his. There was something inside him, something driving his will, something malign and hungry and cold, so cold it might consume all the heat and light in the world.

"Obey me, *master*," Amir urged. "Say it."

Niko wet his lips.

"Fucking say it!"

This wasn't right.

He didn't want this.

"No." That word belonged to him. Just one little word, but it was his and it had power too.

"Ah," Amir said, disappointedly. "Of course, you'd be too damn stubborn to accept it." He produced a fresh needle. "The guards took a few shots before they became my toys. This is your... eighth?" The red liquid sloshed in the cylinder as Amir approached.

Niko should fight this. Why couldn't he?

Another rumble trembled through the broken palace.

The world was coming undone and all Niko could think was how he wanted to drown in the dark.

He couldn't make himself move, couldn't think around the presence in his head. Impossibly, Amir controlled every second, stringing one to the next, leading Niko along.

"No time for finesse." Amir took Niko's hand, turned it over, exposing the wrist, and pricked the needle into a vein.

More heat poured through him, and the hungry cold inside yawned wide, desperate for escape. That was the dark flame. He knew it for what it was, knew he should be raging, screaming, fighting with every breath and beat of his heart to make this stop, but he did none of those things.

"There's a good dog." Amir withdrew the needle. A bead of blood glistened at the entry point. He swept it up and licked his finger clean. "Having you like this is so fucking hot." He stroked his finger down Niko's cheek, his touch hard and cold. "Don't you agree?"

"Yes, master."

Amir's laugh boomed. "Vasili was a fool not to have turned you sooner! I can only imagine my brother found his cold, dead heart somewhere in Seran. It's a shame he didn't find it years ago when I needed him the most. I became invisible to him. No matter what I did, he stopped seeing me. He'll pay for that mistake. He'll *see* me now. But first..." He patted Niko's chest. "I suppose we must see off these elves. I'll show Vasili the true power of a Caville and Yazdan union." He sighed, his expression softening. "Your father would be proud. Not the drunk blacksmith, the other one, Bucland. Pity I killed him like I did your parents before him."

A crack zagged through the ice inside him. Just a crack. The ice held, its touch breathlessly cold.

"Did Maria tell you, hm?" Amir teased. "My treacherous aunt? Did she tell you how Bucland was found hanged from a familiar tree? I made sure she knew. She likes to collect secrets. Thinks I don't know. Like the books with their missing pages. Your captain friend will find nothing but riddles in their pages, but they'll keep him occupied while I fuck your head, heart, and body into submission."

Niko's heart thudded harder. He heard himself screaming, but the sound never reached his lips. His ice prison held.

Amir peered closer. "Hm, you all thought me the fool, didn't you? My brother did too. He kicked me to one side in favor of chasing the flame. All this time... he had no idea I knew about you, about your bitch of a Yazdan mother coming all this way to find Bucland and form an alliance, how they hid you, their babe, in a blacksmith's forge, thinking you'd grow to be strong in the shadow of the palace so that one day, you'd stop the flame." He stroked both hands down the front of Niko's coat. "I watched Vasili try and find you, watched him try and understand who and what you were. It really was so much easier to let my brother do all the work. He has no idea how he played right into my hands." Stepping back, he clapped his hands once, his face lighting up with glee. "Come along then, my beautiful bastard."

And Niko went.

CHAPTER 37

Words fell harmlessly from Amir's lips, but the same words fell like hammer blows from Niko's, building something, shaping it, pulling weight from the shadows and throwing it around them as though the night could be hammered and forged into a weapon. And that weapon was Niko's.

Wrong, but so right.

Cold, dark flame rippled over the cobbled streets ahead of them, hungrily reaching outward. Niko could taste what it tasted. Blood and earth and death in the air. A feast for the flame to devour.

The clash of swords rang through the air.

And then the elves came.

Just three. The first of many...

They burst around a corner and kept right on running at them, blades free, teeth bared, eyes fiery with murderous intent.

Amir placed a weighty sword in Niko's grip. "Kill them and feed the flame."

Amir spoke more words, and Niko echoed them until they became a chant in his head, beating in time with his heart. The sword swung, and the dark consumed. And the elves lay dead, turning to ash at his feet. It was all so... easy. Alive then dead. A blink. Gone.

"More," Amir barked, striding past. He raised his arms, skipped backward, and laughed. "More, Nikolas! Take this fucking city for me and everyone in it."

The streets filled with rushing elves.

Niko looked through the flame and into their approaching charge. No fear. No doubt. The words on his tongue were so familiar now he didn't need to speak them aloud. They were in his head, driving him forward. He swept into the first wave, cloaked in the killing night, cutting them down like they were nothing but falling leaves.

The wind picked up the drifts of ash and made it fall like filthy snow.

Beautiful.

Wrong.

Amir laughed his insidious laugh, and Niko killed, and nothing had felt more right.

Something burst out of the shadows and slammed into Niko's side, crashing him against a wall. Jarred from reality, silence reigned over his thoughts. Blissful silence.

The beast's eyes flashed. The beast that had plowed into him.

Vasili's?

It lunged a second time.

Niko flung an arm up. Teeth sank into his muscles and yanked. It should hurt. His mind told him the blood was his. But nothing about the attack felt like it belonged to him. The beast thrashed its head and Niko coolly observed.

"Amir!" This new voice was real and loud and pissed. "Release him!"

The beast stopped its mauling and dropped back onto all fours. Blood and drool streamed from its mouth.

Niko lifted his gaze to the approaching figure.

All-black armor made his pale hair and skin shine under the moonlight. He stepped over the dead. Stains marked his face too. Red stains.

Amir laughed and clapped his hands. "Dear brother, did you think to have all the fun without me?"

Vasili pointed the tip of a dagger at Niko.

Amir lowered his hands and grinned. "You're the fool, Vasili."

"I swear by Etara, if you don't immediately release him from your binding, I will kill you where you stand, *brother*." Hate burned through that last word, and the flame burned through Vasili, lit him up, calling to Niko to strike it down, to end his life and let it become one again.

Amir ran a hand through his hair. "Nikolas, my darling, kill Vasili."

The flame tingled through Niko's veins, lending him its unnatural strength, and Niko straightened.

Vasili glanced over. Fear made his blue eye shine. "Amir, stop this."

"You made a mistake, Vasili." Amir grinned. "In all this time, you never once fucked up, but you've fucked up now, brother. You gave me the greatest weapon there is in this war, and you didn't think I'd recognize it for what it is."

Niko approached. Blood trickled down his arm and slickened the grip on his sword.

Vasili glanced between them. "Amir, don't do this. We must find a way to keep us both alive, to keep the flame controlled. Neither you nor I can control it alone."

But Amir was beyond reason. Rage warped his face. "You were going to kill me at the shah's funeral!"

Vasili winced. "No, I was going to render you helpless. We're too close to the palace. If you kill me, the flame wins."

"It's already won. It won the day we were born."

Vasili lifted a hand, holding it palm-out toward Niko. "Niko, stop."

Ash silently fell, landing on Niko's lashes. His orders were to kill Vasili, and he was always a good soldier. He always followed orders.

"*Kill him*!" Amir screeched.

He didn't want this.

The screaming in his head grew louder. But the ice held.

Growls bubbled from behind him. Niko spun. Vasili's beast leaped. His blade sailed unhindered through its body, but the beast's mass slammed into Niko like it had before, knocking him down. The sword skittered from his grip. He reached for it, saw Vasili kick it free, and met the prince's icy, blue-eyed gaze. He seemed... defeated. Vasili wouldn't hurt him, not even to save himself.

A fresh crack sparked through the ice.

Vasili... cared.

A gunshot boomed.

The beast howled and wisped into smoke.

"No!" Vasili flung his glare down the street.

Yasir stood some distance away, hat tilted back, his glare locked down the long barrel of a large gun. Salt. He'd fired salt into the beast, thinking it was Vasili who attacked Niko.

The alien laughter started up again in Niko's head. Mistakes, that was how the flame won. Men made mistakes. Humans made mistakes. The dark flame was faultless. It existed. Consumed. And it *hungered*.

Amir laughed. "You surround yourself with fools, brother." Amir reached for Niko and hauled him to his feet.

"Niko?" Vasili held both blades at his sides. They were the only defense he had, but he was fast with them. "Listen to my voice, not his. You're too stubborn for this." His voice hitched. "Damn you, Nikolas. You were not supposed to succumb!"

"He won't stop, brother. He's all mine and he's powerful—can't you feel it? After he kills you, I'll have him fuck your corpse right here in the street and make the elves watch."

Vasili bared his teeth and backed up. *"Amir, gods-damn you! Why are you like this?!"*

"Because I fucking loved you. You were the only right thing in my life, and overnight you just changed. You forgot me. I lost you and had nothing else."

"That's absurd."

"You don't even see it, even now. You're so wrapped up in the flame, you don't give a shit about me."

"Amir, I always cared."

"Bull-fucking-shit. You think I don't know your lies?! You stopped caring when mother told you about the flame, and then Carlo came and she died, and you were gone, lost somewhere in the legends. And then when the elves came, I made sure you really were gone because I couldn't fucking stand to be around you when you looked right through me."

"I looked right through you because of this! I couldn't look at you and know it would destroy us, so I pushed you away, it's true." His face saddened with regret. "I pushed you away to save you."

"Oh, fuck off, Vasili. Niko, before he dies, take his good eye. I want him to truly feel alone just like I've done for my entire fucking life!"

"Yes, master."

Vasili's shocked expression made Niko's insides knot, but he couldn't take the words back. He couldn't stop himself from approaching Vasili, and he wouldn't be able to stop what came next either. The master inside his veins pulled his strings, and he had no means of cutting free.

Amir was back to laughing like all this was perfectly hilarious. "You truly didn't know he's this powerful?"

"No," Vasili replied, his tone dangerously level.

"He's so damned beautiful brother. Look at him."

"You figured it out, Amir." He studiously stared at his brother. "You got there before me."

Amir preened at that. "Finally, you see my worth, albeit too fucking late. One thing I must know, because it's so unlike you to miss an opportunity staring you in the face. Why didn't you give Niko your blood? You know what our blood does to people. So, why not possess Niko?"

Vasili frowned hard. He fought to keep the grimace from his lips but failed and turned his pained expression on Niko.

"Oh fuck... you care about him, you *really* care." Amir spat a horrible, brittle laugh. "You found someone you couldn't manipulate into being your tool and fell for him? I mean, you still fucked him up, but you wouldn't go any further because you like him. Shit, you had a limit after all. I bet that was a surprise for everyone. Cold, heartless Vasili Caville actually gives a shit about someone who isn't himself. Do you love him?"

Vasili's expression subtly altered from pain to regret. "Amir."

"You do, you fucking do." His grin stretched. "My darling dog Nikolas, kill Vasili."

Niko started forward, his body and mind out of his control.

"Hold!" Yasir approached, gun raised for a second time, but this time its barrels were fixed on Amir.

"Aim at Nikolas," Vasili snapped.

Yasir hesitated. "What?"

"*Shoot Niko*," Vasili said.

"No, I'm not—"

Amir chuckled. "Nobody trusts you, brother."

Vasili tossed him a snarl and backed up some more, stumbling over a body. Niko methodically tracked him, and Vasili raised his blades again. "Nikolas, you know I didn't want this."

He knew that, but he also knew this was happening, and despite the screaming in his head, there was nothing he could do to stop it.

"Yasir, shoot Niko!"

Twin gun barrels finally pointed at Niko. "Niko, talk to me."

"He can't," Vasili hissed. "Shoot him, Yasir. He can't stop this. You can."

Amir clapped his hands together and laughed harder. "This is fucking priceless! He's so high on power and spice, shoot him and he'll just get right back up. Nikolas Yazdan does everything I tell him to. He's mine, Vasili." Amir pointed a finger at his brother. "He's all fucking mine, and knowing you love him makes this all the sweeter."

Niko stepped over the body Vasili had stumbled over moments before. The prince had his back at a wall now with nowhere to go. He brandished the blades like a threat, and maybe he'd summon the flame to help, but it didn't matter. Niko was more than the flame, more than Vasili's or Amir's power. He was made to be more.

"Niko, dammit! Stop!" Yasir barked, circling around to face him.

A high-pitched whistle shattered the distant sounds of battle.

An elf call.

Niko knew it. He'd heard it before on the front. Reinforcements. If Amir didn't unleash him on the elves, they'd soon flood into the streets in a wave bigger than the first.

Vasili's head whipped around at the sound. His cheek ticked, and that was all the warning Niko had. Vasili's blade flew. The dagger punched into his shoulder, but barely broke his stride. It all happened too fast, but at the same time excruciatingly slow, as though time was slowing to make him see the terrible thing he was about to do.

He tore the blade free, tossed it away and pinned Vasili to the wall, making the prince bark a cry.

"Kill him!" Amir screamed.

Niko's thumb sank into Vasili's beautiful eye. The prince opened his mouth in a silent scream. He didn't fight, didn't push back, because Niko pushed against the past already branded into his chest. Elves had done this.

Held him down. Took his eye. And now Niko would take the other.

Another crack in the ice. A gasp of freedom.

Horror tried to squeeze the air from Niko's lungs and the blood from his heart. He couldn't... do this.

"Fucking blind him! Make the bitch scream like your mother screamed when I put a noose around her neck and cut her throat!" Amir's manic laughter delivered the final, devastating crack to Niko's ice.

A gun blasted so loud and close that Niko staggered under the weight of fresh fire in his side, his ears ringing. Vasili slipped from his fingers. A kick landed in his gut, and then he was on his back, staring at the falling ash, wondering why it was snowing in Loreen.

Shouts went up, but they had nothing to do with him because none of this was real. It couldn't be. This was all part of the nightmare Amir had him wrapped in.

His gut heaved, folding his spine. He rolled onto his side and heaved up a sticky mass of wet blackish phlegm.

The sounds of a scuffle and blades and gasps tried to pull his focus back into the moment. A battle... he was part of it, maybe... Gods, he couldn't think. Etara, take him now. Why was his skin on fire?

"Shit! Shit, shit, shit..." Yasir's worried face suddenly filled Niko's vision. "Niko... Are you in there?" His hands roamed over Niko's shoulder and chest, burning every damn inch of skin they touched.

Niko let out a low moan. "You shot me."

Yasir grinned. "Move... we have to move. *Now*." He whipped his head up. "Fuck," he said, and was gone, leaving Niko trying to grasp at the falling ash.

The hideous, twisted face of an elf appeared, looming over him.

Fear shot like fresh ice through his veins. He reached for his blade—*gone*. The elf lunged in. Thick, rough fingers vised around Niko's neck and the other hand sank into his hair. The elf hauled him along behind. Niko clutched at the elf's grip and tried to dig his boots into the cobbles. He twisted, grabbed at the road, but his fingers slipped and his nails scraped the stone instead.

The elf let go.

Air. He pulled it over his tongue and filled his lungs, then hacked up more of the foul black stuff and spat it onto the cobbles. The world dipped and swayed, his place in it unbalanced, like he lay on an ocean that might swallow him down.

Boots running. Swords clashing. Moans and cries.

And fire. Real fire, with heat and sparks.

Was he in Etara's hell? It was all too much at once and not a bit of it felt real. He'd dreamed... but what was real and what was fantasy?

Vasili had given him up to Amir and then told him he cared. That was real.

Niko rolled onto his front and pushed up with his arms. Soldiers marched through the street. So many. Loreen guards. If he could just find a sword... he could fight. He knew how to do that.

He got a knee under him. His shoulder throbbed. Get up. Fight. Simple.

An arm hooked under his. He was about to thank them when a cold blade touched his throat and he looked up into a fresh pair of elf eyes. The elf smiled.

A small blade swooped in from behind him and opened

up a second smile in the elf's neck, but Niko's sudden hope was short-lived. The elf dropped, clutching his throat, and Amir grabbed Niko by the arm. "The city is lost," the king whispered close as he hauled Niko to his feet. "You're still mine."

But Niko wasn't. For all the pain and dizziness and sickness, he knew this was wrong, and his body was his own again. And by the gods, his fury was a thing alive in his veins, like the flame, only it belonged to him. Amir had a bloody dagger in his hand. If he could get it from him, he could kill the bastard, but if he did that, the flame would jump and destroy all the control left in Vasili. Better to wait, to play Amir's game, to trap him.

Vasili darted from a side alley, swung a right hook, and landed it square in Amir's already bruised nose. Amir's grip on Niko vanished, and Niko staggered against a wall. If he let go, he'd go down to his knees, and he couldn't afford to drop again.

Vasili landed a second punch, this time in his brother's gut. Amir grunted and buckled over. Vasili brought his knee up, smacking Amir's face again. This time the king sprawled backward, arms flung out and landing like a deadweight in the road, puffing up clouds of ash.

Vasili stood over his brother's prone figure. His fingers twitched around his remaining dagger's handle.

"Don't," Niko rasped.

Vasili turned his head. His face was smeared with blood and ash. His skin was as white as his hair, but his eyes were black. *All-black.*

"No," Niko urged.

The flame wanted this. It wanted to be whole again. Niko knew because he'd heard its voice in his head too. It would play the game of men and women until it was free, no matter the bodies it burned through to get there.

"Don't," Niko said again, louder. He didn't care if the elves heard. He couldn't let Vasili kill Amir.

"Don't..." He staggered from the wall. "We'll find another way."

Vasili's face fell. "There is no other way."

He knelt on Amir's chest.

"Vasili?" Amir wheezed.

And plunged the blade into his brother's heart.

CHAPTER 38

The dark flame erupted out of both Amir and Vasili like it had with Talos, manifesting as a great funnel of darkness so large it threatened to block out the sky and chase all the light in the world. It roared skyward in a spiraling storm and then split into two great jaws and came down upon Vasili, swallowing him inside its vortex.

"No!"

Niko stumbled forward. He had to get to him, to tear him free. He'd tear him from the flame with his own bare hands if he had to. He was Niko's, and Niko needed to keep him safe. He'd always save him. *Always.*

The dark howled and whipped up ash and grit, trying to blind Niko, but he made it through the howling noise to see the flame feeding into Vasili's skin.

Vasili lifted his face to the sky.

Ash clung to the tears on his cheeks.

"Vasili?"

He whipped his head around, but there was no

emotion on his face, nothing but the dark looking back. He had become the storm, and the storm had no soul, it had no heart, it just was.

No... Damn that thing, it wasn't taking Vasili's light from this world.

Niko thrust out a hand.

The dark flame lashed.

Let it take Niko instead.

He was done. He'd lived enough, fought enough, but if he could win this last battle and make it so Vasili lived, then it would have been for something.

The flame reared up to strike again.

He looked through the dark and found Vasili at its eye, caught in a life he'd never wanted under a curse he couldn't control.

Niko closed his eyes and sighed out.

"Take my hand, Vasili..." The storm tore the words from his lips, but he'd have heard. He had to. Niko held out his fingers and, like before, when he'd saved him from the flames, Vasili came fighting through, the storm folding around him. His slim fingers locked with Niko's.

Niko heaved with all the strength he had left, and Vasili fell into his embrace.

The roaring storm quieted. The wind died.

Niko opened his eyes and blinked through the ash stuck to his lashes.

Vasili breathed against him, his body nothing but tremors and gasps. Ash lay in his hair. He looked up, blinked, his lips parted in silent shock. But he was Vasili again. The dark had released him, either because it was done with Vasili or it had won. That was a question for later.

"Are you... all right?" Niko asked softly. It was the most absurd question to ask, but Niko could think of nothing else.

"I'm alive."

Gods, he wanted to hold him forever so nothing in the world could hurt him again. Niko reached out a trembling, filthy hand to pluck a piece of ash free from Vasili's hair, and then Vasili tucked himself against Niko's chest, his head bowed under his chin and, gods, Niko held him so close he didn't know where he ended and Vasili began.

The sounds of battle still rang out streets away, fires still raged, and at any moment, elves might come upon them, but he didn't care.

"You're not alone, Vasili. I have you."

Vasili's fingers tightened into fists against Niko's back. A sob tried to choke Niko, and if it weren't for the striking, gun-carrying figure sprinting toward them, he might have gone to his knees and taken Vasili down with him.

"Go! Elves— Go!" Yasir waved the gun toward a side street, indicating which way to go, and they ran.

THEY FLED Loreen alongside terrified townsfolk.

Niko wished he'd done more. Done... *anything*. He had blood on him and his body bore the aches and hurts of battle, but his memory was full of holes. When he reached for how or why he'd ended up on the street, he saw only Amir's laughing face, and so he stopped looking for the past and concentrated on the winding path ahead. Amir... whose body they'd left on the street. Whose flame had funneled into Vasili...

"This is Bucland Manor, isn't it?" Yasir whispered as they stumbled up an overgrown track to find two great stone pillars marking a treelined entranceway.

Niko frowned at the sign—the words BUCLAND etched in stone, now covered in ivy. He hadn't been aware of any direction, just *out* of Loreen. Long ago, when the trees had been smaller and the track clear, he remembered walking hand in hand with Mah to this gateway. She'd crouched and smoothed his hair back, telling him she'd be home for dinner, and she'd leave him to go inside the enormous house.

"It is."

"We should get off the road," Yasir suggested.

Vasili leaned heavily against Niko's side. He nodded, still trembling, and that was all the encouragement Niko needed.

The track meandered through a forest and eventually brought them into a vast open entranceway to reveal what had probably once been a grand limestone manor house. But like everything else in Loreen, it had cracked and decayed with time. Boards covered all the first-floor windows. The left wing had clearly been gutted by fire. Recently, by the scorched vegetation. But the roof was intact, and Niko's legs weren't going to hold him up much longer.

Yasir pulled off a few of the planks and heaved the front door open. "Welcome home, Lord Yazdan." His voice echoed in the grand foyer and up the sweeping staircase. A pigeon startled from its perch somewhere and fluttered above their heads, losing a few feathers before finding another perch. Considering the thin layer of bird shit coating the once-colorful tiles, the birds had moved in some time ago.

"Lovely," Vasili grumbled, the first word he'd spoken since Loreen.

Yasir readied his gun and set off to search the building for any sign of intruders while Niko looked at the staircase as though it were a mountain to climb.

"The upper floors will make good vantage points," Vasili said as he carefully extracted himself from Niko's arm and used the banister to haul himself up the stairs.

At least the first room they came to was pigeon-free. And it had a bed, albeit a filthy one, with an excellent view of the estate's overgrown approach road. Niko wedged himself against the bay window and peered through the grubby glass.

His thoughts drifted with no anchor. Aches and burns and twinges began to reassert themselves. Looking down, he regarded the lightweight leather armor and had no memory of clothing himself or where he'd been before waking in the street. The entire left side of the armored jacket was torn and frayed, caked in dried blood. Elf blood or his own? He didn't dare look for wounds.

He braced against the wall to stop the room from suddenly spinning.

Firm, cool fingers spread against the back of his neck, offering strength now Niko's had failed.

"You're safe," Vasili whispered. The brush of his lips against Niko's ear spilled shivers down his spine. Gods, he wanted nothing more than to rest on that bed with Vasili beside him and never wake again. "The flame, Vasili," he croaked, hastily looking over his shoulder.

Vasili merely smiled. "I'm fine, really. Your concern is

touching but unnecessary." His fingers stroked down the back of Niko's neck, and Niko leaned into him, needing that anchor.

Fine? The flame had devoured him. He'd seen it. How was he standing and walking and functioning like before? "Loreen?"

"It's lost." Vasili let his hand slip away.

"You did all you could."

"No." He blinked. "I did not. When I saw you, Nikolas—saw what he'd done to you—No, don't talk. Shut up and listen for once—*I* should have been the one to turn you."

"That's not a comfort." That was not what he'd wanted to hear from Vasili.

"I planned to," the prince admitted, his face grim, "right from the very beginning, before we met. I'd pull the rumored Yazdan bastard from obscurity and make him mine, but as soon as I found you, you refused to bend to my will, you refused to follow orders, you were obstinate and brutal, you saw right through the walls I'd built around the truth, and for the first time in my life, I doubted my resolve."

"I, er... thank you? I think." Niko leaned away from Vasili and against the wall. So Vasili wished he'd been the one to fuck him up instead of Amir? Gods, he was tired of the double-crossing, the misdirection and all the little lies.

"You were too stubborn, too damned right," Vasili went on, "too everything that makes you who you are, and I told myself it didn't matter, that when the time came, I'd still make you mine, but that time came and went." Vasili backed off, opening a new gulf between them. One of honesty. "I had every opportunity to turn you. But I couldn't, not even to save the city. Amir... I'd dismissed him as ignorant. I was wrong. Those things he said in the street. I didn't know he felt that way... I should have. And he was right. In all of it. Like you said, I push people away. I don't know how else to live." He looked at the room, with its peeling wallpaper and cobwebs, but then turned on his heel and swept back in, so quickly Niko froze, expecting a dagger in his hands. Instead, his soft hands cupped Niko's rough jaw. "And now his influence is in you, and I'm sorry I didn't see the potential in you sooner, I'm sorry it was him, and—"

"Sorry you didn't get there first?"

Vasili sighed and pressed his forehead to Niko's. "Yes. And no. *You* defy me at every turn, Nikolas Yazdan, and I fear I love you for it. Does that make me a fool?"

Love. Gods, the room tipped, and Niko only barely made it to an old chair before his legs gave out. He hmphed over, bracing his elbows on his knees, and tried to breathe. Questions burned on his tongue, but he couldn't bring himself to ask them, fearing the answers. Vasili's love —the words, the truth—they were a gift, but how could he trust it after everything that had happened?

When he next opened his eyes, morning light filtered through the windows, and Vasili lay fully clothed on the bed, breathing deeply.

Amir was dead.

All the flame lived in Vasili now. Niko had seen it. *Felt* it. But he seemed... calm.

A stabbing ache in his chest doubled him over, leaving him gasping. Amir's laughter filled his head as though the man were in the room with them, but it was surely just a memory—one of the many trying to muscle its way back into Niko's thoughts. Gods, that damned wretched Caville haunted him after death.

He stood, swayed a little, and waited for his vision to clear before approaching Vasili.

His chest rose and fell. His closed eye twitched, dreaming. Niko reached out to stroke a curl of hair from his forehead. He remembered the pool, and the nights in the cabin with Vasili tucked close, and Amir's horrible laughter faded to nothing. A memory viciously stabbed at Niko. His thumb in Vasili's eye and a terrible desire to bury that thumb deep into the man's skull and make him scream.

Niko tore away and staggered from the room, and fell into the stair banister, retching up nothing.

He hadn't...

That hadn't been him?

He couldn't have...

Oh, but he could.

He'd done worse to elves, and in that memory, he'd *wanted* to do worse to Vasili. There was a darkness in him. It had always been there. Maybe that's what it truly meant to be a Yazdan.

"Niko?" Yasir's hand landed on Niko's shoulder. The touch steadied him, cleared his head. He almost sobbed with relief. "Come, let's get you cleaned up."

Once again, Yasir tended his wounds. He made light of it as Niko shivered on the floor in front of a roaring fire. Yasir used torn fabric strips to wrap the peppering of wounds down his right side. The deep, weeping cut in his shoulder took more attention. He didn't recall how he'd gotten it. He *did* recall Yasir shooting him with salt. He remembered the searing pain and waking on his back, staring at the falling ash, knowing deep down inside that he'd created that ash, that those remains had been elves. The rest was too ugly to piece back together and make any sense of.

"I don't know what he did to me... that prick. How long was I with him?" Niko croaked out. Cleaned and bandaged, but back in the unfamiliar leather armor, he still felt as though half of himself was missing. Like he'd forgotten something vital.

He'd tucked himself into an armchair by the enormous fireplace, feeling small and insignificant in the high-ceilinged grand hall.

"A week."

A week with Amir. He remembered the taste of blood and spice on his tongue. He looked at his wrists and saw faded puncture marks.

Julian had hurt him emotionally, but Amir... Amir had *violated* him.

Perhaps it was a good thing the spice had taken most of the memories.

"What happened back there in the street?" Yasir asked. He stood at the fireplace, looking somber in the firelight. He had the gun resting against the wall behind him. He'd had it beside him as he'd helped Niko get cleaned up too. It wasn't for intruders.

Yasir didn't trust him. Feared him, even.

Whatever had happened on Loreen's streets, it had made Yasir frightened of him.

He recalled the press of his thumb in Vasili's eye again

and dragged a hand down his face, trying to wipe the memory away. "Fuck if I know."

"What *do* you remember?"

"Just you shooting me with salt."

"It was justified," he said grimly.

Niko sighed and fought the urge to apologize for whatever he'd done under Amir's control. That could only have been what happened. Amir's blood... He'd made Niko one of his possessed but different than the other guards. *Stronger*.

Yasir crouched, bringing him eye level with Niko. "You cut down elves like you were Etara herself. Shadows flocked to you..." He reached absently for words but trailed off when none would suffice. "If all the Yazdans are like you when they're wielding the flame, we're royally fucked."

"They aren't." He was mostly certain of that, though not entirely sure how he could be certain of something he didn't fully understand. "It's over. Amir's dead. Whatever he did to me... it's gone." He wasn't sure about that, though. There was a gaping hole inside him, but it wasn't empty. Just closed. "Vasili holds the flame," he whispered, afraid to speak any louder.

"Then is it over?" Yasir asked, mirroring his thoughts.

Had Yasir seen Vasili take the flame? Was that what he was asking? Niko's instincts had him wanting to protect Vasili from everyone, even Yasir. If word got out that the prince was now the only source of the flame, every damned Yazdan and elf would do anything to get their hands on the prince.

"Vasili seems fine," Niko said. "Maybe... that's all it is." Even after everything Vasili had done, he still wanted to protect him. Maybe that made him a fool too. A prince and a blacksmith, enemies and lovers.

Yasir sighed and crossed the room to peek through a slit in the boarded-up window. "We're a long way out of Loreen."

"It'll be some time before the elves leave the city to sack the surrounding land." Niko absentmindedly glanced around the huge hall. Its wooden paneling made the air oppressive. A pigeon cooed softly from its perch on a ceiling molding. Mah had once worked here. She might even have walked through the same hall, taking her secrets with her. He waited for some kindred instinct to kick in, some sense of belonging, but the house was just an empty house. He didn't belong here. He wanted to retrieve Adamo from the palace stables and ride north with Vasili until they ran out of road.

"I just... It wasn't supposed to be like this," Yasir murmured.

"What wasn't?"

"I came to Loreen to sell silk."

Niko snorted. "I went to a pleasure-house for a distraction and broke Vasili's wrist instead." He rested his head against the back of the chair and remembered Vasili offering him a bag of coin to kill a man. "I blamed Vasili for everything, but all this began long before him." His gaze skimmed over the limestone fireplace with its intricately carved decoration and up to the mantel with its elaborate swirls and waves. The damned thing was a hideous extravagance typical of Loreen lords—of which Niko was supposed to be now. He chuckled at the thought. "Lord of Pigeons," he mumbled, laughing harder, until every muscle hurt again.

Yasir swung a puzzled glance his way and then let his own laugh trickle free. "Gods, in a dilapidated manor house in the frigid asshole of Loreen is not where I'm supposed to be." His laughter faded. "But I... I don't regret it."

"You should."

"No. Meeting you and Vasili, you gave me a purpose. I've spent too long at sea, drifting from port to port."

"We almost got you killed. Multiple times."

"That is true," he chuckled but quickly turned somber. "We had some good times, though."

"We did."

"Niko, there's something you should know."

Niko's gaze snagged on a griffin carved into the limestone in such a way that it was deliberately hidden, and his laughter fell away. The waves in the stone weren't waves—they were flames. And beside the griffin, the flame licked upward, over a crossed hammer and sword. Three insignias. Three families. Three keys.

"Something I've done," Yasir continued, but Niko was only half listening, "and I'm asking that you please don't overreact, or rather... just take a breath... We can handle it, I think. I should have told you before..."

Niko pushed from the chair and approached the fireplace. The limestone monstrosity was out of place inside the hall. Too big, too white, too obvious. "There, see it? Three families."

"No, I just see..." Yasir examined the fireplace up close. "Oh! You don't think... the three keys? Is it a sign?"

"It's something." The fireplace, the house. What if it was more than just walls and a roof? What if he held some significance in this age-old battle against the flame?

A startling whistle pierced the quiet, sailing in from outside. "Nikolas Yazdan!"

Niko reeled. He knew that voice. *Alissand*?! But how... How had he found them? It didn't make any sense... Alissand couldn't have known where they'd be. Unless... He lifted his gaze to Yasir.

Yasir pushed out his hands. "Niko... Wait... Just wait—"

"You son of a bitch!" Niko lunged.

Yasir grabbed the gun and cradled it high, making Niko peer down its dark barrels. "Wait, dammit!"

"Come out or we'll burn you out!" Alissand declared outside.

No, not again. Not Yasir. "You did this!" He made a grab for the gun, but Yasir backed up, his finger tight against the trigger. "I fucking trusted you. We trusted you!"

"They have Liam!" he blurted.

Niko froze.

"They have Liam..." he said again, ending in a choked sob. "They intercepted my letter... They've had him since Seran fell. All this time. Niko, gods, please... don't hate me. Please. I was just... I was just supposed to get you here. They just want to talk."

"*You* brought us here deliberately? After everything we've been through?"

"You had no idea where to go. I just... I just... They have Liam, and I can't... He's all I have. Please, Niko, please... understand. I tried to tell you. I was going to tell you, but there wasn't time and then... Then you were at the palace and—"

Niko caught the gun and yanked it from Yasir's grip.

He yelped and recoiled, expecting Niko to—what? Pull the shadows in and drown him inside them?

"Gods-damn you, Yasir." He tossed the gun at Yasir's feet. "Go wake Vasili."

"What are you going to do?"

He went to the window and peered through the boards. A dozen riders waited near the tree line. There would be more out of sight. Alissand rode a heavy chestnut charger and waited ahead of his riders. Tied and gagged behind him sat a tired and bruised Liam.

"Talk to them, just like you said." They hadn't come to talk. The Yazdans wanted only one thing. "They don't know who's here, right? Just me?"

"No, I was told to just bring you."

Niko turned and grabbed Yasir by the jacket. "Get Vasili away. Can you at least do that? I'll do what I can to get Liam to safety, but you have to get Vasili away from here *now*."

He nodded, and Niko shoved him away before he struck him for being the damned fool he was.

"I'm sorry..."

He wanted to hate him but knew what it was like to feel helpless when someone you loved was caught in a storm. "I know."

CHAPTER 39

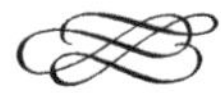

Thick mist hung heavy over the treetops, holding the air still. Niko descended the steps of Bucland Manor. Unarmed, he had little to battle with, but all he had to do was buy time for Vasili and Yasir to escape. The only thing that mattered was getting Vasili far away from the Yazdans.

"Nikolas." Alissand's mouth lifted in a snarl as he took in Niko's rough and battered state in a head to toe once-over. His uncle had never looked more foreboding than atop his horse with his riders spread out behind him.

"You and your men were idle here while Loreen fell?" Niko asked, keeping the anger bubbling in his veins and not his voice.

"Loreen was lost the day Talos was killed."

"Coward." All of them were cowards. They'd watched Loreen fall from afar and done nothing. They didn't care about anything but the flame. "Talos was a fucking lunatic."

"Talos knew his place!" Alissand snapped, briefly startling his horse so he had to rein it back under control. "Unlike his sons."

"Talos was going to surrender to the elves."

"Yes, well. I didn't say he was sane. The Cavilles have always required careful management. It's the flame... it makes them unpredictable."

Niko stopped on the bottom step and spread his arms. "You found me. What do you want?"

"The prince you took from us."

"Vasili? I don't know where he is."

"You're a terrible liar." He jerked his head. "Search the house!" Three of his men demounted and walked up the steps, around Niko, to head inside. The house was big enough for Yasir and Vasili to avoid them and escape out the back.

"Vasili gave me up to Amir," Niko said. "I got free. Been in Loreen ever since. That fuckin' Caville prick can swing by his balls from the highest tree for all I care."

Alissand leaned forward in the saddle, his interest sharpening. "And what of the colorful Captain Lajani? I suppose you don't know where he is either?"

"We met up a few times. I was supposed to meet him here, actually. Seems you knew that, huh? Seeing as you've suddenly crawled from the woodwork."

Alissand straightened again. "Did you kill him?" he asked, assuming Niko had discovered the betrayal.

Liam bucked and moaned through his gag, trying to catch Niko's eye. He didn't know Niko, didn't know how he'd never knowingly hurt Yasir. But if Alissand thought Yasir dead, he'd no longer need Liam.

"No, like I said. We were supposed to meet. He was

pretty insistent. I guess that's because of the extra baggage you have there."

Liam let loose more muffled protests.

Alissand eyed Niko as though trying to decipher any lies. "We've had our differences, Nikolas. The fact you cared for a Caville being one of them. They aren't meant for loving, nephew. They're to be used like the useless vessels they are. Perhaps, in light of the prince's betrayal, you have learned your error?"

"You tried to pour his blood down my throat, *uncle*. And when that didn't work, you ordered me dead. I agree. I've learned a few things."

"You have. I see it in you... the flame. You can't hide it, not from me. I didn't free you, but someone did. Feels good, doesn't it? The power. Feels right. That's because you are a Yazdan, your mother's son. The shah gave you her ring because you belong with us. Come back with us. I'll teach you our ways. You'll be powerful, like the sorcerer you were born to be."

Did they know he was half Bucland blood? Had they seen whatever happened in Loreen that made Yasir so afraid of him?

A scuffle drew Niko's eye back up the steps behind him. Two of Alissand's men had Yasir caught between them. They'd gagged him, and as they dragged him down the steps, he caught Niko's eye and frantically shook his head.

Niko's heart skipped. "There you are, Yasir." He gestured carelessly at Alissand. "We have guests."

Yasir's eyes widened. But then he saw Liam and all the fight drained from his bones. Alissand's men dropped him to his knees in the dirt, and if anyone had any doubt about his fate, they made it clear by aiming pistols at his back.

Shit, they were going to kill them both anyway. "Wait!" Niko stepped forward. Where the fuck was Vasili? Had he gotten away? There was one man still left searching the house. Vasili had the flame. He could easily kill a single man, maybe kill everyone here, but at what cost? He'd barely contained it on the street. What if he couldn't hold it now?

Niko raised his hands. "Just... wait. Uncle, let them go."

"And why would I do that?"

"I'll come with you. We'll do whatever the fuck Yazdans do. I'll become whatever you need me to be. Just let them both go."

"You show your hand too easily." Alissand narrowed his eyes. He pulled his pistol free and aimed it at Yasir's head. "Where's the prince, Niko?"

"Don't!" Niko stepped close still. "Don't... They're not a part of this. You can let them go and no harm is done."

Alissand's grin was a long way from friendly. "You have a big heart, nephew. Leila was the same." Liam openly sobbed, still bound and gagged behind Alissand. Alissand's finger tensed on the trigger. "Tell me where Vasili is or your friends die."

"I'm right here." Vasili's smooth, dulcet tones announced his arrival. He emerged from the house, oozing confidence with every stride, and descended the steps, passing Niko without sparing a glance. "It's me you want." He stopped mid-distance between Niko and Alissand on his horse. "Let them go, including Nikolas. You'll never get him to obey anyway. Believe me, I've tried."

"Vasili—"

Vasili raised a hand, cutting Niko's words.

Did he have daggers on him? Niko couldn't see any, but he rarely did until it was too late. He would be armed. Was his plan to get close to Alissand and end his life with the slash of a blade?

There would be a plan because Vasili *always* had a plan. He distracted with one hand and stabbed the dagger in with the other. His whip-quick mind was brilliant. As much as Niko hated that about him—having been on the receiving end of that mind—he loved it too. He'd fix this.

Vasili approached Alissand's horse and ran his hand lightly down its neck, making it shy. He crooned softly, settling it, and even Alissand seemed transfixed by Vasili. "Besides..." Vasili looked up. "Why settle for a piece of the flame in Niko, when you can have it all in me?"

Just what exactly was Vasili's game telling a Yazdan they had access to all the dark power within arm's reach? He'd just painted a larger target on his back than before.

Alissand frowned, clearly searching for the trap too.

"Let them go," Vasili said again. Softly this time, but it wasn't a request.

Alissand nodded at the guards holding Yasir. They withdrew their aim and returned to their mounts. A third guard reappeared from the house and mounted up too. If Vasili had a trap, now was the time to spring it.

Alissand murmured at Liam, and then used a small, curved dagger to cut his bindings. He tore his gag free, clambered down off the horse, and fell into Yasir's arms. Niko's heart constricted at the sight of the pair embracing, his gaze returning to Vasili.

Vasili crossed his arms at the wrists and offered them up to Alissand. "You let them all go, and you and I will have an agreement. But if I learn you've interfered with them, you'll find me far less compliant."

Wait.

What was this?

"You're handing yourself over?" Alissand asked, skeptical. "Why?"

"Because I am tired of fighting the path history mapped out for me."

Alissand eagerly looped a piece of rope around Vasili's wrists before he could change his mind. "We have an agreement then, prince."

Niko raised his hands. "Wait. Stop."

There was no plan. No game.

Dread plunged through his heart.

Vasili was telling Alissand the truth. He really was handing himself over.

Alissand grabbed Vasili by the bound wrists and heaved him onto the back of his horse. The prince settled awkwardly in place. His gaze briefly snagged Niko's, jaw locked in defiance.

They'd bleed him. Use him.

Why... Why was he doing this?

"Vasili, no." If Vasili wasn't going to stop this madness, then Niko would have to. He approached Alissand's horse. "Release him. Like I said. Take me."

Alissand smiled and tightened his horse's reins, reining the beast backward. "A good Caville knows his place is serving a Yazdan." He pulled on the reins, turning the horse away. "Like it's always been."

"Bullshit. You let him go or I will turn this world upside down to get him back. In Loreen, I commanded the flame—"

"The root of his power is dead," Vasili snipped off Niko's confession. "His power was Amir's, and now it's as dead as my brother. Nikolas is nothing but a burned-out blacksmith. We should leave before elves discover us."

Alissand narrowed his eyes, reading between them both. "Say your farewells, nephew."

There were no words. This wasn't goodbye.

At Niko's silence, Alissand turned his horse from the house.

And now Vasili was close, and Niko saw all the horrible truth in his soft gaze. He didn't expect to ever come back. Vasili fought the regret on his face, but not enough to hide it.

"Don't do this," Niko begged. "You said... You said you cared, you said you loved... If that were true, you wouldn't do this."

He smiled sadly, like he had hope for Niko. "That's why I'm doing this."

Alissand kicked his horse into a gallop.

"Wait! *No*!" Niko bolted forward, plunging into the clouds of dust the retreating horses kicked up. He ran hard, thighs burning and lungs pumping down the track. But it wasn't enough. The sounds of hooves faded fast, and by the time he reached the Bucland gateway, there was nothing ahead but a deathly quiet.

No, no, that slippery bastard... He couldn't do this. Not now. Why? *Why!*

"You wretched— You damned, wretched fucking snake." Niko kicked at the ground, churned up by hooves. Vasili had given himself up for them all. But Caville princes didn't do stupid, heroic things. Vasili didn't surrender. He never surrendered. He had to have a plan, a reason, a distraction, because he hadn't walked back into his own nightmare for Niko. That couldn't be it. Not the vicious, conniving Vasili. "Damn you."

Why.

He should have used the flame, should have killed them all, even though Niko had warned him not to. Why hadn't he fought back?

He could have stopped them all, but instead, he'd crossed his wrists and given himself over to the Yazdans.

He truly had surrendered.

For Niko.

Niko staggered and fell to his knees in the dirt.

They'd tie him, cut him, bleed him. It would be like before, with Vasili locked in silence, his life draining from his veins, and Niko wouldn't be there to stop it. He'd be alone again.

It was wrong.

So wrong.

He'd surrendered, knowing what they'd do, so Niko didn't have to go with them, so Niko could go free, build a cottage somewhere and live a simple life like he'd made him promise. But that stupid prince, he didn't realize Niko had vowed to save *him.*

"Fuck you, Vasili!"

The bastard didn't get to make that choice for him. He didn't want that perfect life without Vasili in it. "Fuck you, my prince." He hunched forward and squeezed his eyes closed against the sudden all-over ache of loss.

Cool tears splashed into his dusty palms. He opened his eyes and looked at those wet splashes.

Dark flame dripped from his fingertips, and his

memory flashed back to the killing in Loreen's streets, to the monster he'd briefly been.

Fear clutched at his heart and stole his breath.

He lifted both hands and turned them, watching the flame pulse. It hadn't gone. It was... waiting. Quickly, he folded his fingers into fists, and the dark flame spluttered out. Controlled.

He had the flame inside him still, leftover from whatever horrors Amir had forced him to commit. His gut said not to use it, to hide it, but his head already knew what had to be done.

Get his fucking prince back.

He looked up the empty road.

Vasili didn't get to surrender, not for anything, and certainly not for Niko. Niko was damn well bringing his prince home, and no vicious elf, no endless war, and no dishonorable Yazdan was going to stand in his way.

The Prince's Assassin series concludes in
Curse of the Dark Prince.

Order now from Amazon.

ACKNOWLEDGMENTS

A huge thank you to all my readers in the Ariana Nash Silkies Facebook group, who keep the stories alive long after they've been released into the wild. And to everyone who takes the time to leave a review on my books. Reviews are like little gifts to authors. If you're able to leave one, please do.

Vasili and Niko's final adventure takes place in *Curse of the Dark Prince*, coming early 2021.

Available to pre-order from Amazon now.

SILK & STEEL EXCERPT

Eroan

The iron door rattled on its hinges and groaned open, spilling silvery light inside. Gloom fled to the corners, leaving behind a figure with broad shoulders. *Male*, Eroan thought. Curious scents of warm leather and citrus tickled his nose. After the wet and rotted smell of the prison, he welcomed any change in the air, even if it meant his visitor had returned.

Eroan kept his head low and his eyes down, hiding any signs of relief on his face. The shackles holding his wrists high bit deeper. He'd been so long in the dark, he'd almost forgotten he was a living thing. The constant, beating pain was a cruel reminder. This visitor was a cruel reminder too.

He knew what happened next. It had been the same for hours now. Days, even.

The male came forward, blocking more light, lessening its stab against Eroan's light-sensitive eyes. He turned his face away, but the male's proud outline still burned in his mind. Other images burned there too. The male's half-smile, the glitter of dragon-sight in his green eyes. Eroan had rarely gotten so close to their kind without killing them.

His mission would have been successful if not for this one.

"You need to eat." The male's gravelly undertone rumbled.

He needed nothing from *him*.

A tray clattered against the stone floor. The sweet smell of fruit turned Eroan's hollow stomach.

Moments passed. The male's rhythmic breathing, slow and steady, accompanied the scent of warm leather rising from his hooded cloak, and with it the lemony bite of all dragonkin. A scent most elves were taught to flee from.

"Were you alone, elf?" the dragonkin asked. The questions were the same every time. "Will there be another attempt on her life? How many of your kind are left in our lands?" More questions.

Always the same. And not once had Eroan answered.

Steely fingers suddenly dug into Eroan's chin, forcing him to look, to *see*. Up close, the dragonkin's green eyes seemed as brittle and sharp as glass, like a glance could cut. His smile was a sharp thing too.

"I could torture you." The dragonkin's smile vanished behind a sneer.

Eroan's straining arms twitched, and the chains slung above his head rattled against stone. *He has me in body, but not in spirit.* He gave him nothing, no sneer, no wince, just peered deep into the dragonkin's eyes. Eyes that had undoubtedly seen the death of a thousand elves, that had witnessed villages burn. If they had souls, this dragon's would be dark. *He could torture me. He should. Why does he wait?*

Eroan recalled that cold look when their swords had clashed. He'd cut through countless tower guards, severing them from their life-strings as easily as snipping at thread, but not this one. This one had refused to fall. This dragonkin had fought with a passion not found in the others, as though their battle were a personal one. Either he truly loved the queen he protected, or he was a creature full of fiery hate that scorched whatever he touched.

The dragonkin's fingers tightened, digging in, hurting, but just as the pain became too sharp, he tore his hand free and stepped back, grunting dismissively.

Eroan collapsed against the wall, letting the chains hold him. Cold stone burned into raw skin. His shoulder muscles strained and twitched. Pain throbbed down his neck too, but he kept his head up, kept it turned away.

"I cannot..." Whatever the dragon had been about to say, he let it trail off and reached for the ornate brooch fixing the cloak around his neck, teasing his fingers over the serpent design.

Eroan wondered idly if he could kill him with that brooch pin. Of course, to do that, he'd need to be free.

The dragon saw him watching and dropped his hand. "You do not have long, elf." His jeweled eyes glowed. Myths told of how the dragonkin were made of glass and forged inside great fire-spewing mountains in a frozen land. Not this one. This one had something else inside. Some other wildfire fueling him.

The dragon turned, sweeping his cloak around him, and headed out the door.

"What is your name?" The question growled over Eroan's tongue and scratched over cracked lips. He almost didn't recognize the rumbling voice as his own.

The dragon hesitated, then partially turned his head to peer over his shoulder. The fire was gone from his eyes, and something else lurked there now, some softer weakness that belied everything Eroan had seen. His cheek fluttered, an inner war raging.

The answer would have a cost, Eroan realized. He shouldn't have asked. He let his head drop, tired of holding it up, of holding himself up. Tiredness ate at his body and bones. The shivers started up again, rattling the chains and weakening his defiance. This dragonkin was right. He did not have long.

"My name is Lysander."

The door slammed, the lock clunked, and Eroan was plunged into darkness.

ALSO BY ARIANA NASH

Please sign up to Ariana's newsletter so you don't miss all the news.

www.ariananashbooks.com

Also by Ariana Nash

Prince's Assassin Series

King of the Dark

Reign of Darkness

Curse of the Dark Prince

Silk & Steel Series

(Complete Series)

"I would expect this series (Silk & Steel) to appeal to fans of CS Pacat's Captive Prince and Jex Lane's Beautiful Monsters." *R. A. Steffan, author of The Last Vampire.*

"A few pages in and I'm already hooked. I can't wait to see the deliciously dark world Ariana has created." *- Jex Lane, author of Beautiful Monsters.*

"The characters yank, twist, and shatter your heartstrings." *- Goodreads review*

Click here to start the adventure with Silk & Steel, Silk & Steel #1

~

Primal Sin Series

"A story of star-crossed lovers, of two men, two enemies, who should never have fallen in love."

Angels and demons fight for love over London's battle-scarred streets.

Primal Sin, Primal Sin #1

Eternal Sin, Primal Sin #2

Infernal Sin, Primal Sin #3

~

ABOUT THE AUTHOR

Born to wolves, Rainbow Award winner Ariana Nash only ventures from the Cornish moors when the moon is fat and the night alive with myths and legends. She captures those myths in glass jars and returning home, weaves them into stories filled with forbidden desires, fantasy realms, and wicked delights.

Sign up to her newsletter and get a free ebook here: https://www.subscribepage.com/silk-steel

Lightning Source UK Ltd.
Milton Keynes UK
UKHW012200070921
390162UK00002B/506